I0675377

DYSTOPIA NOW

HARVEY HIESTAND

Air Raid PRESS

Portland, Oregon

This is a work of fiction. Characters, names, places, and events described are the product of the author's imagination and are used fictitiously. Resemblance to any person, living or dead, locales, businesses, and actual events is coincidental.

DYSTOPIA NOW

Copyright © Harvey Hiestand, 2013
All rights reserved

Published in the United States of America by Air Raid Press, Portland, Oregon

Library of Congress Catalog Card Number: 2012904131

ISBN-13: 978-0989314985
ISBN-10: 0989314987

for Ted and Madeline

Preface

*...[I]n our progress toward a resumption of work, we
require ... safeguards against a return of the evils of the old
order: there must be a strict supervision of all banking and
credits and investments, so that there will be an end to
speculation with other people's money.*

—President Franklin D. Roosevelt

*I have a deep and abiding faith in the destiny of free men.
With patience and courage, we shall someday move on
into a new era—a wonderful golden age—an age when we
can use the peaceful tools that science has forged for us to
do away with poverty and human misery everywhere on
Earth.*

*Think what can be done, once our capital, our skills, our
science—most of all atomic energy—can be released from
the tasks of defense and turned wholly to peaceful purposes
all around the world.*

There is no end to what can be done.

—President Harry S. Truman

*Travel all over the world, to learn to know our brothers
abroad, will be fast and cheap. The fear and pain of
crippling disease will be greatly reduced. The material
things that make life interesting and pleasant will be
available to everyone. Leisure, together with educational
and recreational facilities, will be abundant, so that all can
develop the life of the spirit, of reflection, of religion, of the
arts, of the full realization of the good things of the world.*

—President Dwight D. Eisenhower

i

...[A] strong America cannot neglect the aspirations of its citizens—the welfare of the needy, the health care of the elderly, the education of the young. For we are not developing the Nation's wealth for its own sake. Wealth is the means—and people are the ends. All our material riches will avail us little if we do not use them to expand the opportunities of our people.

—President John F. Kennedy

This administration today, here and now, declares unconditional war on poverty in America. I urge this Congress and all Americans to join with me in that effort.

It will not be a short or easy struggle, no single weapon or strategy will suffice, but we shall not rest until that war is won. The richest nation on Earth can afford to win it. We cannot afford to lose it.

—President Lyndon Johnson

Make the economy scream.

—President Richard Nixon

...I must say to you that the state of the Union is not good: millions of Americans are out of work. Recession and inflation are eroding the money of millions more. Prices are too high, and sales are too slow.

—President Gerald Ford

The gap between our citizens and our government has never been so wide. ... What you see too often in Washington and elsewhere around the country is a system of government that seems incapable of action. You see a Congress twisted and pulled in every direction by hundreds of well-financed and powerful special interests. ... Often you see paralysis and stagnation and drift. You don't like it, and neither do I. What can we do?

—President Jimmy Carter

Our citizens feel they've lost control of even the most basic decisions made about the essential services of government, such as schools, welfare, roads, and even garbage collection. And they're right. A maze of interlocking jurisdictions and levels of government confronts average citizens in trying to solve even the simplest of problems. They don't know where to turn for answers, who to hold accountable, who to praise, who to blame, who to vote for or against.

—President Ronald Reagan

*Now, I know that the only way [Governor Bill Clinton]
can win is to make everybody believe the economy is worse
than it is. But this country's not coming apart at the
seams, for heaven sakes. We're the United States of
America. In spite of the economic problems, we are the
most respected economy around the world. Many would
trade for it. We've been caught up in a global slowdown.
We can do much, much better. But we ought not to try to
convince the American people that America is a country
that's coming apart at the seams.*

—President George H.W. Bush

*For thirty years, family life in America has been breaking
down. For twenty years, the wages of working people have
been stagnant or declining. For the twelve years of trickle-
down economics, we built a false prosperity on a hollow
base as our national debt quadrupled. From 1989 to 1992,
we experienced the slowest growth in a half century. For
too many families, even when both parents were working,
the American dream has been slipping away.*

—President Bill Clinton

*We must have an economy that grows fast enough to
employ every man and woman who seeks a job. After
recession, terrorist attacks, corporate scandals, and stock
market declines, our economy is ... not growing fast
enough or strongly enough. With unemployment rising,
our nation needs more small businesses to open, more
companies to invest and expand, more employers to put up
the sign that says, "Help Wanted."*

—President George W. Bush

...I took office amid two wars, an economy rocked by a severe recession, a financial system on the verge of collapse, and a government deeply in debt. Experts from across the political spectrum warned that if we did not act, we might face a second depression. ...

But the devastation remains. One in ten Americans still cannot find work. Many businesses have shuttered. Home values have declined. Small towns and rural communities have been hit especially hard. And for those who'd already known poverty, life's become that much harder.

This recession has also compounded the burdens that America's families have been dealing with for decades: the burden of working harder and longer for less, of being unable to save enough to retire or help kids with college.

So I know the anxieties that are out there right now. They're not new. These struggles are the reason I ran for President.

For these Americans and so many others, change has not come fast enough. Some are frustrated, some are angry. They don't understand why it seems like bad behavior on Wall Street is rewarded, but hard work on Main Street isn't, or why Washington has been unable or unwilling to solve any of our problems. They're tired of the partisanship and the shouting and the pettiness. They know we can't afford it. Not now.

—President Barack Obama

DYSTOPIA
NOW

Carson Piercy

There's something dumb inherent in youth; he smiles at me in the midst of his. He has moved into my house without my consent, he eats of our food as though it was his, and he calls me *Dad*, though he's not my son. The smell of sex surrounds him, and it makes me think evil thoughts, thoughts of cruelty, thoughts of something tortuous applied to him in the early hours of some soon morning. I blink the thoughts away and take my coffee to the living room, where the fish in the life preserver grins at me. I wince back, deciding the dining room would be better. I go there. The chair squonks along the floor as I sit.

Carson Piercy is the kid I'm bearing with. There's an arrogant look to him, and an Elvis Presley smile that makes women swoon. He's not the right man for my daughter. But it's not my place to say so, I guess. He approaches, holding his own cup of my coffee.

I ask him where Sheila is.

"She got up early," Carson says. "We're going out tonight and she just *had* to do some shopping." He pulls out a chair and sits across from me.

I stare at my cup.

"You know how women are: a hundred things in the closet but nothing to wear."

First of all, my wife had no such neurosis. And second, just who is Carson to call my little girl a woman? Sheila still shrieks with joy when I win her a bear from the crane machine down at Pavilions. Sure, she's taller than me, but she outgrew me before she was even twelve, and—

"Didn't you ever party, Dad? You know, take the missus out and have a blast?"

"Shasta and I were too busy living. *Surviving*."

"Sheila never talks about her mother, you know."

I look up. "Sheila didn't *know* her mother."

"I sure hope *you* did," he says.

You see, this Carson kid has a way about him. *Yeah*— a way with words. A way that makes you want to give him a nose job with your boot. I consider for a moment if I had ever been such an ass. The answer comes quickly: *Yes*. And it has a footnote: *You were worse*. I wash the thoughts away with a double swallow of my coffee.

Coffee that's still too hot for Carson.

"Tell me what it was like," he says before blowing across the brim of his cup.

I take a deep breath and let it out slowly. "What *what* was like, Carson?"

"Back when you were with Sheila's mom."

"What do you want to know?"

"Everything."

"*Everything*, huh?" I think back.

I can tell stories spanning years of my life that, even when told in great detail, would take mere minutes. Ah, but *that* year—the year I spent with Shasta—time was denser. Events unfolded. Lives changed. Carson knows some of what happened already. It's taught in school and played in endless loops on the higher television channels, in programs where they love to blather about *El Consumidor* and *Los Demonios*, about the curfew and the occupation, and about a firestorm that started down the canyon from here and then spread slowly across North America. Watching those programs taught me something: history can be naïve, if not entirely wrong. I look at Carson again. His eyes tell me he's not backing down.

Today was supposed to be *my* day. A day I get to ignore pretentious fops like Carson. A day I get to do the things *I* want to do. But then I think of my daughter and what she would want, as I've done for the last twenty years—a long, *long* twenty years. My girl would want me to play nice.

So I grunt and give Carson the gist: "I had just gotten through the emotional mess from the death of my grandfather. That's when the Hundred Days Riots began. It was an insane, tumultuous time. Shasta and I found each other. We moved in together. We got married. I got her pregnant. Then we moved up here, away from the riots and into the hills, into the house she grew up in. I wanted to name our baby after her mother, but the name *Shasta* always reminded me of the soft drink." Only that's not true—it's the soft drink that always reminds me of her: *Shasta*... Her father once told me she was conceived on a camping trip in Northern California, in view of the ice-capped mountain. Beauty. Beauty without bounds. That was Shasta.

"No," Carson says.

I let that hang for a moment, figuring on more. Then: "No *what?*"

"No, Dad. Tell me the *story*. I want to hear the *story*. It doesn't mean anything when you say it that way. Like, if I go: *Romeo and Juliet fell in love but their families disapproved so they killed themselves*—I mean that's not the story!"

Another grunt escapes me. I have nothing else to do today, other than my laps. But I guess I can skip it. Or go for a swim later tonight.

Carson is bobbleheading with an eager smile.

I give in.

HRW International

1—*That* Is The *Labyrinth*

Shasta and I got to know each other at work, so I should start with my job, and the economic conditions that would create such a job. See—those were hard times back then, Carson, and it felt like they were hard by design. It started with the Great Recession when I was a kid, and instead of ending in slow economic improvement, it just dragged on. Eventually, people started calling it the *Late Depression.* And *that* finally ended, at least here in Los Angeles, with the death of Public Enemy Number One, a rioter and provocateur known as *El Consumidor.*

The depression was a time of loss and lack, of tightening belts and selling valuables, of working long hours and receiving little pay. Still, no one of any real character minds suffering in the short term as long as there's a payoff at some point. That payoff—the hope of modest prosperity—is what keeps society moving and working and producing. I went along daily, as most people did, playing the economic game as though I was at a slot machine, hoping for the one pull that would bring the jackpot.

I had wanted to save my grandfather the burden of college tuition, so after high school I landed a job at HRW International, which has since gone out of business. Well—*scratch that:* I spent long enough in management to know these companies never go out of business. What happens is they get divided into chunks that're devoured by predator stakeholders. So in a way, I guess HRW is immortal.

But its name is dead.

In my tenure at HRW there were two Directors of Personnel. Mr. Chandler was the first one, and he was nice enough to your face—but in reality he was a passive-aggressive type. For instance, there was a switch under his desk that went to the coffee machine's power receptacle. He'd wait for an employee to drop a fiver in the slot, and as the person selected the flavor, he'd flick his little switch off and on again, resetting the machine. Behind his cubicle wall, he'd be giggling like Anderson Cooper.

One time, he posted a job listing at the Tourette Association's office on Wilshire. He hired a half-dozen of the referrals and sat them strategically throughout the office. There was a barker, a shrieker, a swearer, and the rest just kinda let out periodic squeaks. You'd be hard at work when a sudden, blood-curdling scream would startle you out of your concentration. Then: *"Fucker!" "Arf!" "Eeep!" "AAAAAAH!" "Et!" "Nit-nit!" "MURP!" "AAAAAAH!" "Arf! Arf! Arf!"* You never knew how long it would last—the tics could go around for five minutes or two hours before settling down. Incredible turnover resulted from the constant noise, but the ticcing didn't bother Mr. Chandler at all. He would just do his work, laughing and laughing.

See, that was Mr. Chandler's style: attacking while flying under the radar. Even so, he didn't last forever. No, once he was gone there was another personnel director, the *active*-aggressive type—in other words, a Machiavellian prick. He'd play stupid games with interviewees, he'd fire employees who'd done nothing wrong, and, through his negligence, he'd actually killed one of the vendors. Despite embezzling thousands of dollars a month through Accounts Payable, he ran the best numbers in the company. And in the end, his AP scam was a pittance compared to what he stole from the LEGACY account.

And how would I know that?

Well, that second personnel director was me.

One of the Tourette's employees, the barker, was a little hottie named Doreen Crenshaw. At the age of eighteen, she had been in her second year of grad school. Although financial aid paid for tuition and a dorm room, and she worked some hours as a teaching assistant as well, she was always short on food. Two quarters away from her Master's, she got too weak to concentrate. On winter break, she went to the Tourette Association looking for a solution to her difficulties, and instead, she found Mr. Chandler's job posting. She applied and got the job that very day.

She quickly made friends with her closest cubemate, a Chicano kid from East L.A. named Octavio Mendez. Adolescence had been cruel to Octavio, leaving him with a moustache and beard of pits and bumps instead of hair. He'd talked Mr. Chandler into hiring him by promising he'd quit in a short while, to go and work on the harvest. I'd always wondered what type of crop Mr. Chandler thought Octavio could harvest out in East L.A., but I never asked.

Everyone else in Personnel came and went. Soon, the only long-termers left were the three of us. By the time I was twenty-one, I had been there three years, and Doreen and Octavio a little less than two.

Octavio would give Doreen and me rides to work and home again, and in the mornings, he always had sack lunches for us—he was cool like that. Cruising around in his Impala was fun. It was painted diarrhea brown, but he kept it polished like glass. When we drove past, people stared at us like we were movie stars (or maybe gangsters). As poor as we were, that made us feel pretty good.

Since I was the senior one, I worked as Mr. Chandler's administrative assistant. I didn't get extra pay, but that's what gave me access to the magical Accounts Payable envelope. It was a scam I had caught onto a few months after Doreen and Octavio were hired—anything you ever put into the AP envelope got paid, no questions asked. I had been slipping all my bills into it since my grandfather died. Had it not been for that magical envelope, I'd've been on the streets. No doubt about it.

One afternoon, before I earned my promotion, Mr. Chandler was done hiring some twenty employees and was now ordering office supplies. I was sitting beside him in his cubicle, signing *Gary Chandler* for the umpteenth time on all his new-hire paperwork. My hand was cramping and his signature was devolving from a nice copy to a squiggly mess.

The phone rang. Mr. Chandler answered it.

"Oh, hi Bob," he said. "What's up? ... Well, it doesn't surprise me that this region is more expensive than the others. ... It's Los Angeles, Bob: California taxes us for *not* spending money, you know that. ... Right. ... Right." Mr. Chandler recradled the handset. "O-*kay*, Bob."

"What was that about?" I asked.

"Starting next week, we need to keep copies of everything in the AP envelope. Bob wants to audit the invoices to see why our region is so expensive."

I cringed at the thought.

Mr. Chandler tapped me on the shoulder. "Hey," he said. "Do me a favor…"

"What?"

He motioned for me to stand up, and pointed to a large X scribbled in permanent marker on the tile floor. "Stand right there." His eyes were darting around, triangulating.

"What're you doing?"

"A little to your right… *Perfect.* I can't block all of the cameras by myself. Just stay there for a couple seconds, Zeno."

I stood with my arms folded.

Mr. Chandler picked up the phone again. Leaning awkwardly, he dialed a number. "Hey, Rick, how you doing? … Great, how's the wife? … Hey, listen—you know my construction project? … No, I'm not worried about that. What I need is an invoice. … Well, you can estimate, can't you?"

Doreen barked from somewhere.

Mr. Chandler seemed to be getting frustrated. "Rick, I don't care—estimate high. But I need an invoice today. Starting next week, my boss is going to be auditing my expenses. … Okay, thanks—you're a life saver." He hung up.

I sat. "Gonna build yourself an office?"

"No, it's better than that," he said.

At home that evening, I sorted through my bills and stacked them by the door. First thing the next morning, as Mr. Chandler was over by the entrance picking through interviewees, I stuffed those bills into that week's accounts payable envelope. Sure, the cameras were there, but I'd been doing it for a year-and-a-half by then, and there had never been any fuss.

And, as it turned out, there was no fuss this time, either.

The construction began maybe two weeks later. Upon arrival at work, I found myself stuck just inside the door, among the regular sea of applicants, all standing tall by the south entrance and holding résumés in their left hands. They couldn't hear my *excuse me*s because of all the construction noise, so I shouldered my way through. When I breeched the applicant crowd, I could see that all the cubicles had been crammed together, toward the east side of the building, and now the office only filled a quarter of the floor. Beyond the office, a plastic curtain had been erected, concealing what was being so loudly built.

At the entrance to Mr. Chandler's cubicle, a man was screaming at the top of his lungs. "*This is* HIGHLY INCONVENIENT *for my employees, Gary! Your*

PROJECT *is blocking both the* ELEVATOR *and the* STAIRWELL!"

Mr. Chandler shrugged. *"They're not blocked at all! Your people will need to kick through a little sawdust— that's all. It'll all be over in a couple weeks."*

The man continued his tirade as I walked over. *"My employees are educated professionals and I have to bend over backwards to keep them! As poorly as they're paid, they won't put up with this! How are you planning to find me more, Gary? It's not like they can be replaced with..."* The man motioned to me. *"...any* DIPSHIT *off the street!"*

I brought my shoulders back.

Mr. Chandler held his palm toward me, bidding my patience. He faced the man, looking stern. *"Go away, Gordon! The construction will be over soon."*

Gordon stomped off, weaving through the crowded cubicles and then pushing through a seam in the plastic sheeting.

I spoke directly in Mr. Chandler's ear: "What are you building?"

He motioned toward the plastic with both arms outstretched. "THAT *is the* LABYRINTH!" He smiled like a new father.

Later that day, after the construction workers had gone home, I was close to finishing my boss' signatures. As I worked through my hand cramps, Mr. Chandler worked

14

through the computer's security. Since the Help Desk had disabled access to the browser, there was no way to open it explicitly, so he went to the operating system's help menu and followed hyperlinks to open it implicitly. When he found the right link, the browser appeared and he typed in `calottery.com`. Like always, he placed his lottery ticket against the screen as Wednesday's Powerball numbers appeared. He eyeballed the two sets of numbers and then ripped up his ticket, tossing the confetti in the trash.

"Why do you throw your money away like that?" I asked.

"Oh, *no*," Mr. Chandler said. "No, no, *no*. Don't you know what *hope* is?"

"Hope? Like the *I hope she's making steak for dinner* kinda hope?"

"*Hope*, as in: at least one person wins a million bucks every week in this country. It's true. And the only way to win is to hold a ticket."

"Yeah, Mr. Chandler—they sucker billions out of people that way."

Locks of his hair were scourging his face. "No, no, *no*, Zeno. My five bucks doesn't only buy a ticket. It also buys the transformation of my *dream* into a *possibility*. And it's my *hope* that'll transform a *possibility* into an *actuality*."

I looked at Mr. Chandler pitiably as Octavio appeared at the entrance to the cubicle.

"Just you watch, Zeno," Mr. Chandler told me while straightening up a wood carving of a clover on his desk. When he was done adjusting it, he turned to Octavio. "How much longer till the harvest?"

"All the crops *fail* last summer. Tole you that."

"Right."

I stood up. "Have a good night, Mr. Chandler."

"Later, Zeno."

Octavio and I walked off to find Doreen, and it wasn't hard. Her Tourette's had been especially strong that day and we followed the sound of her tics to the snack machine. She was hitting the coin slot with the palm of her hand, over and over.

I gently took her hand in mine and massaged her palm lightly.

"It stole my ten-spot," she said, twitching her neck and blinking. She barked lightly twice.

"I got it," Octavio said. He slid a ten-dollar bill into the acceptor. "What you need?"

I was still massaging her palm.

Though she barked more, she was relaxing. "Some peanut butter cups." She blinked and winced. "Yeah, that would be good."

When Octavio got the candy, I released her hand and hooked my arm through hers. By the time we got to Octavio's car, she was finishing her peanut butter cups, smiling, and ticcing hardly at all.

It took a while to become accustomed to Doreen's tics, but to Octavio and me, they eventually became background noise. It was not the same with the dissonant symphony of screaming circular saws, whining electric drills, and exploding nail guns now playing in the mornings, all of it resonating within the hard cement walls of the HRW building. At the cubicle the next day, Mr. Chandler seemed oblivious to all this noise, leaning low over his desk and studying a scribbled diagram of something. We talked together loudly, and enunciated perfectly.

"How can you put up with all this racket?" I asked.

He blew away some eraser fluff. "Meh."

I looked at his diagram. "What's that?"

"We were bought out," he said, drawing an arrow.

My heart jumped some. "Are we still employed?"

"Yes, Zeno..." He shoved away his drawing. "A buyout doesn't change anything at our level."

That calmed me some. "Then what's the problem?"

Mr. Chandler frowned. "Well, HRW owns a majority share of DDG, Inc., which is fine. DDG, Inc. owns a majority share of the 223rd Bank of Omaha, which is also fine. This is where it gets tricky." He closed his eyes, pausing in thought. "The 223rd Bank of Omaha just leveraged their assets to buy a majority share of HRW..."

It seemed simple to me: "A circle jerk."

Mr. Chandler squinted. *"What?"*

"Never mind."

"Who the hell do we work for?"

"We work for HRW International, Mr. Chandler. You're overthinking it."

With an angry shrug, he crumpled up his diagram and threw it in the trash.

I had a dilemma. I wanted a coffee, but all I had was a twenty. And I'd learned my lesson losing twenties in the coffee machine while Mr. Chandler was at his desk.

"Got any change?"

Mr. Chandler opened his bottom drawer, where he had a cash box. "Paper or plastic?"

"Plastic's fine."

We exchanged the twenty and four fivers.

"Thanks," I said. "You want one?"

He flicked a finger at his water bottle. Then he brought out his wallet and put the twenty inside.

I cleared my throat.

"What?"

I shook my head. "Oh—nothing."

"It's for my lunch at Burger King," he said. "If there's leftovers in petty cash at the end of the month, HRW reduces the fund. They don't care what I spend the money on, as long as I file the receipt."

"You don't have to explain yourself to me," I said, walking away to the coffee machine.

When I got there, Mr. Chandler was away from his switch—he was over weeding applicants by the south entrance. My fiver ticked away beneath the coffee machine's slot; I selected *Mocha*. A cup dropped down and the machine whined and spat.

2—Breaking News

After three years on the job, with two of them as Mr. Chandler's assistant, my work day had become routine. It went like this: coffee, process write-ups for those late to work, read incoming memos and print those requiring Mr. Chandler's reply, coffee, receive supplies from vendors and sign their invoices, file the invoices properly, eat my bagged lunch with more coffee, and spend the rest of the day signing all the lines that legally required the signature of the hiring manager. When I was done signing, I'd massage the knots out of my hand and forearm until Octavio gathered me up to take me home. On this evening—the evening on the day of the buyout—Octavio invited Doreen and me out to the commune. We'd both been regulars over there, mostly because of the free food and beer. But this time it was different—it was the evening I got to know the infamous *Jimenez Loco*.

The enclave known as East L.A. has gone the way of HRW. That is, the way it is now isn't the way it used to be—with all the old shanties, the run-down mid-twentieth-century multiplexes, the apartments built like prisons, and the businesses whose most modern convenience was running water. Back then, people would have told you that going out to the eastside was equal to wearing a sign that said, MUG ME. But it wasn't like that at all. As long as you were respectful, East L.A. was just as safe as my neighborhood in West Hollywood.

Once we were past downtown, there were so many children playing on the streets that Octavio couldn't go more than five miles an hour. And I wouldn't have wanted him to. I waved at the kids as we passed them, and they twiddled their fingers back. The sharp smell of marigolds permeated the air. The cars in the driveways were old, but well maintained. The homes and apartment buildings were lit with purples and pinks and blues, and beautifully detailed murals decorated every blank wall facing the street. It was during this ride that Doreen first noticed the tags—the simplest one was just a spray-painted X. But many of them were beautiful, airbrushed works of art—lifelike crossbones painted on the doors of houses, or on mailboxes, or on sidewalks, or on the walls of businesses.

Doreen asked Octavio about them.

"The *Sureños* mark property with *los tibias cruzadas*. It mean you better not touch."

Octavio pulled into a one-story, U-shaped apartment complex that must have been a motel some forty or fifty years prior. Most of the doors were open and dozens of people were sitting in chairs in front of their units. Scattered out in the lawn within the center of the U were a collection of coolers of all different colors and shapes.

Señor Jimenez was the group's patriarch. Most of the time he was on the road pushing freight, but on this day he was home. With a beer in hand, he rose from one of the lawn chairs and ran toward us. He called to me: "Zeno—*¡Bienvenido!*"

I lifted a hand toward him and got out of the car. He embraced me with a bear hug saying "Good for you to come! You will have *cerveza, ¿sí?* And tamales—*debe probar los tamales de María.* Come! Come!"

Octavio and Doreen pulled some lawn chairs into the long shadows and sat.

As Señor Jimenez and I neared the coolers, we walked over the remnants of a pool deck. There were bolt holes where there had once been a diving board secured to the cement. The center of the pool had been filled in, and growing in the dirt was Bermuda grass and a couple of stunted palm trees.

I clapped the patriarch on the back. "Thank you for having us over again, Señor Jimenez."

"*Llamarme* Carlos, *¿entender?*"

"*Si...*"

"Zeno... Are you *Griega?*"

"No, not Greek. I'm Jewish, actually."

"*Judío...* Same as us then—*compañeros.* Always taking shit for things not our fault, *¿sí?*"

I grabbed a *Negra Modelo* out of the cooler. "Sounds about right."

Carlos looked around and spotted Octavio and Doreen. "*Octavio,*" he bellowed. "*Conseguirme un pañuelo para El Judío.*"

Octavio got up and went inside one of the apartments.

Carlos got out his keys, holding a bottle opener for me. I popped off my beer's cap and then handed the keys back. I used my thumbnail to push back the thin foil still covering some of the bottle's lip.

"Let us sit," Carlos said.

We found a shady spot by one of the apartments. Next door, tables with folding legs had been set up. On those tables, a half-dozen crock pots sat with spoons and tongs sticking up from within. There were paper plates and cups, napkins, and lots of different kinds of hot sauce and salsa.

"That smells fantastic," I said, and took a swig of beer.

"*Si,* María has slaved all day for our feast."

Someone walked up behind me. I took another gulp of beer.

"Stay still," Octavio said into my ear.

There was a flash of baby blue color and then the feeling of cloth being tightened around my head. I kept my eyes on Carlos.

Carlos smiled as Octavio finished adjusting my bandana.

"*María, vamos a comer,*" Carlos said.

María rushed over carrying two TV trays. She unfolded them and placed one in front of Carlos, the other in front of me. She ran back to her tables, preparing two platters of tamales, beans, and rice for us, and she set us up with the food, utensils, and caddies of sauces.

"*Gracias,*" I said.

María smiled and walked away.

Carlos bowed his head and crossed himself; I lowered my head in respect. He prayed in a whisper. When he voiced an *amén*, we unwrapped our tamales.

He unscrewed the cap from a bottle of pepper sauce. "*Que aproveche,*" he said, shaking the sauce liberally on his beans and rice.

I ignored the hot sauce and forked a bite of the tamale. I washed it down with my beer, and then said: "Jesus, this is *really* good."

Carlos laughed heartily. "*María—¡Sus tamales han hecho la llamada Judío para Jesucristo!*" He'd said that her tamales made a Jew call for Christ—I chuckled at this. María yelped joyously, in the way that only Mexican women do. Carlos reached over and slapped my arm.

I cut myself a larger bite as María called out for the others to line up. Many of the children ran, but the adults came slowly, wearing smiles of blissful satisfaction. The men held their women by their waists and the women rested their arms on their men's shoulders.

Carlos looked at me dead-on. "You been coming here for a while now," he said. "Now let me ask you this— *¿Cuando se trata de la guerra, se mantendrá con nosotros?*"

He'd asked if I'd be with them if there was war. "*Si,*" I said.

He smiled and nodded and sipped his beer.

After a couple forkfuls of rice, I asked, "What war?"

"It's coming," he answered. "If you try, you can sense it."

Later that night, after the children had been shuttled off to bed, Doreen was snoozing in a lawn chair. Octavio was extolling the virtues of the 1967 Chevy Malibu, which he swore he'd own someday. That's when the conversation turned to the economy.

I guess I started it.

"I envy you guys," was what I said.

Octavio went *pfffff.*

"Oh?" asked Carlos. "*¿Por qué?*"

"You aren't clanning like everyone else. Every family has their own home. With everyone sharing the expenses, this must be as cheap as clanning."

A portly but strong-looking guy named Manuel leaned forward. "I have my wife and Paco, Marta, and Vida. All five of us. And one bedroom." He jerked his thumb toward apartment eight. "This not a condo in Polanco. Or Beverly Hill."

I turned to Carlos. "Have you ever thought of adding a second story?"

"*Si*," he said, nodding. "I try. But there's too many laws. What do you call it? *Codes*. Only way is to tear it down, start all over."

"That's bullshit," I said. "They need to change the laws."

"How you make them do that, *Judío*?" Octavio asked.

I shrugged.

Carlos spoke: "They say a man can change things with appeals to City Council. Or with a vote. For thirty years we try these things. But, a bank need a bailout?" He snapped his fingers loud enough to make Doreen stir. "A business need a tax break?" *Snap.* "*Policía* need a warrant?" *Snap.*

"Yeah," I said, "kinda backwards."

"*Si*. 'We the People' don't exist no more. Not to government. What happens when you vote? *Nada*. And when you protest in a park? *Pepper spray*. When things get this bad, the people should make *revolución*. But here, it's impossible. The government's too protected. And the people—even the homeless—so *not* angry."

"Apathetic," I said.

"*Si*," Carlos said. "If they don't care, there's no way to change nothing."

"There are ways," I countered.

"If you have no army, the only thing else is terror."

"Civil unrest. Civil disobedience. Civil destruction. They didn't call the rioters in Watts *terrorists*. They were *protesters*. It was *illegal* protesting, sure—burning neighborhoods and stores and all. But it wasn't terrorism."

"Stupid," Octavio said. "They burnt their own homes."

"They burned the *banks'* homes" I said, "homes they were being overcharged for—both in value and in interest. But they weren't hopeless, and no one today is hopeless. They're just apathetic—the only thing they ever yell at is their television. But there are ways, ways to disrupt the system, ways they have no defense against. Like dumping nails out on the 101. Or painting all the freeway signs black. Or shorting out the power lines along the L.A. River. Or with ten bucks, you could go to Radio Shack and get the parts to make a screamer—a little box that broadcasts interference over all the public airwaves. The possibilities are endless."

Carlos began talking *rápidamente* to the others, and the beer was making it hard for my mind to translate. As the sun began lightening the eastern sky, I thanked Carlos for hosting the little party, and then imposed on Octavio for a ride home.

Before taking us home, Octavio grabbed two twelve-packs, one each for Doreen and me—he was cool like that. I stumbled into my house, put the beer in the fridge, and went to bed. I was out until maybe four in the afternoon. When I got up, I rinsed my face, brushed my teeth, and filled up a glass of water. I took it to the couch and flipped on the screen.

An aerial view of a crowd came on. Below the picture was a banner ad: *Get $5 off by logging onto Tide.com within the next five minutes.* When the banner disappeared, an overlay started with a man dressed in a black suit and a red tie, walking on top of the scrolling marquee at the bottom of the screen. A pistol belt held a six-shooter on each of his hips. The words blinked on beside him:

Property Damage at Your Home?

The man unbuttoned his coat, and pulled his coattails behind him. Then he drew from his right hip and shot the caption, making the words fly apart like exploding glass.

Vehicular Damage from Protesters?

Now he drew from his left hip and fired. The shattered words flew apart again.

Lost Wages Due to Demonstrations?

Finally, the man shot multiple rounds from both weapons, making the letters scatter all over the aerial view from the helicopter. When they dissolved away, the man blew a puff from each gun barrel and another banner rose from the bottom of the screen:

Call Your Lawyer:
Thurgood Thurman III, Esq.
(213) 555-9900 or go to TTIII.com
Now!

Thurgood Thurman the Third reholstered his pieces and stood with his hands on his hips, smiling.

Above the ad, you could tell now that the crowd was outside an Albertson's in Pasadena. Sky5 was high above the scene, trying to catch the enormity of the mass of people. They filled the entire parking lot as well as the streets ahead of the store for three blocks. When the camera zoomed in, there was action near the storefront. The people were shouting some one-syllable word, but I couldn't tell what it was by reading their lips. As they screamed it, they punched their fists upwards in emphasis.

The caption onscreen read *Breaking News*. In those days, an actress with a broken nail was considered "Breaking News" by KTLA, so you got to where you ignored that particular phrase. This was clearly more than *Breaking News*, though: the caption should have read *Impending Doom*.

When they switched from Sky5 to the field crew, you could hear the crowd's chant. They spoke loudly, passionately, angrily. And that simple, one-syllable word came across loud and clear.

That word was *"MEAT!"*

A Fox 11 Special Report had aired that morning, investigating why the price of meat had skyrocketed within the prior few months. The industry had given their standard answers: for beef, it was another year of drought in the Midwest; for pork, it was the increase in the cost of feed; for chickens, it was changes due to increasing pressure from PETA; for fish, it was toxic metals. The speculators and futures traders had run with these facts, resulting in sky-high prices for anything meat. Though the grocers and retailers had predicted an initial contraction in demand, they knew it wouldn't last long. After all, the public may balk at high prices initially, but they begrudgingly pay them in the end.

What Fox 11 had uncovered was that the free-range lands were not under drought conditions at all, but were rather experiencing higher than average precipitation. Feed prices were at an all-time low, but the pork producers were having trouble getting their hands on expired and waste foods from restaurants and supermarkets. The stuff usually sold, pound-for-pound, at half the price of feed, and now nearly all of it was being diverted to food banks. Next, the special report pointed out that the chicken industry had been compliant with both governmental standards and PETA's guidelines for nearly a decade. And finally, they quoted from an FDA study published just two weeks prior to the seafood industry's excuse about heavy metals, revealing that the levels of mercury and other contaminants had dropped so low that the government was considering eliminating random testing, saying that the practice was "a waste of taxpayer dollars."

So, who was responsible for the price increases? Someone or some organization was clearly manipulating the market, but Fox 11 didn't dig that far—which was one of the reasons I watched KTLA.

By noon, protesters had gathered at each of L.A.'s supermarkets with signs like:

STOP
UNFAIR
PRICING

and:

LOWER
MEAT
PRICES
NOW!

and even:

SAFEWAY:
SCREWING
MOM AND POP
AGAIN

Twenty or thirty protesters at each grocery store didn't amount to much, and the protestors knew it. So, through the magic of social media, they decided to concentrate on just one supermarket, and the hundreds of little street-corner protests became one huge protest at the Albertson's in Pasadena.

The manager had locked the store.

Now, KTLA's field reporter and cameraman were pressing through to the front, where the store manager stood behind the sliding doors with his arms folded. The glass between the camera and the manager was slick with spit and peppered with sticky snot rockets.

The reporter screamed above the chants of *MEAT! MEAT! MEAT! MEAT! "Sir!"* she said. *"Will you crack open the door and speak with me?"*

The manager shook his head emphatically: *NO.*

"If you'll relate your position, perhaps it will calm the crowd!"

The manager considered this, and reached into a pocket, bringing out his phone. He pushed some buttons and held the phone against the glass. The reporter wrote down his phone number. She then fiddled with some wires between her mic, her phone, and some other device.

"Just a moment," she said. "We'll be going live with the manager in a few seconds…"

I'd emptied my water. It was time for a beer. I got up and grabbed one. When I got back, the reporter had the manager on the telephone.

"Sir, may I have your name please?"

"Greg Kline," he said. One hand held the phone to his ear. His other hand was on his hip.

"Are you the General Manager?"

"Yes." Greg looked incensed. His small, frameless glasses had slid down to the tip of his nose. He wasn't pushing them back up. His eyes surveyed the crowd from above the lenses.

"Mr. Kline, these people seem frustrated over the recent increases in the prices of food—of meat in particular. Do you care to comment?"

"We are a neighborhood store. We pride ourselves on hiring locally. On providing union-protected wages for those in our community. What I wish to say to these protestors is that we are your neighbors. Your friends. Your relatives. If we have to close our doors, I have to send my employees home—*unpaid*. Please let us do our business."

The reporter flicked back a lock of hair from in front of her eyes. "Do you feel these people have a right to be angry about the price of meat?"

"Certainly. But whether you do your shopping with us here at Albertson's or elsewhere, your neighborhood retailer has no impact on pricing. We purchase our goods at the current market levels and add one, two, three cents on the dollar, depending on the item. Some things, especially when on sale, are even sold at a loss. Nearly a third of our meat is priced that way: at a loss. The protest shouldn't be here. We do a fair business."

"Where should the protest be?"

"Not here," he said.

"Are your suppliers price-gouging?"

Greg shook his head. "Albertson's does business with only the best, most trusted vendors. That is all I have to say." He pressed a button and pocketed his phone. His arms went back to being crossed over his chest.

I'd drained my beer already. I got up and came back with three more. I didn't want to miss a thing.

"Mandy," the anchor said from the studio, "can you hear me?"

"The shouting, as you can hear, has gotten louder." The camera swung around to the protesters. Those in the front row were yelling curses at the manager.

"For our viewers at home," the anchor said, "I apologize for the language you're hearing. This is breaking news, live from Pasadena."

All at once, the crowd became silent and still.

The cameraman lifted his camera high above his head and surveyed the protestors. The faces in the crowd were all looking down—checking their phones.

A singular cry went out: *"SMASH THE DOOR!"*

The crowd took up the new chant.

Mandy spoke again. "The crowd has stopped chanting for meat and is now calling for the door to be broken down."

"Mandy, we're going to stay with you…" The screen changed to a split with the anchor on half, coupled with a jiggling view at the Albertson's. The anchor commented for the viewers: "For her protection, our on-site security is taking Mandy Gutierrez a safe distance away."

The half-screen at Albertson's changed back to Sky5.

The crowd had grown even larger since the last aerial view. The sun was below the horizon now and the parking lot's lights were snapping on as the helicopter hovered some thirty stories above.

"Ruben Chavez is in Sky5—"

"Yes, Jerry, the crowd is clearing space for people approaching with shopping carts. Nick, try to zoom in on that..."

"Ruben, can you tell if there's any sign of police?"

"No, and visibility is a good three or four miles." There was a brief pause. "Okay, now three men with carts have arrived at the front door."

The camera was zooming in. Fists were punching the air everywhere. Faces were flushed with anger. One of the men went sprinting with a shopping cart ahead of him.

The door exploded inward.

The crowd lunged toward the entrance. The door became a bottleneck as the protestors in the rear pushed forward.

"The front door has been broken down," Ruben said. "Many have gotten through, while others are being pressed against the storefront. This is a tense, possibly deadly situation, Jerry."

Jerry started in on an "if you're just joining us" interlude.

Ruben interrupted him. "Here we go, if we can pan over. We've spotted a convoy of police vans heading across the 210…"

The camera zoomed into the smoggy distance. Six large armored vans were taking up the right lane on the freeway. Convection from the day's heat was rising in the night; the vans' flashing lights wavered in the distance. As if in accentuation of the apocalyptic feel of the visual, the van in the lead careened into the rear bumper of a slow-moving car, sending it spinning to the median.

"Jerry, these are the type of vehicles we see for transporting police in riot gear. Each one can carry twelve to fourteen officers, along with all their equipment."

"Can you tell me, Rubin—how long before they reach the disturbance?"

"No more than five minutes, another one or two before they'll be ready to engage the crowd."

Sky5's camera panned back to the Albertson's entrance. The second set of sliding doors had been opened. They crowd was flowing more easily now.

"Do we?" Jerry asked someone. "Our field reporter Mandy Gutierrez is now inside the Albertson's located at Sierra Madre and Michillinda. I'd like to remind any viewers who may be travelling tonight into western Pasadena or Sierra Madre to avoid that area. Okay, now we're back with Mandy. Can you hear me, Mandy?"

"Yes, Jerry. I'm standing at one of the checkout stands. Moments ago, I witnessed the store manager, Greg Kline—who we met earlier—lead his employees upstairs. No one in the crowd has turned to follow. Within this melee, they seem more interested in filling their carts."

A ringing bell sounded.

"Right now we're hearing an alarm," Jerry said. "Can you tell what that's from?"

"I can't see past the crowd. I assume the alarm's from one of the emergency exits..." Mandy looked left, right, left again. She stopped someone who had a blue, button-down shirt pulled up over his nose. "Sir, can you please take a few seconds to tell me why—"

"Ain't got time, sweet tits," the man said before disappearing into the herd of bustling arms, legs, and torsos.

"Once again," Jerry voice-overed, "apologies for the language. We are covering this scene live..."

The camera moved into one of the aisles. A quick survey of a cart showed a dozen cans of chili, a flat of cat food cans, several bottles of a colorful confection, a box of Hamburger Helper, a partial rack of teen magazines—most of them identical. A second cart had a stack of disposable turkey roasting pans, armfuls of Little Debbie's, foot powder, bleach, and what appeared to be most of the store's stock of Band-Aids.

Mandy made it to the center aisle and was slammed by a cart filled with milk jugs. An involuntary *"Oooof"* burst out of her, and she backed against an emptying display of Bud Light to get her wind back. The person pushing the cart gave a curt apology and hurried away. Mandy was bent at the waist, holding her arms crossed over her stomach. Tears streamed down her cheeks.

"Oh, *dear*," Jerry said, sounding dramatic, "are you okay, Mandy?"

She bobbed her microphone up and down while her glazy eyes gazed at the camera. The screen split again, with Mandy's cameraman turning from her over to people swiping things—*any*things—into their carts, and Sky5 focusing on looters streaming out through a side door.

Rubin broke in. "Jerry, it seems they have gotten into the butcher's shop. Outside one of the emergency exits, we can see a cart here—it is, yes, that's a *side of beef...*" When the cart was pushed into the street, it appeared to be stuck. The man at the handle was pushing hard enough to lift the rear wheels off of the ground.

"Rubin, is that cart in a pothole or something?"

"No, Jerry. The carts have theft-preventative measures on them. Once you get off the property, one of the wheels will lock up."

A second man lifted the front of the cart as the first man pushed.

"They seem to have found a way past that. How far are the police now?"

"The police have just exited the 205 and are heading northbound…"

Inside the store, there was another moment of stillness while the looters felt their pockets for their phones. Mandy's cameraman panned through the still crowd. In only seconds, their energy was back again— everyone was scanning the store for the nearest exit.

It only took three or four minutes. I was downing another beer and, by the time I'd finished it off, the Albertson's in Pasadena was empty, the crowd's members scattering in different directions toward each of their vehicles. The carts had all been abandoned within a block of the store. Those left partially full were quickly emptied by neighborhood lookie-loos.

The cops arrived.

Ambulances whisked away some walking wounded.

Mandy had recovered and stayed to report on the store, which looked like it had been hit by a tornado. I was well-buzzed by then, and I began nodding off as Mandy Gutierrez and her crew covered every square inch of the ravaged supermarket.

By Sunday morning, three more supermarkets had been plundered and another plundering was underway. What happened there in Pasadena and at the stores that followed became known as *gang grabs*. The map displaying the afflicted stores showed none near Hollywood, but I figured one of these gang grabs could pop up anywhere. So, I decided I should go to Ralph's and stock up.

Problem was, so had everybody else.

Ralph's wasn't surrounded by a mob. Instead, there were hundreds of bored customers patiently waiting in a line looping the store. The supermarket had paid for a contingent of security—there were at least a dozen outside the building. Inside, they limited the number of shoppers so that as a certain number left, the same number of new ones would be allowed in. It was just before noon when I got in line; now, as a mid-spring sunset was turning the clouds pink, I had ten-or-so people left in front of me. Directly to my left, there was an area enclosed by portable, aluminum barricades. A well-used sheet protector had been taped to the barricade containing a notice:

NO BAGS ALLOWED
INSIDE STORE

Unsecured
Baggage
Holding Area

We assume
NO RESPONSIBILITY
for loss or theft of
your items

Within the area were stacks of backpacks and bedrolls. The smell coming from the pile was nauseating.

A scrawny kid with a peach-fuzzed face and untrimmed, unkempt hair was sitting next to the doors going, "Can you spare any dollar-change?" as people entered. A clanned trio exited, their cart stuffed full, with a family pack of pork chops poking above all the bags. The dollar-change kid shot up from his spot, seized the meat, and ran. The trio stood there with their mouths dropped open, asking each other, "What'd he take?" and poking through their groceries like they'd figure it out. They were still sifting through their items when I was finally allowed in.

What I wanted was lots of ramen noodles, some frozen vegetables to cook with them, and some crackers and spray cheese. And maybe some cold cuts that I could dice up and put on the crackers—if the meat was semi-affordable.

When I got to the noodles, the back end of a woman was sticking out of the supermarket shelf. She wore long jean-shorts that on an ordinary woman would have gone several inches below the knees, but on her, they ended several inches above it. Her belt was just a length of nylon rope tied into a square knot inwards of her right hip. On her feet she had pink Chuck Taylors that were so faded that they had turned a pale flesh color. Her lime-green socked pinky toe was sticking out of a hole in the size-thirteen right shoe. Past a rip in her other shoe, you could see an aqua sock. She was mumbling within the shelf, her voice low and froggy, and my view of her upper half was obscured by the cup noodles to her left and the bagged ramen to her right. She was going, "Chicken... Chicken... Beef... Chicken..."

I began filling my basket with Oriental flavored ramen, pulling them strategically, trying to get a look at her face.

Suddenly, she shot out of the shelf, lifting a cup noodle aloft and crying, *"Yes!"*

I stood frozen in place, halfway to transferring another bag of Oriental ramen to my basket. I craned my neck to meet her eyes—if I'd've stood on my toes, I might've been at eye level with her breasts. She was wearing a men's basketball jersey that was threadbare and tied-up in the back, accentuating the curve of her waist. A guilty look appeared upon her face, as though she was a child who just got caught doing something naughty.

Then she modeled her prize smilingly, as though she was performing for a commercial. "It's totally amazing they don't charge more for these shrimp Cuppa Noodles." She shook the Styrofoam cup at me, saying, "These little shrimpies are yummy!"

I gave her an understanding nod, and continued stocking my basket with the Oriental ramen.

Her face took on a look of self-reproach. "Well, that's rude of me, isn't it? Tell you how yummy the shrimp is and take the last one..."

I gave her a closed-lip smile. My face was filling with hot blood. I didn't know what to say, couldn't get my brain working. I just kept stocking up my basket.

"Hey—you want one?" she asked. "I must have a dozen…" She plopped the Cuppa Noodles into my basket.

I held the basket out toward her. "No, no," I said. "I like my Oriental flavor."

She took Cuppa Noodles back with a shrug. "Okay." She paused with it in her hand.

I just stared like a dumb ass.

She smiled again. "Whoa—like, *crickets*…"

I gave her a double-take like, *Huh?*

She chucked her shrimp Cuppa Noodles into her cart and proceeded up the aisle. I never stopped looking at her as she walked away, and she looked back at me— twice.

I had the most peculiar feeling when she looked back that second time, and I guess she felt it too. I mean—I could see it on her face. It was nothing like love at first sight: I think *that's* just a bunch of fairy-tale nonsense. It was a strange feeling of familiarity to me, as though we already knew each other. Like maybe a long time ago. Maybe when we were children. Maybe in a previous life. Now *that's* a bunch of fairy-tale nonsense *too*, but that's the best way I can explain it. It was an electrical moment. It ended when she turned the corner at the end of the aisle.

I walked home from Ralph's well after sunset. Clouds had rolled in from the Pacific while I was shopping and a thunderstorm now raged overhead. I got home drenched. After changing, I cooked some Oriental noodles with green beans and watched more Breaking News on KTLA.

The rain and thunder continued all through the night and, after a couple hours of that Breaking News, I finally splurged on a movie. It must have been awful because I can't remember what it was. No, for the rest of the night, I could only think about that skyscraping girl who was dressed in rags, about my failure to seize the moment, about how I should have taken that Cuppa Noodles she had offered. How I should have invited her to share it with me.

On Monday morning, I finally pried myself off the couch and got ready for work. It was still pouring, but the lightning had stopped. I donned my windbreaker and stood on the porch, listening for the approach of Octavio's Impala.

3—512 Write-Ups

The rides to work were a blur for a couple weeks—on every single trip, I was absorbed with how I could possibly find the Cuppa Noodles girl again. Even at work, I could think of nothing else. The only things I really remember about these days—as work on the labyrinth was finishing up—were the twanging of steel guitars from the Impala's speakers and Doreen's constant pestering. She would ask me over and over again if I was okay, and I would tell her, *Yeah, yeah,* while in my mind kicking myself in the ass: *I hadn't even gotten the girl's name!*

On another gray morning, Octavio parked where he always did, with quick access to the front door. The parking lots surrounding the building had the capacity for thousands of cars, but the only one anybody parked in was the south lot, and there were never more than thirty cars in it. If most of your employees work for minimum

44

wage, there won't be too many drivers—Octavio was the only one in our department.

When we got to the door, a new sign proclaimed:

APPLICANTS AND VENDORS
ONLY
Employees use the
West Entrance

I pulled the door open. Mr. Chandler was standing beyond it.

"*Ah-ah-ah,*" he said musically while wagging his finger. "You step one foot past this threshold and I'll fire your ass faster than a fat chick pops a bonbon." He emphasized the way to the other door by pushing me westbound. I backpedaled off of the entrance's sidewalk and tripped. My tailbone landed on a hard, steel grating covering a riser from the third basement. The impact paralyzed my diaphragm; I rolled over on my side in agony.

I heard Mr. Chandler slam the door shut.

Doreen knelt down beside me. "You alright, Zeno?"

I grunted.

Octavio let out a few curses; the one in English was "This *bull*shit, man."

I rolled onto my knees and waved an arm hoping for help up. Neither of them noticed.

"What does *qué chinga* mean?" Doreen asked.

"It mean *qué chinga*, I dunno."

I pulled myself up slowly, using the window frame. As I tottered westbound, Doreen and Octavio followed.

"Well," Doreen pushed, "what's *chinga* then?"

"I say *I dunno.*"

When we got to the west entrance, it had a sign similar to the other one:

EMPLOYEE ENTRANCE
Applicants and Vendors
Use the South Entrance

Doreen held the door open for me and let out a little bark. I smiled at her and went in.

My tailbone fracture was now a throbbing ache, one that I knew would smart whenever I'd sit. As soon as I had walked in that door though, I forgot about the pain entirely. Ahead of us was a hallway that went for a while and ahead, there was another hall perpendicular to it. Nylon ropes were on the ground labeled with permanent marker on duct tape. The labels said: *Centro, Ascensor, Oficina, Escalera, Salida 1, Salida 2, Salida 3...*

The air reeked of fresh paint. The labyrinth's walls were plain white and, after we had made that first turn—where the entrance door was no longer visible—there was a severe impression of uniformity, of homogeneity, that you could turn corners for the rest of your life and the damned thing would go on forever. We followed the *oficina* rope as it went through L-turns, T-junctions, cross-junctions, and switchbacks. Before long, all sense

46

of direction was lost. I looked up, hoping to decipher directionality from the roof. The tiles and the lights of the suspended ceiling were square, giving away nothing. The labyrinth was awe-inducing, terrifying, and—most importantly to Mr. Chandler—sure to make most of the employees late to work.

After the twentieth turn or so, Doreen tugged at my sleeve. "Shouldn't we be writing this down? Making a map—*something?*"

"You're probably right," I said. "But we're too far into it now."

We continued to follow the *oficina* rope.

We walked for fifteen minutes before the rope led us to the office. Octavio and Doreen headed off to their cubicles, but I wanted my morning cup, and all that was left of the coffee machine were the mop-water stains outlining the machine's feet. I went to the south entrance to talk to Mr. Chandler.

"You're late," he said.

"We were on time until you made us go through your maze."

"You could argue that."

"Where's the coffee?"

"Coffee, water, soda, snacks…" He pointed to where I'd come from. "All in different spots in the labyrinth. Just follow the rope that says *Coffee*. Or whatever that is in Spanish."

"*Café,*" I said.

"Better pay attention—I'm pulling the ropes tonight."

An employee opened the south entrance door.

"*Ah-ah-ah,*" Mr. Chandler said.

I went back to the labyrinth to follow the *café* rope.

I took out a fiver and dropped it in the coin slot. I selected *Hazelnut,* and the machine did its thing. Off to the left, someone had hung a painting. There was a silvery cloud, the type that you would see in old nautical engravings—a squinted face in the cloud's billows, rounded lips, and the suggestion of wind made with dashed lines in swirls and curlicues. The gust was blowing a sombrero over the grassy thickets that form just beyond the high tide line at the beach, and as strongly as that cloud was blowing, the sombrero wouldn't be touching down until it was over the water...

I traced the brush strokes of the painting with my index finger. The sky was smooth, with a feel like wet glass, and when I moved my fingertip over the beach, it was gritty—making me lift my finger to see what was under it. I touched it again. It was as though the artist mixed finely textured sand into the paint. I traced over a blade of sawgrass and a jolt of pain came, like when you get a paper cut. My finger had a minute drop of blood on it. I looked at the painting closer, and closer still.

The sawgrass was paint—nothing more.

I sucked the tiny blood drop off my finger and grabbed my coffee.

I followed the *café* rope back to the office.

As Mr. Chandler interviewed applicants, I went back into the labyrinth to make a map. It didn't take long for me to realize that doing so would be unrealistic. The passages were as narrow as aisles in a convenience store, and the labyrinth itself was a block wide and a quarter-mile long. A map would have taken no less than a week, or maybe two, to complete. Instead, what I made was more of a key, like: *Left, Straight, Left, Right, Right, Straight, Straight, Right...* I made keys from the entrance to the office, from the office to the entrance, from the office to the coffee, and from the coffee to the office. It took me until lunch—I kept running into employees who couldn't translate the ropes.

I got to Mr. Chandler's cubicle with a fresh cup of coffee. I opened my sack lunch and sat diagonally, to keep off my butt wound.

"Where've you been?" he asked.

"Lost in your labyrinth." I peeled plastic wrap away from my lunch.

"Huh." He pointed at my sandwich. "What's that? Roast beef?"

I lifted the slice of bread. "Looks like it." I bit off a quarter of my sandwich at once, trying to end the conversation. It didn't work.

He pulled some onion rings out of his Burger King bag. "I want you to write up everyone who clocked in after 8:30. That way, when they're late tomorrow, I can fire them. I need all of the write-ups signed by the time you leave work."

I nodded my understanding.

Chewing my mouthful, I called up the Late Time Punch Report. 512 people clocked in after 8:15. I swallowed and it went down hard. I sipped some coffee and then talked, spitting moist crumbs: "There's no way, Mr. Chandler."

Mr. Chandler looked at the report and laughed. "Get your two buddies to help. You take Personnel and HR. Octavio can have IT and Security. That'll leave Doreen with Marketing and Payroll."

"We have a *Marketing* Department?"

"Yeah, down on two. There's like 250 of them."

"What do they market?"

"Hell if I know…"

I opened a form-letter write-up and dragged-and-dropped the list from the Late Time Punch Report into it. After a quick keypunch, the printer spat out the paperwork. I finished my sandwich, and hunted down Octavio and Doreen to tell them our afternoon job.

That night at the commune, Mr. Chandler was the topic of conversation.

"He gone *loco*, Man," was Octavio's take.

Doreen opened a beer. "I don't think so. He brings prospectives in through the south entrance, hires them, and then loses them in the labyrinth." She ticced a couple of times and recovered. "Seems like a great way to increase turnover."

I shook my head. "He's created something that, to me, would mean instant unemployment. Like, 'I didn't show up because I couldn't find the place.'"

Doreen took another swig. "Yeah, maybe. But he's not paying a dime for any of these people. I mean, they don't get paid for the interview, they don't get paid to have their info entered into the computer. So, if an employee loses the unemployment, HRW wins. If the employee gets the unemployment, we still win—because we never paid out any earnings in the first place."

"If the employee gets the unemployment," I added, "HRW has to pay a higher insurance rate." I downed the rest of my beer.

Octavio was working on a bottle of Jack. He swallowed, prune-faced. "Blah, blah, blah. You both talk too much. He *loco*. That's it."

Doreen got up for another beer. She smiled at me, and then mimicked Octavio's drunkenness behind his back. I couldn't help but laugh...

I need more coffee.

I stand up.

I can still see Doreen's petite frame, the lower half of which was covered in skin-tight jeans. Her bottom was angled upward as she reached into the cooler, and her blouse was sliding up, revealing those two dimples you see on a girl's back—a couple of inches above the top of the buttocks and an inch-or-so on either side of the spine.

"Excuse me," I say to Carson, and walk off to the kitchen.

There's no earthly reason Carson needs to know about Doreen. I mean, it was one of those heat-of-the-moment things where you're looking and she knows you're looking and you try to look away and you can't and she knows you can't, so she looks up and you're powerless to move and she stands up and kisses you and you're mired in the moment because of all the chemicals—they say a woman secretes pheromones when she's ovulating. And her ovulating chemicals are telling you something and it's mindless, thoughtless, and if it were to come to you in words, those words would be that since she's ovulating, you should be spermulating. There are sexy calls and whistles throughout the commune as you lead her into apartment thirteen and kick the wooden stop into the gap under the door because the doorknob's just a gaping hole and you go back to sucking face and you try to wiggle her out of jeans that're vacuum-sealed to her skin.

She's beautiful; it's not beerful thinking.

No—she's perfect.

And she's not barking.

Her jeans finally pull free and meanwhile everyone's out there and you can hear them out there and you know they know what's going on in apartment thirteen and there's this constant fear you feel as you're tasting the flesh behind her ear and you move the thong off to the side a little and you can smell the odor of your hipwork, but still nobody interrupts, nobody tries to look in through the doorknob hole, and there's no thought of consequence. You just go on and it's the first time in over a year and it must be five minutes before you even unbutton her blouse and loosen up her bra—they are smallish, though still handfuls, the kind that'll never be kneeknockers. You pinch a nipple firmly and she moans softly in reply and she wraps her legs around you, and when she spurs you with her flip-flops, and those flip-flops spring off to regions unknown within that dark apartment, that *does it* for you; it would be another two hours before you'd even think about a condom: much too late—just a little over *two hours* too late. You lift her up and sit her on the kitchenette by an old, noisy Frigidaire and while you taste her, she squeezes your head with her thighs so you can't hear the voices of the commune outside anymore, but you can still hear her breathing and all the times she doesn't breathe (and *good God!* she can hold her breath forever) leaving you with the fascinating sound of the rapid pulse in her thighs. It's her third climax when she curls up, her abs like concrete, and she begs you to stop to stop *to stop* and she's *all* atremble *all* over. You're a little exhausted and a little woozy from drink. So you lift her off the counter and over your shoulder. She's giggling when you drop her on the unsheeted mattress and collapse by her side. When Octavio wakes you in the morning with knocking and a voice spoken in a taunting falsetto, you are awake and oh, so aware. And now Doreen *is* barking, she's barking like a guard dog taunted by children. When she goes in for the morning kiss and you give her her due, there's no love in it, only discomfort.

But she *was* beautiful that night.

Perfectly so.

Carson comes into the kitchen.

"Muffin?" I ask.

"Sounds good."

I fill both our coffees. I put some French vanilla in mine—he just mixes some sugar into his. We each bring our coffee-and-a-muffin back to the dining room.

4—The Fish In The Life Preserver

So, where were we?

Well, there were more paintings in the labyrinth the next morning. We had just gone in through the employee entrance. Directly to the right, a large canvas was hung, showing the surface of an ocean—as an eight-year-old would draw it—with curves painted concave-up, their edges meeting together to form tall little crests. Both the water below and the sky above were blue, but a peculiar hint of color had been added to the sky—perhaps a gray primer meant to take away the gloss. At the center of the painting a life preserver floated, the white, donut-shaped kind with loops of rope on it, and poking up through its center was a funny looking fish with a strange smile. One of his fins rested on the preserver, while the other appeared to be waving...

"That's the painting above your fireplace," Carson says. "It's certainly a McClusky."

"That's right."

"How did you end up with it?" he asks. "Above your mantel?"

"That happened much later, Carson."

"Okay."

I stand and stretch.

Carson cocks his neck and stares.

"Bathroom," I say.

"Ah," he says. "Good idea."

I head off remembering the good times—a soldier had burst through the applicant entrance pleading, *Bathroom? Bathroom?*, and Shasta grimaced at him, fascinated. Soon, she was serving them all. She'd memorized their names, their wives' and girlfriends' names, how many children they had, and especially what they liked to eat.

My coffee seems to be running straight through me.

Sure, it's clichéd, but why can't life come with a do-over?

When I work the handle, the yellowed water swirls down the hole with a *squosh*. I return to the dining room in a confused melancholy.

I sit. Carson arrives shortly.

"Go on, Dad."

The *Fish in the Life Preserver* was just inside, on the right wall. Opposite that, on the left wall, was another canvas. The water and the sky were painted in the same fashion, but on that side there was a dolphin in the water. As I followed the directions I'd written to the *oficina*, there were more dolphin canvasses. Each of them was a little different than the other—comparing them was like inspecting the individual frames of a cartoon show. After a while, I stopped paying attention to my key and kept following the dolphin.

The paintings were hung at eye level no more than six inches apart from each other the whole way through. There must have been hundreds of them, utilizing endless gallons of blue and azure and turquoise. The style was a little cartoony, but each canvas was painted with a sharp eye for highlights and shade, for color and tone, and for depth and perspective. The succession of the frames revealed the dolphin's motion—swimming, leaping from the water in an arc, splashing back down. After we'd followed this dolphin through dozens of the labyrinth's turns, a sombrero came into view, floating on the surface of the water. The dolphin took it in its snout and swam it down to sea floor.

That's where the T-junction was that turned toward the *oficina*.

We walked down that final corridor and stepped out.

On that day, Mr. Chandler was on a hiring-and-firing spree. The downstairs departments had all made it in: Gordon—the guy who called me a dipshit—had painted a big yellow stripe on the floor to mark the path to the stairs. But in Personnel, only forty of us could find the office without the ropes. So, thirty-nine of Mr. Chandler's employees got busy filing the two-hundred-or-so terminations of the ones who hadn't made it.

That afternoon, I was back to signing Mr. Chandler's name again, and now that I was forced to sit diagonally (to this day, my broken tailbone aches if I sit in one position too long), the job had become a strange test of endurance. Instead of just my hand, my whole body was cramping now. As I twisted and squirmed in my seat, Mr. Chandler once again worked his way to the California Lottery website. I watched for his routine of rubbing his hands together, wiping his lips, putting the ticket right on the glass of the screen, sighing, double checking, and ripping the ticket to shreds, but that's not what happened.

What happened was this: Mr. Chandler erupted into a series of coughs, as though he'd accidentally inhaled some water. I pivoted in my seat to face him, and his complexion had taken on an odd, pastel tone—making him look the same way people do on television when you adjust the COLOR slider all the way to one end. He took his ticket and slapped it onto his screen, making a wave of color propagate from there out to the screen's edges. I glanced at the numbers in the browser, and at those on the ticket.

They matched.

As Mr. Chandler stood, his chair was ejected from the cubicle—a caster flapped madly as it shot across the smooth floor. The seat ricocheted off the break room door and then slowed as it put its energy into spinning on its own axis. Beside me, Mr. Chandler bounced up and down, his arms in the pose of a champion. He still wasn't breathing—it was as though respiration had become a non-essential function of his body. It wasn't until maybe the tenth bounce that he finally took an inward wheeze.

"HA HA HA HA, SUCKERRRRRS!" he bellowed in a squeaky pitch. He sucked in another breath. *"TWO POINT THREE BILLION DOLLARS!!! HAAAA-CHAAAAAA!"*

He puffed now, as though in labor. In trembles, he reached into a pocket. He brought out his fob and fought a large key off of it. He slapped it onto the desk. Then, in a sprint, he took off down the first aisle of cubicles. I stood, watching him go. He stopped at each cubicle to brag, "I won the lottery!" When he rounded the first column and started back up the second, he added "—and you didn't!" By the third column, he stopped running and it became, "Ha-ha, I'm rich..." By the fourth column, he was winded and he just shuffled along, going "Ha, ha... Ha, ha... Ha, ha..." as he passed the last of the cubicles.

Some of the employees gathered around me by Mr. Chandler's cubicle. As he tottered back, I expected someone to deck him, but no one did. Mr. Chandler put the winning ticket into his shirt pocket and patted it a couple times. He grinned at me declaring, *"I'm free! I'm free!"* as he took slow, backwards steps toward the applicant entrance. Midway in a turn to open the door, he stopped.

He was frozen in consideration, with deep furrows in his brow.

Suddenly, he was moving again. He dashed to his office chair, lifted it above his head, and walked it over to the window beside the entrance door. When he launched the chair at the glass, a loud, triple-clack sounded, but the window held. Now, Mr. Chandler chuckled in an exhausted fit, pointing at the upside-down chair now at his feet. When his humor left him, he picked up the chair once more, and this time he gave it a running start. The additional momentum worked, and the noise was like a hundred cymbals crashing.

"I'm free!" he said with renewed breath. *"Finally free!"*

More employees gathered now. A few of them motioned feebly at Mr. Chandler, in an abortive attempt to communicate that the chair had disappeared.

Mr. Chandler didn't get it.

He jogged through the empty window frame with his arms raised in victory and vanished. His echoey shriek lasted a mere second or two.

Restrained laughter escaped some of the employees.

I shuffled to the edge of the window frame. The steel grating that had broken my tailbone was gone—the metal thieves must have gotten to it. Way beyond where it used to be—three stories below—was a motionless Mr. Chandler, with his right ankle next to his ear. His chair appeared to have had a kinder landing: it was sitting upright, upon its casters, undamaged.

My eyes sensed motion, and moved toward it. Above Mr. Chandler's wreckage, and only about a story below me, danced that winning lottery ticket. It twisted in the air chaotically, slowly slipping down an updraft.

It was impossible to think of poor Mr. Chandler in this moment. The only thoughts were of escape—escape from the prison of my property taxes, from having to bum rides everywhere, from never having enough money for simple things like meat, from having to eat the nasty, expired junk from the food banks. I could be free—as I'd been when Pop was still around. Back when his pension and residuals and Social Security sufficed, paying all the bills and all the taxes and even the occasional pleasure or two.

The words slipped out of me thoughtlessly: *"The ticket."*

The murmured conversation around me came to an abrupt end.

I was like: *Shit.*

I ricocheted off surrounding bodies until I'd breached the edge of the classroom-sized gathering. I raced for the labyrinth and could hear others sprinting to catch up. At the first turn, I glanced back: only five or six were pressing on, while the others had stopped outside the labyrinth's entrance. I continued at full speed, keeping my eyes on the backwards-swimming dolphin. When I'd backtracked to the employee entrance, I followed Gordon's yellow stripe. (There were more paintings then, unfamiliar ones; there were flashes of a flying squirrel, of ants riding a leaf on the rapids of a narrow, stony stream, of a pair of trees giving each other high-fives... But my determination to get that ticket kept me focused on the stripe.) After fifteen or twenty turns, the stairwell's double doors appeared before me. I pushed through them, and then took the stairs in half-floor leaps. On the third jump, I nearly went headlong into the cinderblock enclosure, so I stopped leaping and descended one stair at a time, though in a rapid shuffle.

There was no sign of it coming—on the last flight, someone body-checked me, making me tumble down the last of the stairs and scrape along the floor at the bottom. I turned to find my assaulter, and my neck spasmed as a short-skirted gal dashed away.

My left side was skinned, and some scratches on my face were bleeding. I dabbed the areas with my sleeve. I moved my limbs and nothing was broken. As I got to my feet, I screamed in agony as my tailbone flared with pain. But in this moment, my intestines could've been dragging at my feet and it wouldn't have kept me from going for that ticket. I moved onward into the third basement. Rapid click-clacks echoed through the corridor ahead of me, making the girl easy to track. When I found her, she was closing the access door to the riser. The ticket was in her hand.

It didn't stay there—she stuffed it into her bra.

"That's not yours," I said.

"It's not *yours*," she replied. She brought out her phone, dialed three digits, and held a finger above the call button. "Touch me, and it'll be *rape*." She wrinkled her nose and bared her teeth. *"Rape!"*

Backing slowly toward the stairwell, she stepped past me, holding her phone in her shaky hands like a ray gun. I was statue-still, strung rigidly, like a catapult. She could have been taken in a pounce. She sure could have...

"Don't move for *two minutes*, or I swear to God, it'll be *rape!*" She disappeared into the stairwell. Click-clacking echoed until the spring-loaded door shut the sound in.

I waited for a few seconds, and then decided I'd been stupid. I should've swatted her cell phone away and taken the ticket by force. I rushed upstairs, where the yellow stripe led me back to the employee entrance. I opened the door and looked out. There was no sign of her. I followed the dolphin back to the office, where I wound my way through the office's cubicles looking for the girl. By the time I got back to Mr. Chandler's desk, it was clear she'd escaped.

It took me two more orbits of the office to convince myself of it, though.

My thoughts eventually reminded me that Mr. Chandler was dead. So, I gave up my search and called 911. The recording's questions were simple and I answered them with zeros. After twenty minutes of being on hold, an unfamiliar employee approached.

"So, Zeno, who got the ticket?"

I shrugged. "Not me, obviously." The phone clicked in my ear; I shooed away the employee.

"911, what's your emergency?"

"My boss is dead."

"What is your location?"

"The HRW building on Pico."

"You think your boss is dead? Is he or she breathing?"

"*Mmmm*, no. He's not."

"Can you check? Feel for any breath? See if his chest is rising and falling?"

"I can't really check."

"Why is that, Sir?"

"Well, he fell three stories down a shaft. I tried to go down, but I got hurt. I think I'd better let your EMTs do it."

"I see. How badly are you injured, Sir?"

"It's just a few scratches."

"May I have your name, please?"

"Zeno Jacobs."

"Zeno? Like Xena with an O?"

Idiot. "Z-E-N-O."

"Okay, Mr. Jacobs. I've dispatched emergency personnel to your location."

Once off the phone, I grabbed Mr. Chandler's clover-shaped carving. It was ugly. I dumped it in the trash.

The phone rang.

"HRW International, Zeno speaking—"

"This is Bob," the voice said. "Can you tell me why Gary broke that window?"

I looked up and behind. The camera was pointed straight at me, and I could feel the zoom lens tightening on my pores. "Well," I said, "he went around to all the cubicles screaming 'I'm free, I'm free...' I'm sorry—*who* is this?"

"Bob Norris."

"Doesn't ring a bell, Sir."

"*Madam,*" she said. "I'm the Executive Vice President of the Western Territories."

I winced and then waved at the camera. "Zeno Jacobs."

"Terminate Gary immediately."

I was going to say "Yes, Ma'am," but the line went dead.

The rain fell hard as we rode in the next morning. When I told Octavio and Doreen we should still go through the labyrinth, they told me I was crazy. At the applicant entrance, the window had been fixed and the grating above the basement riser had been replaced with a hard plastic one. As we entered, the phone at Mr. Chandler's desk began ringing. I answered it before I'd even gotten my coffee.

"HRW Interna—"

"This is Bob. You're late."

I checked my Casio. "*Umm,* I'm thirteen minutes early."

"You will be at work *twenty* minutes early in case I have anything to discuss with you."

I had vaguely wondered why Mr. Chandler was always at work before me, and now I knew. I nodded my agreement at the camera.

"Why didn't you tell me that Gary died?" Bob asked.

"You hung up on me."

There was silence.

I kept my mouth shut.

"I need you to fill out an incident report," Bob said. "Please make it *very clear* that he broke the window when he *very well* could have used the door."

All of that had to be for insurance. Or worker's comp. Or whatever. "Okay, Bob."

"You're the Senior Terminations Specialist, correct?"

That seemed a fancy way of putting it. "Yeah."

"Have you ever sat in on any of Gary's interviews?"

"Every day."

"Okay," she said. "I'm in conference with DDG executives, but I need to fill Gary's position."

"You know Gary just won the lot—"

"We're not talking about Gary, we're talking about you."

Jeeesus. "Okay."

"I can't offer you much for salary. I'll give you $530 a week, and that's 75% of the maximum wage—so that's not bad."

I did some mental arithmetic. "$530 a week is the *minimum* wage."

"Well, that's the starting wage for a Personnel Director. There's one thing to keep in mind, though: as Director, you'll be eligible for a bonus."

"Oh?" A bonus sounded good. "How do I earn that?"

"I'll e-mail it to you," Bob said, though she never did. "So you'll take the position?"

"Sure."

Again, the line went dead. I replaced the handset and then took my dripping windbreaker off. The key to the building was still sitting on the desk. I brought out my keychain and slipped it on the ring.

5—The Chicken Cook

THIS JOB SUCKS
CALIFORNIA'S NEWEST BILLIONAIRE
NINETY-SIX INJURED, FOUR DEAD

If there were any vacancies in the department, the spots around the boss' cubicle quickly cleared out. After all, most people prefer a buffer zone between their workspace and the boss'. But while I'd been on the phone with Bob, Doreen started moving all her things to the cubicle directly next to mine. I didn't know how to communicate to her that I preferred her barking from a distance, so I didn't.

As Doreen pinned items to her cubicle wall, Gordon came in through the applicant entrance. He took off a black jacket—one of those Gore-Tex kinds that the water beads up on. A couple of shakes dried it and he flung it over his shoulder. Underneath, he wore what could be loosely described as a poor man's suit: cuffed Dockers above glossy, black shoes; glossy belt to match those shoes; a plain, white, short-sleeved shirt; and a narrow, all-black tie. He walked past the break room and went into the men's bathroom. The door didn't close all the way, and beyond the doorway's gap, Gordon beckoned softly.

"*Psst, psst!*"

I turned to my computer to check my mail.

"*Psst, psst!*"

I let out a heavy sigh, and went into the bathroom.

Gordon slammed the door shut behind me and rested his back against it. He extended his hand. "Gordon Goulet," he said through a nervous smile. "I'm the Director of IT."

He must have forgotten calling me *dipshit*. I decided to drop the issue and shake his hand. "You run the Help Desk, right?"

"Them too," he said, releasing my hand with a jerk. He immediately went to the sink and washed his hands, scrubbing them with liberal amounts of soap. After rinsing, he turned toward me, holding his hands up like a surgeon.

I motioned to the air dryer.

He looked at it, and then back to me. "Incubators. For germs."

"Ah."

"Rumor is you'll be offered the Director spot."

"Yeah, Bob just called."

Gordon took his position again, with his back against the bathroom door. "Did you accept?"

"Yeah."

"Right." He took a brief visual survey of me and made a face that indicated he found me wanting. "You won't get any training from Bob. It's sink-or-swim with her, if you know what I mean."

I nodded. It already seemed that way.

"IT is down on two. We share the floor with security. You know the cameras have been on you."

I thought it was only Mr. Chandler who was being watched. "So?"

"You any good at math?"

His non-sequiturs were confusing me. "Good enough for this job, I guess."

He nodded. "I'll send you your targets on webmail. But I need something in return."

"What?"

"Don't fuck with my people." With that, Gordon got off the door, opened it with his foot, and left.

The mail he sent had a bunch of equations, labeled Productivity, Labor$, Labor%, Labor Hours per Termination, Turnover%, and so on. It listed what had been Mr. Chandler's current numbers, and it showed weekly and monthly goals as well as where I was expected to end up for the year. I printed the targets and searched the desk for some thumbtacks. Unable to find any, I stole one from Doreen's side of the wall and tacked the printout up. As I did, I noticed the prospectives gaggled near the applicant entrance, going from foot to foot, holding papers that I knew were résumés. It was time to start hiring. I looked over the equations once more, and then walked over to introduce myself. I guided the seven of them over to my cubicle, and sat. They all held their résumés in front of them creatively, as though they had a bet to see which one I would reach for first. When I didn't reach for any of them, they lowered their arms one at a time.

"Hi! I'm Shaqueena," one of them said.

"I don't care what your name is," I said, and burst into a short, plosive laugh.

Shaqueena left without further ado.

"Very good," I said. "Somebody tell me how badly you need this job."

A plain, chunky girl raised her hand.

I stood and gave her a high-five. Then I sat again.

"Now somebody tell me how bad you need this job!"

"I've lost my home," one of the guys said, "and I'm trying to keep a roof over my wife and kids' heads. I need this job very badly. I'll work very, very hard for you, Sir."

"Okay," I told him. "You can go."

He blinked at me. "Go where?"

"Go away!" I said, giving him a backhanded wave.

He shuffled backwards slowly, looking confused, and then left. A second one followed him.

"Come on—don't any of you just need twenty bucks for some crank?"

They all went wide-eyed. Another one walked away silently.

There were three left now. Over the years, I actually *had* paid attention to a thing or two. As Mr. Chandler's sidekick, I had always been interested in what he called *The Numbers*:

"I understand most employers will give you some kind of test," I said. "But I'm not the least bit interested in how well you can read, what kind of personality you have, or any of that stupid crap people test applicants for. Instead, I'm interested in just one number. That's what we managers manage: *Numbers*. This one's called *Loss Potential*. It's measured in *Jobs per Year*. What you do is take the number of jobs you've ever had in your whole life and divide it by the number of years that you've been in the workforce. For instance, I've had only one job in my life—*this* one—and I've worked here three years. So, my loss potential is one-third, or point-three-three-three."

They were all doing arithmetic with their fingers—a good sign.

"Feel free to use my calculator..." I said, motioning to my ten-key.

They each lined up one at a time, calculated their number, and stood back again.

I pointed to the chunky lady. "Okay, what was your number?"

"Zero-point-zero-nine," she said.

"Yikes," I said. I pointed to the old guy. "And yours?"

"Zero-point-eight-three."

"Better..." I pointed to the last one, a young kid. "And you?"

"Twelve."

I shook the kid's hand. "Congratulations! You're hired!"

I had hired six more before lunch. One of them was to fill a position downstairs, but the rest had been mine. I spent the first part of the afternoon signing on the lines, and took a half-hour to massage the knots out of my arm.

It must have been around three when the phone rang.

"Hi, this is Tammy from the Home Office. Is Gary in?"

"No, he's no longer with us."

"Oh. Are you the new Director?"

"Yes—I'm Zeno Jacobs."

"Is that with an X?"

Moron. "No, a Z."

"Okay, Zeno. Once a week you're supposed to FedEx your paperwork to us. Once every period, you send the employee files of those that were termed within that period. I haven't received yours yet."

"What's a period?"

There was a pause. Then she said, "Oh, my..."

"Hello?"

"Do you see a calendar around anywhere?"

I looked for one and didn't see it. "No."

"Okay," she said. "Well, a period is four weeks. With fifty-two weeks in a year, that means there's thirteen periods per year. Every week I need your invoices, cash receipts, and new-hire paperwork; once every four weeks I need all of that as well as your terminations. Do you see those large, colored envelopes in front of you?"

I looked toward the camera—it was pointing at me again. I turned back to the hutch. "Yes..."

"The red ones are for invoices. The green ones are for your cash receipts. The 8850s, the I-9s, the 2320s, and the LAC-70s go in the blue ones—do not send the whole employee file. You keep the files of your current employees there, except for the forms I just mentioned. When you or your staff terms someone, put the person's file with the termination form into one of the expandable orange envelopes. Every Friday, place the red, the green, and the blue envelopes in one of the pre-addressed FedEx boxes, seal it, and have it picked up right away. Every four Fridays, you need to add the orange envelope to the packet. Understood?"

"Okay. Sixteen people never came back to work the day Gary died and—"

"He died?"

"Yeah."

"At work?"

"Yeah."

"Did you fill out an incident report?"

"I actually don't know how…"

The mouse pointer moved around on my screen. "It's here: push on the Pioneer, then go to *Director Functions* and then *Accident/Incident Report.*"

"Oh."

"When you get it filled out, make sure to put a copy in the orange envelope with the terminations."

"Right. How many files will fit in there?"

"The orange envelope is expandable. I think it'll fit sixty or seventy. If you ever burn through more than that, just use another one."

"Okay. Think I got it."

"Call me if you need any more help, Zeno. The corporate phone tree is under *Director Functions* as well. Okay?"

"Sure." We said goodbye.

I was worried I'd forget what the colors meant, but the envelopes were labeled with what had to go in them. So, I rifled through the desk and the hutch and everywhere else I could find paperwork and receipts and the right forms and stuffed the envelopes full of them. I'm fairly certain some trash ended up in that first packet I sent off, but once it was sealed in, I didn't care. I called the number on the FedEx box and left the box by the door.

I stayed late that day, trying to get comfortable with how all of the numbers worked, and calculating productivity and labor percent and turnover longhand. Octavio and Doreen had left hours earlier—must've been around eight when I started clearing off my desk. The applicant door opened. An old man in loose jeans and a light blue shirt shuffled in. He didn't see me at first. He walked over to a closet I'd never noticed, opened the door, and brought out a broom. The weight of the broom seemed to add to the curvature in his back. He started in the far corner *swish-swish-swish*ing away.

I stood.

He caught my motion. "Oh, hello there!" he said.

I waved.

He ambled over, in the careful steps of a man afraid of breaking a hip. "It's so rare I have any company this late at night. Except for those Help Desk folks—and they're questionable company for sure."

I offered my hand. "I'm Zeno Jacobs."

"Samuel McClusky. Pleasure. What you do round here, Zeno?"

"I'm the Director of Personnel."

"Oh—*important man.*"

"You wouldn't know by the size of my paycheck."

Mr. McClusky humored me with a laugh that came out like he was clearing his throat. Then he coughed thickly. "Last time I seen the personnel director musta been ten years ago."

"*Whoa*—ten years is a long time, Mr. McClusky."

"Ten years is but a flash in the pan, Son. Listen—I've been tryin to make it in durin daylight hours for the better part of six months. Ain't never woke up on time, though. Been needin to put in for retirement."

"Retirement?" I asked, skeptically. It was inconceivable that HRW would offer such a thing to a director, not to mention a *janitor*. Benefits were special incentives for executives and government employees, not for us lowly grunts. "How long have you been with us, Mr. McClusky?"

"Been with this company since the nineteen-sixties. Back then, there was no Personnel Director—just the owner, Mr. Kaufman, and seven or eight of us young kids."

"Wow," I said, doing some mental arithmetic. "That's well over fifty years."

"Yep. I was hired as a cook. Back when you knew what the company did, what it was called, and who owned it. Did you know this company started out as a restaurant?"

I made a smile of disbelief. "*What? Seriously?*"

"Yep. It was called Pioneer Chicken. Best dang chicken in the world, I thought—put Kentucky Fried to *shame*. And those buttery corn cobs... Excuse me," he said, wiping his chin, "I think I'm droolin."

I pulled up the second chair and offered it to him.

He shook his way down into the seat and smiled at me. "Legs tremble like a nine-pointer, but thank God my hands are steady."

I sat as well. "So, what happened to Pioneer Chicken?"

"Whole mess had to do with franchisin. Mr. Kaufman wanted to grow his business, and he did—there were over two hundred stores in the nineteen-eighties. But he was wastin a lot of time on other projects, and his franchisees were throwin fits that he wasn't spendin no time or money on maintainin Pioneer. So, Mr. Kaufman asked some lawyer friend for help with his troubles, and that lawyer got a bunch of people together to buy the chain out from under him—some friend, *huh*? Most of the locations got took over by Church's, if memory serves. There's still a coupla independent owners round today, right here in Los Angeles, but you can drive right by em and never notice. Anyhoo, the new big-wigs transferred me over to tend a local office of AFC Company, which stood for 'America's Favorite Chicken,' who operated Church's. Then the First Islamic Bank bought up the place. Soon, the new owners changed their name from FIB to Arcapita to make it sound less turban-*escent*. Through all these years, I'm gettin shuffled around, not really sure what company I'm workin for or what I'm supposed to do. After Arcapita split some divisions and sold em, my job went over to some venture folks named Harris, Dixon and Lauder. Then another company called Miller, Reece and Wilcox did some inbreedin with HDL—well, in business parlance, I think they call it a merger. But anyways, their little baby was Harris, Reece and Wilcox—the initials on the roof. Every week or so I check the sign to make sure it's the same."

"That's crazy—you were continuously employed through all that?"

"Yep—the whole time. All that corporate hanky-panky left me dizzy, but it also left me well paid. Yep, well paid, indeed. Along the way, the different companies had different policies and different benefits. I signed the ones I wanted to. And I *didn't* sign the ones I *didn't* want to—*y'know?* Through it all, I got medical, dental, life insurance, disability insurance, cost-of-livin increases, and a *pension*—none of that 401K hooey. While I'm here, I'm guaranteed a raise of four percent above COLA every year, no matter what. Last year I cleared 105-large—not bad for an old janitor, *huh?* And nobody would know if I took an unannounced day or two off, would they? Well, nobody now exceptin *you.*"

"Wow," I said. "You made quite a niche for yourself."

"You can say that again. What really tickles me is when I git my stub in the mail, the darn thang says I'm still a *cook.* A doggone *chicken* cook, for cryin out loud! I ain't cooked no chicken since, *what*—1989, musta been. Bet you ain't even been *born* yet!"

I hadn't been. "Nuh-uh."

"Got me a rent-controlled villa up on Hampton and Gardner. Just $550 a month. May as well be free for that price. Yep—ain't shamed to admit—I done good for myself over the years. Allowed me to spend time on my paintins."

"Oh, yeah? What do you paint?"

"Canvases, mostly." He was staring at the numbers I had tacked to the cubicle wall. "*Turnover per Day?* Sweet Jesus! What is it that HRW does now?"

"We terminate people for profit."

Mr. McClusky broke into a barrage of deep, phlegmy coughs. I asked him if he was okay. He held up a hand to confirm that he was, so I looked away from him, to give him time to recover.

He shook his way onto his feet and took in some deep breaths. "Oh, damn," he said.

"Sure you're okay?"

He nodded.

I considered Mr. McClusky—he must've been a handsome man, back in the day. The best way I can describe him is like a seventy-year old James Bond. He was lean and fit with a face that was handsome beneath the wrinkles. He was six inches taller than me, but the curve in his back brought him down to my level. And when he was seized by one of his coughing fits, the blood would drain from him; his tone would turn to ivory and his lips would go blue. Presently, the blood was slowly returning to his flesh.

"Do you need the evening off, Sir?" I asked. "Perhaps you should see a doctor…"

"Nah," he said. "It's the damn chain smokin I did when I was a youngun. That and our lovely Southern California smog. Doctors don't never do nothin but give me pills and inhalers. I'll be okay." He took a couple of deep breaths. "Explain this terminatin people for profit thang."

"The different levels of government have incentives to push employment where they want it to go. There's the Work Opportunity Tax Credit, which gives HRW a tax break every time we hire someone young or on welfare. And there are cash incentives. The State of California gives us $5800 every time a new employee is hired—their goal is to get everyone able-bodied to work so that they will pay income and sales taxes. The Federal Department of Labor pays $5250 whenever an employee is terminated with cause—which is actually a bargain to them, since it's only a fraction of the payout somebody gets while on unemployment. Then there's county and city incentives we cash-in on as well. When we hire someone, we figure out all of the incentives we can take advantage of, we file the paperwork, and the sooner we can terminate the person, the more money we make. If one of my employees gets halfway to the break-even point, I'll make them a special project—but most of them leave well before then."

Mr. McClusky was thunderstruck. "HRW makes no product?"

I shook my head. "None at all—we hire people so they can fill out the terminations of the people they're replacing."

He was silent for a short time. When he spoke, it came out accusationally. "That's not sustainable."

"What do you mean?" I asked.

"Even if you had a thousand employees, by the time each of them terminated one person, they'd all be out of a job!"

I understood what he was getting at. "No, Mr. McClusky. Not only do we terminate our own people, but we are contracted to do the filings of over a thousand corporations throughout the southwest. And believe me—we have plenty of work."

"I see," he said, looking as though he was sucking on a lemon.

I stood. "Well, I was just on my way home. I'll look into your retirement paperwork, but I've never done any before. So, it might be a couple of weeks."

"That sounds fine." Mr. McClusky extended his hand without standing.

I shook it. "Nice to meet you, Mr. McClusky."

"Niceta meetcha too, Mr. Jacobs."

I left on the long walk home.

The next morning, Gordon was coming out of the employee entrance as we pulled into the lot, and I hurried ahead of Octavio and Doreen to catch up with him. When he saw me, he quickened his step toward his car.

"Hey, Gordon!"

He got to his car and began patting his pockets. When I stepped up alongside him, he gave up his search for his keys and used both his hands to hold an object away from me—it was Mr. Chandler's cash box.

"Bob told me to take it," Gordon said, moving the box against his body until he was hugging it to his chest.

"Why?"

"She said if you have to spend any money, you can file an expense report. She said you're too green for petty cash."

"What's an expense report?" I asked.

"If you have to spend money for work, you fill out the report and they reimburse you on your next paycheck. Just go to the Pioneer, *Payroll Functions, Expense Report...*"

I reached for the cash box just to see Gordon flinch. And he *did* flinch—so majorly he almost fell down. I asked: "Hey—as the IT guy, can you do me a favor?"

"What?"

"On all our terminals, the desktop image has the corporate logo on it."

He let out a huff.

"I want all of the desktops to have a bright white background. Then in big, block letters, I want it to say 'THIS JOB SUCKS'. Have the screensavers say that too. Okay?"

Gordon glared at me.

"Thanks!" I said, and walked away toward the employee entrance.

Later that day, I decided we needed some office supplies. I called down to Gordon to find out how to order them. While the phone rang, I watched the screensaver bounce around the screen:

THIS JOB SUCKS

I laughed quietly.

Gordon answered his phone. He instructed me between long exhales. "[*sigh*] Click on the Pioneer... [*sigh*] *Manager Functions*... [*sigh*] *Ordering*... [*sigh*] Now select the product supplier you want... [*sigh*] It'll open up a browser with the supplier's website. Sign in with your username. It's your regular username preceded by HRW... [*sigh*] Find what you need and add it to the cart..."

"I'm sorry—*preceded* or *proceeded*?"

"[*sigh*] *Before*. Then just use your normal password."

"Thanks, Gordon. You okay?"

It wasn't a sigh this time, but a moan. He hung up.

I found the thumbtacks I needed and added them to the cart. The break room had cabinets that stocked the rest of our office supplies. I went in there to do a quick inventory. Doreen followed me in.

She was staring at me.

"I'm busy..." I said as I poked through the shelves.

She gave me a pouty look and left.

We went through reams and reams of paper—so I ordered a dozen cases. Then I added a bunch of other stuff to the order—file folders, Scotch tape, pens...

After that, it was getting late in the afternoon. I spent the rest of the workday signing new-hire paperwork. Octavio and Doreen were going to hang out at the commune and asked me if I wanted to come along. This time I declined, saying I would be soaking my hand in ice water and going to bed. So, Octavio took me home before he and Doreen headed out. I did ice my hand, but the news on TV kept me awake.

KTLA was in need of a filler. It would be a few minutes as Sky5 and the ground team raced to another gang grab. So, they segued to a celebration at the Van Nuys office of the California Lottery. A dainty little woman wore a gigantic grin—her smile was so wide you could see her wisdom teeth. I didn't recognize her at first because of that smile. She had been lax-faced around work, and frowningly tense the one time she had been standing directly in front of me. Below her, a caption flashed: *California's Newest Billionaire.* A person in a fancy suit handed her one of those enormous, ceremonial checks, below which I could see her legs and shoes—the same ones that had gone running past me as I skinned my way along the floor in the third basement.

In all my life, I've only met one person as contemptible as she. I poked both of my middle fingers at her image on the TV. Of course, she didn't care, not one bit. She just kept smiling and smiling. Her name was on the check—Grace Van Horne. I hoped her smile would give her wrinkles, and I hoped she'd choke on some caviar or something.

A reporter asked her a question.

"The first thing I'm unna do," she gibbered, "is getta car. But I never even hadda license, so I'm unna havta do that first!"

I had to turn the television off to keep myself from throwing something heavy and angular at it. I went to the fridge and popped open a beer.

By the time I turned on the TV again, they were back to covering the gang grabs. The banner at the bottom said *#KTLAUnrest.* Soon, it transitioned to the *Thurgood Thurman the Third, Esquire* spot again.

Sky5 was above a large, undulating mass of people at what looked like a truck stop. The crowd was held back by the property's chain-link fence. Parallel to the ground was a huge banner being held aloft by the mass, reading: *#FeedLA.*

That made me hungry, so I turned up the volume and went to heat up some water. In the distance, I heard the anchor's voice.

"In a moment, we'll be covering the governor's speech. Since a good portion of the California National Guard has been activated, it's possible that some form of martial law will be declared. As we broadcast the press conference from Sacramento, we will continue coverage of the disturbance in Santa Fe Springs at the Safeway Distribution Center."

As the water heated, I went back to the TV.

The distribution center's property defined what looked like a right triangle. Thousands circled the property, and from Sky5, the gathering looked festive—but when the camera zoomed in, you could see squinting eyes, lines in faces, and lots of white teeth inside of lips that were anything but smiling.

"The streets around this scene are packed with parked cars, Ron," Ruben Chavez said. "Some of these protesters have parked as far as a mile away. The question is this: if they're planning on breaking into this food warehouse, how will they possibly carry away what they're taking? I mean it's all bulk food here, and—"

"That's an interesting observation, Ruben, but right now Governor Harris is approaching the podium. Again, the governor is expected to discuss the deployment of our National Guard troops. We're now going live to Sacramento…"

I went back to the kitchen and dumped some Oriental noodles and mixed veggies into the pot. By the time I'd returned to the TV, the governor was on the left side of a split-screen, with the view from Sky5 on the right.

"Good evening. On Sunday night, thousands of your fellow Californians received a phone call. They are fathers and mothers, doctors, mechanics, school bus drivers. They are hard workers who contribute successfully to the economy of our Great State. As I'm sure you know, it was necessary to activate our National Guard to quell the unfortunate unrest that a small number of our citizens seem pressed to cause..."

On the right side of the screen, the crowd found a weak point and the fence surrounding the warehouses fell. The crowd trampled the downed fence outward, so the collapsed portion widened. Hundreds of people were now flooding toward the long series of rollup doors.

"What I wish to communicate to you tonight is that we will not be suppressing any of your rights or liberties, we will not turn our cities over to military rule, we will not be declaring martial law or imposing a curfew..."

It was only seconds before several hundred people were at the doors of the large southern warehouse. Those gathered outside of the northeast side of the property began to flow around to where the collapse was still widening. In the meantime, the ground reporters had shown up—the image changed from Sky5 to a scene among the crowd as it passed through the fence.

"There are those who believe that when a society fails to support everyone but a select few that the answer is found in wrath…"

The loading bays filled the right side of the split-screen. Three of the bays had semi-trailers pulled up to them. The area in front of the other four bays was filled with people, and before them, the rollup doors began opening.

"I believe differently: Violence is not the default condition of man. When there is scarcity, we still have love, companionship, camaraderie…"

Beyond the rising doors, leather boots and black shin guards became visible.

"Those of us with abundance share with our neighbors in need. I have seen families with room take in the homeless. I have seen laborers dressed in patched-up coveralls giving cash to the elderly and the mentally ill. And I have seen doctors coming off of twelve-hour shifts just to spend another six hours in a free clinic…"

Cries lit from the crowd. Its movement tried to reverse, but the people were pressed forward by the inertia of those behind them. The doors revealed knee pads next, then riot shields, then rifles and shotguns, bulletproof vests, and finally helmeted faces hidden behind the insectoid appearance of gas masks.

"And what reward do these selfless people get for their acts of kindness toward their fellow man?"

Gas grenades were launched from the loading bays down into the crowd. Some of the speeding, outgassing canisters conked off the heads or shoulders of people before twirling down to the cement below. Whoever was controlling the audio at KTLA cranked the input from the field team, because you could hear the crowd's high-pitched, frantic screams. Beneath those screams, the governor continued his speech.

"I tell you that the reward for kindness and civility *is* society, and society will replace what you have lost. If we do not give in to violence, if we do not let our love degenerate into hate, if we do not allow our charity to turn into selfishness, our reward will be a full restitution of our economy..."

You could hear the cameraman speak through his stuffy nose: *"Oh, God in heaben, sweet Jezuz, I can'd breeethe..."* Just then, through the dense white smoke, what looked like a bright red mask came into view. It was a young, Asian woman who had a river of blood pouring down her face.

"We will have prosperity..."

The cameraman was choking—

"We will have abundance..."

—then retching—

"No soul will want for a job..."

—then the full flow of vomit and its splashing could be heard.

"No soul will want for food..."

The split-screen image changed back to Sky5.

"No soul will want for anything…"

A fraction of the crowd—perhaps ten percent—were left outside of the fence. Those that hadn't made it in had backed away onto the street. Now, with the weight of the people off it, the fence was erect again and leaning inward, acting as a trap.

"We will take the lessons learned from this recession and teach them to our children…"

The police were rushing out of the warehouse now, dropping down to the level of the crowd. They were holding orange shotguns. Firing them at will.

"We will ensure that this will never happen again…"

No one in the crowd was resisting.

"For the health and welfare of our citizenry, the National Guard is being deployed to set up more food banks. This food will be provided free of charge to anyone who needs it…"

Sky5 zoomed in on a man who was on his knees. As the chopper swung around to the north, you could see the man's face. His eyes were bloodshot and streaming, his eyelids swollen flaps. Snot ran in runnels from his nose and foaming drool streamed from both corners of his mouth. One of the bug-faced officers aimed at this man's head. He shot a beanbag point-blank at it.

"The National Guard will provide more than the ordinary food-bank fare. They will provide flour, beans, eggs, milk, cereals, rice, pasta, and all manners of canned goods. They will provide fresh citrus fruits…"

The man flopped limp onto the cement, and then the split-screen switched back to the camera among the crowd.

"Again, these products will be provided for you and your families free of charge…"

Despite the clouds of gas, despite the crowd's blurry vision, you could tell many of them saw that man get shot. Panic was on every face the camera landed on.

"Beyond their duty to man these neighborhood food distribution sites, I am also charging the National Guard with the duty to protect our neighborhood grocery stores…"

The crowd's reaction to the beanbag-to-the-head incident was to reach for their phones. Every one of them was doing it.

"Most of us have seen the images of these so-called *gang grabs*. Let me tell you this—what you have seen are lawless hooligans taking what is not theirs. And they are taking it at the expense of you, our law-abiding citizens…"

The blind, defenseless crowd held up their phones— cameras pointed out. They were holding their phones like the police held their shields.

"You are already being asked to pay what many people call an unfair price for certain items, and we cannot have that price increase even more because some people cannot maintain the peace..."

The police continued firing at the crowd, beating with their batons, caving in noses with their shields, and spraying everyone, even those motionless on the ground, with pepper spray.

"I have prepared a press release, detailing this program further. This information, as it applies to your area throughout our Great State, will be disseminated to your community by your local news outlets..."

The crowd wasn't running to protect itself, as a herd of antelope would do against a fierce lion. They just stood or knelt or sat, frozen in horrible dread. A mass message went out to the phones within the crowd. The fence had been breached at the southeast corner of the property. Some in the crowd shuffled that way; but many others continued to stand like mannequins in a shop window.

I didn't stop watching until my dinner was filling the house with smoke. I substituted the rest of my beer for dinner. The tally was given two hours later: ninety-six injured, four dead, eighty-two arrests under felony charges. There were no police injuries.

6—#HundredDays

Governor Harris' oratory performance, and the police's physical one, were showcased by the news outlets. CNN and Fox News played the KTLA segment in what seemed like a continuous loop, so it wasn't long before every Los Angelino had seen it. The aggressiveness of the police hadn't just nullified what the governor said—to most people, the violence on the other side of the split-screen punctuated his sentences, transforming him into an odd caricature of himself—into a patronizing and sarcastic fascist, like Hitler.

Word had gotten out through social media that there would be a meeting at Echo Park at three the next afternoon. Octavio and I left work early to attend. We wore our bandanas over the bridge of our noses—his dark blue, mine the baby-blue one he had tied around my head the night I sat for dinner with Carlos. When we got there, we waded through the crowd until we were under a cloth banner hung from two trees. It had black-painted words, reading:

#HundredDays
#CienDías

Mandy Gutierrez was there with her crew. She shoved a microphone in Octavio's face and asked for his name.

"I ain't nobody," he said.

She found Carlos, who was also disguised. He wore the same color as Octavio.

"Sir," Mandy said, "will you speak with me? Can I have your name, please?"

"My name is George Washington," he replied, pronouncing *George* as *Horr-hay*.

"Can you explain, for our viewers, what your demands are?"

"*Demands?* We have no demands. Demands come from governments, not from people like us. All we are doing is reacting—we are like a reflex. The police have injured and murdered our friends—our families. We react to ninety-six injured and four dead. That is a hundred innocent people—a hundred citizens attacked by police. And why? Because they were hungry. Everyone is hungry.

"So, we don't demand—*we call.* We call for a hundred days: one day for each of those attacked by the police. For a hundred days we will resist the State. For a hundred days we will disrupt the institutions. For a hundred days we will attack the interests of the banks and the corporations. For a hundred days we will have our lives back and our pride back. And for a hundred days we will take what is ours."

Carlos put a megaphone to his mouth: "*Declaramos que todos los bienes de las empresas están ahora propiedad pública!*"

A great chorus of cheers and whistles came.

Mandy found another man with a bandana on. He was an African-American, with a hard body like a wrestler; his meaty arms threatened to burst the hems of his T-shirt's sleeves. He too wore a bandana to conceal his face. His was red.

"Can you tell me your name, Sir?" she asked.

The man spoke in a deep, raspy tone: "I'm William Whipple."

"What do you hope to accomplish here?"

"I just want to be free again. I wasted fifteen years working. After those fifteen years, I have nothing to show for it. All of my labor went to taxes and interest. And to more taxes. And to more interest. Someday, sit down with your pay stubs and your bills and your receipts and figure it out—you'll *see* it's true. At the end of the thirty-year term on my mortgage, if I add up the equity in my house and my other assets, I will own property equal to three to five years of income. This is not the result of a free-market economy. Theft of any kind is illegal for the people, but the State doesn't protect the people from that same behavior—of *theft* and *usury*—by the corporations.

And the State doesn't even follow its own principles—everyone is double-, triple-, and even quadruple-taxed.

"When governments become corrupt, when they serve only a privileged few, it's our right, it's our *duty* to overthrow such government. A great man once said this. His name was Thomas Jefferson."

Carlos spoke from the megaphone again: *"Declaramos la nulidad de todas las formas de deuda contraída por el pueblo!"*

After more cheers, the anchor questioned Mandy from the studio: "What is being said over the loudspeaker?"

"He says that all corporate properties belong to the people, and that every kind of debt is null and void."

Mandy plunged into the crowd, searching for another interviewee.

Carlos waved to us.

Octavio and I came to him.

Carlos pushed a piece of paper into my hand. *"Este es mi nombre y contraseña de* Twitter. *Ir para mí y enviar este mensaje. Él le llevará inicio."*

I nodded my agreement.

Octavio and I walked away as Carlos used his megaphone to coax the crowd into a fervor. When we were well out of the range of the news cameras, we took off our bandanas. I stuffed mine into my cargo pocket.

As we rode into Hollywood, I asked, "Are you going back?"

"The *policía* declare war last night. So, yeah, I go back."

I was nervous for him. "Be safe."

He put on his cowboy hat. "Nice knowing you care."

As we pulled onto Vista, Octavio spoke again. "Tomorrow, no ride. Hope that's okay…"

"Yeah, I can take the bus. You gonna make it to work?"

"I dunno. Hope so."

He dropped me off in front of my driveway. I went inside and read Carlos' note. It said:

http://www.anonymous.ly
luego http://twitter.com
@JimenezLoco, coheterojo16!

Tweet: 11838433768 1930 #Day1
#HundredDays #Día1 #CienDías

I navigated within the anonymizer to Twitter, where I logged in and sent his message. Then I dragged and dropped the alphanumeric code into Google.

It was a set of coordinates.

It was the Bank of America Center, downtown.

I thought it was risky for them to announce a target publicly like this. So, I sank myself deep into the couch, ready for a good show. I guessed that the second sequence of numbers was the time to be watching: 7:30 PM. It was still more than three hours away, so I set a large pot of vegetables to boil and watched a gang grab go down at a shoe store. When the store was empty, there was Breaking News showing several of the smartphone videos from the night before, but none of them were better than the KTLA footage.

I stuffed myself full of mixed veggies as I watched Twitter traffic tagged with *#HundredDays*. Most of it was just static, like:

> *@JohnnyBoi223:* `Fuck the cops`
> `#HundredDays`

But some of the posts stood out:

> *@Grand_Moff_Harding:*
> `I.Thought.All.Was.`
> `Copa-seti.cal.`
> `#HundredDays #CienDías`

When I narrowed the search to the strange punctuation, I hit the jackpot. What appeared now was operational traffic:

> *@Al_Hamilton:* `826679;`
> `881673; 826666;`
> `. . . .⁻. .`

I Googled the numbers—they were coordinates of gas stations, which left me wondering what that could possibly have to do with Bank of America.

As seven o'clock rolled around, I moved from the computer back to the couch, anticipating the coming action. As I'd suspected, the police arrived to protect Bank of America Center, and every news outlet was there to report on the event. Though an angry mob of perhaps one- or two-thousand amassed on the streets, they made no move to enter the corporate tower. They only shouted at the police and fought for room to show their signs to the cameras. A couple of slogans I remember were:

Student Loan
Forgiveness
NOW

and

Reenact
GLASS-
STEAGALL.

Then it happened, right on time—at 7:30 PM, though not at the Bank of America Center.

No, not there.

My first impression was of rapid flashes of light, like when a big star takes to the red carpet at a movie premier. Onscreen, the cameraman scanned the Bank of America building, and then up and down the street where the protesters were. The picture jiggled and panned, and there was no sign of any damage.

My house's windows shook.

I went out to the front porch. To the southeast, a half-dozen crimson fireballs rose on columns of smoke. I gaped at them until the mushroom clouds dimmed and began to spread thin, blending into the evening's ceiling of stratus clouds.

The news crews scrambled to pack up their equipment so they could move to the sources of the fireballs, and in the meantime, KTLA's anchors engaged in hypothetical small talk. Within a minute, they had narrowed down the source of the fireballs as underground gasoline storage tanks. Just how Hundred Days had burst them open was a mystery, but KTLA found experts to appear on camera within another five minutes. They speculated that the tanks had been exposed with dynamite or C-4. One said that such a task could only have been accomplished by the military—who had access to the more precise, more focused polymer-based explosives.

All this talk made me curiously tense, but not in the sense of danger. No, there's a certain feeling you get when there's some *real* Breaking News—something that you know will be a part of history—and I was feeling that way now. It was some excitement mixed in with a lot of trepidation, because I knew I was mixed up with those Hundred Days people. Admittedly, mine was a passive role—all I ever did was post a message for Carlos—but I had chosen a side, and my side had one hell of a kickoff.

I sat watching interviews until 1 or 2 AM, when my adrenaline finally wore off and I drifted away.

Into dreamland...

...where L.A. had become deserted. The power had been off for days. Rain fell through thick, black clouds above. A fire truck drove past me slowly, its lights blinking, its water cannon spraying the roofs of houses. As the water streamed onto the shingles of the house across the street, it spattered and steamed, sounding like something wet dropped into a deep-fat fryer. Then the whole roof burst into flames. I turned away from the heat and toward the south, toward where the fire truck had come from. In that direction, thousands of homes were joining together in a conflagration, with whirling winds that lifted glowing embers high into the atmosphere, up to where the jet stream blows steadily eastward...

The following morning, I didn't wake up until 8:30. Which meant I was already 50 minutes late to work. I cursed myself and rushed to get dressed. I brushed my teeth with three or four strokes of my toothbrush and then staggered outside into the morning's lavender smog rays. The late-spring showers were gone at last, so I took off my windbreaker, flinging it back at my front door, where it landed in a heap. I walked with a little extra spring in my step, but also with a little panic in my throat. The fact that I needed to take the bus to work infuriated me. *Why don't I make enough money to afford a car? How is it that I've risen to a position in management and I still can't afford anything?*

The cameras were on me as soon as I came in the door. I waded through another sea of people with résumés in their hands. Not even two seconds passed between when I got to my cubicle and when the phone rang.

Of course it was Bob.

"I don't want to hear any excuses, Zeno."

"I have no excuses, Bob. But if the National Guard detains me on the way to work, what can I do?"

There was silence. I didn't care if she bought it or not. I felt aware of Bob's eyes on me, or rather on my image displayed on the video screen she was watching, wherever *that* was. I kept my back to the camera.

"It's two weeks into the period, Zeno, and it looks like you will miss your targets."

"Right. I've been tracking my numbers."

"Your TPD is down some two percent," she said, referring to *Turnover Per Day.* "That has the potential to cost us thousands of dollars. Tell me what you're doing about it."

I stared at my screen saver, the words

THIS JOB SUCKS

bouncing around tirelessly. *How many people were termed this week?* I couldn't remember, I wasn't sure...

I exhaled loudly into the handset's microphone.

"Okay, Zeno. My bonus is based on what my directors bonus. When you don't bonus, it costs me money. So, if you can't tell me what you're doing about it, then I have another question. If you can't or won't answer me this time, I'm going to fire you, okay?"

I said nothing.

"What do you think I'll do to you if you cost me money?"

I still said nothing.

"You have five seconds or I'm going to let you go…"

It was the first thing that came to mind. "Cut my balls off?" I asked.

"No, try again."

The obvious: "Fire me?"

"No, Zeno. That would be too easy. Think about money…"

"Charge me for your losses?"

Bob grunted. "Since you're not getting close, I'll tell you."

I couldn't figure out why this bitch had to play games. She wouldn't train me, she expected me to perform well without any help, and she never returned any of my phone calls. As far as I was concerned, that made whether or not I bonused her problem—not mine.

"What I'll do," she continued, "is make your targets easier to hit. That way, we both bonus. It makes sense, *doesn't it?* But, in the meantime, I'll have you train your own replacement. See: you don't want me to make your job easier, Zeno. Not *ever*. So, you think hard about how you're going to fix your TPD this month."

The line went dead.

I turned around and scowled at the camera. Then I faced my desk again, tapping my fingers and thinking.

Doreen's head popped up above my cubicle's wall.
"You okay, Zeno?" she asked.

I shot to my feet. *"What!"*

She barked loudly.

I barked back.

Her face flashed with shock. Then pain.

"I'm sorry," I said weakly.

She went *pfff* as she turned away from me. "You are a *bastard.*"

My brain was going a million miles an hour. I looked at the equations on the cubicle wall and keyed some figures into the ten-key. I only needed to term five people. But I needed to get it done *today.*

Do I just pick five people indiscriminately? "Hey—you, *you, and you: You're fired." Do I accidentally spill some coffee on someone and when they swear at me, term them for violating our standards of conduct?*

I swirled my coffee cup—*empty.*

Nah, I thought. *In both cases, they'd probably get unemployment.*

I thought about logging onto Twitter as *JimenezLoco*:

> *@JimenezLoco:* BOMB THE
> UNEMPLOYMENT OFFICES!!!
> #Day2 #HundredDays
> #Día2 #CienDías

If that happened, new unemployment filings wouldn't show up for months—if ever. But then I was like, *No, I would be betraying Carlos' trust. I won't do that.*

I thought about unemployment. *What are the qualifications?*

I wiggled my way past the Help Desk's security and got on the unemployment department's website. After an hour of reading legalese, one thing stood out: you needed a minimum period of employment, a period in which your job paid into the system. From this, I identified four targets for termination. Three of them were working at HRW as their first job, and none of them had worked for us long enough to qualify for unemployment. The fourth was a woman I had hired a few weeks before, who had reentered the workforce after sixteen years of being an at-home mom.

I called down to security.

"Security. Eddie speaking."

"This is Zeno Jacobs. May I borrow one of you to escort some terms out?"

The camera whirred, turning toward me. I flashed a thumb-and-forefinger circle at it.

"Right away," Eddie said.

A fat guy exited the labyrinth five minutes later. I waved at him and walked over, list in hand.

It had become one of those days. I made it into work late, I made my boss mad, I made Doreen hate me, I fired a bunch of people to save my own ass, and I needed to fire one more to earn my bonus. I thought things couldn't get any worse. The last thirty-or-so people I'd hired weren't the best candidates and I was certain some of them would stick around awhile. As I pondered who else I could pink-slip, a kid named Matt approached me.

"Uh, Zeno…" he said.

"Yeah."

"I need some money."

I turned to face him. "If you didn't get paid, payroll's downstairs."

Matt shook his head. "That's not it. It's just not enough." He slipped his hand into his jacket pocket. When he pulled that hand back out, it was gripping a handgun. He sat in the chair next to me, resting the thing on his leg.

To say I was terrified would be an understatement. At that moment, it was as though my organs were manufacturing strange and exotic chemicals. My spit tasted like metal, my heart seemed both faster and slower, my kidneys felt bound with rubber bands, and my balls retreated like the limbs of a threatened tortoise. My lungs were no longer on automatic—I had to consciously breathe in and out. I felt sweat poke through my skin everywhere and I was hot and cold at the same time—the same way it feels when you're suddenly nauseated. I was hanging onto a delusion, though, that somehow I could disguise my panic. And sometimes when you're panicked and under stress, you can say the strangest things...

"*Heyyyy,*" I said, "is that a *Luger*?"

He looked down at his pistol. "Yeah."

"You only see those on TV, you know. Usually the bad guys have them."

He flopped the Luger up and gravity pulled it back down to his lap. "Yeah...look Zeno. I need some money or I'll be homeless. You understand." Again, he waved the Luger placidly from his lap, to my direction, to his lap again.

"I'm not an ATM machine." I looked up at the cameras hoping security would be on their way. All six cameras were pointed elsewhere for a change—just my luck. "You know, with the economy the way it is, everyone's either home*less* or home*ful*. Find a little place with eighteen or twenty roommates—your share will be less than a hundred and fifty."

Matt was calm—all business. "I'm either getting a hundred dollars from you, or you can eat a bullet."

I waved at the cameras; Matt didn't seem to care. The cameras made no move toward me. I considered for a beat. "Okay," I said. "What I'd like to do is buy you a cup of coffee. Afterward, we'll go somewhere for some cash. Yeah, we can do that. Okay?"

Matt nodded and stood. "Okay."

I took him into the labyrinth and followed the sombreros. When we got to the coffee machine, I put a fiver into the coin slot, and it ticked away in the machinery. As Matt selected his flavor, my body stilled and I realized my terror had passed. I said, "Gimme that," and took the Luger from his weak grasp.

He raised his hands.

"Put your hands down, dumb ass," I said. I thumbed the safety and fired at the coffee machine's lock.

"Jesus Christ!" Matt bleated. *"What're you doing?"*

I turned to him, and pressed the barrel of the gun into his chest. "You had a round chambered? *Fucker...*" I went back to the machine and tried the lock: dented but serviceable.

I took a precise aim at the lock and fired again.

"Shit!" Matt exclaimed, holding his hands over his ears.

That time, the lock popped free. I twisted it counterclockwise. The front of the machine opened. I safetied the Luger and put it in the waistband of my pants. The coin box was mostly full. I reached in and pocketed a handful. Then I took out the box and held it out for Matt.

"You're fired," I said as he took the box.

While Matt shook the box of fivers, estimating, I pulled stacks of bills from the back of the acceptor. After I'd stowed the cash, I took Matt's coffee. "Payroll will have your final pay deposited in two working days," I said, and then I followed the sombreros back.

He came along. When we entered the office, I expected the 200-or-so employees to be astir with panic from the noise of the gunshots, but they were all busy processing terminations. Matt had stopped and was staring at me. I held my arm out, directing him toward the applicant entrance. He left with his coins.

I kept a gun on me, or close at hand, from then until the HRW building burned down.

7—Kill the Banks

#*NOGRANDMAS*
FOOD GIFT FROM THE PEOPLE
THE CURFEW BEGINS

Friday night was more TV. The FBI declared Hundred Days a terrorist organization. The purposes of such a declaration are *legal* purposes, of course, as doing so instantly deprived any members of rights under both the Constitution and the Geneva Convention. That night, Hundred Days was doing something extraordinary, though you'll hardly find any mention of it on websites or TV programs detailing the time. They actually followed my advice—they were destroying all of the freeway signs. That may sound like a minor thing, but the next time you drive the 405 for instance, just consider how self-similar that freeway is along its length, with its khaki cinder-block walls and its Eucalyptus trees, and how all the buildings you can see from it look the same.

Anyway, the sign assault continued through the night and then it was Saturday—a day, in my traditions, to relax, to kick off my shoes, to go around the house in my underwear. It was now day four of the Hundred Days Riots, but that Saturday was also the day of the Crestline Quake. It was a 6.2 up in the mountains, and still really strong down here. I had, once again, fallen asleep on the couch, and when the shaking roused me from a dream, it was around 5:30 in the morning. My initial impression was of being trapped within the stairwell at HRW, with its walls crumbling around me.

Once I'd realized I was at home, my second thought was that Hundred Days had set off more bombs. As I got up, it was impossible to keep my feet under me and I began to fall. My tailbone screamed at the prospect of reinjury, so I performed a mid-air pivot to protect it and landed on the cushion of my left glute. In front of me, the coffee table's legs jackhammered the floor. The television swayed fore and aft on its table and the picture was breaking up into little squares. Nevertheless, the audio kept playing, blending into the creaking sounds in the walls, the jittering of the furniture, and the crashing of glass in the kitchen. Above all that racket, KTLA's weekend-morning anchors were shrieking like children.

Earthquakes stretch every second into its own minute, and the chaos seems to last forever. But it was probably only thirty seconds before the shaking was over.

I stood and went on a quick survey of the house as the news team blathered on in a self-congratulatory tone—proud that they had pulled through, ignorant of the cowardly display they had put on moments earlier. The computer tower was leaning under my desk—I righted it. Most of Pop's books were all over the floor. I kicked them over along the baseboard. I checked the bedrooms, the living room, the dining room—no broken windows. In the kitchen, I had to step over Ma's prized carnival glass collection, now shattered all over the floor. In there, the range had moved away from the wall by several inches. I sniffed around it—no rotten egg smell.

I went outside and checked the gas pipe at the meter. Again, okay.

As I walked back around to the front door, I saw a thin halo off past the house across the street and toward the horizon. That firelight was barely discernible from the sienna nighttime smog-and-streetlight glow—but it was there.

Distant sirens wailed.

I went back inside.

Above me was the only damage I'd ever found to the house: in the living room, a thin crack zigzagged in the ceiling's plaster, going from the front door to just above the fireplace. I told myself I would patch it.

But I never did.

The words *"This just in..."* brought my attention back to the television. A graphic filled the screen as Nichole Garza did the voice-over: "As you can see here, the epicenter is located approximately three miles east of Silverwood Lake, just north of Crestline. Initial estimates by the USGS place the quake's magnitude at 6.4. We are expecting the greatest effects to have been felt in San Bernardino to the south and Hesperia to the north. We have ground crews *en route* to cover this Breaking News this morning..."

As I waited for video of the damage, I brought in the garbage can. I remembered the years and years that Ma always warned me. *Carnival glass is collectible. It is a sound investment. It keeps its value ahead of inflation. Special care is needed whenever there's an occasion to use it.* Now I was sweeping it up by the dustpanful. And each time I thought I had it all, I'd spot another shard somewhere; so, I swept one last time methodically, starting in one corner and covering every single spot. When I was done, I wheeled the trash back outside. Why I hadn't sold that glass before then, I don't know. I guess I'd always thought of it as part of the house.

Back in the living room, the TV's image from Sky5 showed a toppled interchange in the early morning light. Nichole began talking over Ruben. "I need to break away from you for a moment and go to Jessie Cole at the News Desk, where she has more Breaking News for us..."

"Thank you Nichole," Jessie said. "We have been monitoring emergency radio traffic this morning and, within the numerous requests for assistance due to the earthquake, we have noticed reports of arson breaking out throughout the metropolitan area. Right now, I have a witness to one of these arsons on the phone—her name is Monica Lutz. Monica, are you there?"

A photo of a teenaged Monica appeared onscreen, wearing a bikini and holding a martini. The byline said *Courtesy of Facebook.* "Yes," she said, "I'm here."

"Where are you right now?"

"Market Street and Hillcrest in Inglewood."

"And you witnessed an arson occurring there?"

"Yes, at the Wells Fargo Bank."

"Can you tell us what happened?"

"I was on my way to the bus stop on La Brea—cuz I, like, take the bus to work, y'know. And there was this old blue truck flying a huge pirate flag. A guy in the back had a bandana over his face. The truck drove up onto the sidewalk, y'know, closer to the bank, and the guy in back started throwing bottles..."

"Are you at a safe distance?"

"I think so, yeah."

"Can you tell us if the bank is still on fire?"

"Uh, yeah, it's getting bigger."

"Was there anyone in the building that you know of?"

"Uh, no. It looked closed. The lights were off and stuff..."

"Where did the truck go when it left?"

"It flipped a youie and went south."

"At this point, can you tell if any emergency services are on the way?"

"Not that I can tell. I called 911, but they got me off the phone real quick."

"Okay, thank you very much. That was one of our viewers, Monica Lutz, live from Inglewood. Before we go back to earthquake coverage, we are continuing to receive reports of structure fires at bank branches all over the city…" Jessie flipped through some printouts. "Two in East L.A.… One in Gardena, three in Santa Monica, another in Alhambra… Six in Pasadena, two in Glendale. Our viewer's description of the vehicle, once again, was an older model, blue pickup flying a pirate flag. If you see this vehicle, or any others involved in these widespread arsons, please contact the authorities right away."

I went to the computer and searched *#HundredDays #Day4*:

> *@JimenezLoco:* Matar a los bancos, no toque las cooperativas #Day4 #HundredDays #Día4 #CienDías

There it was, spelled out in clear Spanish: *Kill the banks.*

I fiddled around on Twitter for a while, where I found:

> *@JeftyLA9156:* #GangGrab at Beverly Center now! #NoGrandmas

116

I searched #GangGrab, sorting by most recent. There were endless pages of Tweets, with calls for gang grabs on every kind of company you can think of.

I changed my search term and found:

> *@La_eMe:* Todos ustedes
> deben mostrar su
> solidaridad con la
> #CienDías

which meant that the Mexican Mafia had just endorsed Hundred Days.

I closed down my computer's browser. The National Guard's food bank was due to open at eight o'clock that morning and I was hoping that the earthquake wouldn't force the soldiers that were manning it into emergency services. If they had to leave, I wanted to get what I could beforehand. I got up and took a shower.

I'd brought a backpack to the food bank, but I had to go back home to get the wheelbarrow.

The National Guard's food bank was just a semi-trailer in a small parking lot on Melrose and Fuller. Unlike the civilian food banks, all they had was bulk food. The rice and beans came in huge, fifty-pound sacks. The oranges were in twenty-five-pound sacks. There were cases of pears, grapefruit, lemons, cauliflower, radishes— those were labeled *Please Take Only What You Need.* There was elbow macaroni in two-pound boxes. Eggs nestled in stacked twelve-by-twelve holders. Ten-pound bags of sugar, flour, and powdered milk. Five-pound bags of iodized salt. For meat, there were huge canned hams—like Spam on steroids—which I passed up. There were large lumps of irregularly cut cheese, where the sign said *One Per Family, Please*. I took two because of the swine. Each person was also authorized to take one case of Humanitarian Daily Rations, which are like a five-course meal in a bag. This time when I tried to take two, one of the soldiers pointed at the sign. I put the second case back.

There were crates of candles. The sign above them said, *Take One Per Room In Your House.* I grabbed a dozen.

The Guard soldiers were friendly. Then again, they were the ones with the rifles. When I had brought down what I'd needed, I lifted up the handles of my wheelbarrow, and one of the soldiers shouted an *Excuse me, Sir*, so I lowered my load.

"Don't forget your bundle," the soldier said. He reached up into the trailer and grabbed a rubber-banded stack of pamphlets out. He handed it to me.

I said *thanks*, and thumbed through them. It was a bunch of `Ready.gov` materials like *Managing Food Without Power, Build Your Disaster Supplies Kit*, and *Surviving When Disaster Strikes.* I dropped the bundle in with the food.

The soldier angled up to me and pointed to my cargo pocket. "Sir," he whispered, "not that I blame you, but next time it would behoove you to leave your peashooter at home."

I nodded. I hadn't known the Luger was so obvious.

I wheeled my load over the short distance home and into the garage. I didn't feel like cooking, so I opened up the case of rations and pulled one out. On the outside of the bag, an American flag was printed. Below it, a caption read:

Food Gift From The People Of The
UNITED STATES OF AMERICA

"Thank you very much," I told myself.
"You're very welcome," I replied.

I munched away on an unfrosted Pop Tart, and the Breaking News rolled in like the waves in Malibu. Los Angeles had fallen into pandemonium, and that would be putting it gently. There was no way that any of the stations could cover everything that was going on now. KTLA continued to cover the quake onscreen as the news desk commented on everything else via the marquee crawling just above the advertising banner at the bottom of the screen:

—THE WHITE HOUSE IS SHOWING CONCERN THAT WITH THIS MORNING'S EARTHQUAKE, THE UNREST IN LOS ANGELES WILL BECOME UNCONTROLLABLE AND WILL REQUIRE FEDERAL INTERVENTION. IN THE MEANTIME, THE GOVERNOR HAS DECLARED A STATE OF EMERGENCY IN SAN BERNARDINO COUNTY, RIVERSIDE COUNTY, ORANGE COUNTY, AND L.A. COUNTY, OPENING UP THOSE REGIONS

FOR FEDERAL ASSISTANCE. A CONFIRMED 32 BANK OFFICES HAVE BEEN SET ON FIRE THIS MORNING, WHILE THE UNCONFIRMED ARSONS OF BANK BRANCHES ARE NEARING 100. UNCHALLENGED RIOTS HAVE BROKEN OUT IN LONG BEACH, EAST L.A., COMPTON, INGLEWOOD, AND ANAHEIM—STAY SAFE AND AVOID TRAVEL IN THESE AREAS. THERE HAVE BEEN 13 CONFIRMED DEATHS AS A RESULT OF THIS MORNING'S QUAKE; UPDATED NUMBERS ARE EXPECTED FROM LAC AND SBC OFFICIALS WITHIN THE HOUR. VISIT KTLA.COM FOR A CURRENT LIST OF FLIGHT CANCELLATIONS AT LAX. PACIFIC POWER IS EXPERIENCING 10,000 CALLS AN HOUR DUE TO OUTAGES, SPOKESPERSON ASSURES THAT ALL LINEMEN ARE ON DUTY TO GET POWER RESTORED TO CUSTOMERS—

I was startled just then—a book fell off a shelf and landed flat, resulting in a loud *bang*. I looked around and realized that it was an aftershock. It was over as soon as I'd gotten to my feet; I stood for an uneasy few seconds, unsure of what was still shaking. I found that it was my legs. I plopped back into my seat. With nothing else to do in the moment, I tore into another packet of the humanitarian meal. It was some kind of lentil gruel. Served cold like that, it was a little bitter.

The television changed its own channel—there was a flash of the Home Shopping Network before the screen went black. After a moment, text from the Emergency Alert System appeared. The klaxon and tone sounded. What followed was the longest alert I'd ever heard:

State or local authorities have issued a civil emergency message for Los Angeles County,

San Bernardino County, Ventura County, Orange County, Riverside County until 7 PM Pacific Standard Time.

A civil curfew has been activated in your area. Effective immediately, you are required to remain indoors between the hours of 7 PM to 7 AM daily, including weekends. All businesses, excluding certain emergency and governmental services, are required to close by 5 PM daily to allow employees time to travel home from work. During non-curfew hours, the failure of any person to carry government-issued identification will result in immediate arrest and detention. Civilians in public areas after 7 PM are subject to immediate arrest and detention. Except in the case of religious expression, the act of disguising one's face, in whole or in part, will result in immediate arrest and detention. Anyone engaged in public disturbances including, but not limited to, protesting, rioting, looting, and inflicting damage upon public or private property are subject to immediate arrest and detention. Engaging in such acts after dark may result in the use of lethal force.

The U.S. Geological Survey has detected an aftershock, magnitude 5.3, centered 25 miles east-northeast of San Bernardino. Aftershocks may continue for days or even weeks after a major seismic event. For your protection, ensure that your main gas valve is turned off. Inspect your home for damage and move to your local Red Cross shelter if any of the following has occurred: shifting of a wall from its foundation, bowed or fractured floor or ceiling joists, shifting of the roof from the exterior walls of the building.

A civil unrest warning has been activated within the following communities: Los Angeles, East Los Angeles, Pasadena, Glendale, Pico Rivera, Southgate, Watts, Compton, Gardena, Long Beach, Los Alamitos, La Mirada, Irvine, West Covina, Chino, Colton, San Bernardino. If you reside in these areas, you are encouraged to restrict your movements and remain indoors until local police have responded to the situation...

The alert went on for another five minutes. When the television changed back to the news, the anchors repeated the Breaking News of the curfew.

Which didn't matter to me. I wasn't going anywhere for the weekend.

I hoped that HRW didn't fare as well as my home did. The earthquake could have collapsed the place all the way to the third basement, for all I cared. At least that way, I could have qualified for unemployment.

8—Time To Do Some Shopping

In Complete Denial

Of course, the earthquake did nothing at HRW but knock around some knick-knacks on people's desks, and fling some of my office supplies onto the break-room floor. After thirty minutes of clean-up, I went back to my constant hiring. The afternoon started out poorly. I got a certified letter from OSHA about Mr. Chandler's fall, but Bob wouldn't return my phone call, and I couldn't reach Tammy from the Home Office. So, I had no idea what to do about that. And I needed to move on Mr. McClusky's retirement, but didn't know where to start.

Once I got done with my new-hire signatures, I decided to handle Mr. Chandler's fall first. It was probably my tenth call trying to reach somebody who could help me with the OSHA problem. Someone at the Home Office finally answered:

"Hi—is Tammy there?"

"Uh, no. Who's this?"

"Zeno Jacobs from Region 601."

"*You* again. 601?"

"Los Angeles."

"Right..."

"Look—is there anybody I can talk to about OSHA?"

"What's that?"

"Occupational Safety— Who are you?"

"Lizzie..."

"Okay, Lizzie. Why do you sound like you're twelve?"

"*Hey*—I'm *seventeen*. And a *half!*"

"Is there anyone there, *older?*"

"Naw. I got 'em all the job."

"How many?"

"There's six of us. And me too."

"What do you all do?"

"When we get the bills we pay them in the computer."

"I thought that's what Tammy did."

"Naw, she's always busy on the phone. With people like *you.*"

I stopped myself from snapping at the girl. "When's Tammy coming back?"

"Got me. She caught strep or some shit."

"Great."

"Can I go?"

"*What?*"

"Are you done?"

"I guess."

The line went dead.

I switched to my other pet project: Mr. McClusky's retirement.

At HRW, there was a fine line between Personnel and Payroll. For instance, the job code that an employee worked under was entered by Personnel. But to give somebody a raise, someone from Personnel entered the raise, it was forwarded to the VPs for approval, and once the approval was done, the new wage was finalized by Payroll. So, I could view someone on the payroll screen of our computer system, but changing anything would create a cascade of alarms throughout the company. That was something I wanted to avoid.

The payroll screen normally showed the employee's name, their job title, and their wage. Mr. McClusky's didn't look ordinary:

McClusky, Samuel C., LEGACY
(4114), ???

I spent an hour looking through the system for the meaning of those codes. I found nothing. As I worked methodically through the system's drop-down menus, Bob returned my call—one of only two times *that* ever happened.

"This is Bob. What do you need, Zeno?"

"I was calling about this OSHA issue—"

She blew static across the line to me. "Just type up a quick page saying the grating's fixed. You investigated Mr. Chandler's accident and found that if he wasn't in the process of damaging company property, he wouldn't have found himself falling fifty feet down a shaft. Why is that so hard?"

"Okay—I've just never dealt with OSHA before."

"Respond to them *today*, Zeno. You don't want them crawling around that old building looking for violations."

"Got it. Is anyone going to be replacing Tammy from the Home Office?"

"Ah—since I have you on the phone, she needs to be put on an LOA. She's scheduled for surgery next Monday."

"Surgery—for what?"

"Zeno, we have privacy policies. I mean, how long have you been with us now? You know that."

Talking about Tammy's illness was surely no violation, I mean it was "strep or some shit," but it's not like I actually cared. I'd asked because I was hoping to get to know Bob a little bit. Nothing helps that along like a little gossip. But she refused to gab.

"Okay," I said. "How long will she be out?"

"You don't need to enter how long into an LOA request. Just enter it in and I'll approve it. You have any other burdens for me?"

"Yeah." I paused—and *savored* the pause. "Mr. McClusky wants me to file his retirement paperwork—"

"*What?*"

"Mr. McClusky. *Samuel* McClusky—the janitor."

"We don't have benefit packages for employees."

"We do for this one—"

"Zeno—I've been with this company for twenty-two years and in all that time, we've never offered benefits to our hourly employees. So, you're wrong. Just terminate him and code it as a voluntary separation."

I was going to tell Bob that Mr. McClusky had her beat by a couple of decades, but I could hear the irritation in her voice. I wondered if terming him would automatically start his retirement benefits in the computer. That would make sense. I decided to bring the subject up with Payroll instead of pushing the issue with Bob.

"Anything else, Zeno?"

"Yes."

On the phone, her breath sounded like an explosion.

"Have a nice evening, Bob."

She hung up.

I typed the response to OSHA, put Tammy on an LOA, and then started in on the retirement issue again. Since it was now late, I decided the visit to Payroll could wait. But since I still had a half-hour, I dug around a little more.

At HRW, every type of expense that involved the transfer of money, from the income generated by the coffee machine to the payout of an employee's child support, was tracked on this huge digital spreadsheet called the General Ledger. I opened it and minimized its scope so I was only viewing Region 601. It wasn't very descriptive. It showed things like:

601-15900 A/C Repairs 001459607-1086045320 1154.00

This is what Tammy's department did all day—they coded these things in the computer. When the account was paid, the computer created an entry in the General Ledger.

I opened up the search box, and typed in LEGACY. It said *Search Item Not Found.* I typed in 4114. This time it found hundreds of items. But all these items were embedded within other numbers. I opened up *Options* on the search box. I limited the search to *Whole Words Only* and tried 4114 again.

It said, *Search Item Not Found.*

I thought, *Why is Mr. McClusky coded differently than everyone else?* I continued to think about it in silence as we drove out to Octavio's that night.

Doreen stayed busy knitting with a couple housewives. Octavio had disappeared. I found Carlos and asked where he'd gone.

"Octavio is *shopping* for a car," he said with a measure of sarcasm. "You'll see. You and me are going out. Got your *pañuelo?*"

I pulled the bandana from my cargo pocket. "Where are we going?" I asked.

"Time to go shopping," Carlos said. "You come along, ¿si? Octavio will be there, and afterward he can drive you home."

I didn't know where we were going, nor did I know exactly what Carlos meant by *shopping.* I'd say at that point I was still in complete denial about Hundred Days. It was easier to be in denial, I guess.

There were six little pickups in our convoy. We stopped alongside a curb near a westbound freeway entrance to the 60, which was far enough from the earthquake-ravaged Pasadena to be open. Octavio found us and pulled into the lead spot in a sparkly new Ranger. The truck still had the dealer's advertisement in the license plate frame. Carlos and I were in the truck directly behind him, with me riding shotgun.

I saw Octavio wave through his back window, and then he accelerated away. Carlos didn't follow—instead, he cut the engine. Octavio weaved sharply across the road and disappeared up the eastbound ramp. The four other pickups stayed alongside the road, lined up behind us.

Carlos drummed his fingers to some mariachi playing softly through the truck's speakers. He didn't speak at all; we sat for what seemed like a half-hour. I hadn't noticed the walkie-talkie on the bench seat beside Carlos. When it crackled with a brief burst of static, I almost yelped.

It was Octavio's voice. *"Tengo camión de Vons. Pasará en dos minutos."*

Carlos started the truck; I must have looked terrified.

He slapped me on the shoulder. "It will be alright, *El Judío.* Now watch." We were wearing our bandanas on our heads, *hausfrau* style. "Do as I do, yes?"

I mimicked him, pulling the corners from underneath the knot in back, and drawing them up and down over my face. I tugged it down until the tight edge of the bandana was on top of the bridge of my nose.

"Good," Carlos said from under his mask. "When we are done, you will just do the same backward. *¿Si?*"

"Yeah."

The walkie-talkie crackled again: *"Treinta segundos."*

Carlos put the old Toyota in gear and floored the gas as he released the clutch. While taking the onramp, he cut off an Escalade—it steered wide and into the concrete wall of the overpass. Carlos let out a muffled chortle as he continued forward. Behind us, the Escalade was blasting an angry pattern of honks as our other four pickups passed it by. When we neared the top of the rise, all of us were in a close, nearly bumper-to-bumper, formation.

Carlos turned up the music as we drove into the merging lane side-by-side with a long, white sixteen-wheeler. It moved over to let us in. Carlos pulled into the slow lane and let off of the throttle. After the truck had cleared us, it signaled and moved back into our lane, directly ahead. Now, through Carlos' open window, I saw Octavio's Ranger flash by—he must have been going ninety or a hundred.

"Watch out now," Carlos said, *"nos será frenado duro."*

9—The Bad Guy

THE MEANING OF LIFE
EVERYONE—EVEN YOU—IS INVOLVED ALREADY

I was no longer in denial.

I checked my seat belt. I grabbed onto the door handle. My hot breath was being redirected in my face.

The walkie-talkie crackled again: *"¡Ahorita!"*

Carlos crushed the brake pedal. The walkie-talkie was airborne. It bounced off of the ashtray and seemed to disappear. I was flung hard into the locked shoulder belt. My teeth were bared underneath my disguise. The roaring of tires muted the mariachi.

I saw the semi's brake lights flare at the same time that chunks of glass and plastic and metal flew past. A tire was spinning in the air to the left of the semi.

The sign on the back of the semi was getting closer. It said:

VONS
Ingredients for life

132

Our tires continued their constant, ear-piercing scream, while the semi's tires emitted a rapid series of woofs.

The distance between the back of the semi and our truck was closing. Quickly.

The airborne tire landed somewhere on the eastbound side of the freeway and then it bounced up again, gaining distance from us. As we continued to slide in the lane, I was sure the semi was going to push the engine compartment onto our laps. But we impacted the back of it gently.

And all was still.

The mariachi played over more screeching tires from behind.

Carlos opened his door. "Come, *El Judío.*"

I slid across the bench seat, exiting through the driver's door. I looked behind for any traffic. The other four pickups were blocking the freeway's lanes and stopped cars were piling up behind them. I hurried forward, looking for Carlos.

The semi driver stepped down from his cab. He was as big as a linebacker. Suddenly, he flopped to the ground. I sprinted the distance of the semi's trailer until I was beside Carlos. He was squeezing the trigger of a tazer. Its wires were embedded in the belly of that huge man, who was flailing and yelping on the hardtop.

Carlos dropped the tazer and climbed into the truck's cab.

I rushed forward to find Octavio. The bed of the Ranger was accordioned above the rear window of the cab. He was in the driver's seat with an airbag flat on his lap; he worked the door handle to no avail. I yanked from the outside. The door squealed in protest as the two of us forced it open.

When he got out, he slapped me on the back. "*Bueno.*"

We hurried over to Carlos.

Octavio pointed at the stirring driver. He told me to watch him and rushed away with Carlos to the semi's trailer.

The truck driver rolled onto his back.

I reached into my cargo pocket and brought out the pistol. I pointed it at him.

The driver propped his huge body up on an elbow, and squinted at me. "Is that a *Luger?*"

"Shut up," I told him.

I looked up the freeway and back down. I scanned the slowing traffic on the other side. CHP had to be coming—I was sure of it. And there I was: a bad guy standing on a clogged-up freeway, bandana disguise over his face, holding a gun on a defenseless citizen.

It seemed forever before Octavio came back, but like with the earthquake, time's moments had expanded.

"*¿Es eso una Luger?*" Octavio asked.

I stared at him.

He took the gun from me. "Boss need you."

I said *okay* and ran back to the trailer. There was an open door in its side, and the Toyota that Carlos and I had come in had been pulled up below it. A bucket brigade of masked men was transferring goods.

I called up: *"Carlos?"*

Carlos appeared in the doorway with an index finger over his lips. I raised my eyebrows, but said nothing.

Carlos dropped his hand. "We don't use names, *El Judío*, understand?"

"Yes, boss."

"Come," he said. "Take what you need."

I hopped up into the trailer. Toward the cab end, where a cold wind came from some fans, there were sides of beef. I hoisted one off its hook and the weight of it sent me on a direct trajectory to the trailer's metal floor. Two of the other guys hoisted it off of me. I got up, searching again, and toward the middle, I picked out a case of Charmin. When I passed it off, there were gales of laughter.

Carlos slapped me on the shoulder. "*Sí*, my friend. Eating and shitting—*estos son el significado de la vida*," he said, which meant those are meaning of life. He hopped down to the pavement, put his fingers to his mouth, and whistled sharply.

As the *banditos* made their way back to their pickups, I went to Octavio. He handed me my gun, which I held with my arm slack.

"Sorry, man," Octavio told the truck driver. "Hope you don't get in no trouble." Then he ran off to one of the trucks blocking traffic.

I shrugged at the guy and hurried back to my seat, riding shotgun to *Jimenez Loco*.

Carlos started the truck and, as he floored it, he asked "Is *that* a fucking *Luger?*"

We stopped at a parking garage, where we reapplied the license plates I hadn't known had been removed. Next, we slapped magnetic signs onto each of the pickup's doors, with the branding:

Jimenez Landscaping

just call

(213) JIMENEZ

for all your landscaping needs!

We transformed our masks into head scarves again. The spoils were divided up into the different pickups' beds.

Carlos came to me and shook my hand saying, "Well done, *El Judío*." Then he pulled me aside, and spoke to me quietly. "We are fighting a war, Zeno. But it is a *different* war. We fight the corporations and we fight the corporate government. Our tools are spray paint. And fire. And maybe some explosives. These are the tools we need to kill the corporations. But the only purpose of a bullet is to kill a *person*. Bullets are what this corporate government uses to keep people afraid. We don't need no bullets to fight this war, Zeno. It was *your* idea—you should know this already. So, leave your gun at home."

I nodded.

Carlos gave me a quick shoulder slap and got into the passenger's seat of Manuel's pickup. Octavio motioned me back to the Toyota. He dialed-in a country station and cranked the volume. We circled the garage, and then sped out the exit—westbound toward my home. When we got there, I set up one of my Pop's folding tables in the living room and lined it with wax paper. Octavio helped me in with my side of beef, and then he brought in some of his own booty, stacking six twelve-packs of *Dos Equis* in my garage.

He was cool like that.

"*¿Quieres ayudar?*" he asked, staring at the beef as though it were mooing.

"*Nah*—curfew's in a half-hour. You'd better go."

"We'll be grounding power lines tomorrow," he said. "Your idea. You should come."

I stood with my mouth open, shaking my head. "I got a lot going on, man. I can't get involved right now."

Octavio began to turn away, but his gaze was fixed, so now he spoke to me from over his shoulder. "You will see: everyone—even *you*—is involved already. You should not be afraid to act."

I crossed my arms over my chest. "Octavio—one of these times, you're going to go out and they'll be waiting. Not with pistols, but with machine guns. If you guys won't carry weapons—*real* weapons like rifles—you're gonna be slaughtered."

"Maybe." He took out his keys and walked to the Impala. As he got in, he bellowed, *"Buenas noches, El Judío."*

I waved and shut my garage door.

I stepped inside the house. The side of beef was there. No way would it fit in my freezer like that. I got out some knives, popped open a warm beer, and went to work.

10—CRISIS In Los Angeles

KTLA had announced a primetime special, promising to detail how the federal government would be assisting those Los Angelinos in need. At 8 PM, it started with a trumpet fanfare and the headline:

CRISIS in Los Angeles

It was Mandy Gutierrez again, and at the upper left corner of my TV, it said *LIVE.*

I had never cut up a cow before and, now only a quarter-way done with the task, I was astonished by how much work was still ahead of me. By this point, I had brought in six or seven saws from the garage for different functions and necessary angles. As I worked my way through a hip bone, Mandy spoke.

"Good evening," she said, smiling like a used-car salesman. "I'm reporting to you from the beautiful Mojave Desert within Joshua Tree National Park..."

Carson has a sour look on his face. He's staring away.

"Need more coffee?" I ask.

"Yeah. You can skip over Camp Liberty. I was born there. Raised there."

I take our cups and go to the kitchen. He doesn't follow me this time. I make my coffee my way, and his an approximation of his way. I set up the percolator for another pot and then go back to the dining room, where Carson still seems distant.

I place his coffee in front of him and sit. "Want to tell me about it?"

"There's not much to tell. I was born there, like I said. My parents divorced there too. Everyone was crowded together in open bays and we'd always see Mom with this strange man…"

"Did you have any siblings?"

"There were seven of us." Carson thinks for a while. Maybe a minute. "It wasn't fair."

"When did you finally leave the camp?"

"I was fifteen…" Carson blows on his coffee. "But this isn't my story, Dad. Go on."

The Reader's Digest of it was Mandy pitched the camp, its luxuries and amenities, its schools and sports fields. How its gates were open to any resident of Southern California, and how anyone who moved in would receive free food, free clothing, free housing and utilities, and free education up to an associate's degree—all within that huge compound. But their biggest amenity, as far as I could tell, was safety.

Then again, there was this feeling I had.

That it was an internment camp.

I didn't sleep well. I kept seeing all that raw meat. And the pistol at the end of my outstretched arm, pointed at that truck driver. There's a point you reach when you give up on trying to go back to sleep, and for me it's usually an hour before my alarm goes off. That's when I got up and took an extra-long shower. After drying off, I watched the early-morning news.

Hundred Days was already hard at work—the power in and around Riverside had been out since 4:30 AM, due to the grounding of that high-tension line along the 10. The neighborhoods effected by the blackout were being listed when I began to wonder if Octavio would be showing up to give me a ride. But soon, I heard the Impala in the driveway.

When we arrived at work, Octavio and Doreen stayed outside the labyrinth, talking. I went in and as soon as I got to the office, my extension rang. I looked into the camera and motioned to it, like: *What! I'm just getting here!*

I picked up the handset: *"Hello!"*

"This is Bob," she said. "We have a problem, Zeno."

"Right—I'm short on my terms by seven people. I'll have them by Friday."

"I know that, Zeno. With the riots and the earthquake there, it shouldn't be that hard. But right now we have a different problem. Los Angeles is going to be evacuated."

"My impression is that it's voluntary."

"Your impression is wrong. I spent all day yesterday trying to get an exception for our employees. And right now, your congresswoman's office is very busy."

"Did you get one?"

"Yes. I need you to send a roster to the address I just mailed to you. The subject line says *Essential Personnel...*"

I opened my inbox. "Okay—found it."

"Do you know where the Police Administration Building is? Because you need to drive out there."

I didn't mention my lack of wheels. "Yeah. It's downtown."

"They will give you 2,000 clip-on badges—these are not just for each employee, but also for each of their family members. And Zeno?"

"Yeah..."

"You are down to sixty percent staffing. I suggest you bring on *every* person that walks through your door over the next few days. Because after that, there won't be anyone else to hire."

The line went dead.

When Octavio went past, I walked him straight into the labyrinth again.

"*¿Qué pasa?*" he asked.

"I need a ride downtown."

We exited the building and then got into the Impala. He drove east. Octavio was quiet until we passed Hoover Street.

"So, you got the address?"

"100 West First Street."

"What's that? City Hall?"

"Police Headquarters." We went over a bump. Octavio looked grave. "You fuckin shittin me, Man."

I winced. "No…"

"I park at City Hall."

Turned out there was nowhere to park, not even at City Hall. Every curbside spot within blocks was taken, and every parking garage was coned or barricaded off.

"Give me your phone and go home," I told Octavio. "I'll call Carlos when I'm done."

"Okay, but call María—*Carlos está en de camino.*"

"Right." I brought out the Luger and put it under his front seat. Octavio looked around guiltily as he dropped me off in front of the Administration building, where I entered, went through security, and found a handmade banner hanging from the ceiling that said *Essential Personnel Badges.* The line coming from there zigzagged in a roped-off queue. I found the end of it and got in line.

Three hours later, Octavio pulled up where he had dropped me off. I loaded the cases into his back seat and opened one, grabbing a box of fifty. I got into the passenger's seat and put the box in his glove compartment.

I said, "Those are for *los compañeros.*"

Octavio nodded and put his Impala in gear.

I had Octavio park at the applicant entrance. I retrieved the Luger and stuffed it into my cargo pocket. Each of us carried a case of the badges to the applicant entrance. When I pulled the door open, the lobby was crammed full of desperate-looking people. In the midst of them towered the Cuppa Noodles girl, holding her résumé in her left hand and smiling nervously.

Shasta MacCalistaire

11—Interviewing Shasta

TENSION WITH DOREEN
UNREALISTIC SCENARIOS
WHERE THE CAMERAS ARE POINTED

I don't know if she remembered our run-in at Ralph's.
I'm just an ordinary-looking guy (by which I mean
slightly overweight—in the American fashion), with the
face of a modern Jew whose ancestors have diddled with
the Gentiles some. In other words, my appearance, my
countenance, my visage, so to speak, is entirely for-
gettable. So, I wouldn't have been surprised if she didn't
remember the whole Cuppa Noodles thing.

But I remembered.

I remembered it well.

Nevertheless, at times like these, when life or fortune
or chance or destiny throws you together with someone
for a second time, it never happens randomly. No, something, someone, some force out there makes sure your
lifelines cross with peculiar timing. It always happens
when you least expect it, when your mind is busy tracking

something else, and *most definitely* at a time when you are most capable of making a complete fool of yourself.

Octavio had proceeded onward. But I was frozen a couple of feet away from her, staring upwards.

"Are you okay?" she asked, wearing one of those strange smiles where you only see the person's bottom teeth. She waved a hand in front of my eyes. *"Helll- oooooo?"*

I blinked and took her résumé. In doing so, I fumbled the case of badges and all the boxes inside spilled out. I dropped to my knees and started gathering them up.

She joined me.

As we shoved the boxes back into the case, they didn't fit together the same way, so she held the extra few.

"I'm the personnel director. Can you help me to my desk?"

"Totally."

"Thank you so much," I said. I set the case outside my cubicle, where Octavio had left his. She set her boxes on top. I motioned inside. "Take a seat."

"Okay."

I sat next to her. "My name's Zeno."

"Shasta," she said with a little wave.

I consulted her résumé with flagrant regard. "Yes, Shasta MacCalistaire. Why'd you leave UCLA?"

"I was starving."

I thought of Doreen—same story. "I don't understand why our schools are allowing their students to starve."

"*Not their problem*—one of my financial aid counselors told me that. Every quarter, I'd buy the $8,000 meal plan, but it would run out three weeks before finals, and they'd be like, '*No problem! Just add some more money to the plan!*' And I was like, '*What money?*' So, you either needed a rich family or a job, and I couldn't keep up with the homework and the practice and the job..."

"Practice? Basketball?"

She gave me a stern look, full of rebuke. "Everyone *always* says that!" Then she smiled embarrassingly. "I'm too clumsy to play ball. I play the marimba. *Well*—used to."

It sounded familiar: *A kind of drum?* "What's a marimba?"

"It's like a xylophone. I can play that too."

Ah. "The xylophone's not a clumsy person's instrument."

She shrugged.

I looked at her résumé again. "You've had lots of jobs—none of them for long. Why'd you leave McDonald's?"

She crossed her arms across her chest. "Because it's *McDonald's*."

A chuckle escaped me—it occurred to me just then that she actually *was* the ideal candidate. "I see..."

"I mean, they wrote me up for snacking on a Quarter Pounder from the waste bucket. They must throw away twenty pounds of food a day and they don't even let their own employees..." She put her hands on her knees and leaned forward, with desperation in her eyes. "Please, I just need to make enough money to find my family in Montana. They moved up there three—"

"You're hired, Shasta."

She leaned back in her chair, showing her bottom teeth again. "Cool," she said, but it almost came out like a question.

I opened the new-hire screen on the computer and we spent five minutes entering in her info. When I finalized it, the printer spat out her file.

I stood. "Welcome to HRW, Shasta."

She followed. "Thanks."

I called out: "Hey, Doreen?"

"Yes, you bastard?"

I cringed, but then smiled dismissively, treating it like an inside joke. "Will you show Shasta to a cubicle and get her started please?"

Doreen came around and guided Shasta away. The other prospectives were blocking the applicant entrance, so I called the group over and did my thing with them.

When I'd hired the ones I wanted, I peeked over my cubicle.

"The Help Desk is on their way up, Doreen. I've got two cases of badges. You need to write the employee's name, license number, and 'HRW International' on the lines. Then you just fold over the plastic thing and snap the clip on it. Okay?"

She rolled her eyes.

"Okay?" I asked again.

"Oh-*kay*, you bastard."

I almost yelled at her, but then stopped myself with a deep breath. "You need to be quick. IT will be up at 3:00, Security at 3:15, Payroll at 3:30, Marketing at 3:45, HR at 4:30 and there will still be all our people—"

She barked lightly a few times, and responded: "*Great.*"

"Make sure you tell every single person they have to wear their badge at all times in the city."

"Not just at work?"

"Right. Rumor is there will be mandatory evacuations now. They also need an additional badge for each of their family members, so just give them however many they ask for and let them fill out the info."

Doreen got up and brought the cases into her cubicle.

I stood. "Oh—I need one for Mr. McClusky."

"Who's that?"

"The janitor."

She handed me a badge.

I made up a note with an explanation for Mr. McClusky. I pinned it along with the badge to the outside wall of my cubicle.

When it was time to go, I tried to find Shasta. I wanted to ask her how her first day went, but she had left already.

That night, Hundred Days went south into Long Beach and continued their attack on the power lines, leaving thirty percent of the metro dark. The loss of power in Long Beach was what touched off the civil riots there. And those riots were the most destructive and, in the end, the deadliest nationwide. While Octavio and Carlos were out planting seeds that would sprout as discord, dissent, disruption, and inevitable death, I spaced out, trying to imagine Shasta's face, longing to know what it would feel like to hold her, wondering how far her feet would dangle past the end of my bed, and playing out unrealistic scenarios where we'd happen to fall in love...

In actuality, I kept my distance. I didn't want to play the creepy stalker, so I stayed in my cubicle and did my work, interviewing people, asking dumb questions, putting the newbies' info into the computer, and sending them to Doreen to get their badge. At one point, Doreen goes "Hey, you bastard?"

"How *long* are you going to keep up with this?"

"Look over there," she said.

I stood and looked over my cubicle wall, to where Doreen was pointing.

The cameras were looking that way too—they were all pointing at the cubicle where Doreen had put Shasta. A group of my male employees were gaggled there, resting their arms on the cubicle's walls. I walked over. When the man-herd sensed me, it bounded away, leaving Shasta alone inside. A box of copy paper was nearby; I dragged it over so I could stand on it and talk with her from over the cubicle's wall.

She was busy processing a termination, wearing a bustier, an extremely short skirt, and high-heeled shoes.

"Hi, Shasta," I said, feeling my heartbeat quicken. "You sure look good today!"

She smiled. "Hey." Now, along with the smile came an adorable flush of embarrassment.

I couldn't stop myself from smiling back, but I played my part, saying, "Your outfit must be a ploy for termination."

She turned and typed a few keystrokes. "Oh, you know. A girl can only try…"

"Unfortunately, it would be a termination for cause."

She turned back to me, her arms folded just below her bustier. "Not at all," she said. "I can make a fairly good case, I think. The employee handbook, the one sitting on the shelf in the break room, says—and I quote—'Clothes chosen to be worn by employees must be in good taste.' *Chosen* means *choice*—in other words, I can choose what to wear. However, the handbook never defines *good taste*. My top is a Scaasi. Look it up: there's no better taste than a Scassi."

I examined her top. "Your Scassi has a torn seam."

She pulled on its straps. "Yuh, well it's a Goodwill Scassi."

I cleared my throat, trying to talk to her face instead of her breasts. "Showing so much skin is bad taste. In an office environment, at least."

"*Oh,* puh-*lease*. I'm wearing at least three times the cloth worn by a swimsuit model. Hey—do you like my heels?" She lifted one up to the level of her seat cushion.

My eyes flicked to them. They didn't stay there. "Uh-huh."

Now she stood and posed like Miss America. "Come on. Is this really *bad taste*?"

It was involuntary—I asked, "Do you think you could learn to forge my signature?"

"I…*guess?*" she said, and sat again.

"No, get up. Bring your things."

From then until I termed her, she worked with me.

12—Dolphins And Sombreros

The next day, I ran into Shasta at the entrance to the labyrinth. Octavio held the door open for Doreen and lingered to lick his lips at me from behind Shasta's back. I shooed him away with a commanding flick of my eyes.

It was just Shasta and me now. She looked great in a knee-length skirt, a red button-up blouse that was buttoned down to show a modest amount of cleavage, and a sharp little coat that was cut just right to accentuate her wonderful curves.

"Hey, Shasta!" I said, feeling like a Playboy Bunny's garbage man.

"Hi...*oh*, how embarrassing. It was something exotic..."

"Zeno," I said hopelessly.

"Ah. That's it. So, yesterday, Terrance guided me through, but I'm afraid I don't know the way by myself."

I wondered who the hell Terrance was. I pushed away the thought, and whispered: *"Don't tell a soul*—the paintings are the key to the labyrinth. Just follow the ones with dolphins on them."

"Hmm," she said with a tilt of the head. Then her face transitioned to an adorable smile. "Sounds like you want to keep me around."

I opened the door for her. "No, but I'd rather you quit than get lost in here." My lie was part of the job—I'll admit it. I took her arm. "Go ahead and guide me through."

In our fifteen-minute walk through the labyrinth, Shasta commented on each of the paintings. She asked me how old they were, who the artist was, and what the paintings meant.

I had no answers for her.

We eventually found our way to the office. "So where can I get a cup of coffee?" she asked.

"It's back in there. You follow the sombreros."

"Ah."

I started to walk toward my cubicle. "You coming?"

"I have to get changed," she said, and took off toward the bathroom.

Shasta was in that duty uniform of hers. As she strutted toward me, her thighs pulsated with every strike of her scuffed, spike heels, and their height made her calves rock hard. It seems funny to me how it took until I'd met Shasta to discover how sexy legs can be. I stared frozen in lust as the cameras whirred above me. Finally, she stopped in front of me, asking, "Coffee?"

I produced a fiver. "Yes, please."

Leaving her hand out, she cleared her throat.

"Oh, of course." I fished around my pocket and found another one.

"Thanks, Zeno!" She clicked the fivers against each other as she went to follow sombreros.

The security voyeurs and I watched her butt work—left, right, left, right. Having Shasta as my occupational companion instantly made my job a simple heaven. I no longer spent the early mornings dreading coming to work. I didn't feel like killing myself as I plodded through daily interviews with all those needy people. And—let's face it—I had THIS JOB SUCKS put on all of the computers because it was true. Only it wasn't true—not for me, not anymore—all because of Shasta.

What I was aware of first were her breasts by the side of my face, stuffed into that ornamental bra—she was setting down the coffees. When her hands were free, she handed me my fivers back.

I stared at the coins. "How'd you pay for the coffee?"

Shasta sat and crossed her legs. She blew steam away from her cup. "Somebody broke the lock."

Oh, I thought, *I forgot about that.* "Wonder who would do that?"

Shasta shrugged, and the motion tugged her breasts into a jiggle.

Shasta finished all the signatures of the latest hires. It had only been a day and her signature had become a nice forgery of mine. She leaned back in her chair and faced me.

"Tell me about your clan," she said.

"There's nothing to tell," I replied lamely.

"Come on, there's got to be something. I want to hear about your clan, Zeno."

"I don't have a clan," I said. "I own my home."

"Bull—*shit*. Nobody working *here* owns their own home."

"I do."

"How could you possibly afford it?" she asked with a raised eyebrow.

"I inherited it."

She blinked at me rapidly. "Okay, all the inheritance taxes add up to like seventy-five percent. So if your home's worth two-mill, you would have had to pay one-point-five to stay in it. That means you would have inherited six-mill in cash just to pay up the house. Then there's the electric—the bill on a house has to be more than you make!"

"Yeah," I admitted, "you're right about all that."

"*So!* You don't really live alone, then."

"I do."

"*Explain!*" she demanded, pounding her fist on my desk.

I pulled an envelope off of the hutch. It said:

Weekly Paperwork
AP
Region 601

"I put my bills in here. And they always get paid."

She said it again: "BULL...*shit.*"

"Okay, you don't have to believe me. Why don't you bring me a bill? I'll put it in and we'll see what happens."

"No," she said. "The accountants will see it's a personal bill and I'll be fired with cause—no unemployment."

"They're not accountants, Shasta—they're hired the same way you were. This company is so focused on keeping within their labor targets that they can't afford accountants, and they can't afford to file the invoices once they're processed. Some poor gal working for minimum wage—just like us—sits at a terminal in the home office's basement, she transfers money into the account shown on the bill, and when she's done, she throws the bill into the incinerator and moves onto the next one. She doesn't care what the bill is for, and she doesn't care who it belongs to. Bring me one of your statements and I'll prove it."

She looked at me thoughtfully for a moment. Then she said, "Okay."

On Friday, she returned with a bill from one of her clan.

"Don't you want to pay off one of your *own* bills?" I asked.

"This will prove to me that what you're saying is true. And they can't fire *me* because of this—my name's not Veronica Peabody. But they *will* fire *you*. They'll think Veronica is your lover or something. Unless they truly don't look at what they're paying for."

"You'll see," I said. I slipped the bill in with the other weekly invoices, called FedEx for the pick-up, and forgot about it. Shasta didn't.

13—Shasta's Clan

LIFE WITH THE CLAN
A VOICE FROM THE LABYRINTH
I WANT HER *TERMINATED*
THE UPS GUY

It was Wednesday of the next week, and as Octavio parked, he pointed at a Sparkletts water truck parked along the building's sidewalk.

"It was there yesterday, too. It break down?"

"No idea," I said. "He never came to me for a signature."

As we got out of the car, I stepped on my shoelace. As I knelt, Doreen took Octavio's arm, dragging him away to the employee entrance. Octavio glanced back at me like, *"Man—she angry with you!"* When I was done tying my shoe, I rushed to catch up with them—and I did—but Doreen excluded me from the conversation all the way through the labyrinth.

She'll get over it, I thought.

When I arrived at my desk, Shasta was there, dressed in slacks and a button-up blouse. Her hair was up in a bun, accentuating a professional look. I was going to call

161

Sparkletts, but Shasta smiled when she noticed me—and that's right when I forgot about the truck out front.

"Feeling a little modest?" I asked.

"Well," she said, *"you weren't falling for it."*

"Right." I sat beside her.

She landed a kiss on my cheek with a wet smacking sound.

My heart stopped and then made up for it by going three times as fast. It felt like something strange had migrated to the top of my chest—my spleen, perhaps. I cleared my throat with a low grunt. "What was that for?"

"Veronica's dental bill's paid off. I don't *like* her much—but that's absolutely awesome!" She wheeled over in her chair while pulling a letter from her purse. It was a demand for payment-in-full of her defaulted student loans—$435,000.

I wondered momentarily if the amount would set off any alarms.

Mr. Chandler's invoice for the labyrinth never did.

I slipped the bill into the AP envelope. If I got a kiss for Veronica's debt, surely I would get something more for Shasta's student loans.

I looked at her. Because I lived in Hollywood, I had seen my share of gorgeous women. But I had never seen anyone beautiful like *that*. There's all different kinds of attractiveness, sexual beauty, and looks: you know, *hotness*. And what people are attracted to differs from person to person. For my tastes, Shasta was the absolute pinnacle—every other woman just couldn't compare. Inside, I didn't know how to handle my attraction to her. I could have just shut down and done my work, for fear of ruining everything, or, just as easily, I could have gone on a long-winded soliloquy about unrequited lust, about how I would love to do for her what she was doing for me, or about how we could spend forever together. Of course, I didn't do any of that. But I felt compelled to say *some*thing—*any*thing. What came out was, "Tell me about your clan."

She smiled and, again, I'll tell you how beautiful she was. Her teeth were little porcelain statuettes, lined up in perfect formation. Her lips were red like plums and for the first time I realized that she wore no makeup—she didn't have to. There wasn't a flaw *anywhere* to cover up. She had Mona Lisa's nose—not too big, not too small. And her eyes were the color of shallow water at a white-sand beach. "There's forty-seven of us," she said. "All girls."

I'd never heard of so large a clan. "How big's the house?"

"Two bedrooms."

I gasped.

"*Yuh.* And Karissa—she owns the place—has a bedroom all to herself. She charges each of us $150 a month. She's been prepaying her fifteen-year loan and she's going to evict us when she burns the mortgage. We've only got three months left."

"What're you going to do?"

She gave me a blank stare. Then she said, "I don't know."

I returned her blank stare.

"Some of the girls have been sleeping with her, trying to gain favor—maybe let them stay in the spare bedroom until they find a place. But Karissa knows why they're doing it. I think she's going to give all of us the boot."

"I'm sorry—minus Karissa, that's forty-six women in the equivalent of a one-bedroom house—where do you all fit?"

"Someone lies down on the floor, and everybody else lies down next to her. Eventually the room fills up and spills into the kitchen, the dining room, and finally the back yard."

"You have no bed, no couch, no nothing?"

"Well, I pay an extra fifty dollars for a special privilege."

I cringed, figuring on something sexual. "For what?"

"I get the bathroom."

"Oh," I said. As I imagined it, *yuck* went through my mind.

"It's carpeted—which, I know, is strange for a bathroom. I sleep on the carpet in front of the sink. All night long, the girls come in to use the toilet, but it doesn't wake me up unless it's unusually rank. If it is, I'll be like, *'Shit, girl, light a candle,'* and she'll go, *'Shut the fuck* uuuup, *Shasta.'*"

That made me laugh—but it was *with* her, not *at* her.

"So, *yuh*," she said, "the *American Dream*, you know?"

Yeah. The American Dream.

She continued with her story—*Life with the Clan,* I call it.

"Almost every night, some dude gets dragged into the place. You know, with forty-six girls, at least *one* of them is going to find a guy to bring home that night. No men are allowed—Karissa's militantly anti-male. But she's really, like, *fat*—so, once she's in her bedroom, she's there until morning. Some of the girls sleep naked in anticipation of a visit, with just a sheet covering them. Rule is that whoever brings him gets him first—then it's every woman for herself.

"I made the mistake of coming out of the bathroom some night when all that was going on. This dude was on top of Mary Beth, Julie was on her knees with her junk shoved in his face, and Janeera was lying nearby, taking in the smell and moaning, *'Do me next, boy, do me next...'*

"So, after ten o'clock or so, I stay curled in a ball, dressed from head to toe in the bathroom. Sometimes I'll set the toilet to run so it drowns out the noise. But when I do that, I always wake up to Karissa screaming, 'I just don't get what's wrong with this *fucking toilet!*'

"The weekends are the worst. They'll have ten or twelve guys over and it becomes a total fuckfest until the sun comes up. I can always count on one of them being a perve and trying to undo my pants while I sleep. Sometimes I can get them to go away. Sometimes I have to fight."

I found that I barely had the breath for a question. "Can't you lock the bathroom?"

"Rules say I can lock it only when I'm using it. Rule's the same for the other girls—only they can't ask me to leave. So, a lot of times I'll be leaning against the tub reading or something and one of the girls will come in, lock the door, and just drop their pants and go. I could probably win the record of seeing the most women shit."

She changed the subject. "Do you really think they'll pay off my student loans?"

"No doubt," I said. "What did you major in again?"

"Music. I was gonna be a teacher."

"You haven't been able to find a job as a teacher's aide or anything?"

"Nobody in the education system is retiring. The way inflation is, Social Security hardly pays the rent. Not to mention electricity and gas and water and the trash. And if you work more than twelve hours on Social Security, they reduce it dollar-for-dollar by the amount you're paid. So teachers teach until death. All the new graduates become substitutes and teacher's aides while they're on the waiting list."

"*God,*" I said.

"They tried to put a cap on the teachers, you know. Forced retirement in twenty years or something. But the teacher's union stopped that."

Shasta looked despondent.

"Tell me about yourself," I said.

She looked puzzled. "That's about all there is to know…"

"Well, no, like, *Where were you born?* and *Who are your parents?* and *What do they do?* you know—that kind of stuff."

"Ah." She smiled. "I was born here, in L.A. My parents owned a nice home in Whitley Heights. It was paid off, too. My childhood was magical. *Very* magical. Anytime I think back, it comes to me like a fairy tale. I was raised in a beautiful house with a beautiful garden on a beautiful hill. We had a pool with a diving board and a slide. And we had two dogs—Mitzy and Tipsy. I miss them the most, sometimes. I had two older brothers and a younger sister. I don't know where they are anymore. Other than somewhere in Montana.

"When I was eighteen, there was the financial crisis. Even though my parents made good money, it wasn't enough to keep up with the bills. We did everything to cut back. Unplugged anything not in use. We spent most of the time in the dark and ate by candlelight. Mom and Dad sold their cars and bicycled down the canyon to work. That eliminated paying for fuel and insurance, but it still wasn't enough. My brothers and my sister found work, but they were menial jobs. I myself never did find a job while my parents were here—not even at a fast food restaurant or a convenience store. Eventually, Mom and Dad got a mortgage just so we could eat. And they couldn't pay on it—so they lost the house. They packed up what they could into the RV and put the rest up in a garage sale. They left what they couldn't sell. It was a horrible time—I cried every day.

"When the eviction day came, Mom and Dad gave us a choice to live with them in the RV or to give it a chance on our own. Simon, Nicholas, and Cassie went with them. They left to live on federal lands where they'd get rations and cable TV. I decided to stay in school because UCLA said they would change their cost-of-attendance to allow for other expenses. They did, but they didn't lower the tuition and there's a maximum you can get in loans…"

"When was the last time you heard from your family?"

"I looked up one of Dad's friends over at the ad agency. He told me Dad called from a payphone in Helena, needing something for HR at a new job. That's all I know."

I reached out to Shasta and she pulled back, but I asserted myself. As I wheeled toward her, I placed my hand on her shoulder and squeezed. "I'm sorry, Shasta."

The corners of her mouth moved up—almost imperceptibly—but that was okay. Although it was slight, it was there. And that was encouraging.

Late the next day, I was following sombreros when I heard a voice reverberating from within the walls.

"Help me, please! I'm lost..."

I managed to hold a snicker in. Another newbie wandering on his first day. What a shame.

"Please! Somebody help!"

I walked on.

When I got back, I did some general housekeeping: clearing off my desk, checking my numbers—those kinds of things.

As we left work, I noticed the Sparkletts truck again. Barry delivered our water every Tuesday, normally telling a dirty joke or two as I signed the invoice. The voice I heard in the labyrinth didn't have his deep, gravelly tone, so I once more shrugged off the truck's presence as Octavio pulled out of the lot. Of course, Barry may have taken a sick day, or he may have been put on a different route, but I'm saying this in retrospect. At the time, I thought if Sparkletts was missing a truck and a driver, they would send someone out to investigate. Why they failed to do that, I'll never know.

By Friday, Shasta had decided to dress scantily again. I was sitting close—I could smell her hair: *jasmine.* When the phone rang, she answered it: "HRW International, this is Shasta, how may I help you Sir or Madam?"

Even though the phone was at Shasta's ear, I could still hear my boss' voice: "THIS IS BOB. GET SOME CLOTHES ON YOU FLOOZY!"

Shasta's reply was immediate. "I'm sorry, Madam. I own a minimal wardrobe, and it's one I can't afford to upgrade or expand—especially at the wages that are provided for *this* job. If *you* prefer me to work with different clothes on, then I suggest *you* provide me with a uniform."

The way she was speaking to Bob made me clench my teeth. Sure, I felt it was a sound argument, and the silence from the phone made me feel like perhaps Bob thought so too. Nevertheless, I could imagine the color of her face at the other end of the phone line—red as a third-degree burn.

Shasta pushed the handset at me, saying, "She'd like to speak with you."

I looked up at the cameras and waved. "Hi, Bob."

"Buy that bitch a uniform and I don't care how you do it, but I want her *TERMINATED* by the end of the period. *Do you understand?*"

"Yes, Ma'am," I said, and I had just squeaked it in before she'd hung up.

On the mornings of the next week, the Sparkletts truck gave me fresh reminders to call their business office. On Monday, a couple of the roll-up doors were broken into and the water jugs from within had been stolen. On Tuesday, all the doors had been forced open. On Wednesday, it looked like someone had worked over the sheet metal with a baseball bat—but, strangely, they didn't break any of the glass. And on Thursday, the vehicle's dashboard was gone.

That morning, Shasta was wearing jeans and an off-sized tube top. Having forgotten once again to call the Sparkletts office, I was busy getting nowhere with Mr. McClusky's retirement while Shasta interviewed people. At around ten o'clock, a UPS guy came stumbling out of the labyrinth, looking as though he was the victim of some atrocity. He stood like a mannequin.

Eventually, I walked over. "You okay man?"

He continued to stare at a point ahead of him and slightly above my shoulder. I took the little signature pad from his hand, whipped across it with its stylus, and put it back in his hand. When I kicked the boxes off of his hand cart, he turned to go back into the labyrinth.

I grabbed him by the shoulders. "No need for a second go at it—it already whooped you once." I walked him to the applicant door and let him out.

I picked up the three boxes and carried them to my cubicle. Shasta was interviewing a guy who looked the same as the UPS guy—eyes all wide, staring intently, in another realm. The kid held his hands together in a double fist as though he was pleading. But instead of holding them up in supplication, he held them down over his groin.

"And how long did you hold that job?"

The kid blinked his way out of his trance. "Uh, three months."

"Oh," she said, sounding disappointed. "Three months seems like an awfully *long* time. We really need people that *don't* want to be here. How about you show me—show me how much you *don't* want to be here."

His stare held on Shasta's breasts.

"Your uniforms are here," I said.

"Zeno—get this dork out of here."

I obeyed and took the kid by an elbow. After I'd escorted him out, Shasta ran to me, bent down, and kissed me hard on the lips. I got lost in the moment. Her lips tasted sweet and her breath had hints of strawberry. I wished that the kiss would go on forever, and that's right when it ended.

"I don't believe you," she said. "Roxy, Chico, *Victoria's Secret!* Will any of it fit?"

I was numb, but managed a response. "I've got a handle on your size, I think."

She giggled as she gave me another smack on the lips, and then took her boxes to the bathroom. Of course it all fit—perfectly.

14—Sparkletts Aflame

Friday had rolled around again. Only it was different *this* Friday. Octavio was a little late picking me up because Doreen had been asleep when he arrived—she had been up all night with a stomach flu. As the two of us pulled into the lot, we could see everyone standing outside the entrance to the labyrinth. And I mean *everyone*—all the departments, every floor, close to a thousand people. As Octavio parked, I noticed this day's changes in the Sparkletts truck: the windshield was caved in, more tags were spray-painted on the roll-down doors, and one of the side mirrors was sitting on the pavement.

As Octavio and I walked up, Gordon was talking on his phone: "I can't help it, Bob. ... No, there's no way downstairs without going through Gary's maze. ... I don't know, a broken sewer line maybe?"

I spotted Shasta towering above everyone, looking spectacular in her new clothing. I angled up beside her, asking, "What's up?"

"Um, *yuuuh*," she said. "It's the smell."

"What smell?" I asked.

Since Shasta had started interviewing the new hires, I didn't know most of the employees' names anymore—they just came and went so quickly. But there was this guy, and the only reason I recognized him was because I would see him going out the utilities exit all the time on smoke breaks. He was smoking now, of course. He took a drag and puffs of smoke punctuated his syllables: "Dude, I can usually stand anything, but I could only get to the *Fish in the Life Preserver* before I blew chunks—*everywhere*."

"Uh-huh," I said. I reached up and tugged on Shasta's sleeve. She followed me toward the entrance, but wouldn't get closer than ten feet.

I gave the door a try.

The moment a crack formed in the doorway, an odor wafted past me on the tails of a thousand ghosts. It was vile, to say the least, but putting it in words minimizes how bad it was. I'll give it a try though: it had the sharpness of spoiled beer, it had the alien stench of another person's farts, it had the eye-watering sting of a freshly sliced onion—and if a smell can bring an image to your mind, the image would be squirming maggots ingesting rotted fish guts.

Yes.

It was that bad.

"Shasta," I said, "try the applicant door and see if it's the whole place or just the labyrinth."

She gave me a raised eyebrow, but then she went.

She came back with tears streaming down her face. She was rubbing her tongue with the sleeve of her shirt. *"Aack—I can still taste it,"* she said, and then continued rubbing.

I found the smoking dude. I gave him a hundred-dollar bill and told him to purchase a respirator from the hardware store up the street. "And if you don't bring me both the receipt and the change," I added, "I will take it out of your paycheck."

He lit a fresh smoke and went.

"Okay," I said loudly, "Personnel Department: follow me, please." I led them over to a shady spot under a large Eucalyptus. There were about 150 of my people, which was shy by a quarter. I wondered how many of them quit when they smelled it. "Since I didn't interview many of you, I'd like to get to know you a little bit. My name's Zeno Jacobs. And most of you know Shasta Mac-Calistaire—" Shasta twiddled the fingers of her left hand while she continued to wipe her tongue with her finger. "—though for many of you, this might be the first time you've seen her fully dressed." With that, she balled up a fist and struck me—surprisingly hard. "Now, let's work our way around. Tell me your name and, let's see, how about a hobby? Yeah. Tell me your favorite hobby." I pointed to one of them and said, "Go ahead."

"I'm Jolene Sommers," a blonde girl said. "I like to cook. Nowadays it's always rice and beans and corn—you know, the government stuff—but I cook it good."

"Thank you, Jolene." Octavio was to her left. I pointed to him. "Octavio?"

"I'm Octavio Mendez. I work on cars."

I thought of the Ranger and suppressed a laugh. I continued to go through them one at a time. It was a good time filler. When we were done, the smoking dude was back with the respirator, the change, and the receipt.

I told my people to hold tight, and I put on the respirator. I entered. Within a few steps, I had to go around the smoking dude's puke—*way* around, because he'd had a large breakfast. At the end of the first corridor, my eyes began to sting and I wiped away the tears that came. As I continued, other passages would bring fresh tears, and I turned when that happened. It took about thirty minutes before I reached a corner where there was a painting of a giraffe holding a dagger in its right-front hoof. A bloated and discolored body in a Sparkletts uniform sat against the wall below it. The buttons running down the front of the shirt had all popped, and the sewn-on nametag said HANK. While I stood looking down at Hank, his voice came to me clearly, as though I was hearing it from his rotten corpse: *"Help me, please! I'm lost…"*

I grimaced under my rubber mask.

I worked my way to the office and dialed 911. I put it on speaker while I waited: *"Thank you for calling 911. Your emergency is important to us. If this is not an emergency, please hang up and call your local police or fire department. If this is an emergency, please do not hang up as calls are answered in the order they are received. There are* nine-hundred-eighty-nine *callers ahead of you. The average wait time is* seven-hundred-forty-four *minutes. We thank you for your patience..."*

I fiddled with my computer and discovered mail from HR. I opened it.

> Zeno,
>
> I've noticed that employee complaints have decreased significantly under your tenure. While this is not unexpected from a new director, I wanted to bring this matter to your attention since it is a significant factor on how your performance is judged.
>
> If you have been afraid to be aggressive in the performance of your duties, please be assured that HR always takes the side of our Directors as long as they are acting legally. If you need time to discuss employ-ment laws and practices, feel free to call anytime.

Sincerely,

Gillian Frohm
Director, Human Resources
HRW International

I winced at that idea—to me, dealing with human resources always seemed a little like dealing with the devil. I deleted the e-mail.

The money I spent on my respirator came to mind. I filled out an expense report, printed it, and put the receipt together with the report into the green envelope. Then I tapped my fingers on my desk, thinking of what other busy work I could accomplish.

A few hours later, I set my head down and slept.

Somewhere deep in my brain, a neuron or two kept track of the recording's progress. My sleep was dreamless and I awoke when there was only *one* caller remaining. I was sweaty and disoriented, and I almost pulled off the respirator—but then my mind got the situation sorted out.

"Los Angeles County 911—what is your emergency?"

"Errs a ed odee earr." *Damn.*

"I'm sorry Sir, I can hardly hear you. Can you speak up?"

I took a deep breath and lifted the respirator. "There's a dead body here." I put the respirator back on and breathed. Even the small amount of air that had entered the facepiece was horrible. I almost hurled as the smoking dude had done (and I can't imagine what would've happened if I *did* hurl with that mask on), but somehow I kept the nausea at bay.

"A dead body?" the 911 operator asked.

A deep breath. Up. "Yes." Down. I breathed out, breathed in…

"What is your location, Sir?"

I did the routine each time. "1900 Pico Boulevard, Santa Monica."

"Okay, 1900 Pico Boulevard. The person is not breathing?"

"No. Actually, he's been dead for a while. He stinks."

"Oh, I see. Okay, I'm dispatching police to you, but it may take some time."

"Right. Okay. Thanks."

I hung up and went out the applicant door.

It was dark out except for the parking lot lights. Everyone had gone home—everyone except Shasta. I spotted her on the curb by the Sparkletts truck, where she sat playing with something in her hand. I raised the respirator so it rested on my head.

"Hey—don't you know it's past curfew?" I asked.

"I always thought these sparkletts were made of metal." She had taken one of the blue sparkles off of the branding on the back of the truck. It was a disk about the size of a ten-spot, colored a glossy, ocean blue. With hundreds of them hanging on little pegs, the sign projected a perfect illusion of flowing water, even in the slightest breeze. I'd always loved looking at the Sparkletts trucks when I was young, as they drove past making deliveries throughout the neighborhood, and I'd always wanted to snag one of the disks Shasta was playing with now. Even the orange lights in the parking lot glinted blue in it.

"Well, what *is* it made of?"

"Thin plastic, I guess." She palmed the sparklette and stood, flashing me a smile. "I was afraid you'd died in there. What happened?"

I pointed at the truck's smashed-up cab. "It's the Sparkletts guy. I guess he couldn't find his way out of the labyrinth. He's all puffed up." I gave her a *yuck* look.

She returned it with an *ewwwww* look. "Oh."

"So I called 911. I was on hold that whole time." I sat down beside her.

She scooted away. "*Oh.* I mean, *whoa, dude.* I think— I think your clothes absorbed the smell. *Oh.* I'm sorry." She held her nose and pushed away from me some more.

"I need to stay until the police come. You don't have to, though."

"No, I want to. Just don't get too close, okay?"

Those words, in any other circumstance, would've broken my heart. In this case, it didn't. "Okay," I said.

"Maybe the cop can give us a pass or something, or even a ride. You know, since I was on the phone so long."

"Hope so." Shasta let go of her nose briefly, for a test sniff. When she verified she couldn't smell me, she dropped her hand. "What're you going to tell them?"

"I guess the guy got lost. Nobody knew it until the smell. That's about all there is to say."

"Yuh," she said.

"Yeah," I said.

I don't know how I got up the strength to ask, but it kinda slipped out of me. As though the momentary silence was an empty space and the words from my mouth got sucked into it. I've tried to replay the moment in my head and I still can't figure out *what* got into me.

"Would you like to clan?" I asked, stretching a finger toward her, not daring to get too close.

Her mouth dropped open. "I was sure you'd never ask, Zeno."

She pinched her nose shut again, and reached over, touching my index finger with hers. When she retreated again, she was blushing the way I had when I'd first seen her, back at the Ralph's, after she pulled herself out of that shelf of noodles.

The two of us sat engaged in small talk.

In a while, a kid wearing a red bandana approached. "Hey—yo truck?"

Shasta and I shook our heads. "No."

181

"*Awright!*" he said gutturally. "You folks mi wanna stand back. Ain't no splosion wit diesel, but is hot. Dem tires'll shake up da hood—*knowIsayn?*"

We both stood.

"Hey," Shasta said, flipping the sparklette from finger to finger, "could you get me a few more of these from the back? I want to make something out of them."

"Well, sure, Sweetcheeks!" He disappeared behind the truck and returned with a dozen of them. He motioned to me with a thumb, but kept his eyes on Shasta. "Want me to take im out, Sweetie? You en me could have lotsa fun!"

Shasta put on a pouty face. "Naw, I'm pregnant with our baby..."

He nodded. "Yep. I unstand," he said. He gave the sparkletts to Shasta, brushing her palm lightly with his fingers. "Now you folks injoy the Hunded Day Riots!" The kid unscrewed the gas cap on the tank and wedged a crowbar inside.

"Hey—what day of the riots is it?" Shasta asked.

He paused, looking up. "I think is senty-tree. Yup, *senty-tree.*" When he pried on the filler neck, something popped out. He pulled a rag from a pocket, dipped it in the tank, and then switched it around, placing the dry end in with the wet end hanging out. He lit a Bic and set the rag aflame. "You folks hab a good night, now," he said and ran off.

Shasta and I backed off a distance and, because she could smell me again, she backed off a little further. The cab of the truck was engulfed within a minute. By the time the ambulance arrived, the fire was just reaching its full intensity. The EMTs got out of their vehicle and stood beside us.

"You know," one of them said, "this came over dispatch as a dead body, not a fire."

"Yuh," Shasta said pointing at the employee entrance. "The body's in there."

The squad car arrived as the Sparkletts truck was in full splendor. Both the police and the EMTs were nonplussed by the situation. They let the truck burn and, as it was doing so, they had me lead them to the body. They photographed it. They bagged it. They took it out on a stretcher.

We asked the cop to write us an excuse for the evening, and he regarded us as though we were two silly children. But he wrote the note, so Shasta and I left without even making a statement. We were at the edge of the parking lot when the Sparkletts truck's tires blew. The noise was like two shotgun blasts, maybe five seconds apart.

I looked at the note the cop had scrawled:

> Dear fellow keepers of the peace,
>
> Please give these two lost souls free passage home on this fine evening.
>
> Officer Blakely
> Badge #8712

I passed it off to Shasta. She backed away from me after taking it, and then had the giggles for a while.

KARISSA'S HOUSE
THE ROAD HOME

15—As The Wild Do

We walked and talked for an hour. It was a fine evening
for it; a late July's sea breeze blew warmly and I had
never, ever expected to be able to stroll on such empty
streets where, on that night, the world was ours and ours
alone for the enjoying. I feared being stopped by soldiers
with rifles, or by angry and overworked policemen, or
even to come upon a place where a gruesome creature
jumped out of a shrub and requested a toll. But we were
left alone and it was such a quiet evening that a jet, far
above, probably passing over on its way to San Diego,
sounded like a mighty rocket. The transformers in the
street lamps buzzed within the riot smoke drifting up
from down south, and walking through that lamplight
was like weaving slowly through rows of lacy, flesh-
colored curtains. After the jet had passed, the scraping of
our shoes and the sound of our breath seemed so loud.
So, we spoke in whispers to each other, as though using
our voices would shatter the wonder of it all.

All I wanted to do was take her open hand in mine, to feel her fingertips close softly around the back of my hand, to be lost in the electrical sensation of our first real touch. But I was well-aware of the gruesome stink surrounding me, and as someone with a newly missing tooth will hide their smile, or as someone who has been unexpectedly tasked with hard, sweaty work will keep their arms at their side, I kept my distance, and I dragged my feet hoping the night would respond in kind—by dragging out time forever.

But eventually, we stopped in front of the home where she lived. She paused, in what seemed like a moment of shame. It was a one-story dwelling with a wide front porch—the kind you sometimes see with rocking chairs on them, or a swing hanging off to one side. But there were no rocking chairs, no swing. The porch *did* have two full garbage bags, and passed out against them was a twig of a woman. Her waistband was around the cup of her ass. Shasta stooped to pull the woman's pants up and the woman groaned, mumbling things that sounded like they were said in a foreign language. Her drunken eyes rolled as she sipped from an alcoholic energy drink that, even in her stupor, she'd managed to keep a grip on. When Shasta stood again, consciousness left the woman and she slumped against the garbage again.

"Zeno, this is Veronica. Veronica, Zeno."

I grimaced. I tried to get a look at Veronica's dental work, but her face was too far sunken into her uncomfortable looking pillow.

"You might want to stay here, Zeno."

"No—I'll come with."

She opened the door and I followed her in. When Shasta had described this place to me, I expected the story to have been an exaggeration. After all, most people over-describe to dramatize what they're saying, to give what could be boring or commonplace a little spice so people will listen—everyone's done that a little in their life. But in this case, Shasta had minimized how bad it was. There was a peculiar odor in the living room. A little sweet. A little sour. A girl in a muumuu farted. There were twenty-odd women scattered about, most of them dressed a little, a few reading or poking at old phones, but many sitting cross-legged on the floor idle—doing absolutely *nothing*. A couple of the women had taken spots on the fireplace's hearth, looking as though they'd deck anyone who dared take their spot. A younger one, no older than nineteen, appeared to be naked under a sheet. She had bright red lipstick and an unnatural shade of neon-blue eye shadow smeared in a raccoon mask around her eyes. She grunted at me, and speared me with a lustful look.

As we entered the hallway leading to the bedrooms, I still felt watched. I looked back and raccoon girl was up on an elbow—on that side, the sheet had fallen to expose a breast. She hissed inwards through her teeth, and then turned away.

I focused ahead. We stepped around three more women on the floor, leaning in odd angles against the wall of the hallway. Two of them were dressed, but the other one, a thirty-something woman with her head shaved, wore only a pair of mismatched socks. I looked up and down the hall for her clothes or a sheet or anything. The only things in the hallway, other than those women, were a syringe and an empty box of Pop Tarts.

Shasta opened the door to the bathroom and a woman was sitting on the toilet, flipping through a porno mag. As we entered, the woman looked at me and said, "Hey."

My eyelids fluttered at her.

"Come on, Zeno," Shasta said, "help me get my things."

We gathered Shasta's belongings, filling a couple duffel bags. When we were done, I avoided looking at anything else. I just kept my eyes about two-thirds up the wall, all the way out.

We went north from there, each of us with a duffel bag slung around our bodies. Shasta had also shouldered a purse, a well-worn bag that had torn remnants hanging from it. We were silent for a while—until I couldn't bear it anymore.

"I hope you never go back there," I said. "It's like an asylum. I've never seen the likes."

"You'll never unsee it either, that's for sure."

"If you left anything behind, just name it and I'll get you a new one."

She smiled at me. "*Oh, God!* I left my one-carat diamond ring back there!"

"Yeah, maybe one-carat zirconium…"

"The bastard told me it was *real!*"

I laughed. It helped push away the images. A little. I angled closer to her and she shoved me away.

"You still smell like the Sparkletts guy! Yuck!"

I saw her gaze upwards, toward the Hollywood Hills. Tiny little lights dotted the hillscape, running in irregular curves and arcs. Those lights came from the windows of important people whose salaries were impossibly high. I tried to imagine a future where I could be in a position to provide like that for our little clan.

"I wonder if there's still magic up there," Shasta said.

"I hope so."

"There's certainly none of it down here."

We walked. In a couple miles, I motioned up my driveway.

"This it?" she asked.

I brought out my keys. "Yeah."

"Were your parents movie stars?"

"Grandparents. They were film editors."

"Must be good money in editing."

I held the door open for Shasta.

"First thing you're gonna do is shower," she demanded as she went inside. "And take those clothes and throw them out the bathroom window."

There was no window in the bathroom, but I understood what she meant. "Yes, Ma'am."

I set the duffel on the living room table. As I took off to my bedroom, Shasta turned on the television. I put the Luger in a drawer and threw my clothes out the window. I thought they looked funny draped over the hedges, but I didn't care what the neighbors thought. I went into the bathroom and turned on the shower—nice and hot.

I came back out in shorts and a T-shirt, with a tube of Ritz from the kitchen. I sat close to Shasta, but not hip-to-hip. We munched on crackers as some rioters were looting a Wal-Mart in a 500-person gang-grab. At some point, someone started a fire in one of the changing rooms. Even after twenty minutes, when the whole clothing department was aflame, there was no sign of firemen—I imagined that the store manager was listening to *"There are* six-hundred-fifty-one *callers ahead of you..."*

Shasta slid closer. She had to shift her hips until they were nearly to my knees so she could lean her head on my shoulder. We watched the riots for a while and, as she fell asleep, she said, "We don't have to clan—we could be a family..."

I kissed her head gently. We slept on the couch together.

In the small hours of the morning, Shasta woke me with a kiss. We tore into each other's clothes and cast them away; they were unimportant, undesirable barriers—like candy wrappers. In the varying glow of the television, we indulged in each other. We were nervous, trembling—imbibing in the dim, kaleidoscopic look of our bodies while self-conscious of our own nakedness. But as a co-familiarity came, we touched as romantics, tasted as connoisseurs, moved as the wild do.

16—It's Friday Night, Bitches!

"Whenever I think back upon it, I know *that* will always be the best night of my life..."

I may be looking at the china cabinet behind Carson, but that's not what I see. It was the next day around noon when I woke to a soft tapping at the door. I put on my boxers and answered it. Doreen was on the porch, halfway down the stoop.

"Oh, hey," I managed, wiping sleep from my eyes.

She was in a wavy, flowery summer dress adorned with white lace. Her makeup was done as though she was headed for church, and her hair was in loose curls instead of the ponytail she wore to work. She smiled nervously, and it dawned on me that she was gaining weight. She walked up the two steps and stood close by. "Hey, Zeno.

192

I didn't mean to wake you. I'd've called, but neither of us have a phone, y'know..."

"Yeah."

"Yeah."

I raised my eyebrows and bit my lower lip.

She cleared her throat. "So, it's my twenty-first, y'know. I was going to ask at work, but then I got sick." It looked like she was ticcing, but somehow she swallowed it down. "Anyway, I thought maybe we could get a beer before curfew or something. It'd be fun, yeah?"

Shasta walked up behind me.

I couldn't tell if it was the Tourette's or not: Doreen jerked her head to the side and spat *"Fucking BITCH!"* Then she looked back up, smiling forcibly. "Hey, Shasta."

I guess Shasta took it as a tic because she was cool about it. "Hey, sweetheart," she said.

Doreen blinked at her, and then said, "I'd better go..."

"Nonsense," I said, "it's your birthday and I got a twelve-pack with your name on it!" I reached out for Doreen's hand. "Come on in!"

Shasta slapped my arm down, shouting: *"ZEE-no!"*

I froze.

Shasta put her arm around Doreen's shoulder, which was about level with Shasta's waist. She took Doreen down the stairs, whispering in her ear. They continued on together, down the walk, and then Doreen darted off alone, going southbound and barking rapidly.

(No, she wasn't barking, asshole—she was sobbing.)

"She's getting thick around the middle," I said.

Shasta punched me—hard. "*God,* Zeno—you're a dum-dum."

"What!"

"*Duuurr,*" she said, "she's like three months pregnant!"

My jaw may have fallen as far as my chest.

"And I think she looks pretty good, Zeno." Shasta turned and went inside.

I went down the stoop and out to the sidewalk to look after Doreen, but I didn't see her anywhere. Actually, I never saw her again.

I continue my story for Carson.

"On Saturday afternoon, there was nothing on but the riots. As I watched the civil rioters take to the streets in Long Beach, Shasta kept herself busy next to me on the couch..."

...stringing together something. She had sorted through her socks, looking for the one with the biggest hole. After she unraveled it into threads, she went to work pulling apart an old, beaded blouse that had been worn to death. She collected the beads in a small bowl. On the table in front of her were the sparkletts she'd rescued from the water truck. It wasn't long before my curiosity became overwhelming. Finally, I asked, "What are you making?"

"A necklace," she said, as though it was the most obvious thing in the world.

"Wouldn't it be easier to buy one?"

She gave me a sour look.

"I'm just saying..."

"Zeno—the two of us can't even afford the utilities and taxes on this house. How could I possibly afford to buy a necklace?" She turned toward me with her hips, but leaned away with her back. "And, you know, if I *could* afford it, why would I buy one? Every time you buy something, you buy into the system as well. And our broken economy is something that none of us can afford." She pointed at the television, at the looters with their arms full. "They can't afford it. We can't. Even the rich can't, I suspect. Not anymore."

I nodded, but had nothing to say.

"Anyway Zeno, I can make a necklace out of an old sock and little bits of plastic and be just as happy as if it were gold. Happier, even. And by doing so, I've deprived our broken government of the taxes they would have collected from me uselessly blowing my money."

Since she was on the topic of finances, I thought it was a good idea to share what all the household expenses were. What was paid up, what wasn't—all that wonderful stuff. "Speaking of money—"

"Yuh, Zeno. I think I need a different job."

I hadn't expected that—and it hit me like a slap. Without Shasta at work, my days were going to return to being long and lonely. But as firmly as Bob insisted on me terminating her, I knew it was inevitable. *Better to get it over with,* I thought. "I'll make sure you can file for benefits."

"Won't Bob be angry about that?"

"Yes," I said. "But I don't think it's a terminable offense. She said she didn't care how I did it."

"Oh. Good."

After that, I decided an outlaying of the monthly bills could wait. I turned back to the coverage of the riots and Shasta sat beside me, working on her necklace. We relaxed together for the rest of the weekend until, finally, Monday rolled around again and I woke cursing the adage that *nothing lasts forever.* It was an adage that I was hungry to beat. To find a way, somehow, to be free. To be able to stay home a few extra days with my new girlfriend if I wanted. To be liberated from this constant wage slavery called *work.*

I considered this liberation as Octavio pulled in to give me a ride.

"Doreen say she quit, Man."

I buckled my seat belt. "Nonsense."

"No, Man. Swear to God. Had suitcases and all that shit."

I looked at Octavio.

He was nodding rapidly at me.

"Go by her house."

He did. I knocked on the door, and questioned the guy who opened it. As he answered me sternly, the others in her clan gathered right behind him, murmuring and giving me a death-stare. When it was clear that no one would tell me where she'd gone, I got back in the car silently.

"Tole you, Man." He shifted the car into gear and we drove to work.

When we got there, I paused at the door for test sniff, but the air was clean, with the sweet smell of bleach. Mr. McClusky must've scrubbed the floor and aired the place out. First thing at my desk, I put Doreen and Shasta in the termination queue. For Doreen, I selected *Job Abandonment or No Call/No Show*. For Shasta, I selected *Other*. In the explanation box that popped up, I typed *I just don't like Shasta's clothing*. Then I hit SEND.

I sat silently, pondering why Doreen would leave without saying *goodbye*. The ringing of my phone jerked me away from those thoughts.

"HRW International, this is Zeno—"

"*Zeno. This is Bob.*"

I tried to sound enthusiastic and failed. "Hi, Bob..."

"'I just don't like Shasta's clothing'? *Really?*"

"You said you didn't care how I termed her..."

"*YOU'RE THE ONE WHO PURCHASED THOSE CLOTHES!*"

I held the phone away from my ear for a moment. When I was sure the tirade was over, I spoke: "Okay. But this is the last week of the period. I wanted to have it done."

"She's going to get unemployment, Zeno. I hope you're proud of yourself."

Actually, I was. "I'm so sorry, Bob. I won't let it happen again."

The line went dead.

Without Shasta, I was now back to signing every single scrap my printer spat out. By late afternoon, my hand cramps had become debilitating. So, I went to into the ordering menu and purchased a stamp with my signature on it; finally, I would be able to do my paperwork without pain. I stapled and sorted my new employees' files by their last names. I was on the last stack when I ran out of staples.

I went to the break room and couldn't find any. There were none in Doreen's desk, and her stapler was missing. There was simply no way we could do our work without staples, so I went back to our ordering site, found the cheapest staples, and finalized the order. When I did, a window popped up:

APPROVAL REQUIRED
Enter Password
＊＊＊＊＊＊＊
—

That was strange since I had just purchased that signature stamp. And I'd never needed approval for office purchases before.

I logged off my terminal and logged back in. I reentered the purchase, and the window popped up again. I tried ordering other things. Still, the pop-up appeared. I tried a different site (we ordered different things from different suppliers depending on who gave the largest kick-backs to the executives). The pop-up appeared for glass cleaner, for toilet paper, for *everything*.

My password didn't work for ordering—it said, APPROVAL DENIED. I e-mailed Bob. Near quitting time, she still hadn't responded. I opened up the webmail, typed "I NEED STAPLES," and hit send. Then I typed "I NEED STAPLES" and hit send. I did this for like ten minutes before the phone rang.

"HRW Interna—"

"THIS IS BOB. STOP THAT!"

"Why do I need approval to buy staples?"

"It is *MY JOB* to protect the budget. What's this $435,000 coded to *Other Expenses*?"

Uh-oh. "Did you ask Accounts Payable?"

"They don't know what it is—once it's coded and paid, they discard the invoice. Haven't you been keeping copies?"

Here it comes, I thought. *She's gonna fire my ass.* "Uh, no, *Bob*. No one ever said I *had* to keep copies. You know, it wouldn't hurt if you spent a day or two training me. You know, a little—"

The phone clicked.

"Bob?"

My phone sat silent for the rest of that week. I figured Bob and I had ended at an impasse, and that I could ask for staples as soon as she got over me not saving copies of the invoices. By Thursday, everyone in the office was sharing those tiny groups of two or three staples—you know what I mean: those little cast offs that collect in office drawers—the ones whose primary purpose is to jam the stapler. Since they were yet to pay me back for the respirator, I wasn't about to spend any of *my* money on staples, so I endured the inconvenience.

When I came in on Friday, one of those funny golf carts the meter maids drive had pulled up in front of the Sparkletts truck. The lady tried to attach a ticket to the windshield wiper, but the wiper arm was a curled-up mess and there was no windshield left. So she rolled the ticket up and pushed it into the door crack, making it protrude in a malformed bloom. She applied a 24-hour tow warning to the scorched door. It had a check next to VEHICLE PARKED IN A FIRE ZONE.

Later that morning, as I conducted interviews, a UPS guy came in. I went over to the applicant entrance and he appraised me distrustingly, as though he'd heard a nasty rumor—and he probably had. He handed me the signature pad.

I whipped the stylus, but there was no package. "What am I signing for?"

"I'll bring it in," he said.

What he wheeled in, on one of those hand-operated forklift things, was a pallet of boxes, with my rubber stamp sitting on top. When he pushed a lever, the pallet thumped on the floor, and he wheeled his little contraption away. I opened one of the boxes, and inside was an array of more boxes. Inside each of those were twelve extra-large binder clips.

I took one, swung around its arms, and operated it. *What the hell are these for?* I thought. I brought the binder clip with me to the desk. As the half-dozen interviewees stared at me, I called Bob. The phone went to voicemail.

"Hi, Bob. We received an order of 10,000 extra-large binder clips. What am I supposed to do with them? Thanks."

As I hung up, a shout came from a cubicle a couple rows down. "ELAINE GUTHRIE?" The kid's head appeared above his cubicle wall. *"ELAINE GUTHRIE!"*

I weaved past my applicants and walked over.

The kid turned to me, shoving papers into my hand. "Can you explain this to me, please?"

"That appears to be termination paperwork," I said. "What's wrong?"

"The name: Elaine—"

"—Guthrie, that's right."

"You put her in the terminations queue? She's in the hospital!"

"No one called to let me know…"

"*I* did. I told you on *Tuesday*."

I actually didn't think I'd ever seen the kid before. "There's a policy we all sign when we're hired that says we must call into work personally—"

"She blew her FUCKING *appendix!*"

"I'm sorry—who are you again?"

"David!"

Didn't ring a bell. "David...?"

"*GUTHRIE YOU FUCKING IDIOT! And you're terming my MOTHER!*"

Ah. "Well, pack up your things. Calling your boss a 'fucking idiot' is definitely termination for cause—don't you think so *David Guthrie?*"

He put up an index finger: *Wait.* He put his hand atop a cross-stacked pile of forty-or-so unstapled employee files. His arm moved slowly and deliberately, dumping the stack on the floor. He began tap-dancing on top of the mess.

I laughed. "David—do you know how many people will quit while sorting out your mess? What a *service* you're performing for me!"

He stopped, turned red, and went straight out the applicant door.

I set several people to the task of sorting out the papers. One of them actually *did* quit.

When Octavio pulled in to drop me off home, Shasta was standing at the door, wearing a pink robe that was tightly cinched at the waist. She waved excitedly. I couldn't wait to enjoy another weekend with her. I waved back and smiled.

Octavio let out his breath harshly. *"Ave María Purísima."*

"Qué sé yo," I responded.

As Octavio pulled away, Shasta ran into my arms.

"I got my unemployment," she said. "And food stamps."

"Guess your time at McDonald's paid off after all."

Shasta slugged me in the arm, where a bruise would eventually form. I answered her punch with a kiss and we went inside. She darted away to the kitchen and I followed no more than a step behind. She hung her robe on the pantry's door handle and was now dressed in something that was barely a top and something else that was hardly a skirt. And she had finished her necklace. Five sparkletts gleamed above her breasts.

As she stirred some concoction atop the stove, I walked up behind her and took hold of her hips, pulling her against my chest. I got on my toes, trying to stretch far enough to plant a kiss on her neck. Instead, my kiss landed between her shoulder blades. "What're you cooking?" I asked.

"Hodgepodge, I suppose. I bought some things—all of them on sale—and it still cost $250. And it's only like two days of food."

"At least it's not corn and rice and beans." I breathed in along her spine.

"That tickles... Wait till after dinner, okay? Go turn on the TV."

I squeezed her hips gently and obeyed reluctantly. As soon as the television fired up, the caption flared:

Long Beach Under Siege

"Hundred Day Riots" Crowd Pushes
National Guard Back and Takes
Control of Long Beach

Actually, Hundred Days had nothing to do with it—it was civil rioters who had seized Long Beach. The only time Hundred Days was anywhere near the city was back when they grounded the power lines. During this week, real estate offices were their target—and the ones they torched were all along the 10, east of L.A. I remember a photo on Yahoo! News from a burned-out insurance office in Redlands. In the picture, fire hoses snaked all over the building's lawn. Poking up through the hoses, a card-board sign on a wood stake demanded:

STATE FARM:
Insure Thyself

You see, whatever Hundred Days did, they did it with a message. Like with the Vons truck, when the message was: *You can't guard everything.*

I called out: "Shasta. You gotta see this."

She rushed into the living room. "*Oh*—what're they burning?"

"Looks like Long Beach State."

"*That's horrible!*" She plopped down next to me. "God…"

Yes, these were the civil rioters: the kind you see swinging fists after a sports game, the kind that climb up signal poles and statues to try to get cheers from a crowd, the kind that set fire to someone's car because it's fun, the kind that kick a guy when he's down (usually with a steel-toed boot and usually in the head), the kind whose answer to their bad behavior is *because I can.*

The video changed to a Target Superstore, where looters were exiting with unbagged merchandise. They did nothing to disguise themselves while strolling past the cameras with shopping carts full of goods. One of them actually changed his path to get in front of the KTLA cameraman, where he shook fistfuls of $500 bills. "Look, ma!" he screamed, "I'm a *millionaire!*" He snickered off, but another one followed. This one was ecstatic: "*I never owned a vacuum before! Ding-ding-ding-ding-ding! I WIN!!!*" After him, a kid in a Kings jersey, one that still had the tags flapping on it, waved his hands to attract a pan-and-zoom. The kid soon filled the screen. He made some kind of gang symbol with his fingers, and shouted, *"Hey! It's Friday night, bitches!"*

My stomach growled, so I got up and spooned out two bowls of Shasta's hodgepodge. I brought them out on a couple of trays and sat. Shasta leaned over and kissed me, saying, "Thanks, Babe." It was ramen noodles and veggies and some kinda stuff that resembled sausage, but wasn't.

"What's this meat?" I asked.

"It's that stuff in the freezer—you've got a king's ransom of beef in there."

"Yeah… What'd you do to it?"

"Ground it, added some spices."

A man came out of the Target with a cart full of basketballs.

"Oh, *what the fuck!*" Shasta said, spitting flecks of hodgepodge. "He doesn't *need* that."

"Rioting isn't about what you need."

"Well, it should be. If *I* were rioting, I'd be taking shampoo, wine, cheese, *yeast.* You know—I wanted to make some bread with that flour in the garage. But do you know how much they're charging for a simple packet of yeast? *Ten fucking dollars!* For like a *quarter-ounce!*"

I patted her on the knee. "It's okay, Babe."

"Sorry. *Food, clothes, firewood*—necessities. *Cash,* maybe. But you wouldn't see me stealing basketballs."

"Yeah," I said agreeably, "you're a good woman."

It was instantaneous: "So, when are you going to marry me then?"

I set the tray down and shifted around to face her. "Well, let's set a date." I meant it. There was nothing more that I wanted to do than marry her. But, you know, women have dreams, expectations of a certain dress, of a particular flower arrangement at each of the guests' tables. They want special china and glassware and silverware and all that. It was going to take a lot of money to have the marriage she deserved rather than one that was more my style: a ten minute legality before a justice of the peace.

"Yes, let's," she said. The corners of her mouth travelled out and up. And again I'll say I loved that smile—I'd have done *anything* to see it. I did my best to match it. We set our trays down. We both tasted like hodgepodge, but that was okay—we kissed for a while and we both got kinda hot, so we made love again on the couch, with the news blaring the latest reports from Long Beach.

We did set a date, but it didn't work out that way.

I got up sometime in the night and got a glass of water. I checked my computer, and #HundredDays was getting a lot of traffic. I limited the tweets to @JimenezLoco and found:

> *@JimenezLoco:* Hoy nos atacan
> las propiedades de los
> bancos #Day81 #HundredDays

#Día81 #CienDías #ROE
bit.ly/5yT9U7

I clicked on the Bitly link and a browser window opened with the address ciendias.org.mx/reglas_de_contratacion.

The window had two links: English and Español. I clicked English.

The rules were simple. Hundred Days was going to go through all of Los Angeles burning homes. To keep a citizen's property safe, the home owner was expected to mark the home with the crossbones, or just an X—like the homes were marked in East L.A.

Without the mark, a home would be considered bank-owned by default.

Something twinged within me. It was a feeling that we—all Los Angelinos—would never be the same again. We were teetering right at an edge, and the tiniest shove—or even the slightest of breezes—would put us straight into a freefall. All the way to Hell.

Pop's home wasn't marked.

I made a mental note and then warmed up next to Shasta.

We awoke together, covered by a scratchy knit blanket. The volume on the television was still where we'd left it in the night—*fucking loud.* Shrieks jolted me upright. I squinted at the bright picture: smoke was pushing past some people leaning out of a window. Whoever was at the camera was making me nauseous, bumping and jerking around. But finally the picture settled on a fire truck as it extended its ladder toward the home's upper story.

JimenezLoco's tweet came back to me as I watched.

The three faces, those of a woman and two children, radiated terror brighter than the flames that were dancing behind them. The three seemed familiar to me—I'd seen them—perhaps not recently, but certainly regularly. It wasn't in East L.A., for sure, and it wasn't Doreen's clan—I didn't remember seeing any children there.

I blinked my eyes, trying to place it.

Shasta grabbed the remote saying, "*Uff*, not till I've had a cup of coffee…"

I recognized something. *"Don't shut it off."*

Shasta froze with the remote out, her finger hovering over the power button. She eyeballed me, confused.

On the screen, an address number flashed by: *826.*

"God," I whispered. I jumped over to the big picture window behind the TV. Even though I was naked, I ripped the curtain wide open. Shasta hid her face from the glare.

I looked at the TV. Out the window. TV. Window.

It was the house across the street.

"Shasta. Get dressed. *Now.*"

She looked up, and when her eyes adjusted, she said, *"…the fuck?"*

"Go, go, go!"

17—Behold *Los Demonios*

I was pulling up some socks; Shasta threw me a shirt and it hit me square in the face. The TV was still blaring: "Why are you burning homes? *People's* homes?"

I recognized Carlos' voice instantly. "*People's* homes? *Seriously?* These aren't *people's* homes. One in five homes in West Hollywood sit empty and the others are either rented or mortgaged by the banks. They ask ridiculous prices for homes all over Los Angeles—prices that no one can afford. Instead of allowing the market to determine the price, instead of allowing people to refinance—or even to rebuy the homes as they're auctioned off—they let them go *empty. Empty!* Listen— when the United States began, businesses had less than one percent of the wealth in the nation. Now the corporations hold *ninety-nine percent* of our cash reserves. And they hold the deeds to our homes and our properties. What's next—our *sons and daughters?*"

"Still," the reporter said, "you can't deny that there are people living in many of these homes."

"We issued a statement, but fine." Carlos turned to the camera. "If you own your home in Hollywood, Brentwood, or Beverly Hills—paint a really big X on the front door and *we won't burn it.* I have to go."

I stood. I went to the door and Shasta followed. I opened it.

It wasn't just the house across the street. The whole neighborhood east of our house was in flames. The sky was marred black, the sun eclipsed. An orange luminescence was the only light to see by. Across the street, the mother and her two children were stepping down the fire truck's ladder. Shasta and I ran down the steps and onto our little front yard. A news crew was arranging some equipment there while a cameraman took footage of a pickup four houses down the street. A huge pirate flag waved from a whip extended off of the cab's roof. Two men with bandana disguises were throwing Molotov cocktails from the back.

"Shasta, we need paint."

"What?"

"They won't burn a house with an X on the door. We have some old paint…" I dashed away to the garage.

Shasta yelled as I went. "Zeno—we don't have *time!"*

When I got back with the pail, Shasta was standing in the doorway, waving her arms. The pickup was alongside the curb in front of the house. The firemen across the street screamed obscenities at the pair of masked men in the pickup's bed, but they kept their hoses on the burning home. One of the guys in the bed—it was Manuel—saw me walk up beside Shasta as he ignited his bottle. His eyes squinted at me as Shasta yelled at him: *"Hey!"* She raised her arms above her head, her hands in fists, forearms crossed to form an X.

"¡El Judío!" Manuel screamed. *"¡Eres demasiado pequeño para semejante mujer!"* He was making fun of the size difference between Shasta and me. He trilled loudly and then laughed.

Shasta looked down at me, her arms still crossed above her head.

I shrugged up at her as though I hadn't understood the guy.

Manuel slapped the roof of the pickup's cab twice, signaling the driver to move on. Right then, one of the firemen turned the hose on Manuel, the pressure on *full blast*. He was instantly ejected from the pickup's bed, and his *compañero* scrambled out in avoidance of the same treatment. When Manuel got back to his feet, he found his burning cocktail and flung it into the fire truck. It was like *whump!* and the entire cab of the ladder truck was filled with flame. The pickup pulled away and the two men scrambled down Vista to catch up with it.

We were both speechless and terrified. I used my keys to pry the lid off the gallon of paint. Inside the can, it appeared that the solvent had evaporated, but I plunged my hand into it anyway. A half-inch crust gave way to liquid. I pulled my hand from the goo and slapped it against the door, painting a diagonal slash across it. I did it once more, making a really big X on the dark maple— an X that I hoped would save our home. Shasta slammed the door shut and locked it behind us. She dragged me to the kitchen. After scrubbing my arm clean, she kissed me—a long, arousing kiss—the kind you get after a long separation. Or maybe right before one. I don't know why she did that just then, with the whole neighborhood ablaze and all, but she did—we were terrified, I told you.

And that had made things better.

When we made it back to the window, huge chunks of glowing ash—some as big as a hand—were drifting by. I thought: *Our home will catch fire soon.* I went back onto the porch to survey things. The air outside was murky, and breathing it gave me a feeling of pin pricks in my throat. Even though it was just before noon, the streetlights were on.

I stepped out of the path of a drifting ember and the top floor of the home across the street collapsed. As its roof sank, huge coals rocketed into the sky, making glowing sparks precipitate in a block-wide circumference. I jumped inside and slammed the door shut once again.

"Zeno—watch."

I drew in some clean air and coughed heavily. I joined Shasta in front of the television. Sky5 was showing a man hosing down his roof. The homes all around him were ablaze and flames from a nearby carport licked at his home's eaves.

"You heard it first on KTLA," the anchor said, "the leader of the Hundred Days Riots said they will spare any home with an X painted on the front door."

"But that may not be protection enough," a co-anchor said, "since fires are now spreading from home to home. What you are witnessing, live from Sky5, is a man working hard to keep that from happening." The man had his shirt's collar pulled up over his nose, and he was hopping feverishly from place to place with his hose. Every time he sprayed down a hot ash, fresh flame would erupt somewhere else on his roof.

"Shasta," I said, "maybe I should put the sprinkler up there."

"Yuh," she said, "good idea."

A thick cloud moved past the front of the house, turning the living room dark as night. Shasta dashed off toward the bedroom and I heard her thump into a wall. She made it back with a couple of my T-shirts, which she soaked under the kitchen faucet.

"Water pressure's a little low," she said. It looked fine to me—the shirts were saturated in a couple of seconds. She folded them and gave one to me.

"You should stay here," I said.

"I'll stay on the ground and help—in case the hose hangs up or something."

I nodded my agreement. We went out through the garage, each of us taking an end of my grandfather's ladder. There was a wind now—West Hollywood was becoming a firestorm. Fifteen or twenty mile-an-hour winds blew and gusted up to thirty, or maybe even forty. And when one of those gusts hit, it felt like a blast of air from an oven.

I took the full weight of the ladder and then leaned it against the side of the house. Shasta ran to the front porch to get the sprinkler. She screwed it onto the hose, turned it on, and handed it up to me. I pulled it with me to the top of the ladder and dragged it onto the roof. Embers had settled on the asphalt shingles and the wind wasn't blowing them off again. Instead, in the gusts they just glowed brighter and hotter, sinking through the asphalt tiles and down to the plywood. I dragged the sprinkler to the far end of the roof and there was steaming and sizzling as the hotspots cooled. I rushed back to the ladder and a sooty puff stung my eyes.

I squinted over the side, waving. *"Shasta—get the sprinkler from the back yard too!"*

She nodded and ran to the back yard. Her scream was immediate. I stepped down the roof's slope to see, and she was brushing her arm. As a wave of relief washed over me, an arborvitae in the corner the yard transformed into a column of fire. She rushed over to the spigot and turned on the hose. She thumbed the flow from the hose into a fan and sprayed the shrub. It was extinguished quickly—more from having burned through its foliage and less from the water. She left its smoldering branches and located the sprinkler. By the time she arrived at the base of the ladder, she had lost the soaked T-shirt somewhere and was coughing. As she screwed the sprinkler onto the hose, water gushed and spurted all over her in protest. But she persisted and got it attached. I climbed halfway down the ladder so she could hand it up to me and I set it on the near side of the roof. I hurried down, leaving the ladder there, and we went back inside.

As the anchors continued their commentary, the two of us hacked and wheezed and wiped tears from each other's faces. Then the tone of the anchors' voices changed suddenly, making us look.

"We've just received word that our News Team's James Rohm is live in the Hollywood Hills. We're switching to him now."

"Thank you, Jerry. I'm on location near Laurel Canyon with the leader of the Hundred Days Riots. You prefer to remain anonymous—is that right, Sir?"

The camera zoomed out to show a masked man beside the reporter. I could tell instantly—it was hardly the leader, though he was a trusted lieutenant. In front of the camera, being interviewed by James Rohm, was the masked face of Octavio Mendez.

"I'm an American," he said. He was speaking the clear speech of a Southern-California-raised television star, dropping his Chicano accent entirely. "A working, taxpaying citizen, a voter, and a *consumer*, as they like to call it. Perhaps you should call me *El Consumidor*." He smiled under his bandana. But his eyes: they remained the same—all business. I was seeing a side of Octavio I had never witnessed before: one of extreme intelligence and cunning.

"When will the burning end?"

Octavio seemed confused. "The burning has just started. It will stop when the fuel is used up."

"What are your demands?"

Octavio shook his head. "There are *no* demands. We are holding *nothing* for ransom. Those are things that governments and businesses do. This is just the effect."

"The effect of what?"

"This is just what happens when you starve your people of meat. When there is no bread. When there's no home of your own to live in—no place to grow food, no place to bed your lover. No yard for your children to play in. No gas for the car.

"Do you know a fifth of the produce on the supermarket shelves is being discarded due to spoilage? Yet they refuse to lower prices...

"More and more people can't afford to drive because the price of gas is triple what it costs to refine. But the oil companies refuse to give up the margin...

"There are businesses—right here in *Los Angeles*—whose only business is to *make people quit!* They hire the desperate and the young and make them quit so they can cash in on the government incentives. This whole society has become *insane!*

"How much do you get paid, Reporter?"

The man mumbled an incoherent reply.

Octavio shook his head at him. "It doesn't matter. The people are deprived. *People*—men, women. They work. They work and *work.* But they get *nothing!* When you deprive people, eventually they burn. If you deprive them enough, they *burn* and burn." He faced the camera. "All of you watching who make six, seven, *eight* digits in salary: *We come. We come to burn. We come to burn and burn.*

"If I had a demand, Reporter, it would be only this: *Look below.* This is not your *Los Angeles* anymore."

The masked Octavio stretched out his arms as the camera panned back for a panoramic view of a thousand smoke columns rising from the city.

"*Yes! Look below!* Behold *Los Demonios.*"

As though on *El Consumidor*'s command, the power went out.

Shasta whispered in the darkness. "*Jesus, Zeno...*"

I found her.

Held her.

The smoke outside had thinned some, and now the light through the front window colored everything a dim hue of amber. It was barely enough light to see, and in the garage, I had to locate the wheelbarrow by touch. I handed several of the candles to Shasta and gathered up an armful myself. We brought them to the living room, where I lit one and then went back into the garage.

I found an old radio—a multiband shortwave. I turned it on, but it was lifeless. Inside, the battery compartment was filled with white flakes. I shook all the old batteries to the floor. Back inside, a kitchen drawer was stocked with batteries pilfered from the break room at work. The radio swallowed eight of the double-As. I turned it on, and it squealed creepily as I turned the dial. I switched the selector to F.M. Unbelievably (or perhaps not), KROQ was playing "Disco Inferno." On the A.M. band, I found a news station and set the radio down.

I hoped that if Shasta were doing something, it would keep her from panicking. Since smoke wisps were entering the house through its cracks and crevices, I went to the garage once more for duct tape. When I got back, I handed the roll to her.

"Seal up the doors and windows—the smoke's getting inside."

"Kay," she said.

As Shasta tore lengths of tape, I prayed for our safety, but imagined the house burning flat.

"—in Melrose Heights are being looted. There's no police, no National Guard here to stop it. They've been called into the hills to stop the advance of the Hundred Days rioters. The latest news is that their commander, the man identifying himself as *El Consumidor*, has ordered his men to set fire to Topanga Canyon—"

"That was Lou Dobbs, reporting for us from the Melrose District. Breaking in live from Malibu, is Terrence Davis. Terrence, what are the latest developments?"

Crackling gunfire came across the radio. "Hundred Days rioters have been engaged by the California National Guard along PCH at Tuna Canyon Road. I am standing perhaps five-hundred feet away—"

Thunderous shots came in rapid succession: DUNN-DUNN-DUNN... DUNN-DUNN-DUNN... DUNN-DUNN-DUNN-DUNN...

"Those blasts are from the main cannon of one of the National Guard's M3s, also known as the Bradley Fighting Vehicle. Two of the Hundred Days' pickups have now been, more-or-less, disintegrated. A third one is immobilized, and it looks like the driver is surrendering—"

Pickups, I thought. *Oh, Lord—those are* los compañeros!

DUNN-DUNN-DUNN.

"Uh, the driver's been immobilized as well..."

Knock-knock-knock.

Shasta came near, her eyes wide with fear.

"What?" I asked as the reporter continued his commentary.

Knock-knock-knock.

In my mind, I hadn't separated the knocking sound from the gunfire. Shasta spoke in a whispered scream: *"There's someone at the door!"*

I stood there in thought for a second. "Just ignore it."

Shasta faced the door.

Knock-knock-knock.

I tugged her sleeve and mouthed the word *NO.*

I turned off the radio and for a moment, everything was silent.

"We can see you through the window."

I lunged for the half-taped front window and, with one tug of the string, the curtains flew closed. When I backed up again, I accidentally shouldered the television over. It hit the floor hard, and with a loud snap. I held my arms open and Shasta entered them. I gripped onto her in an embrace that was probably more for my comfort than for hers.

"You have the only house left. If we clan, we'll protect you. But if I have to break in, I will kill you. And I will have your woman."

I released Shasta and approached the door.

This time it wasn't a tap of the knuckles. There was a BOOM—BOOM—BOOM on the door that shook the whole front of the house. I stepped back, expecting the door to fail. The guy must've had a mallet, or a sledgehammer, or something else really big.

Fear was with me once more. My hands and arms and legs shook, and my heart bounced like a terrified bunny desperate to escape a tiny cage. But I managed to get my voice working, though its pitch varied at the same frequency as the rest of my body's tremblings. "Let us have ten minutes to gather our things. Then we'll give you the house and leave."

"We can't breathe: OPEN THE FUCKING DOOR!"

I picked up a candle and ran to the bedroom.

"Zeno—Zeno!"

I wasn't gone long. I came back with the gun.

Shasta looked at me with bug eyes. She whispered, *"Ohmygod—is that a* Luger?"

I reached up and squeezed her shoulder. "I won't let them hurt you. Okay?"

She'd stopped breathing. She just kept looking at the gun.

I shoved her lightly away. "Stay behind me." I moved beside the door, on the opposite side of its hinges.

BOOM-BOOM—

18—Melrose

—Craaaack!

The door flapped open. Before me stood a large, bald man; my instant impression was that he was Mr. Clean. He had big, gold loops dangling through gauges stretched open in his ear lobes. He'd overestimated the strength needed on the eighty-year old door—he was dumbly bent over at the waist, and the weight of the picket-pounder he was holding had forced his upper-half in through the doorway.

I'd been standing at the ready. I thumbed the Luger's safety.

I fired.

Strangely, I've never recalled hearing the sound of the gunshot. What I noticed first was a forceful splat blown onto the door. It was red and lumpy. The gun leapt in my hand, feeling suddenly like a fish trying to escape my grasp. Finally, sound returned to me: the pounder made a single *DONG* on the tile floor, Shasta shrieked, and Mr.

Clean slumped to the floor with a thud. The others on the porch—there were four of them—looked at me as though I was Freddy Krueger. As I swung the gun toward them, they spat curses and jumped off the stoop, down onto the lawn. It seemed by the time I blinked, they'd all scattered away.

Shasta stood trembling beside the couch.

I went and took her by a wrist, rushing her to the bedroom. "Quick—get packed up."

She walked weakly and stared blankly. I dragged her old duffel bags out from the floor of the closet.

I spoke patiently: "Go on, now."

Shasta slipped some jeans over her short-shorts. Seeing them disappear under the denim filled me with disappoinment, even in the terror of our situation. She pulled her clothes from the closet in bunches, leaving behind rocking hangers. I went through a few of my drawers, gathering my clothes, socks, underwear, and all my papers: birth certificate, social security card, deed to the house—those types of things—as well as all the cash I'd taken from the coffee machine's bill acceptor.

"Don't leave anything you need behind, Babe," I said. "We need to go."

"Go... *Go where?*"

I gave her a one-armed hug. "Back to work."

The body must've weighed 220, 250 maybe. But in the state I was in, I could've moved an elephant if I had to. I dragged Mr. Clean off the porch and dumped him off at the curb—in the same manner as I left the trash there on Thursday mornings. Part of the X that I had painted, which was still wet, was now obscured in bloody clots. I shut the door, but the frame had busted where the catches were. Shasta followed me into the garage where I rifled through Pop's shelves, gathering nails, a hammer, and an old, discarded plank. We nailed the front door shut.

Just then, I remembered Pop's knife, a knife I'd been specifically prohibited to ever play with. I found it in a kitchen drawer and withdrew it from its sheath; it was like Rambo's knife—serrated on one side and extremely sharp on the other. I attached the sheath to my belt and resecured the knife. We left out the back door, locking it behind us. I surveyed the sky. The heavy smoke was now a couple blocks west of us. I turned off the two sprinklers.

I mounted the bags on myself as Shasta strapped her purse diagonally across her chest. We walked down the driveway and went southbound on the sidewalk. We looked back at my grandfather's house.

"It stands out like a bull's eye, Zeno."

"I know." I figured it wouldn't be long before it was just like the others. Another smoldering ruin among the thousands of others in Los Demonios. Or it might become the seedy hideaway for a forty-strong clan of outlaws. But I didn't dwell on it—not just then, anyway. We looked forward and proceeded away, leaving my inheritance behind. Around us, where there had once been modest but beautiful mid-twentieth century homes, there was now a black-and-white flatness. The smell was industrial—the pungencies of combusting all of the synthetic compounds of modern American lives, all the televisions, the computers, the carpets made with Stay-Cleen textiles, the curtains made with PermaPress cloth, and the toys made with anti-microbial chemicals mixed into the plastic.

It's a smell I will forever associate with Hundred Days.

Shasta went to turn right on Melrose. I tapped her arm lightly with the back of my hand and started going east.

"That's the wrong way," she called.

"No, it's not."

Shasta skipped her way up to me again. Then she was like, "Good God."

I nodded in agreement. The shops along Melrose weren't burned—they were smashed, shattered, stomped, and sorted through. We walked along the sidewalk, my left hand holding her right, and my other hand on the butt of my knife. I was looking for a particular store, but as wrecked as everything was, I wasn't sure I could identify it. But a couple blocks up, I did.

We entered the jewelry store crunching on the jetsam of bashed display cases. It was as though a gang high on PCP had gone on a rampage, because it wasn't just the displays—they had gotten to the fluorescent lights above, they'd torn down the suspended ceiling, they'd beaten the walls until they were bare studs. The top of a cash register drawer had been ground off with some sort of power tool. Display fingers and false busts were cast around everywhere. With all the anger shown in the destruction of the place, I hoped the looters had missed some of the jewelry. I kicked through some of the fingers and found what I was looking for.

No, they weren't gold. See? It's just plain silver. But it's got these cool little designs…

Anyhow, I held them up and they looked like a nice set. There were other ones, and I was about to sort through them.

But Shasta said, "Those are *soooo* cool!"

I turned to her, with those bags on my back, in the midst of all of that destruction. With all the glass on the floor, I didn't drop to a knee—standing beside Shasta was like being on my knees anyway. But I did speak—in what had to have been the least romantic proposal in the history of mankind: "Will you marry me, Shasta?"

She bent down and kissed me. Said *yes*. My ring fit—hers didn't. She put it on her pinky finger, laughed, and kissed me again.

It came to me that not ten minutes ago, I'd shot someone in the head. You know—the horror of that should have made all this impossible. If not for me, than certainly for Shasta. But that's the funny thing. I'd always wondered how any babies came to be born in 1945, within war-torn Normandy. Or the same thing in 1946, after the bombings of Hiroshima and Nagasaki. The two of us were in the midst of a local apocalypse, and we were looting jewelry from a smashed-up store on Melrose. And kissing! In dangerous times, you may not think there is time for passion or love. But those things have deeper meaning within loss and danger and uncertainty. I can say I loved her more later on, especially when she was giving birth to Sheila, but I never loved Shasta with more urgency than I did in that jewelry store. Back when we were still acquaintances, still exploring each other, still uncertain of things. And that love, born in urgency, has lasted even till now.

With our rings, the two of us crunched back out, walking arm-in-arm, now going the right way on Melrose, toward Fairfax, where we'd cut south and go on toward Santa Monica and HRW.

It was early Saturday night, and the sun disappeared into haze well before it sank below the Pacific. Gray and orange pyrocumulus clouds surrounded Hollywood to its north, west, and east. When HRW's plain cement walls came into view, Shasta got quiet, and she was visibly nervous. I asked her what was wrong.

"This might be the wrong place to go, Zeno. The gas stations and the grocery stores have the National Guard to protect them—*we don't*. If the rioters come here looking for the man in charge, it'll be *you*. And they will *kill* you."

I had considered that, actually. After Octavio's rant, HRW was sure to become a target at some point. But it was either HRW or Camp Liberty now. To me, freedom was always the better option—regardless of the risk. What Shasta didn't know was that *El Consumidor* was just Octavio. And I was his *compañero*. Although that meant nothing to the civil rioters, it was protection from attack by Hundred Days.

"We'll be safe here right now," I said. "Let's stay for a few days and feel it out, and if we can't make it work, we'll go to Camp Liberty. Okay?"

She nodded.

Above us hung the huge metal framework that held the green glass-fronted letters of HRW International. The lights inside them were off. I unlocked the applicant door and looked in, and it was so dark I couldn't see any of the cubicle walls. Though the emergency lights were on, their batteries were giving up their final drops of juice, and the bulbs illuminated nothing but themselves.

"Hold my hand," I told Shasta. "There's a backup generator where the smokers go out for a break."

The door clicked as it locked itself behind us.

We walked past the first emergency light, and I guided us close to the wall to clear the rear cubicles. I smashed my shin against something and cursed. I felt the object: it was an office chair, and someone had adjusted it so that the seat was all the way down. I pushed it away on its wheels and it thumped against something. We moved on, toward the second emergency light.

There was a brief tap—the strike of a wood stick.

"Hello?" I called out. My voice echoed softly in the room. Shasta's hand had become moist, and it was squeezing mine strongly.

A gritty whisper came out of the darkness. It sounded as though it was right in front of my face. *"Leave me alone. You'll go away, if ya know what's good for ya."*

Shasta whispered my name. I unsheathed the knife with my free hand.

"Whoever you are, you don't belong here."

There was another strike of the stick. *"Go away!"*

We approached the third emergency light, shining dimly above the row of vertical files on the east wall past the bathroom. My eyes had adjusted so that the tips of the hair on my forearm looked like a line of light scratches in the darkness. The edge of the blade in my hand glinted, though only in my peripheral vision—when my eyes landed on the knife directly, it turned dark again. I continued to scan the room, and the only light of any significance came from the reflection of the two dim floods in the sparkletts of Shasta's necklace.

I took another step.

Shasta was panting in shallow puffs.

I became aware of my heartbeat pulsing through my ears, and a step further took us directly below the third emergency light. Something whooshed by my face leaving a faint odor of straw.

The voice wasn't a whisper anymore. *"God damn ya lawless freaks I'll kill every last one of ya!"*

Shasta yanked my hand, pulling in the direction of *OUT*.

I smiled and sheathed the knife. "Mr. McClusky?"

That's when he struck me in the face.

Shasta shrieked as I fell to the floor.

19—He's Got Meat

A RALPH'S DELI FEAST

After he'd taken me down with the broom, Mr. McClusky asked, "Mr. Jacobs? That you?"

Shasta was on the floor feeling around for me and grunting in horror.

I sat up. "It's okay, sweetie, it's Mr. McClusky."

She found me with her hands. We helped each other up.

"I'm sorry, Mr. Jacobs," he said in the dark. "Wasn't expectin no one here durin the weekend."

"That's alright," I said. "Can you help us find the utilities exit?"

He had a small flashlight and he blinded each of us with it. He held it on Shasta and she squeezed her eyes shut against it. "My name's Samuel."

She squinted a look and said, "Shasta."

"Pleasure," Mr. McClusky said. Then he led us along the filing cabinets to the door on the northeast side of the building. He pushed it open, saying to Shasta, "Keep a foot on it so it don't latch shut."

Shasta did as she was told.

The rusty moon cast enough light to see outside. We were within a walled-in area outside, easily a hundred feet long, but only about ten feet wide. There were electrical panels, a row of ten air conditioning units, a huge generator, and a six-foot tall fuel drum.

Mr. McClusky started flipping switches, first in the electrical panels and then on the generator. "Figured having the generator on would attract attention."

"Hopefully the walls muffle it," I said. "Just make sure the sign on the roof is off."

He turned off the sign and said, "Oh, yeah," and jammed down the big handle that said MAIN. "Don't do that and you're likely to start powerin the whole neighborhood." He pushed a button. The generator coughed a few times, and banged twice. Then it purred softly—hardly making a sound at all. He adjusted a couple dials that made the engine labor briefly, and then it smoothed out again.

We went back in, where the fluorescents were soothing to the sight.

Mr. McClusky rushed over to a panel of light switches and turned them all off. We were in the dark again, but there were splashes of light as the computers within the cubicles booted up. Mr. McClusky came back over.

"Why'd you do that?" Shasta asked.

"We gotta black out the windows first, so we don't attract no attention. You kids come with me." Mr. McClusky led us into the labyrinth, keeping his flashlight's beam on the pictures. A dolphin was in the air, then it breached the water, then it swam backwards just below the surface. At the end of the passage, there was a T. We went right. To the left side, the dolphin was swimming tail-first, away from the sombrero. On the right side, a crab appeared, picking up a pair of eyeglasses from the sea floor and putting them on. The crab walked sideways with the glasses in front of its stalky eyes, and continued out onto a beach until it was under a palm tree. A coconut fell onto the crab and at the end of the next T, the coconut was bouncing away and the eyeglasses had splashed back into the water. We followed the eyeglasses. They sat below the water for a couple of frames and then they started rising. A motorboat appeared, going backwards through the water. Spray from the boat's wake seemed to reapply the glasses to a kid who was leaning over the side railing. Next, as the boat reversed away, a smiling sun appeared in the frame.

"Zeno—*this is sooo cool!*" Shasta whispered, taking my arm.

Mr. McClusky circled the sun with his flashlight. "The sun leads to the elevator," he said.

"How do you know, Mr. McClusky?" Shasta asked.

"Well, I'm the man who hung all these here pitchers."

"You paint them, too?"

Mr. McClusky cleared his throat. "Yep. Many, many years ago. Let's move along now…"

We followed the sun.

There was only one button: DOWN. Mr. McClusky pushed it and the arrow glowed. When the door opened, we all squinted in the sudden light. I was the last one on and my weight made the damned thing tilt toward the back, jolting me with sudden panic. Mr. McClusky hit B3. The door scraped on worn bearings as it shuddered closed. After a screech, we were momentarily weightless. As gravity returned, the floor vibrated beneath us. A loud humming accompanied our descent. I had a vision of us falling like Mr. Chandler. Shasta and Mr. McClusky seemed at ease, though.

Shasta was warming to Mr. McClusky. "What did they do to you, Mr. McClusky?" she asked.

"Call me Sam, young lady," he said.

"Okay, Sam."

"They who?"

"You said you would kill them for what they did."

"Oh, *them*," Mr. McClusky grumbled. "They threw one of those burnin cocktails through my neighbor's window. At the time, I was lyin down for a nap. My neighbor, old Mrs. Kemper, been on oxygen for the last five years or so. I saved her, and we barely got outta there alive. The flames spread to my roof as the firemen got there, and they hosed it before my place burned down.

Still, the place ain't livable no more. Had to pack up everythang—a lifetime of paintins, drawins, doodles—and probably ten-thousand in supplies. Six-hundred in food went to waste. And now, I gotta live in the motor coach."

"I'm so sorry, Sam."

"Well I appreciate that, Shasta."

The elevator groaned to a stop and, as the door opened, the floor positioned itself as if to trip me.

"This thing's a death trap," I said as I stepped up the gap.

"Naw," he said, "if you knew how it worked, you wouldn't say that."

"Still," I said, "I think we should take the stairs up."

Mr. McClusky grunted.

It was well-lit in the third basement, with plain walls made of textured white paneling. He led us down a series of corridors and stopped in front of a door labeled MAINTENANCE. He took out some keys and worked the lock.

Inside, machines were lined up along the left wall: floor buffers, a wet/dry vac, several stand-up vacuums, and a few things I couldn't ascertain the purpose of. On the right side of the room there were chemical buckets, chemical dispensers, and spray bottles all hanging by their triggers on a rack. We walked further into the room. I felt like we had stepped into an aisle at Home Depot. There were huge spools of wire, shelves with open boxes of plumbing and electrical supplies. There were toolboxes, tool cases, tool belts. We went around a corner, and Mr. McClusky found what he was looking for. He wheeled over a handcart and loaded two rolls of what looked like thick, black construction paper. Then he went to a shelf and grabbed a few rolls of duct tape.

"Okie-doke," he said. "So, do we haul this up three flights of stairs or can we risk the elevator again?"

Those rolls looked heavy. Shasta and I both said, "Elevator."

I wheeled the cart out of the maintenance room, and Mr. McClusky closed up behind us. When the elevator door opened, the cart thumped as it dropped the two inches to the floor. We all stepped in and the elevator sank another inch.

Mr. McClusky was standing by the buttons. "Goin up!" he said, pushing L. My grip tightened on the handcart as the elevator shook us back to the labyrinth.

The door opened to blackness. Pushing forward, the cart's wheels wouldn't go over the gap. I let Shasta and Mr. McClusky out so I could pull the cart up. The door tried to close on my arm, and when the sensor was triggered, the door shook violently before retreating. I got the cart out with a yank, glad to be free of that infernal thing.

Mr. McClusky's flashlight was back on the paintings. We watched the opposite sequence of what we'd seen before.

"I *love* your paintings, Sam," Shasta said. "I want to see them *all*."

"Thank you, Dear," he said. "Perhaps I can give you a tour sometime later."

We reached the T-junction where the dolphin had the sombrero in its teeth. Going down that corridor would leave you with that series of paintings on your right. Mr. McClusky moved his flashlight to the left wall of that corridor. It was a coral reef animated with colorful fish. Within the scene, a sea horse was looking questionably at a beach ball floating above it. And in the distance, a small island with palm trees poked out of the ocean.

Mr. McClusky loaded me up with a roll of the black paper and two rolls of duct tape. "You do the office windows. We'll do the windows in the maze."

"How can I see without the flashlight?" I asked.

"Just follow your nose, Mr. Jacobs. The exit's ten feet *thataway*." He began to push the cart, with Shasta at his side. "When you're outa the maze, you'll see well enough in the computer light."

In a few steps, the office glowed ahead of me. When I exited the labyrinth, there was an echo reverberating toward me—it was the sound of Shasta laughing hysterically. When I turned to look back into the labyrinth, all that was there was darkness.

I finished with a half-roll of tape to spare. When Shasta and Mr. McClusky came out of the labyrinth, the way she was giggling made me think he'd pinned her down for a tickling. But they were walking arm-in-arm: Mr. McClusky was quite the charmer, that's for sure. When the two found me, I actually wished that he'd continue his act, but she let go of him. She took a spot beside me and planted a gentle kiss on my lips.

"You need to be careful of me, Mr. Jacobs," he said. "I just may steal your girl."

Shasta grinned broadly in the gloomy monitor light.

"She's not just my girl—she's my fiancé."

Shasta pouted and nodded her head: *Yuh, sad but true.*

"Means less today than it used to," he said. "Let's turn on the lights."

We walked together to the light-switch panel. Shasta flipped them up and the fluorescents popped on asynchronously. I invited them to my desk where they took the two rolling chairs.

"So, what now?" I asked, standing on the fading X that Mr. Chandler had scribbled on the floor.

"Well," Mr. McClusky said, "we have shelter and clothes and air and water—the only necessity of life that's left is food. For that, a friend of mine is payin me a visit when he gets offa work."

"Oh, yuh?" Shasta asked.

"And he's got meat. Sure to be dry as jerky, but he's got meat."

I had regretted leaving all that beef in the freezer back home, and I was sure we'd be on government rations from then on. But actually, we never had to eat rations again. I had no idea what Mr. McClusky had in store for us, but if it was meat, it was a good thing.

Shasta and I shared a smile.

Mr. Chandler's trick got the internet on my terminal. I found the KTLA stream and clicked on it. A video window appeared with a spinning circle. Mr. McClusky and Shasta were in an animated conversation and, every so often, she would burst into laughter and I would look at her and smile. I hadn't seen her so happy since I'd met her, and that made me feel good.

A knock sounded at the applicant door. Mr. McClusky got up to answer it, holding his broom as a weapon. A young man carrying a clear trash bag walked back with him. It looked as though someone had taken a bunch of clean wax paper, crumpled it up in balls, and filled a trash bag with it. He set it down just outside my cubicle. The nametag on his apron had the Ralph's logo on it, and it was engraved with the name MICHAEL.

"These are my friends," Mr. McClusky said. "Shasta and Zeno."

Michael smiled at me, and asked, "The philosopher or the emperor?"

"I like to think the philosopher, but I didn't know my parents."

"Well," Michael said, "it's a cool name. I'll bet no one forgets it."

I looked at Shasta. She gave me a guilty smile.

Mr. McClusky took out his wallet. He pulled out two $500 bills. "This is for the food," he said, giving Michael the first bill. Then he gave him the other one. "And this is for the family."

"It's too much, Mr. McClusky," Michael said.

I unzipped a pocket in one of our duffel bags and took out a fistful of fivers. I slapped the coins into his hand. "Here's some more."

Mr. McClusky clapped Michael on the back. "You be a good man and take it—I got so much in the bank that I couldn't possibly spend it before I pass on. But you— well, you're just startin out. You feed that baby of yours. Just remember us if you got any more in the future. And *don't git caught.*"

Michael made all the money disappear. "Thank you. Thank you all," he said. He left out the applicant door.

Shasta emptied out some of the wax paper wads, and then burst into a voiced inhale. She sunk both hands into the trash bag. She brought out a huge plastic-domed tray of fried chicken and lowered her nose to it, inhaling once again. Her breath came back out in an ecstatic moan. The chicken was passed off to Mr. McClusky, who set it on the desk. A plain box was lobbed at me, full of plastic forks, paper plates, napkins, pats of butter, and packets of ketchup, salt and pepper. Then out came another domed container—Chinese—broccoli and beef on fried rice. She pulled out more and more tubs: mac and cheese, coleslaw, mashed potatoes and gravy, Swedish meatballs, pasta salad, and a huge mass of jojos. Lastly, there were tons of chicken strips. She gobbled one up right away exclaiming *"Sweet Jesus!"* with her mouth full.

I tried one of the chicken strips as well. It was juicy and still warm—almost straight-from-the-fryer hot. We all made huge mounds on our plates. Mr. McClusky ate only his firsts. I took seconds once. But Shasta, who seemed to have a bottomless pit for a stomach, had more than the two of us put together. She was working on her fifth piece of chicken when KTLA started giving the casualty count.

"—of the rioters are confirmed dead, 387 residents of the greater Los Angeles area are confirmed dead, and six members of the California National Guard are also confirmed dead. The Governor has requested the assistance of Federal soldiers who are on their way from Fort Irwin. Further units have been dispatched from Fort Lewis in Washington State as well as Fort Hood and Fort Bliss in Texas. Their arrival is expected within the next forty-eight to seventy-two hours. Further requests for federal assistance are expected to help quell riots in Colorado, Oregon, Texas, Louisiana, Florida, Michigan, and throughout Southern New England."

Another reporter spoke. "In the meantime, National Guard soldiers have failed to penetrate roadblocks in their effort to resecure Long Beach. Lars Pearson is joining us live from Sky5."

The screen changed to an aerial image circling around a large pyramid. Two men stood near the top, fighting its steep angle. They both held five-gallon drums, pouring a liquid so that it cascaded down the four sides of the roof.

"It's taken them days to do it, but the Hundred Days rioters at California State Long Beach have managed to remove most of the blue aluminum that makes the Walter Pyramid so distinctive."

I pushed my plate away. "Those people *aren't* Hundred Days!"

Mr. McClusky wiped his mouth with a napkin. "Now, what makes you think that?"

"Hundred Days has particular targets—they're not interested in destroying schools."

Both Mr. McClusky and Shasta dismissed me with *pffff* sounds.

Lars spoke again: "Can we zoom in on that?"

The picture tightened on one of the men. You could read the text on the can: *KEROSENE.*

Lars said the obvious: "It appears that these people are pouring an accelerant onto the exposed roof."

One of the men slipped. The camera caught his fall until he tumbled off the edge of the roof and smacked the concrete below.

"Well, good riddens to him," the unseen anchor said.

"Yuh, *totally*," Shasta agreed.

The other arsonist crab-walked down the pyramid toward a hydraulic lift below. He stepped onto it and lowered himself to the ground. The helicopter orbited to get a better view. When the picture settled on the man again, he'd gotten off the lift and grabbed a flaming bottle. The camera zoomed in on his face—he was a young, white guy with a beard trimmed so that it's just a pencil line along the jaw. He saw the chopper and flipped it off with his free hand. Then he wound back like a baseball pitcher and threw the bottle in a high arc.

Shasta had stopped eating—she watched with a slack jaw.

"Well, there it goes," Lars said.

The bottle exploded and fire splashed up the wooden roof. Though the kerosene caught, the spread of the flames was slow. It took a full five minutes before the whole pyramid was blazing. When the camera found the arsonist again, a mob was standing around him celebrating—patting him on the back.

"If I could shoot that horse's ass through the computer," Mr. McClusky said, "I would."

Shasta ran a finger along her necklace. "Yuh, right in the nuts."

20—HELL

Calorie overload left Shasta passed out, drooling on the desk. Mr. McClusky gathered up the leftovers and put them into the fridge in the break room. Meanwhile, I could only maintain semi-consciousness, and my brain flickered on and off as I waited for the flaming pyramid to collapse.

"It's okay to sleep," Mr. McClusky said. "These are my workin hours. I'll stay up for the night watch, and then you two can keep an eye out while I sleep in the mornin."

"Alright," I said. I set my head down on the table, next to Shasta's.

A sudden gasp from dozens of people stirred us, and Shasta and I lifted our heads at the same time. There were people gathered all around my cubicle. I recognized some that were my employees, but there were also children now, as well as other faces I didn't recognize. I glanced around groggily, and my first impression was that all these people were all staring at me. But I followed their eyes, and what they were looking at was my computer monitor.

It was morning, and the civil rioters were knocking down the Hollywood sign. The Y and the W had already fallen, leaving HOLL   OOD, and now the D was tipping precariously. Above the sign, an older man with a striped shirt and an unzipped parka was running toward a guy who was obviously a lookout. The old man slowed as he neared the lookout, turning his energy to yelling and gesticulating with his arms.

"Oh, no," Ruben said from Sky5, "what does this man think he's doing?"

The lookout produced a large, shiny revolver. He leveled it at the now-frozen-stiff old man and fired. The old man collapsed in a heap.

The employees and their families gasped again, and a few shrill cries lit from among them. For me, seeing that murder brought full alertness—no coffee needed. Rubin began speaking like a scratched CD: *"Oh no oh no oh no oh no."* The camera zoomed in on the murderer, who smiled above the body and kicked dirt in its face.

The camera panned back to the sign as the Os from OOD fell simultaneously. By then, the D was hanging upside down, and a chopping motion by one of the men made it drop. A team of two secured a cloth around the O from the remaining elements of HOLL. As they tightened up the lanyards, the cloth formed an E. The men, nine in all, then hurried up the hill. The camera panned from the HELL sign, following them.

The group approached a curve on Mt. Lee Drive, and as they passed the body of the old man, the lookout joined them. A couple of the men laughed along with the lookout. As the group got further up the road, they spread out among a series of tankers crowded together on a pullout—most of the brand names of the fuel companies were represented on the tanker's sides: Shell, Chevron, Mobil, ARCO... But two of the nine tankers were different—they were cylindrical—which meant they were either natural gas or propane. In short time, fuel from the gasoline trailers spilled everywhere. When a white panel-van pulled up, the driver handed a backpack out to someone. As the others filed into the van, the man with the backpack got it strapped to the side of one of the cylindrical tankers. Then he ran back and got into the passenger's seat. The van sped away eastbound toward Griffith Park, and the camera didn't stay on them for long. It returned to the spilling gasoline. And that backpack.

"Judas Priest," Ruben said. "We're gonna need some distance, Derek."

Everyone was staring at my monitor—even the children. I told Shasta, *"Come on,"* and grabbed her hand, leading her out the applicant door. We walked to the east side of the building and the HELL sign was there in the morning light, blatant—even through the rusty brown smog from the continuing brush fires. Even so, Mount Lee itself looked peaceful from where we were. Though the hills and the distance hid the fuel tankers from us, neither could hide the result of whatever was in that backpack.

In an instant, Mount Lee was transformed.

We'd not only shut our eyes, but reflex brought our arms up for protection. We were miles and miles away at HRW, but the fireball radiated so strongly that the hairs on my arms were singed. In a few moments, I dropped my arms and opened my eyes. Above the mountain, a red ball bigger than the sun blazed, casting a maroon glow on all of Los Angeles. The HELL sign had been obliterated in the explosion, and everywhere around it, the mountain's brush was ablaze. When the explosion's report reached us, it was surprisingly soft—sounding like ripping off the top of a cardboard box. As the fireball rose, its radiance faded slowly to black.

"Oh my God, Zeno. When's this going to end?"

"What day is it?"

"Eighty-two? Eighty-*three*? I don't know…"

"I can't imagine another eighteen days of this."

Shasta buried the side of my face in her chest; I held her tight. As the black mushroom pushed into the brown sky, others began to file out of the building to have a look. They gathered around us, and everybody was shouting, gesturing, weeping.

Occupation

21—A Place Called Hobart Yard

The others quickly returned to the HRW building. I'm sure they continued to watch the streaming video from my computer, but there's always a smaller measure of horror to something onscreen as opposed to the same thing seen with your bare eyes. Shasta lingered outside, though. Her face said she wanted to confront me.

"What about Camp Liberty?" she asked.

"All this is going to end. You saw the news—the Army's on its way. They'll secure the city, and we'll be okay."

"Living in a war zone—*really? 'We'll be okay'?*" She looked toward Mount Lee, where the fire had already spread to Cahuenga Peak. It fed a looming smoke cloud as large as any thundercloud I'd ever seen, one that was now blacking out the sun in the northeast quarter of the metropolitan area. Above us in Santa Monica floated rusty gray clouds from the thousands of home fires now burning in Venice, Marina Del Rey, and Culver City. She looked directly at the dimmed-out sun and didn't have to

251

shield her eyes to do it. She asked, "Honestly, Zeno: does the HRW building have to *burn down* before we go?"

I didn't answer because I was watching a large vehicle as it pulled into the west driveway of the parking lot. As it got closer to the building, I could tell it was a Hummer—not one of the ones you see the rich farts driving—a *military* one. It had two big antennas that were whipping around unsecured, at twice the height of the vehicle's roof. I pulled Shasta across the lawn until we were flat along the south side of the building. The Hummer drove to the employee entrance, and then its engine stopped abruptly. Shasta and I advanced to the southwest corner of the building so we could get a better look. As we neared, we stepped lightly, close to the wall, not wanting them to see us. I got to a knee and peered around the corner. The driver was out already—he wore a camouflage uniform, including a bulletproof vest and helmet, with a rifle in his hands. He walked to the other side of the Hummer and opened the passenger door, where another soldier got out. This one was older, and he held a large map. Instead of a rifle, this one wore a pistol on his hip. Shasta took a peek from above me, her hands resting on my shoulders.

"Wow," she whispered, *"score one for you."*

The soldier with the map leaned back into the Hummer and brought out something that looked like an old telephone handset on a curly wire. He barked into it for a few moments and then tossed the handset back inside.

Shasta and I were maybe a hundred feet away. The two soldiers walked toward the employee entrance. I figured it was no big deal—it was Sunday, and the employee entrance would be locked. But it wasn't. By the time the soldiers were inside, there was nothing we could do to prevent it.

"Come on," I told her, and we walked to the vehicle. The two antennas oscillated on their springs and the cooling engine ticked. I looked for some kind of identification, like you see printed below the cockpits of fighter jets. But all I saw were nonsensical combinations of letters and numbers stenciled on the bumper.

"What could they possibly want from HRW?" Shasta asked.

"I don't know," I said, "but we'd better find them before they're lost in there."

We entered the labyrinth and followed the dolphin. After a few turns, we could hear the soldiers talking, so we tried to follow their voices. But we kept taking turns that made them seem farther away. Finally, we just stopped and listened.

"What the hell is this, an art gallery?"

"I think we're in a maze, Sir."

"No shit, Corporal."

"Hello?" I called out, and again louder: *"Hello!"*

There was silence for a moment before the reply came: *"What is this place?"*

"You're in the labyrinth."

"Who are you?"

"My name is Zeno Jacobs. Can you describe the painting you're nearest to?"

"There's an airplane with bird's wings. Feathers."

I looked at Shasta. She gave me an *I dunno* look. "Okay," I told her, "go find Mr. McClusky." She nodded and backtracked to the dolphin.

I yelled in the direction I thought their voices were coming from. "Just stay where you are. I'm getting help."

"Help? Why should we need help?"

"The last person who got lost in here died," I said, and instantly regretted it.

"What's your name again?"

"Zeno. Zeno Jacobs."

"Roger. I'll be putting a bullet into you, Mr. Jacobs. Unless we're out of here in ten minutes."

That was the second time I'd been threatened with a bullet at that job, but this time, the threat seemed dire and certain. I followed the dolphin quickly.

Mr. McClusky was asleep in the break room. Shasta sat beside him on the couch, shaking him gently. "Sam, we need your help—wake up."

His eyes opened and he blinked a couple of times. "Oh, hello beautiful," he said.

Shasta grinned.

Mr. McClusky sat up in a coughing fit.

Shasta waited patiently for him to breathe well again. Then she said, "Some soldiers are lost in the labyrinth and we need your help."

"Anythang for you, my dear."

I cleared my throat. "They said they'll shoot me if they're not out in ten minutes."

Mr. McClusky put his arm around Shasta's waist. "We should find them in eleven, what you think?"

She balled up a fist and struck him on the leg.

Mr. McClusky winked at me.

Shasta stood. "Come on. They're somewhere with an airplane—"

"—with feathers on the wangs," Mr. McClusky finished. "Not too far from one of the exits, actually."

We left the break room and walked toward the labyrinth.

Mr. McClusky motioned to all the families. "Who are all these people?"

"You were the one on watch," I said, "remember?"

He gave me one of his low grunts. We entered the labyrinth and the paintings did their funny forward-time, reverse-time thing. We eventually came upon a school of fish, swimming backwards from our perspective. Then the sea floor changed, with the water getting shallower and the fish spreading out. A beach rose up. Sticking in the sand were three surfboards—toward their tops, they were all grinning. You could see their incisors, their canines, and the first of their molars. They had no noses or eyes—just smiles. After another turn, there was a cityscape in the dark of night. The windows were full of Art Deco silhouettes of people engaged in different activities: drinking, eating, dancing, kissing. Shasta giggled at one—the shadow cast by some kid picking his nose. In the sky by that window, the fringe of a feather glistened in the moonlight.

"Just follow the feather," Mr. McClusky said.

After a few frames it had disappeared. "It's gone," I said.

"No it's not," Shasta said, motioning to the opposite wall. "It just blew over there."

We followed the feather as it rose into the air, and when we found the airplane it had dropped off from, the two soldiers were there. Their helmets were hanging off their canteens, held in place by the chin straps.

"Hello, gentlemen," I said. "I'm Zeno Jacobs."

The older one stepped forward and offered his hand. "Colonel Emmons."

I shook his hand. Fearfully, to tell the truth.

"I'm the commander of the Third Cavalry Regiment. I'm here scouting a location for an HQ. I need your parking lot for my troops."

I was glad there was no reason to object. "It's all yours."

"Very good," he said. "Why haven't you folks moved out to Camp Liberty?"

I showed him my clip-on badge. "We've got a pass."

"Right," Colonel Emmons said. He glanced around at the ceiling, the walls, and the paintings. "Now, tell me—*what the hell is this place?*"

"This is HRW International," I said, "currently the worst place to work in the world." I turned to Mr. McClusky. "Sir—will you please take us to the office?"

"Right this way," he said.

Mr. McClusky yawned hoarsely as he led the way. Colonel Emmons and I walked side-by-side. And Shasta walked with the corporal, the two falling further and further behind every time Shasta exclaimed, "*Checkitout! This one's so cool...*"

"The perimeter will be secured," the colonel said. "We'll fence in your parking lot with concertina wire. If any of your employees need to leave, they'll be able to sign in and out at the gate."

"Okay, that sounds fine," I said.

"Do you have a cafeteria?"

"No, just a break room."

"Well, for letting us use your property here, we'll offer free chow. I have a box of pins for you to give your employees. Anyone wearing one is free to help themselves to the DFAC."

"Sorry—what's *dee-fack*?"

"Means Dining Facility. It'll be open 0730 to 0900, 1130 to 1300, and 1700 to 1830."

I tried to decipher the military time, but with them stacked back-to-back, I failed. "That's really neat, Colonel. Thank you."

"Don't mention it."

We turned a corner. "Why does the Guard have to set up a headquarters? I thought they had little posts here and there."

The colonel laughed. "Oh, we're not the *National Guard*." He said *National Guard* with a thick measure of sarcasm. "And we're not the *Reserve*, either. We're the real deal—*U.S. Army*, active-duty all the way. We're going to kick the shit out of these rioters and looters. I've always thought the looters were the lowest form of scum."

I glanced at my wedding ring. Then I nodded. "Right."

The colonel walked backwards for a few paces. "SMITH—WHAT KINDA HANKY-PANKY ARE YOU ENGAGED IN BACK THERE! TIGHTEN IT UP!"

Smith's voice echoed to us: *"Moving, Sir!"*

In twenty seconds or so, I could hear the thumping and scraping of the corporal's gear. He and Shasta soon ran up behind us.

"Sorry," Shasta said, "my fault."

"Not a problem, Ma'am," the colonel said.

"Oh, I didn't notice the moon in these before—it's so cute!"

Colonel Emmons gave me an awkward glance. "You *Angelinos* are a strange bunch, aren't you?"

"I've never travelled, so I wouldn't know."

"Just what does this business do?"

I paused, wondering if I should tell him. Then I figured, *What the hell?* "We hire people and make them quit."

The colonel's eyebrows shot up. "Sounds un-American."

"Quite the contrary—" I started, but Colonel Emmons gave me a death-stare that was fifty times worse than the one Doreen's clan had given me. "*Un*-American. Yes, Sir." I cleared my throat. "We're also one of the rioters' primary targets."

"I'll keep that in mind."

The corporal asked Shasta what she did around here. I glanced back at him. He was blushing.

"Oh, I don't work here, but we had to abandon the house because of the emergency. I'm actually the boss' fiancée—he's kind of short and a little weak, but he's still got all the hair on his head!"

I looked back at her, but her focus was on the corporal. I faced forward.

"Can I see your helmet?" Shasta asked. Then she called, "Hey, Zeno!"

I walked backwards in the labyrinth's final corridor.

Shasta gave herself an underbite and spoke in a growl: *"They slipped out in the night, but the smell—that gasoline smell—the whole place smelled like... Victory."*

The corporal laughed, but I wouldn't understand the reference until years later when, on one lonely night, I downloaded *Apocalypse Now*.

Shasta gave back the helmet. "You got a fiver, Zeno?"

I flipped her a coin.

"Coffees all around—except you, Sam. Go back to bed." She disappeared into the labyrinth, following sombreros.

Shasta came back with her arms full. She handed the cups out and we all muttered our thanks.

"So, when will your soldiers arrive?" I asked.

"They're rail-loading as we speak, due at a place called Hobart Yard on Tuesday morning. I need to recruit someone that knows Los Angeles forward and backward, someone who knows all the shortcuts from here to Palm Springs, and on down to San Diego." He nodded at me. "You think you can help us out?"

I shook my head. "Oh, not me. *No.* But you're free to ask any of my employees. If none of them will do, there will be a lot more tomorrow morning. Most of them work Monday through Friday."

"Okay. I appreciate it." The Colonel began mingling with the families.

"We saw the Hollywood sign fall," the corporal said to Shasta. "And the fireball—looked like an airstrike."

"Nuh-uh," Shasta said, "it was a bunch of fuel trucks set off with a bomb."

"How do you know?"

"It was on Channel 5."

I interrupted them. "Have you ever been sent out like this before?"

The corporal sipped his coffee. "Sure. We deploy to the field at least four times a year. Maybe once or twice a year to NTC or JRTC. We even went to Africa once—that was three years ago, though."

I didn't ask him to translate his acronyms. "What I mean is here at home," I said. "In the States. In the cities."

"Uh, no urban deployments. This'll be my first."

"What can we expect—like what do you do when you set up?"

"We usually form the vehicles in a defensive posture. Like a circle—for protection. Everyone stands guard until we've secured the location. We set up concertina wire in a triple stack around the perimeter. We set up land lines for communication. The 25-X-ray commands the squad that gets the satellite, radio, and line-of-sight up. Then the sergeant-major gets all the platoon sergeants to make up a guard roster. Once the guards are in place, everyone's free to get to work on other things like maintenance, ammunition, the DFAC, sanitation and water facilities, and so on. While the men take care of all that, the NCOs are usually in the CP getting intel from the officers, finalizing and fine-tuning the mission. We're usually up and running within an hour, and ready to do a mission briefing for the troops in ninety minutes—tops."

"All that in our parking lot?"

"Actually, we've squeezed into spots a lot smaller than this."

The Colonel walked up with Octavio. "This is our man. We're going to borrow him as a guide. You are to take no personnel actions against him—do you understand?"

I nodded, but I was shocked by Octavio's presence—I hadn't known he was with us. Moreover, what was he doing at work on the weekend? Had *los compañeros* abandoned the commune? These were things I couldn't ask right then, but I looked at Octavio questioningly. He returned my glance with a tilt of his head.

The colonel and the corporal took Octavio outside, and I followed. The corporal ran off and then pulled the Hummer up by the applicant door. Octavio sat on the curb while the two Army men talked on the radio, thumbed their phones, and drew lines on a map.

I walked over beside Octavio. "Why're you here?"

Octavio looked up at me and spoke in a low voice. "The Guard is shelling East L.A.!"

"Why are you going with them?"

Octavio stood and grabbed my arm. "*Man,* you still afraid to get involved?" He released me with a disdainful push.   I looked him in his predatory eyes, and my adrenaline surged at the sight.

Colonel Emmons folded his map.   He motioned Octavio toward the back seat and Octavio responded meekly, opening the door and getting in. When he closed the door I couldn't see his hands anymore, but by his posture he seemed to have them folded politely on his lap. As Corporal Smith shifted the Hummer into gear, there was a hint of a smile on Octavio's face.

22—Brave Rifles

By Monday, I had locked the employee entrance and posted a sign there directing people to the applicant entrance. But now, everyone who worked downstairs couldn't find the stairwell, so all the departments' people were in personnel's cubicles goofing around while Gordon painted a fresh stripe—this time orange—on the floor of the labyrinth.

Many of the employees were missing. There were usually two hundred in my group alone, and between the other departments, there should have been another eight hundred. So from a thousand-or-so down to the hundred that were hanging around in personnel that Monday was a big cut. I didn't gripe about the lack of work going on. Even though it was a workday now, it was the first after a very stressful weekend, and because of that, I figured we kinda *should* goof around. I waited for Bob to call and chew me out while Shasta dipped cold chicken strips into ranch.

And Bob *did* call, as I thought she would.

"This is Bob. I'm having several issues this morning—I was hoping you could help me out."

A paper airplane sailed overhead. "Happy Monday, Bob!"

"I'm trying to be calm, Zeno. I've taken my blood pressure pills…"

"Well, Bob, let me help. Please."

"Okay. I thought you termed that floozy. So why does she have her feet up on your desk?"

"She's not a floozy, Bob. She's my fiancée." That got Shasta's attention, and she watched me as she continued to munch on chicken strips.

"*You're marrying her?*" Bob asked. "Never mind—that's beside the point. Did you rehire her?"

"No."

"Then why is she there?"

"Haven't you seen the news?"

"The *news* is the only thing on, Zeno."

But Bob wasn't in Los Angeles, and she couldn't know what it was like live—and in 3-D. "Look around in that camera of yours, Bob. Everyone you see here is homeless. Los Angeles is burning to the ground. So, we need to open our doors to our employees and their families. It's just a temporary measure, but a necessary one. Unless you want me to just term everyone and shut the place down."

"But how do you get them to quit if they *live* there, Zeno?"

"As I said—it's temporary. The company should be able to write off any loss in profits due to the riots. Hopefully we'll be back on track next month."

Bob let out a deep breath. "All right, Zeno. But you remember this is a *business*. We can only be human-itarians as long as it suits *our* interests. If I sense *for a second* that you're not mitigating our losses, I'll make you process your own termination. *Understand?*"

I knew if I answered that question, she'd hang up on me, so I asked, "What are all of these binder clips for?"

"You didn't answer my question, Zeno."

"Can you tell me what these binder clips are for?"

"Unlike staples, binder clips are reusable."

"And about a thousand times more expensive—good call, Bob." This time I hung up on her.

"Still calling me a *floozy*, huh?" Shasta asked.

"You know Bob."

When Mr. McClusky awoke late that morning, he came over to the cubicle and spent a while clearing his lungs. When he'd recovered, he put a hand on Shasta's shoulder.

"Hey, pretty lady," he said, "how about that tour of the maze?"

She bounced several times in her seat. "You mind, Zeno?"

"No. Not at all." I tugged on Mr. McClusky's sleeve. "You sure you're up for it?"

He scowled at me. "Yes, Mother," he said, leading Shasta away.

I stayed at the cubicle and watched the Santa Monica Pier sway some and drift out with the tide. Then the rioters moved south and started sinking yachts in Marina Del Rey. In the meantime, the firefighters were busy throughout the Santa Monica Mountains putting out brush fires that kept popping up like trick candles. On the news, they announced that more firefighters were due to arrive from Washington, Idaho, Montana, and even Alaska, but I know if I lived in any of those places, I wouldn't have wanted my firefighters leaving. Hundred Days riots, perpetrated by new members subscribing to *Jimenez Loco*'s online manifesto, were breaking out all over the country—even in Hawaii.

The National Guard couldn't help much. With most of the Guard units attached to supermarkets, food banks, and now gas stations, there were only a dozen teams left to actively engage the rioters, which was nowhere near enough—in a city like Los Angeles, twelve teams could hardly secure a city block.

And where were the police? You'd see squads of cars speeding here and there. I sometimes think that's all they did—you know: line up in a convoy of ten or twelve cars, turn on the lights, and speed as fast as they could to the other side of the city, blasting their sirens at every intersection. But no, in reality a lot of people were dying, and for every dead body produced in the riots, a police officer must have had the job of filling out the paperwork. So, I imagine their lives were frighteningly grim in those times—primarily made up of the tasks of doing what you could to identify the dead and then shuttling the corpses off to a medical examiner who hadn't slept in weeks.

Soon, Gordon declared the labyrinth's floor-paint dry. He called the other department heads over, saying they could gather up their employees. When he was done chatting with them, I approached.

"Hey, Gordon."

"What now?"

"Can you tell me anything about what to do when somebody retires?"

He cast a look upon me that made me feel stupid. "How could *you* possibly have a retiree?"

"It's Mr. McClusky."

"Oh." The look he'd given me migrated back to his brain, and his face returned to its default state of utter boredom. "Take McClusky's file to payroll. Give them three days to get everything sorted out before terming him."

"Thanks," I said, and I meant it. The computers came to mind. "And can you do me a favor?"

His jaw clenched, and little muscles by his ears twitched.

"Until the riots are over, it'd be nice if you'd allow the internet browsers to work on the network. Just in case, so we know it if a gang with torches and spears are coming..."

Gordon walked away, following his floor stripe.

Between the bathroom entrance and the utilities exit was the long bank of vertical files I mentioned, like the kind you see in medical offices. It was where we held the paperwork of our current employees. I walked along it until I found the label **Mc**. Mr. McClusky's file was the thickest one there. Inside were hundreds of forms, with typewritten pages, carbon-papered signature sheets, and thin copies printed in a faded purple ink. It smelled of cheap paperbacks and formaldehyde.

I followed Gordon's stripe, wondering if I'd run into Shasta and Mr. McClusky. At the point where the coconut falls onto the crab, the stripe turned to follow the rolling coconut. For the length of a long stretch of wall, the coconut did nothing but sit there. Then Gordon's stripe went in two directions at a four-way junction. To the right, the story of the coconut continued, but in several feet Gordon had ended his stripe and painted OOPS on the floor. Above his orange OOPS, the coconut had split, and a palm sprout was sticking up through the crack.

I'll ask Shasta later, I thought. But I never did.

I went back to the four-way junction, going in the direction of the second stripe. It was a place where the ocean seemed to have nothing of significance within it or upon it. After twenty or so frames, a Styrofoam cup appeared, floating upon the water. It drifted and drifted and drifted, until finally joining a great gathering of trash upon the sea. Little packing peanuts began to congregate together like a swarm of little shrimp, swimming together into a large, yellow raincoat. As the raincoat filled, it began to stand erect above the island of floating trash. When it got to its full height, it reached its arms to the sky, where a large thunderstorm was building…

I followed the stripe away from the flotsam island. In a couple more turns, the orange stripe joined the yellow one—the one I had followed the day Mr. Chandler died. The day that bitch Grace Van Horne stole my lottery ticket. The thought made me angry in a flash. I made it to the stairwell quickly, and as I took the stairs down, I kept looking behind me. And it occurs to me now that I always look behind myself in stairwells.

I guess it became a habit.

The walls of the second basement spoke to me. Their words were devoid of meaning or intent. They screamed whiteness, sterility, boredom, a complete lack of utility other than to hold space. The air was stuffy and scentless. I followed the hallway through a ninety-degree turn at the midpoint of the south wall. The turn led to the centroid of the rectangular building, where the hallway ended. Straight ahead were two doors, and each of the adjacent walls had one apiece. From left to right, they were labeled: MARKETING, HUMAN RESOURCES (NO ADMITTANCE), LEGAL, and PAYROLL.

I opened the door to payroll and went in. Five feet in front of the door there was a counter with a window, like in a check cashing store. No one was at the window, but a camera stared at me from the ceiling.

I waved at it.

There was a door off to the left. I tried it, but it was locked.

I spent some time pacing. Soon, I started exaggerating my walk, at first all stiff and erect, like a stuffy businessman, but then all loose and stooping, like in a duck walk—with my butt on my heels. I flapped my arms like wings and quacked like a fool.

"Couldn't you have called?" a voice said.

As one often does when caught in a moment of imbecility, I froze in place. A plain-looking girl was at the window, the kind with glasses that make their eyes look like billiard balls. Her name was Pam or Pat or Pat*sy*—yeah, that was it. Anyway, I had hired her, so, I was like "Hey, Patsy," as I stood, blushing.

She gave me a sour look. "We're already a day behind, Mr. Jacobs. What do you want?"

"I have an employee whose retirement needs to be started."

She held out her hand on the other side of the glass.

I stuffed the file into the dip under the window. It barely fit.

She yanked it free and disappeared with it.

I stood there for a few minutes, not knowing if she'd come back. When she didn't, I went back upstairs and followed Gordon's stripe to the office.

That evening, I listened to Breaking News while figuring out how poorly the month's numbers were going to turn out. The funny thing about the way they measured turnover was that you could lose a bunch of people, but if you didn't hire more to replace them, it wouldn't show in the numbers. We had termed something like 215 people from my department alone that month, but since my staffing was so depleted, I wasn't getting credit for it.

"Howya doing, Zeno?" a voice asked from behind me.

I turned. Michael was there, looking like a skinny Santa Claus in his Ralph's uniform, only without a beard. He heaved the full trash bag from his shoulder to the floor.

"Good, Michael, good," I said. "How're you?"

"Alright. Is Sam around?"

"Somewhere. He's been in the labyrinth all day." I looked at the clock in the monitor's taskbar—they had been gone for over ten hours. Even with the enormous size of the labyrinth, and even with the hundreds of paintings within it, I couldn't imagine a tour would take that long. I mean, Shasta was excitement prone with a lot of the scenes in there, but I would've thought Mr. McClusky would tire from such a long time on his feet. He couldn't even sit down without shaking like he had Parkinson's, for crying out loud. The whole tour-of-the-maze thing was starting to grate on me, badly…

"The *what?*" Michael asked, for probably the third time.

I blinked at him. "Oh—the *labyrinth*. It's a maze my old boss installed so the new employees would get lost."

Michael's eyebrows arched.

"Be thankful for your job," I said.

"I got laid off."

Uh-oh, I thought. *This will be the last of our food, then.* "Why?"

"They closed my store. With the city emptying out, they're only going to keep two locations open. So, I'm considering taking my family to Liberty. Can you tell Sam to hit me up on my cell?"

"Sure, Man, sure," I said. Michael looked like he really needed to talk to someone, and I was about to offer him a seat, but then he just turned around and walked away. I stood to call after him, to offer his family a cubicle to sleep in, but by the time I did, he was already out the applicant entrance.

I sat again. Steam was billowing past the trash bag's opening. I wrote a quick note for Mr. McClusky with Michael's message, and taped it to the break room door.

Moments later, I was enjoying barbeque ribs and potato salad.

It had been another long day. I emptied the fridge of the dried-out leftovers from Michael's first visit, and then loaded the new stuff in. Around eleven, I began to wonder if Shasta had been by, and that maybe I hadn't noticed. But I didn't think she had.

I watched KTLA's streaming feed. Most of central Los Angeles seemed to be calming at this point, and now the bottle brigades were invading eastward into Riverside. As I listened to Martin Mason comment on the torching of the Mission Inn, I leaned over, resting my head on my arms.

Shasta woke me with a kiss to my temple. Must've been two in the morning. "Thank you," she said while messaging my back. As I drifted, I wondered, *Why the hell were you gone so long? The labyrinth isn't that big... What could you have been doing for* fourteen *hours?*

But I never got the answer. I never asked.

I woke up early, craving my morning cup. I went into the labyrinth as Shasta continued sleeping with her head on the desk. I followed the sombreros and came back with my coffee. I could hear a diesel engine idling outside the applicant entrance, so I went out expecting to see the colonel, the corporal, and Octavio. Instead, what I saw was the upper half of a soldier sticking through the roof of a different Hummer. The guy pivoted the largest gun I ever saw at me. The barrel measured longer than both of my arms stretched out, and the hole bored into that barrel was aimed directly at my chest. A chain of rounds hung off the side of the gun—each of them the size of a cigar.

I assumed the position of *I surrender.*

Hot coffee dribbled down my wrist, and I flinched some, but kept my hands up. A soldier exited from the passenger's side. He motioned flat-handed, up and down a couple of times. The gunner pivoted the barrel upwards and away from me.

"I'm looking for Zeno Jacobs."

"That's me." I lowered my arms and sucked the coffee from my wrist.

"I'm Lieutenant Colonel Hathaway. We've all had a very bad morning."

Mine wasn't turning out so well, either. "What can I do for you?" I asked.

The colonel motioned to his driver, who came out with a box.

"My advance party will be here in an hour. We're going to secure this facility and shut down the roads in a two-block perimeter around it. If any of your people own vehicles, tell them to move it over there or the wrecker's gonna haul it away."

Of course, none of the cars were parked where he was pointing. "I'll let my people know."

"Very good." The colonel took the box from his driver and pulled a pin out of it. "I want each of your people to wear one of these. Do not give any of these out to people who don't belong here. Do you understand?"

"Yes, Sir."

"We'll need access to your electricity until our generators are up. Is that okay?"

"Yes, Sir."

"Good man." The colonel shoved the box into my hands, and then he and his driver got back into his Hummer. They drove away.

In the box were hundreds of the pins he'd shown me, wrapped in plastic like candies. I pulled one out—it had a round face with a gold trumpet on top of a 3, and on a scroll that ran around the trumpet were the words BRAVE RIFLES.

I went inside and woke my people up. I called security telling them to make sure everyone downstairs came up for an immediate meeting. I briefed the employees and they passed around the box. We all put on our pins. Then Gordon gathered up everyone who owned a vehicle and coordinated the car-parking situation. Within that group, Mr. McClusky spoke to himself, griping that he didn't want his property so far from the building.

Shasta just had to tell me about the paintings, and in doing so she kept my attention away from the current news. She was animated, describing with her hands and miming with her face. A hollowed-out tree housed tens of thousands of ants, and they all worked together with strange, miniature tools to convert the tree into some kind of machine, and she had tried as hard as she could to figure out what the purpose of the machine was but she couldn't and Sammy refused to tell her what it did—he said it was a matter of interpretation... She continued in continuous description like this until the soldiers came.

A few minutes after the noise of twenty or thirty diesel engines became apparent, a soldier burst through the applicant door. He held a long extension cord and was going, "Outlet? Outlet?" I pointed to the receptacle by the door, where he plugged in the cord and left. Because of that cord, the door wouldn't shut all the way, so all anyone could hear now was the noise from the engines. There was one vehicle in particular that was louder than them all, and when it throttled up, it was as though God was roaring. It made the whole building shake.

Mr. McClusky had been napping until then. Now, he walked out of the break room barefoot with droopy, bloodshot eyes. *"What is that horrible noise?"* he barked.

"That's the Army," I said.

Mr. McClusky went *"Hmpf"* and turned back toward the break room.

Another soldier burst in through the door. "Bathroom? Bathroom?" he asked.

I pointed to it.

Shasta put both of her hands over her bladder, mimicking *"Bathroom? Bathroom?"* Snickers began hemorrhaging from her.

Another soldier entered. He wore strange oversized gloves, glasses with huge, brown frames, and he carried his rifle over his shoulder like a purse—it fell off twice as he stepped over. When he got to my cubicle, Shasta lost complete control, letting out enormous guffaws at the poor specimen.

The soldier looked slightly wounded but mostly confused. "I'm PFC Garrett," he said in a thick, southern drawl, "the POL guy. LT says to fill up yer generator."

I left Shasta to her giggles and showed the guy to the enclosure. He found the tank and gave it a few taps. "Yep, near empty. Smells like mo-gas." The soldier turned around a couple of times, like a dog chasing its tail. "Ain't no door? How you git a hose to it?"

"Over the wall, I guess."

He followed me back to the office. Shasta looked serious, but she couldn't keep her breath from exploding past her pursed lips. Again, she calmed momentarily, saying, "Ahm PMJ Shasta, the HRW lady…"

The soldier gave her a sour look and exited.

I humored her with a laugh. When we'd exhausted ourselves, I helped her to her feet. "Come on, let's see what's going on out there."

I was leading her toward the applicant entrance, but she pulled me back, saying, "I've got a better idea—"

"—the ants lead to the roof."

"Oh, yeah?"

"We can get a bird's-eye view up there. Come on!" She took my hand and dragged me into the labyrinth, where she was walking so quickly I had to jog to keep up. "You follow the sea horse, it pushes the beach ball, the ocean turns into a murky swamp, and on the last picture there's a tiny ant crawling along a leaf. When you turn there, the swamp'll turn to soil, and you'll see long line of 'em. The ladder's in a dead end right before the tree!" She took me through turn after turn, through a distance of maybe a half-mile. Every so often, she would go, "I really like this one," but she didn't stop to admire anything, nor did she slow any to let me take a look. She just kept going, and turning, and then going some more.

I started to get a real grip on just why the Sparkletts guy died in here. I would certainly never find my way back from where we were. But Shasta had it down now— memorized. After one final turn, the ladder stood before us, bolted to the cement slab of the southern wall. Shasta shot up its rungs, calling down to me: *"Hurry, Zeno!"*

I climbed up. Next to the ladder, about three-quarters the way up, a telephone box stuck out of the wall. Three lengths of conduit went from the box all the way down to the floor, each of them a different size, and each of them labeled. The fattest one said *RJ-45*, the middle-sized one said *RJ-21*, and the smallest one said:

LEGACY

My muscles knew what I'd seen before my mind did— rigor froze me stiff on that ladder. I shouldn't have cared anymore—Mr. McClusky's retirement was payroll's issue now, but I couldn't give up my curiosity about the way he'd been coded in the computer. What was LEGACY? And why did my computer list his job code as a series of question marks, while his paycheck continued to refer to him as a chicken cook? Then, there was that word itself: *LEGACY.* Something you're proud to have, something you want to pass onto your children, something that shows you've made a mark on the world.

Shasta called down again: *"Come on, slow poke!"*

I continued up. At the top there was a landing with a door. It opened onto the roof. I walked out.

In each of the parking lots, soldiers were lining up hundreds of vehicles. On the south side of the building, I looked down to the lawn and upon it, teams of soldiers pitched interconnected tents. Across from there, beyond the north end, the tops of tall antennas jiggled as the soldiers below staked them to the ground. Well beyond the building, out past all the parking lots, shoulder-high coils of razor wire were being connected together in the streets. To the west, at the entrance to the parking lot, something that looked like a strange tow truck arranged barricades, each of which looked like a huge toy jack. An engine started nearby. I looked again toward the south parking lot directly below me, where a different wrecker attached itself to the Sparkletts truck—it throttled up and the two vehicles rolled slowly toward the barricades.

Shasta walked to the far end of the north side, where the generator laid below. I followed. Below us, the soldiers unrolled nets, and on top of them a vinyl ruffle had been attached, cut in wavy forms that made it look like leaves. There were both hexagonal and diamond patterns to the netting, and they were being zip-tied into some sort of arrangement. The lawn extended a good distance from the building on that side, and at its edge laid a curbed sidewalk, where a soldier measured the width of the pavement between the curb and the islands that bordered the close end of the north lot. He began talking into a helmet-mounted headset.

A few moments later, God moaned somewhere in the distance.

"What *is* that?" Shasta asked.

"An engine—loudest one I ever heard."

"Where?"

We looked around. On top of the moaning sound, there were screeches, and this other noise like *tickle-tickle-tick-tick-tickle-tick*, and when the moaning increased to a roar, another sound came like the dragging of a hundred full suitcases on carpet. We finally saw it—a humongous track vehicle the size of a house was approaching from the east. All the way up front, a helmeted head poked out of it, and in the vehicle's center, the full upper torso of a soldier manned one of those huge guns that shoot the cigar bullets. At the tank's front end was a spade—like a bulldozer. The vehicle worked its way around to the north lot, never going faster than ten miles an hour. Without the slightest pause, it drove into a tree that was in one of the parking lot's islands. This wasn't a little landscape tree, mind you—this was a full-grown, fifty-year old Eucalyptus—as tall as four or five stories. The machine pushed its spade into the tree until roots as big as legs came popping out of the ground. The tree crunched as it swayed, and when it fell, it whacked the asphalt hard enough that we could feel the tremor travel through the roof. The Eucalyptus massacre continued for a half-hour along the whole length of the north lot. When they'd toppled the last tree, the guy at the machine gun got out and hooked a monster chain—each of its links as big as a torso—around the tree's trunk. The guy hopped onto the spade and the vehicle dragged its victim away to the far end of the north lot. When it got there, there was a quiet moment as the chain was disconnected. That's when Shasta called down to one of the men assembling the net below.

"Hey," she said, twiddling the fingers of her right hand. "What you doin' down there?"

"Assembling the S-2," was the soldier's reply, not that we knew what *that* meant.

Shasta didn't let that stop her. She pointed to where the men were unchaining the tree. "What is that big-ass thing?"

The soldier looked in the direction she was pointing. "Oh, that? That's the Hercules."

"Why is it killing our trees?"

The soldier smiled and nodded. He pointed to the lane between the sidewalk and the parking lot's islands, and then motioned along the entire length of the building. As he did this, he shouted up to us: *"Airstrip."* Then he returned to his work.

"He's screwing with us, Zeno. That's *totally* not wide enough for a runway."

The Hercules screamed as it pivoted on its track toward our direction. As it crawled back, a long flatbed semi drove down the lane. Strapped to its back were three airplanes. None of them big enough to hold a pilot, but they were airplanes, nonetheless.

They were drones.

23—My Army Friends

SPECIALIST DOOLEY
MOVING TO THE LABYRINTH
LOUD AS GODS
CHOCOLATE KISS
HOUSEKEEPING TASKS

As the soldiers elevated their camouflage nets, huge elements of even more vehicles began streaming into the lots. They looked like steel boats, but with four axles, and each of them had both the big guns and the springy antennas. As they were busy parking them like the other vehicles—in neat little rows—Shasta and I went back down.

When we exited the labyrinth, several cries lit from within the cubicles. Gordon had turned on the internet browsers by then, so I looked in at one of the monitors:

Universal Studios Taken

Hundred Days Rioters Shoot Security Guards
Six Confirmed Dead

I huffed at the subtitle, remembering Carlos' speech to me about the Luger. An older soldier came in through the applicant door and took off his helmet. As his eyes searched the room, I walked over.

"Hello," I said.

"I'm Major Kass. How many people do you have here?"

"A hundred. More or less."

"And most of them are living here?"

"I'd say all of them."

"Right. AER has arrived with some supplies. You want to help me prop the door open?"

Again, I ignored the acronym—through all this, it seemed easier that way. "Sure."

A civilian guy brought in a pallet on another one of those hand-operated forklift things. On it were cots, collapsed into compact little packages, placed five wide onto the pallet and cross-stacked as high as my shoulder. The guy butted the pallet right against the one with the binder clips and was out the door again. When he came back, it was with a pallet of wool blankets. Next, he brought in a huge, corrugated, open-top box. When he wheeled his forklift out, I stood on the edge of the pallet and peered inside: pillows. A similar box was next, this time filled with linens. A folding table came after that, and the major worked with the guy to set it up. They motioned to us and we helped them bring in four five-gallon beverage dispensers and a case of paper cups. The major signed the guy's paperwork and the guy left.

Shasta had an arm resting on one of the beverage dispensers. "So, what's in these?"

"Chow won't be ready until evening," the major said. "They're still getting the kitchen set up, so until then, its soup."

Shasta spoke in a happy groan: *"Cooooooool."*

The major plopped his helmet back on. "Don't forget—chow's 1630 to 1800. I think Dooley's making pot roast. Don't want to miss that."

"We'll be there," Shasta said.

"Good, good," the major said. "Hey—would you guys happen to know where there's a fire hydrant? I've been tasked to locate one so the men can fill the water buffalo…"

Shasta shrugged.

"There's one outside of the generator enclosure," I said.

The major blinked at me.

I translated into military speak: "Over where they're setting up the S-2."

"Hooah," he said with a wink of understanding, and then he left.

Shasta looked confused. "Water buffalo?"

I shook my head at her. "I have *no* idea."

Shasta tore open the case of cups and pulled out a sleeve—they were a plain khaki color. She filled one under a nozzle, and the soup steamed as it streamed out.

I grabbed a cup as Shasta blew across the top of her soup.

She tasted it. "Wow!" she said. "That's *some* chow!" At that moment, the words *food, meal, breakfast, lunch,* and *dinner* had all left Shasta's vocabulary. From then on, it was *chow.*

She turned to face the office cubicles. *"HEY, EVERYBODY! Come get some soup! And for chow tonight, they say it's roast beef!"*

In the streaming video, every kind of person—young and old, male and female, friendly- and scary-looking— marched around Universal Studios producing mayhem. For a moment, Sky5 panned around a lot where people were demolishing a facade with axes, but eventually the camera found a scuffle going on behind some shrubs.

"Oh, for any of you at home with children, please turn them away. This is horrible, just *horrible…"*

A large Asian man had his pants down below his butt. He appeared to be raping Marilyn Monroe.

"God, Zeno, I can't watch this…" She left and went into the bathroom.

I couldn't stomach it either, so I began reading the marquee along the bottom of the screen:

…3rd CAVALRY EXECUTIVE OFFICER WARNS THAT CURFEW HAS BEEN EXTENDED FROM SUNDOWN TO SUNUP. ANYONE FOUND ON THE STREET DURING THAT PERIOD MAY BE DETAINED. ANYONE WHO IS ARMED OR LOOTING CAN BE LAWFULLY SHOT ON SITE.

YOU'RE WATCHING KTLA 5, SOUTHERN CALIFORNIA'S NEWS LEADER. CELLULAR, RADIO, TELEVISION AND EMERGENCY SERVICES SEVERELY DISRUPTED BY SUNDAY'S BLAST ATOP MOUNT LEE. RIOTS ARE BREAKING OUT IN SOUTHERN LOUISIANA AND MISSISSIPPI AS THOSE STATES' NATIONAL GUARD PROTECTS BUILDING SUPPLIES. THIS SEASON, THREE HURRICANES HAVE MADE LANDFALL IN THE SOUTHEASTERN STATES. HURRICANE MALIA'S STORMTRACK PROJECTS THAT IT WILL STRIKE GULFPORT, MS ON THURSDAY MORNING AS A CATEGORY 4 HURRICANE.

I looked up from the marquee. The rapist was now hitting Marilyn repeatedly in the face. She wasn't fighting back anymore—she was either unconscious or dead. I went back to the scrolling text:

...KTLA 5 BREAKING NEWS: FIREFIGHTERS ARE TRYING TO STOP THE SPREAD OF HOME FIRES IN GLENDALE, BUT THIS SUMMER'S LACK OF PRECIPITATION—

My eyes had to flick back up—*had* to.

The man was rebelting his pants and staring down at Marilyn's motionless body. Sky5 zoomed in on his face until it filled the entire screen. A loud concussion sounded through the studios, and Sky5 left the rape scene to see what had caused it.

Shasta came back. "What happened?"

"Marilyn's dead, I think."

"I hope my Army friends will kill him."

I hoped so too. "Yeah."

An EAS icon started flashing in the notification area of the taskbar. I clicked on it and a window opened:

Civil authorities have announced an immediate evacuation of the Greater Los Angeles Metropolitan Area effective 1:20 PM Pacific Standard Time. Roads and highways inbound to the Metropolitan Area will no longer allow public traffic as of 3:00 PM Pacific Standard Time. Commuters who live outside of the metropolitan area are urged to go home immediately. North- and southbound traffic out of the metropolitan area will cease at 7:00 PM Pacific Standard Time. After 7:00 PM Pacific Standard Time, all traffic will be diverted onto eastbound Interstate 10. The civil curfew remains in effect for the Greater Los Angeles Metropolitan Area. Evacuees will be allowed travel after curfew, but should remain in their vehicles at all times. Those people without vehicles will receive bus transportation to Camp Liberty at no expense. Civilian pick-up will occur at the National Guard food banks established within your community. Each person is authorized travel with up to fifty pounds of personal items. Essential personnel, working certain governmental, medical, and critical infrastructure jobs, who are not evacuating are encouraged to wear their EP

*identification at all times. Evacuees must
bring all personal records with them, such
as identification and birth records, social
security cards, insurance policies, deeds and
titles, inoculation records, banking and financial records, as well as any outstanding
debts or bills. Before leaving your resi-
dence, please ensure the main circuit
breaker for electric power is OFF and
ensure that natural gas is turned OFF at
the main valve located by your meter. Any
questions regarding property and/or personal items left behind will be addressed by
processors at Camp Liberty.*

After that, the message gave a list of the affected communities.

"Do you think it's time to go?" Shasta asked.

"I don't know," I told her. "I think we're better off
here—with the Army."

"Maybe," she said.

A large trailer was now just outside the applicant door.
Shasta dragged me out there a half-hour before service so
we could be the first in line. A sign was staked into the
grass in front of it:

3d Cavalry Regiment
DFAC

"Blood and Steel"

"That's not a very good advertisement," Shasta remarked.

We heard a strange noise—it sounded like jets. Both of us surveyed the sky, but it was impossible to tell what direction it was coming from.

"Oh! Look!" she said, pointing east.

A thin, dark shape was a couple hundred feet in the air, gaining altitude and turning south.

Shasta followed it with her eyes. "Long Beach, you think?"

"Probably."

We heard another one throttle up. It went east and just kept going that way, and another one flew out going east at first, but then turning north. We'd only seen three of them on that big flatbed trailer, but more trailers must've arrived after we'd come down off the roof. A dozen of the drones had lifted off by the time a friendly-looking soldier opened the door for us.

"Welcome, welcome," he said. "My first guests! Come in!" He went behind the counter and picked up a large, stainless spatula. He twirled it around his finger at the spot where the blade bent. "What's yo name, young lady?"

"Shasta," she said through a grin.

"Wanna tiny appetizer, Shazza?"

"Sure," she said.

He took the spatula by the handle and balanced a cherry tomato at its tip. "Now open yo mouth and be so still," he said. "Okay, raise yo head a little—good." He turned around so his back was to us. With a little jerk, the tomato was airborne. It landed right in Shasta's mouth.

Shasta chewed it. "*Mmmm,* how'd you do that?"

He turned back to us, smiling warmly. "Juss a little trick I pick up in da Middle East."

I looked down the line at the other three cooks. As I met each of their eyes, I received a nod and a smile from each of them.

"Gots da famous pot roast today, season to taste, or if you prefer, Michaelson has prepare a steamy chicken gumbo."

"I'll have the roast beef," Shasta said.

"Me too."

The cooks wore bright white uniforms that were pressed and starched, and black name tags were pinned to their shirts. Our host's name tag said DOOLEY. He produced a large carving knife from a sheath attached to his belt, and he wiped it with a spotless, bright-white rag. He twirled the blade in his hand a few times and then quickly drew it down the roast diagonally, trimming off an end. He kept the knife moving and his actions were rapid—he'd carved perhaps fifty slices of equal thickness in a half-minute. There was a stack of cardboard platters off to his side, the kind with dividers for the different parts of the meal, and he spread out a pair. He slid a couple of slices upon each, and then grabbed a pepper mill.

"Fresh groun peppa for da lady?"

"Yes, please." Shasta was staring at Dooley's hands, entranced.

He ground the pepper mill, moving it in circles.

"For da jennelman?"

"No, thanks."

"Himalayan sea salt for da lady?"

"Yes, please."

"No, thanks," I said.

"Gravy's made from da roast's own drippins. Tell me when…"

Shasta paused until most of the ladle had been emptied out. I only waited a moment.

"Outta da whole day I spenn on dis evenin's meal, I spenn most my time on da slaw. Dressin near took an hour—done from scratch." Dooley gave us both a scoop. "Fo dessert, dey's chocolate or carrot cake. I'm sure is chocolate fo da lady—*always* chocolate fo da ladies."

Shasta was almost drooling now. "Yes, please."

Dooley put a square of a plain cake onto the platter.

"There's no frosting…" Shasta told him, nearly in a whisper.

The answer *was* a whisper: "Oh, yes, *dey is*." Behind Dooley, there was a steel pan on a hot griddle with another ladle in it. He drizzled hot frosting on top of the plain cake.

Shasta grabbed my arm.

Dooley then sprinkled some dark chocolate shavings on top of gooey frosting and handed Shasta her meal. She took it and gasped. Her color had gone pale—I'd never seen anyone go into shock over a meal before.

"I'll take the carrot cake, please." When he handed me the tray, I said, "Thank you, Sir."

"Nodda *Sir* in dis life, fraid. Dis time is *Specialiss*. Or you can juss call me Dooley."

Soldiers were beginning to file in. "Well, thank you, Dooley."

"You welcome." His smile was huge, proud of the reaction he'd gotten from the lady. "See you folks in da mornin."

We went on down the line. The next cook gave us a bowl of salad and some ranch packets. Past that there was water, milk, or coffee. We both filled a paper cup with milk, and we went down the stairs and back into the building.

Shasta started on the cake first. She savored it, swishing it around in her mouth, moaning in long *Mmmmmmmmmmmm* sounds. When she'd finished it off, she seemed reluctant to move on to the other parts of her meal. Instead, she fingered up traces of the frosting, saying, "*Shit, Zeno. Why didn't I join the Army?*"

When Shasta had finished her meal, she said she was going to get chow for Mr. McClusky—and try for a second helping of dessert.

I watched the news. It didn't take much for Hundred Days to have made a spectacle in Glendale. They just lit a couple vacant houses at the base of the Verdugo Hills, where the brush was less like vegetation and more like kindling. The fire spread both ways, down toward the city and then up to the ridgelines. From the cameras aboard Sky5, the hills looked like a volcanoes erupting from the outside in.

In a while, Shasta came back with Mr. McClusky. They both sat and Mr. McClusky started on his slaw.

"Are you comfortable in the break room?" I asked him.

"Slept in worse places," he said, and forked some more slaw. "I'd sleep in the coach, but it's fulla boxes."

"We have cots now."

"Couch is just fine, thanks."

I turned to Shasta. "I think we should move into the labyrinth."

She nodded her agreement—her mouth was full of more hot-frosted cake.

Mr. McClusky tapped Shasta's arm. "You kids should move to the dead-end with the pink fox. Member where that's at?"

Shasta nodded again.

"It's about the furthest place from anything else in there. Good and private."

"*Mmmmm,*" Shasta said, "Thanks, Sam."

It was exactly 7:30 PM when we heard the sound. A thousand soldiers were screaming in unison, all in the same words:

Brave Rifles!
Veterans!
Baptized'n Fire,
Blood and Steel!

Shasta and I twisted our necks toward the applicant entrance, where the cement wall and the metal doors failed in attenuation. The fear instilled in me was something I'll never forget—it was less of an emotional fear, and more like the Biblical kind—like the fear of God.

When it was over I stood, and heads with curious eyes began rising above cubicle walls only to recede again, making the office look like a life-sized version of Whac-a-Mole. Shasta took my hand, and I had to peddle my legs to keep up with her as she rushed to the door. She started by opening it a crack, and then she slowly widened the gap. When the opening was wide enough, she slid outside and pulled me through.

As I said, I'm not good at estimating crowds, but the number of soldiers was three or four times the number of employees that had been outside the labyrinth on the day the poor Sparkletts guy started outgassing. They were standing dozens deep in an arc stretching from the west side of the building to the DFAC trailer. We walked past the trailer and out into the lane between the grass and the south parking lot's islands. In the center of the arc, Major Kass was giving orders. Lieutenant Colonel Hathaway was standing atop a wood crate, and beside him was a young soldier with a bugle.

"First few rows," the major said, "get on your ass. Next few rows, take a knee. We don't have all day, ladies." When the soldiers had settled in, he took his spot behind the colonel.

Colonel Hathaway stood erect on that crate in his full gear, except his helmet had been replaced by a black cowboy hat.

"*Shit, Zeno,*" Shasta whispered, "*there's so many of them...*"

"Yeah."

A grizzled and wrinkled soldier appeared and took a spot on the other side of the crate from the bugler. He called out: "*Specialist Lutz!*"

The reply was immediate: "*Here, Sergeant Major!*"

"*Private Willows!*"

"*Here, Sergeant Major!*"

"*Corporal Smith!*"

There was silence.

"*Corporal Smith!*"

Shasta whispered, "That's the soldier we met in the labyrinth..."

I nodded.

The sergeant major yelled once more: *"Corporal Smith!"*

The bugler put his instrument to his mouth and began playing. Even I, who'd never had anything to do with the military, could tell the tune by its very first note: *Taps*. It was played softly and slowly, and the colonel, the major, and the sergeant major stood motionless, staring straight ahead all the while.

Some of the soldiers sniffed and wiped their eyes.

When the bugler was done, he stepped back a few paces.

Shasta bent to my ear: *"Wonder what happened..."*

I shook my head, thinking of Octavio's slight smile.

"LISTEN UP!" Major Kass growled.

Colonel Hathaway began speaking; there was no podium or lectern in front of him, and he held no notes: "Been goddamn hundred and fifty years since the last time active-duty soldiers were deployed in combat against fellow Americans. But we've all sworn an oath, and that oath is to support and defend the Constitution against *all* enemies—foreign *and* domestic. This is the first time the enemy has been domestic in a *very* long time, longer in fact than the sergeant major's been alive."

There was some laughter among the soldiers.

"For real now, during the Civil War, his great-grandparents hadn't even been born yet. So the point is, it's been a long, long time. And what's kept the peace here in the States so long? If you go down into Central and South America, and across the seas to Africa, civil warfare is the norm. See—assholes with ideals are common, but they're no different than any flavor of the week. If one of these assholes with ideals seizes power, the civilians may like it at first, but it's not long before they're looking for something better. What they're looking for, even if they don't know it, is the freedom and the liberty and all the other things guaranteed to us by our Constitution. What they're looking for is what we have here in the U.S. of A.

"The peace we've had through many generations is due to the Constitution you've sworn to defend. Sure, these are difficult times, and it's difficult worldwide. But what we Americans do in hard times is lean in, put our back into it, and work even harder.

"Right now, a few assholes with ideals have found some people who will feed on the diarrhea issuing forth from their mouths. These assholes want to destroy the banks that protect our hard-earned pay. These assholes want to burn the homes our families are raised in. These assholes want to destroy the businesses that employ our brothers and sisters, our mothers and fathers, and all the good, hard-working citizens we defend. And—believe you me—they would replace our Constitution with a third-world document that would bring us down to a third-world level: a level where life is desperate, a level where food and water is scarce, a level where all the good things in life are unobtainable."

Colonel Hathaway shouted now: *"Will you fight this enemy?"*

The thousand soldiers shouted: *"Hooah!"*

"I'll take no action against any one of you who refuse this fight. Raise your hand now and I'll send you back to my staff-duty desk, where you can sit and drink pop with the queers in the rear." The colonel waited a few moments.

"Each and every one's a proud soldier, Sir," the sergeant major said.

"Very well," Colonel Hathaway said. "Our enemy has engaged our citizenry and our Constitution. They are traitors. And we're their rider on a pale horse: we shall release upon them a great plague of lethality. They shall fear us greatly, hiding in caves and praying for death, praying for the rocks to collapse upon them so they can avoid our wrath—nevertheless, we shall find them, and make them snort our sulfur and swallow our steel."

Again the soldiers cried: *"Hooah!"*

"Through all this, I want to remind you that we are civilized, professional soldiers. You will shave when the opportunity arises. You will not act the part of the barbarian—those who do will be dealt with swiftly and harshly. You will protect and defend non-combatants, and you will give quarter to any of our enemy who surrenders. Understood?"

"Hooah!"

"Good. Sergeant Major—do you have anything further?"

The sergeant major cleared his throat. "There's gonna be some pain, Troops. Never been a battle without some. Each and every life comes to this world through pain. Think of what your Momma endured pushin you through her *hoochie-cooch*—that's the kind of endurance I need from each and every one of you. In that way, y'all will do your mommas proud, *hooah?*"

"*Hooah!*"

"Alright," the sergeant major commanded, "First Sergeants, have your troops fall back in."

As the soldiers snapped to their feet, I led Shasta back inside. We sat at my cubicle, and soon the soldiers cried out again, loud as gods.

Shasta had assembled our two cots side-by-side, directly under the lights of the dead end with the pink fox in the snow. She got into her cot, and I got into mine. We lay on our sides facing one another for an hour, talking about the soldiers, about what the colonel and the sergeant major had said, and about the war that was starting in the night. Finally, she leaned toward me, and when she kissed me, she still tasted like chocolate. I told her to wait, and then I stood on the cot, opened the lens of the fluorescent lamps above us, and tuned the bulbs until they went out. There was still a little indirect light from outside our little dead end, but it was nice—like mood lighting.

After breakfast the next morning, I watched the news at my desk, but it wasn't really sinking in. I had dreamt about LEGACY in the night, and my mind was dwelling on it now. I was sure the wire labeled with the word went down to IT, so before making a trip down there, I needed to figure out what to do about Gordon. As I was contemplating, a soldier found me and gave me a FedEx envelope.

When the soldier left, Shasta stood. "Seeya for chow. I'll be looking at Sam's paintings."

I nodded and she left.

The letter was from Bob. It was a few (stapled) pages with a sticky note on top. The sticky note said:

> Zeno,
> Post Immediately—Bob

I ripped off the sticky note and read the memo:

> Los Angeles Team:
>
> I've tearfully watched the violence and destruction unfold in Los Angeles over the past couple of weeks. I understand that many of you have had to leave your homes to escape this violence and I want to assure you that I approve of you and your families staying temporarily within the relative safe-ty of the HRW Building. I also understand that the Army is moving into the sur-rounding area, which adds an additional layer of security for you and your loved ones.

Please be aware, though, that HRW Los Angeles has some important corporate duties. For example, payroll for the entire western region is handled at HRW L.A. If we do not continue some basic housekeeping tasks, it is possible for the crisis in Los Angeles to disrupt the entire company.

For now, I am approving a half-day work schedule so you can get basic tasks done. For this you will still receive your full pay. Please review the attachment for other critical housekeeping duties.

Thank you,

Bob Norris
Executive VP, Western Region

I wrote a short addendum and printed it:

There will be a mandatory meeting after lunch today at 1pm. If any of your family members are interested in working for us until the end of this disaster, please have them see me before lunch starts at 11:30.

Thanks, Zeno

I made a hundred copies, passed them out to my employees, and called downstairs to have people come up to get copies for their departments.

24—Shovel It Down And Taste It Later

Thunder-Six
I Want His Trash

We had our meeting. The soldiers had launched several volleys of howitzer fire through it all, but I managed to communicate above the noise. The most pressing issue was to train the family members, and to solve that problem, I paired up the newbies with their own families.

Their half-day being over, the families all relaxed in their cubicles, but I had mounds of paperwork to sign, so I went through the papers one at a time, stamping my name on the appropriate lines. By dinner time, I had a thick stack of new employee files.

That being done, I went into the labyrinth to find Shasta. I tried my best to locate the ants, but ended up lost instead—there was no sense left in me which direction was which anymore. I wound up in a dead end where the moon went to blow its nose, but blew a bunch of meteors out from its craters instead. It was nowhere close to *anywhere* I'd *ever been* in that damned labyrinth.

I saw fleeting images of the Sparkletts guy, and I smelled fleeting odors of his bloated corpse.

At this point I just wanted out. I turned around and walked, making two left turns. Right then, I entered a square room with a passage exiting at the center of each wall. These passages defined eight walls within the room, and upon them were eight enormous canvases—each of them at least four feet wide and ten feet tall. Shasta was standing in front of one, tracing the line of a waterfall with her finger. She startled for a second, and then calmed when she realized it was me. Her smile was broad and mysterious, and I could only see it in profile—she looked at me from the corner of her eye. She put her finger back to the surface of the waterfall. "Hey, Zeno," she said.

"Hey," I said.

"It's so timeless here. I love this place."

"Actually, it's not timeless at all. Do you know what time it is?"

She looked excited. "Time for chow?"

"Yeah, it's almost four o'clock."

"*No*—it *can't* be past one."

"Come on, Babe," I said, but then the waterfall caught my attention too. It was a large stream freefalling off the side of a cliff, and the way it glimmered, the way it was painted in long strokes of the brush, and the way the texture had formed when it dried gave an impression of motion. I looked closer and it appeared as though tiny granules of glitter had been mixed in with the paint. I stared up to down, and left to right at the misty rush, and the glitter's sparkling travelled with my vision.

Shasta placed her hand over mine. "Timeless, Zeno," she said, tracing the waterfall with our fingers intertwined. "Or maybe it's time*ful*. Either way, there's something magical in Sammy's paintings, dontcha think? I want to know what it is." Her stomach made an audible growl. "But right now, let's get some chow."

"Okay."

Shasta thrust a thumb in my direction. "He was a *horrible* boss. Always trying to get me to quit…"

Dooley laughed. "Well, we *do* use civillens in da rear and I *do* need a prep cook, thas for sure. But can't do nothin without talkin to my platoon sergeant. So, I'll aks."

Shasta shot him a gracious smile and curtsied.

Sometime after lunch, out in the south lot, they had set up a dining area in an air conditioned tent big enough to hold a circus in. Instead of taking our meal to the cubicle, I motioned toward the tent, and Shasta shrugged and nodded her agreement. We went inside. There was a center aisle, and to the left and right of it, picnic benches had been set up side-by-side in rows. On the far side of the tent, a captain was going over last-minute plans with his troop.

"Regulator will commence at 2100 hours," the captain said to his soldiers. "By then we'll be at the rally point lining up for our advance to Objective Delta. Can anyone tell me our rules of engagement?"

"Let's sit here," Shasta said while we were still close to the tent's entrance. "No need to disrupt our Army friends."

We sat.

Meat loaf was that evening's fare, with potatoes and greens. I'd never had greens before—there were little flecks of lamb swimming around in it. I ate a forkful. They were a little tart, but the meat added richness to the flavor. "You should try the greens, Babe. I don't know what it is—definitely not spinach, but its good."

Shasta smiled.

"Do you really want to work in the Army kitchen?"

Her smile changed to show a hint of embarrassment. "I should learn how to cook for my family. And I think Dooley's the best cook *ever*."

"Yes," the Captain said, "just a bandana over the face qualifies the person as the enemy. But remember—we cannot fire upon them if they're unarmed and not engaged in destruction—you will detain those people for transport to Camp Liberty. Anyone engaged in destruction may be fired upon."

A soldier asked, "What's armed, Sir? Just guns? What about rocks or sticks?"

"Good question," the Captain said. "A weapon, for our purposes, is anything that can do damage to personnel or property. So, it goes back to the concept of *engaged in destruction*. If someone's holding a stick, don't fire. If someone's waving the stick at you, feel free to fire.

"Now, the vehicles the arsonists use have been described as light pickups. They use a code of two crossed bones to keep from harming each other's homes, vehicles, and property. You may also see a pirate flag..."

"You're right," Shasta said, "these greens *are* good. I'll have to ask Dooley what they are."

"Okay, Troop," the captain said in a broadcaster's voice. "Shovel it down and taste it later. We load our gear in ten, ready for the final mission briefing in thirty." He marched right past us and out of the tent.

A pair of soldiers came in with their platters and sat down in the table right behind me. One of them was oldish, the other was young—very young. If he wasn't in the Army, I'd have said he was fourteen or fifteen.

I started in on my meatloaf. It was moist, flavorful, divine.

The kid started sobbing. "I'm sorry, Sir. Smith was my best friend. And seeing the colonel dead too..."

My brain went, *What?!*

The soldiers at the rear of the tent began filing past. One of them flung his tray at the garbage can by the exit.

"*Three points!*" he exclaimed, dancing around in a circle with his arms up in fists.

"Why would God allow that to happen, Sir?"

"I can't say, Son. There's many times in the Bible where the Lord intervened in human affairs. But most of those times, the people turned away from Him. It's almost as though our faith is facilitated by Him remaining uninvolved. But remember, sorrow and grief are pains only the living bear. Colonel Evans and Corporal Smith are in a place of joy and happiness, a place of abundance and plenty, a place of infinite love and peace."

I looked up at Shasta. She was listening intently.

"Forgive me, Chaplain, but you *all* say that. We don't really know."

Shasta reached across the table and shoved my shoulder. Then she motioned in the direction of the chaplain.

"Don't allow their murders to rob you of your faith, Son. If you do, that evil man, that *murderer* will have won."

I whispered: "*Shasta—we don't want to get involved.*"

She didn't whisper back. "What are you talking about, *Zeno?* We *are* involved!"

I rubbed my forehead with the palm of my hand, and turned around in my seat. "Excuse me, Chaplain. When you're done, may I have a word with you?"

The major looked at us. The chaplain. Us again. Then he lifted his arms at their elbows, shrugging his shoulders like: *What the fuck?*

We were in the S-2, under the camo net, and the backsides of Hummers were pulled up all around, with people in the backs of them flipping switches and turning knobs and monitoring monitors. Mounted onto the cement wall of the backside of the HRW Building were a series of huge television screens. One showed a detailed map of the Los Angeles area, where there were labeled dots in some places moving around. The other screens showed live aerial images. One of the howitzers went off, making the camo netting above us shiver. Fifteen or twenty seconds later, there was a big flare of light from one of the televisions, where an explosion bloomed within a crowd of people.

"Roger, King," a voice said through one of the Hummer doors. "Fire for effect, I say again—fire for effect."

Three more howitzer rounds were fired, and each of the concussions made it feel as though you were being tackled by a 300-pound linebacker. I coughed, and Shasta cleared her throat.

"Chaplain, you have horrible timing," the major said.

"Sir, these civilians know who murdered Colonel Emmons."

The silence lasted only two seconds. The major grabbed a radio handset. "Thunder-six-two, Thunder-six, over."

"Thunder-six-two."

"Report to the S-2."

"Roger, Sir. Over."

"Thunder-six, out. Ghostrider-six, Thunder-six."

"Ghostrider-six-delta."

"You got a twenty on your six? Over."

"Roger, he's at the DFAC. Over."

"Relay that he's needed at the S-2. Time: Now. Over."

"Roger, location: S-2, time: Now. Over."

"Thunder-six, out."

The major regarded us with cold, cunning eyes. He threw the handset and it skipped off the plywood table like a flat stone skipping on a pond. It hung now as a pendulum on its curly black wire.

The major was an animal with his teeth bared, ready to lunge at the throat and then tear: *rip and tear.*

A sound like a popcorn popper came across the radio.

"God, shit! Remington Base, Crazyhorse-one-three. Over."

"Remington Base."

There was screaming in the background. *"...hit by an IED, one— FUCK! I'm blocking one-five and one-six."* There was a large boom; screaming came, and some more screaming. *"...going to need to move out. Break."*

311

"Crazyhorse-one-three, Remington Base. Over."

"—ger *Remington Base. My Delta's missing half his face. Wait one.*"

Shasta was shaking, breathing shallowly through her mouth.

The major raged at the chaplain. "Get them *the fuck* outside! What're you thinking? *Civilians in the S-2? What the fuck?*"

The chaplain took us out onto the airstrip. We walked out past it and sat on the curb of one of the parking lot's islands where a tree used to be.

"I'm sorry," the chaplain said, "it won't be long."

Even from where we were, we could hear Thunder Six roaring: *"LISTEN UP! I WANT EVERY MOTHER-FUCKING ASSET THAT'S NOT CURRENTLY EN-GAGED ENROUTE TO CRAZYHORSE. THAT INCLUDES SKY AND BLACKSMITH. GET SCALPEL READY FOR CASUALTIES. DISPATCH REMINGTON NINER-ZERO, TIME: NOW! ARE WE FUCKING CLEAR?"*

A collective *"hooah"* resounded from under the camo net.

"Chaplain?" I asked. "Is it true that you can perform a marriage?"

Shasta and the chaplain looked at me like I was crazy.

And I was like, "What?"

A soldier followed Shasta over to my cubicle, and I guided a different two into the break room. I stared down at Mr. McClusky, who snored away on the couch. When I took a chair at the table, the two soldiers sat across from me. One of them had a lot of sergeant stripes and one of those black armbands with white letters: MP. The guy to his right was tanned, lean, and muscular—the type that would whoop anybody's ass in a bar fight—and he had a gold rank on the center of his chest.

The MP spoke: "I'm Sergeant First Class Tillman, and this is Major Knight, the acting Regimental XO. I'm an interrogator, but interrogation isn't what we'll be doing here. You and I are just having an interview. That's all. I need your answers to be precise. No bullshit. If you don't know, say you don't know. Just tell me the whole truth—don't leave anything out, but don't speculate either. Do you understand?"

"Yes," I said.

"Will you consent to being searched?"

"You don't need to," I said. I unstrapped my knife's sheath and put it on the table.

The MP slid it over to the major.

"That's all I have on me," I said, the gun weighing heavy in my cargo pocket.

"Do you understand why we feel a little tentative?" the sergeant asked.

"I understand the colonel and the corporal were murdered."

"How did you become aware of that?"

"We heard the chaplain discussing it with a soldier in the dining tent."

The MP nodded at the major. The major opened a folder and took out two pictures, placing the first one in front of me. It was the colonel's and the corporal's heads—still in their helmets—severed from their bodies. The faces were pale and their cheeks were sallow, and both of their mouths were gaping; the pale tip of the colonel's tongue jutted past his teeth. The corporal's eyelids were half-open, but the only thing showing of his eyeballs was white. The two heads lay next to each other, facing skywards, and kept from rolling by being propped against a railroad tie.

My stomach squeezed. I burped silently.

The major shoved the second photo across the table. It showed the Hummer with its door open. On the front seats were the two headless bodies—still belted in. Blood had fountained from their necks all over the dashboard and the windshields.

I had to squeeze my eyes shut—*had* to.

When I opened my eyes again, the Major had taken the photos back. "I understand you told the chaplain you may know who did this."

"Yes," I said. "Colonel Emmons wanted to take one of my people who knew the area. So they could get around easier. I had never heard of the rail yard or whatever—*where*-ever they were going. The colonel started asking around. An employee of mine volunteered and left with them."

"What was his name?"

"Octavio Mendez."

The major produced another photograph. It was a security still. A face passing by some sort of guard shack.

"We got this photo from a security camera at Hobart Yard. I need you to be very certain—if you can't be a hundred percent certain, I need to know. Is this your employee?"

I looked at the photo. All the acne scars. The face. And *oh, my God,* the blood covering him everywhere.

"Yes. One hundred percent certain. No doubt. That *is* Octavio Mendez."

The MP spoke: "I need everything you've ever had on him. Give me his personnel file and any work he's done. I want anything with his signature on it. I want his trash."

"Sure. You can have it all."

The two soldiers stood and the major held the door open for me. Shasta was alone at my desk.

"I need Octavio's personnel record," I said.

"I gave it to him already. And I showed him to his cubicle."

I escorted the major and the sergeant there. The officer who had questioned Shasta was at Octavio's desk, wearing gloves, and going through Octavio's trash can.

"I'll let you know if we need anything else," Major Knight said. He handed me my knife and dismissed me with a shooing gesture.

25—Trust Your Army Friends

NO TIME LIKE THE PRESENT
TWO ARE BETTER THAN ONE
YOU GOTSTA BEAR IT
TRACKING THE LEGACY WIRE
THE 6300
APPRECIATION

Major Knight and his soldiers worked quickly. It wasn't even an hour before Octavio's bloodied image had hit the news and, even though I had seen the picture before, the broadcast of it was still a shock. Then the image changed to a less gruesome picture of my friend.

"This is a photograph from California DMV records of Octavio Mendez," the reporter said, "also allegedly known as *El Consumidor*. Army Intelligence analysts based at Fort Huachuca, Arizona were able to make a positive identification based on the results of facial recognition software. The FBI has placed Mendez at the top of its Most Wanted list of criminals. He is currently wanted for at least two counts of murder, twelve counts of inciting a riot, and an as yet unknown number of counts of first-degree arson. We remind the public that Octavio Mendez is considered extremely dangerous and, if you

316

see him, you should not approach him but should call 911 immediately."

"Oh, God, Zeno. He came here to kill you. You *must* know that…"

"Colonel Emmons made a better target."

"What if he comes back?"

"He can't. Every single soldier is going to have his picture. He'd be mowed down before he even got past the first coils of wire. We're safe here."

"What if they don't catch him?"

"If they don't, it'll only be because he went to Mexico."

"I don't know."

"Trust your Army friends. We're safe."

The applicant door opened and the chaplain walked in. He was carrying a plain, manila folder. I waved to him and he walked over.

"How did the interviews go?" he asked.

I stood, saying, "Just fine."

Shasta nodded her agreement.

"Well," the chaplain said, "I appreciate you guys letting us know. Colonel Emmons wasn't just our CO— he was very special to us—to all the men." He held out the folder. "This is the paperwork you need. Just fill it all out, find me at chow in the morning, and we'll set up a time for a ceremony."

I opened the folder and there were a few forms inside. I put them on the desk and extended my hand. "Thank you, Chaplain."

He shook my hand. "No problem, Sir. See you in the morning."

It seemed sad to me: processing Octavio's termination made me the last long-termer in personnel. While I readied a third orange envelope for that period's terminations, Dooley's platoon sergeant had Shasta fill out some paperwork. She had to get a security clearance just to prep vegetables.

Later that night, Shasta and I were both lying awake, staring at the ceiling. "You deserve a full wedding, with a dress and flowers and your family there. We can wait."

Shasta turned on her side, facing me and wrapping her arm around my waist. "No time like the present, Zeno."

She closed her eyes.

It was omelets and hash browns in the morning. I gave the chaplain the paperwork and he asked when we'd like to do the ceremony. Shasta told him *right away*, and the chaplain said he could be ready by ten o'clock.

We didn't have any nice clothes—we wore what we had on that day. As we entered the chow tent, we exchanged our rings and Shasta left again quickly. At the far end of the tent, an arch made from Eucalyptus branches stood, and as I approached it, the fragrance became powerful. To this day, that aromatic scent reminds me of our wedding.

The chaplain's assistant dinged out a tune on a portable piano the size of a suitcase. I turned around.

Mr. McClusky was dressed in a tuxedo, with an arm hooked around Shasta's, which he braced himself with so he could stand fully erect. Now he *did* look like James Bond, albeit at a very late time in life. Shasta was just beaming, and even if she had worn a wedding dress, I wouldn't have seen it. All I remember of this moment was her face, and that hypnotizing smile I loved so much.

Mr. McClusky gave Shasta away, and I received her.

The chaplain didn't soliloquize, he simply read from Ecclesiastes:

Two are better than one
because they have a good reward for their labor.

For if they fall, the one will lift up his fellow.
But woe to him that is alone when he falleth,
for he hath not another to help him up.

If two lie together, then they have heat.
But how can one be warm alone?

We exchanged our vows. Put our rings on each other's fingers. And kissed.

A couple weeks after the wedding, Dooley found Shasta saying she could come to work. She was overjoyed. She started the next day at the crazy hour of five-thirty in the morning. The earliest she'd ever finished was seven at night, but she loved the work, and she was always excited to tell me all the wonderful things she was learning. I was glad that she was enjoying herself.

The different troops of the regiment would go out for a week at a time, but they always got their chow. Shasta told me about all the food they made. Even though all of it was prepared in that funny trailer, only a small amount of it was served there. Most of it got packed up in airtight, insulated crates and driven out by the supply soldiers to where the troops were. The privates in supply would tell the cooks all the stories of what was happening at The Front—where the troops were actually engaging the rioters and destroying the remaining pockets of resistance.

One of the Stryker elements—the soldiers in the boat-looking vehicles—came back right as dinner was starting. Shasta and I talked as she heaped spoons of chow onto my tray. I wasn't interrupting her work or anything, but I did come in for my three meals a day, and she'd tell me what she'd prepped, what she'd peeled, and what she'd pureed. She had just handed me my tray when her face went white.

The soldiers of Grim Troop were filing in the door. Their uniforms were dusty, torn, and some of them were bloody. They took off their helmets as they came in. Their hair didn't have the familiar high-and-tight cut to them. Many of them hadn't shaved in days. They all looked beat.

One standing beside me had a bright, blistering burn across his face.

Dooley dragged Shasta beside one of the ranges and faced her away. He was grinning in that smooth, easy-going way of his.

"Listen here, Shazza," he said. "Dese are men fightin fo us. Keepin us safe. I know how you feelin when you see that. But you gotsta bear it: smile now, cry later. Unstand? You clean yo face."

She wiped her tears away.

"Now you got yo gloves dirty. Change em."

Shasta snapped off the old gloves and put new ones on.

"Good. Now let me see yo pretty smile. Is what we do here."

Shasta smiled pretty.

"Okay. Keep it up now." He turned to the soldier with the burned face. "You gonna love our fresh turkey today, Sommers! Better den Thanksgivin—so *moist!*"

"Can I have a drumstick, Dooley?"

"Sho can, my man. Tell ya what... We gots eight turkeys fo here in da rear—I'll give ya *two* drumsticks. How's dat?"

The kid smiled. It looked uncomfortable, but he didn't appear that way at all. "Thanks, Dooley. You're the best!"

"Naw—ain't nothin like you guys. You know dat."

I left the trailer. As the door closed, I saw Shasta gleefully spooning out mashed potatoes.

It's a hard admission, but it was nice having Shasta busy at work because I still hadn't hunted down where that LEGACY wire came out downstairs. I wanted to see what it plugged into, and I didn't want to have to explain my obsession to anyone—not even Shasta.

I knew the dead end where we slept was close to the ladder, so I started at the cots and, after grabbing a pen and paper, worked my way from there. I'd found the ladder in just a few minutes, and now I needed to estimate how far it was from the ladder to the stairwell. I couldn't tell with the labyrinth's walls in the way. I climbed the ladder to the roof and paced the distance from the edges of the building to where the conduit was below.

I went back down and began working my way to the stairwell.

It took about an hour to find Gordon's stripe. When I made it to the stairs, I went down to the first basement, home to Security and Gordon's IT Department. I stayed close to the south wall, which is where I hoped to find the conduit poking through the ceiling. I went west until the corridor ended, and paced my distance eastward. A wall was in the way, about ten paces short of my goal.

In that corridor, I could only turn left, so I did.

Halfway to the north side of that floor, there were two glass doors. The one to my left said:

SECURITY

Authorized
Personnel
Only

To the right, the other door said:

Information Technology

Gordon Goulet,
Director

I entered the IT department.

The room was alive with one-sided conversation, though from the department's entrance, you couldn't see anybody past their cubicle walls. I scanned the room looking for anything standing out, denoting where Gordon worked, but there was no secretary's desk, no office-in-a-corner, no nothing. The outsides of each cubicle were adorned with similar riff-raff: greeting cards, printouts of internet cartoons, pictures of children.

Way off to my right, I spotted the three conduits poking through the ceiling, so I walked over. The thick one went to a large, locked box with hundreds of thin wires coming out of it, and from there, all those wires ran into a cabinet. The medium sized conduit went to another locked box labeled *Pacific Telephone.* The small-sized conduit ended about two feet down from the ceiling, where dozens more of the tiny, colorful wires fanned out and led to the back of an antique PC. The branding on that PC said *AT&T*. I figured LEGACY must've had something to do with the old phone system we had—I didn't know AT&T ever manufactured computers. Sitting on top of the PC, a monitor was partially blocked by a note:

DO NOT TOUCH
—Gordon

I flipped the note up and out of the way.

On the screen was a dumb prompt, in monochrome peach:

>   >_

Taped on the desk was a cheat sheet. Both the paper and tape had yellowed, and the ink had smeared through hundreds of coffee rings, but I could still read what it said:

BACKUP C:	Record backup on tape drive
LOTUS LEDGER.XPS	Start Accounts Ledger
TRANSMIT	Send files to Home Office
SOD	Do start of day processing
EOD	Do end of day processing

The computer's keyboard was a boxy thing with cubic keys. I typed LOTUS LEDGER.XPS and pushed EXECUTE, which is what that keyboard called the

ENTER button. A spreadsheet opened up, and I scoured the menus for a search feature and found one. I searched for 4114.

In column DG, or *way* the hell off to the right, it said LEGACY ACCTS-DO NOT USE. DH said Pioneer. DI said AFC. DJ, -K, -L, and -M said FIB, Arcapita, HDL, and MRW.

At DH-4114, there was an entry:

2,306,971,455.86.

Below it was an account number. I scribbled them both down, and selected File and Open. A list of hundreds of accounts was there. I scrolled through them until I found the one matching it.

The account activity showed two entries per month:

```
XFR LABOR MCCLUSKY, S      (10,250.00)
INTEREST ACCRUAL           11,534,857.27
```

I stuffed the paper and pen into my pocket as I scrolled through years—*decades*—of entries like this. There were no entries other than Mr. McClusky's labor and the interest accrual since the early 1980s. I scrolled all the way back to the top of the spreadsheet to the account name. It said, ACCOUNT 4114 - FRANCHISE FEES AND CASH RESERVES.

I closed that file and found another called ACCOUNT HELP. It was a long list of the account numbers, followed by their titles. I scrolled until I found ACCOUNT 5000 - LABOR. Accounts 5000 to 5099 were job codes for

Pioneer's corporate positions. 5100 said REGIONAL MANAGER. I kept scrolling. 5110 said AREA MANAGER. 5111 said RESTAURANT GENERAL MANAGER. 5112 said ASSISTANT RESTAURANT MANAGER. 5113 said SHIFT MANAGER.

And then, there it was: 5114 - CHICKEN COOK.

I'd seen enough—I moved the highlight on the screen toward Quit.

A hand yanked on my shoulder. *"WHAT ARE YOU DOING!"*

It was my first instinct: I swear it had no malice in it. I reached over, flipped off the computer, and turned around. Gordon stood no more than an inch away from me, puffing through his nostrils, with several veins on his face looking ready to burst. I was sure a fist would soon be thrust through my face.

"YOU CAN'T SHUT OFF THE 6300!"

"I'm sorry, Gordon..."

He started with a low growl, and in a continuous exhale, it went from that low growl to a high-pitched wail.

I slid away from the computer and away from Gordon. In that instant, every phone in the place began ringing. I started hearing, "HRW, this is *so-and-so*, how may I help you? I'm sorry, the 6300 went down momentarily, we should have you right back up. I'm so sorry..."

As I stepped slowly backwards, Gordon flipped the computer back on and faced me.

"You just killed the 223rd Bank's operations from coast-to-coast!"

"Oh," I said, continuing to step back. "At least Hawaii's still up, huh?"

Gordon was experiencing his own private earthquake.
I ran out of there. Fast.

The next morning, Shasta got up at her God-awful time.

Out past the dining tent, the regiment had a trailer with a dozen shower stalls. The soldiers had made "female time" 5-6 AM or 10-11 PM. So, she was up at five, into the shower, and prepping for breakfast a half-hour later. That morning, I found it hard to fall back asleep— my mind kept replaying Gordon's freak-out. I finally gave up at seven and got some breakfast.

When I got to my desk, I had an e-mail from Bob:

Zeno,

With much consideration due to the current events unfolding in Los Angeles, HRW International has decided to discontinue our operations in Region 601. We feel that a) Los Angeles currently does not have the proper infrastructure to support operations, and, b) the state of the job market after the crisis has concluded will lead to high costs.

This does not mean we do not appreciate all of our Los Angeles team members and what they have done for us. We have leased a building in Denver where there has been little civic disruption. Should any members of your team wish to relocate, we are offering to reimburse them for any expenses incurred in doing so.

If any members of your team do not wish to relocate, they will need to be involuntarily terminated (code 55: laid off due to business closure). This will leave them eligible for benefits with the state employment division.

The closure of Region 601 will be effective next Friday evening, at 5 pm. Until then, I have enclosed guidelines on packing up the corporate equipment and paperwork as well as how to ship it to the new location in Denver.

Again, let me reiterate: I appreciate all that you and your team do!

Sincerely,
Bob Norris
Executive VP, Western Region

Unless Shasta and I moved to Denver, I would be unemployed in two weeks.

All those clichéd phrases of instantaneous action drifted through my mind like echoes: *carpe diem*, opportunity never knocks twice, no time like the present, never put off for tomorrow that which can be done today, if you snooze you lose, the early bird gets the worm... I decided now was the time to take a chance.

I wrote a memo. It said:

> To: Accounts Payable
> Re: Acct. #001004601-0596174114
>
> Please transfer the funds from the account number above into Acct. #114000674-5529877227.
>
> Sincerely,
> Bob Norris
> Executive VP, Western Region

I put the memo into the AP envelope and assembled the rest of the period-ending paperwork. I called FedEx for an immediate pick-up and walked the box to the soldier at the gate.

26—Don't Go, Zeno

HEY, FUCKFACE!

When I came back from the gate, the phone was already ringing. I answered it while giving the camera a guilty look.

"This is Bob. Gordon's been sending me a bunch of long e-mails. In every one, each paragraph has the name *Zeno* in it, along with some very derogatory remarks. Do I have to read all this, or do you want to tell me about it?"

This is it, I thought. *It's been a nice run, but now I'm thoroughly fucked.* My hands were shaking and the vibration was being picked up by the handset's microphone. I moved my neck so the handset was between my ear and shoulder, and pivoted away from the camera so I was facing my desk. "I accidentally shut off Gordon's precious computer."

"Yeah, everyone at 223rd went crazy over that."

"It was an accident. I bumped the power switch, and Gordon freaked. It was like watching the Hulk transform."

"He said I should fire you. That you were going through account numbers."

"Not true. An account number showed up as part of a global search—that's all. I was searching for Mr. McClusky's old file."

She was silent.

"Mr. McClusky," I repeated. "I told you about him. He's retiring."

"Right—you thought he had benefits…"

"And he *does.* He's been working for this company since the 1960s."

"What?"

"Yeah—and he *does* have retirement. You should call Payroll. They've got his file now. It's out of my hands."

There was a pause. "Okay, Zeno. Good job getting all that sorted out. But I'd stay away from Gordon for a while."

"Alright." I continued to face my desk so she couldn't see the relief wash over my face. My rapid pulse slowed, the weak feeling in my chest abated, and the trembling in my limbs calmed.

"Did you see we bonused?" she asked.

I hadn't looked up the numbers in so long, I had no idea—but it didn't seem possible. Other than some family members, we hadn't hired anybody in a good long while, and presently, we weren't even one-third staffed.

"By the skin of our teeth, Zeno—but we bonused."

I was going to ask *how*, but she hung up.

I immediately looked up the numbers.

Bob had adjusted the targets, making them easier to hit.

It was a day in the middle of the next week. Shasta had gone to work and I was in my cubicle watching the news. The President was approaching the podium, live from Washington, D.C. Out there, it looked like a beautiful day. Here in the West, the day hadn't quite started yet.

Text crawled along the marquee at the bottom of the screen:

> **BREAKING NEWS:** 12 RIOTERS AND 1 SECURITY GUARD DEAD AFTER AN OVERNIGHT ASSAULT ON MGM STUDIOS. SECURITY GUARDS SUCCESSFULLY DEFENDED THE STUDIO AGAINST APPROXIMATELY 100 RIOTERS—

"Good morning," the President said. "Today, I'd like to talk to you about jobs. There is nothing I do of greater importance than job creation. There is no task I take on more seriously than job creation. There is nothing more vital to our families' welfare than job creation.

"This month, as July draws to a close, we have seen more jobs created than at any other time in history.

"America is going back to work.

"And so, my fellow Americans, this long-lasting lull in consumption, this scandalous squeeze on finances, this Great Recession of business is now finally over.

"We need not worry about how we're going to feed our children. Consider Arthur Durant of Biloxi, Mississippi. He started a business building fiberglass boats in his back yard two years ago. This month he added twenty-six new workers to his payroll. All of them well-paid manufacturing jobs.

"We need not worry about home ownership. In Coeur d'Alene, Idaho, Michaela Brown started her own construction business, focusing on energy-efficient, Green technologies. This month she added 110 people to her payroll—and the homes they manufacture sell for only $80,000.

"And we need not worry about employment in general. Yesterday morning, I talked with Roberta Norris, of Denver, Colorado."

At this, my ears perked up.

"As Vice President of a large company, she was responsible—since January—for creating 2,800 jobs in Los Angeles, 1,100 jobs in Seattle, 850 jobs in Reno, and 600 jobs in Los Cruces..."

I was like: *Woo-hoo! My department created the most jobs!*

But then I was like: *Who are you kidding? No one's creating jobs here. It's the same job over and over again! I'm just turning them, burning them, faster.*

And I thought of those jobs in Biloxi and Coeur d'Alene and wondered if they were any different than the ones here at HRW. Or, if any job is really any different. Maybe it's all busy work. Busy work until death—when you may rest at last.

Shasta was on a ten-minute break when she found me. "Sammy's got to talk to you," she said.

I was packing up files for Denver. "Can it wait, Hon?"

"Nah," Mr. McClusky said, "don't think it can wait none."

I swung toward him in my chair.

"With the evacuation and all, seems as though it's the right time for me to go. Got all my goods packed up in the motor coach anyways. And..." Mr. McClusky pointed to the monitor, where cops were dragging a family out of a makeshift shelter erected beneath a freeway underpass. "You can see everythang here's goin to hell at a furious pace. So, I'm gonna git before they force everyone to go to that damned camp in the desert. Wanna lay my doormat down in Lake Havasu City—ever heard of it?"

"Spring Break," Shasta and I said in unison.

"Yup—that's right. I hope to git on the road tomorrow. Michael and his family are waitin on me."

I considered what I'd discovered about LEGACY. I worried Mr. McClusky's retirement would come from the account I was in the process of stealing. "I'm sorry, I just need to go down to payroll and see if they've wrapped everything up."

"Yes, she told me you gave them my file. Lady said long as you terminate me with the code 'Voluntary Retirement,' it'll go smooth as silk."

I clicked on the Pioneer, selected *Personnel Actions*, and *Terminations*. I put Mr. McClusky in the queue. I selected the category he mentioned and the printer spat out his paperwork. It was a thin stack—I finished stamping it within a minute.

I gave him a copy of his termination.

Mr. McClusky took it and verified it had been done correctly. "You kids should come with me," he said.

Shasta looked at me, scanning for my reaction.

"This is our home," I said.

She let out her breath harshly. "I have to go back to work." She turned to Mr. McClusky. "Don't leave without saying goodbye, Sammy."

Mr. McClusky smiled. "Don't you worry—I won't."

There was a long line for lunch, and I was at the end of it, a good hundred feet from the trailer. The soldiers were in high spirits, although many of them looked like they'd been tied to a bumper and dragged down a cobblestone road. I waited and thought of Shasta standing behind that low glass counter—and smiling. She was so beautiful, you see, that every single one of these men waiting in line ahead of me bothered her when they got to the grill.

With those soldiers came their smell. It was a pungent man-musk. You smell musk on animals and it doesn't seem so strange. It's not body odor—that man-musk was a strange, highly individualistic odor. Only composed over weeks of hard work, from day and night fighting and maneuvering, from the chemicals of muscle exertion secreted from the pores, from the dust and dirt and environmental grime, from the continuous sweat absorbed by their uniform, from the natural skin and hair oils, from the incomplete bowel movements because they had to stop shitting to fight, and, yes, from the piss in their pants when the fighting became especially fearful. It makes your eyes water. But, you see, it's the smell of a man who does dangerous things, who risks his life, who goes ahead and pisses his pants but then blows the kneecaps off of the dickhead who's kept him and his brothers frightened for so long. And all these men, when they filed past Shasta—they did their little routines, but I couldn't blame them for it—they thought she was hot just like I did. I moved slowly forward within that fog of musk, holding my breath at times—and even gagging at other times—but I eventually made my way inside the trailer.

"Hey there, good lookin!" I said. Shasta was on the grill that day. "Wanna go for a tour of the shower with me?"

"For *you*, totally," she said with her occupational smile.

"Cheeseburger."

She dropped down a patty. It sizzled spatteringly.

"Shasta," I said.

She looked at me. "Zeno, we should reconsider Sammy's offer."

I ignored that. "I need to go out this afternoon."

Her chow-hall smile disappeared. "*What?* Why?"

"HRW is closing down the Los Angeles region in two weeks. I need to see how much money is in the bank, and I want to check on the house."

"No," Shasta said adamantly. She flipped the patty and put a slice of cheese on it. "Don't go, Zeno." She opened up a bun and put it on a plate.

"I have to, Shasta. If I don't, we'll be forced to go to the camp."

"Or we could go with Sammy!" She lifted my patty, put it on the bun, and passed the plate to Private Folsom. He tonged a heap of fries beside the burger.

"I'll be back for dinner," I promised, but I wasn't sure she heard me—her smile had reappeared as she took a soldier's order.

I went to my cubicle and set down my lunch. I watched the coverage on KTLA for a while. It was brutal.

Back when Long Beach had fallen to the rioters, people had flocked to the university and claimed it as spoils. Pilgrimages to the burned pyramid arrived daily, and as the press interviewed the travelers, they would ask where they had come from. Some had travelled short distances, like from San Dimas, East L.A., or Riverside. Others had travelled from as far away as Indio, San Diego, or San Francisco. Most of these people weren't rioters—they were just fools who had become enamored of a movement. Many of them had even brought their children. And each of these people wore their colored bandanas proudly, even on this morning, when rioters, protestors, and fools alike were slaughtered *en masse*. I watched it live. As the Stryker troop arrived, the few rioters within the crowd of fools began throwing their Molotov cocktails. The machine guns on top of the Stryker vehicles were on remote control—there were no helmeted soldiers sticking up through the turrets' hatches—and they began firing, mowing down everyone there. Those huge cigar bullets didn't just blast holes in the people they struck. No—the people exploded like water balloons, and those water balloons were bursting by the hundreds.

This was the *Massacre at Long Beach*. And it was the soldiers of the 3rd, headquartered at HRW, that did the killing. Was it wrong? Well, would *you* bring *your* children into the center of a warzone?

I don't think answers exist for those questions.

When I finished my burger and fries, I turned the monitor off.

"Mr. Jacobs?"

I turned around—it was Dooley.

"They's cameras here, yeah?"

I nodded.

"Where can we go?" he asked.

I stood. "Follow me." We were both silent as I walked him through the labyrinth to the coffee machine. I said, "We're good here."

From under his apron, he produced a pistol. He released the clip, checked it, cleared the pistol, and put the clip back in. "Mag's full."

"What's up, Dooley?" I asked nervously.

"Take it. Ain't on da books. Is an old M-9 thass listed as destroy. Armorer's a buddy a mine. You use it if you need it. Go on, show me how to slide it back."

He was holding it out to me, but I didn't take it. "I've got a gun, Dooley." I reached into my cargo pocket and brought it out.

"Lawd, is *that* a *Loogah?*"

"Yeah—it's a Luger."

"You need to ditch dat shit. They lookin for a white boy with a Loogah—held up a grocery semi."

I felt a surge of adrenaline. "Well, it wasn't me."

"Don't matta. Dey ain't doin no trials. Trade me—I'll dissemble it and scatta da pieces."

He took the Luger and gave me the M-9.

"Thass the safety," he said, pointing. "Be careful cuz when da safety's off and da hamma's cock, juss a little presha set it off."

"Why're you doing this, Dooley?"

"On count of yo woman. She love you. She scared shitless." He elbowed me. "Now you hide dat good—dey shoot anyone gots a gun in they hand."

"Okay. Tell Shasta she'll feed me chow tonight—I promise. Okay?"

"Yes, Sir."

"Alright. Thanks, Dooley." I showed him out of the labyrinth.

I left through the applicant door and walked to the gate. I told the sergeant of the guard that I'd be back late in the afternoon. He said *whatever* and continued thumbing through his phone. The Sparkletts truck was now being used as a barricade. Once past it, I was out on the streets of Los Angeles.

I'd never realized visual cues were how I got around, but I became acutely aware of it once I'd gotten a few blocks north. Most of the larger commercial buildings still stood, but all that was left of the residential neighborhoods, other than rubble and blackened trees, were street lamps and telephone poles. As I continued on my walk, I slowly recognized what businesses had been targeted. Every restaurant and convenience store had been smashed. Every cash store, pawn broker, coin dealer, and jewelry store—the same. Every real estate office, insurance agency, and utility company was hit as well. But very few of the sole-proprietorships had as much as a broken window. I wondered, with the civil rioters, how things could work out that way. I wondered if it was an effect of social media, but there was no way to know.

There was no chance any banks within walking distance had survived. But since the grocery stores were protected by the National Guard, I hoped they still had ATMs. I would go home and see how bad it was, and from there I would walk to Ralph's and check my account.

I knew the major streets, so I stuck to them. When I passed under the freeways, I was amazed by the lack of traffic. There had been two semis and a car that passed above me the whole time I was within earshot—and that was it. I stayed on Pico until it gets to where it wanders south, skipped over to Wilshire, and then took Fairfax north into West Hollywood.

I spared myself another trip down Melrose and proceeded into the flatlands that used to be my neighborhood. It still had that artificial stench to it. I wondered where all the people had gone, I wondered how they would ever be able to rebuild, and I wondered how the hell my house at 825 North Vista Street still stood.

As I got closer, it looked less and less right. I couldn't see any reflections from the windows, there were no sprinklers on the roof, and the landscaping had changed somehow. I crunched through a neighbor's property until I was onto the sidewalk of Vista Street. Mr. Clean was gone—I gave thanks for that. I walked over to the curb where I'd dumped his body, and discovered a code that had been spray-painted in orange on the asphalt in front of it:

$$\Delta 892$$

I wondered what that could possibly mean, then I turned and went up the driveway.

Behind me, a vehicle ground to a stop. I turned. It was a cop. He didn't get out with his hand on his gun— he got out with his gun already pointed at me.

"*Hey, fuckface!*" he said.

I immediately raised my hands.

"Where do you think you're going?"

"This is my house, Officer."

"Right." Now he brought his left arm up to join his right one, and he was squinting along the gun's sight.

"The address is on my license. Can I show you?"

"*Put your hands on your head.*"

I did.

"*Don't move.* Where's your license?"

It was funny—instinctively, I went to reach for it, but at the same time, his instruction for me not to move kept my hands on my head. The result was a small jerk of my elbow and nothing more. "It's in my back pocket."

"Face away."

I turned my back to the officer. I heard him walking, and then I felt the barrel of his gun on my back.

"You even so much as twitch and your right lung is going to have a ventilation hole. Any drug needles or anything? You're gonna die if I get stuck."

I thought of the gun. It was in a cargo pocket down by my knee on my right pant leg. "No needles—swear to God."

His hand went into my back pocket. He retreated down the driveway with my wallet. "Keep your hands where they are. Face me again." He compared me with my picture. He searched around the front of the house for an address. My address numbers weren't there anymore, so he checked the sidewalk.

I saw his eyes go to them.

He holstered his gun. "Well, shit, Sir. I don't know how many hundreds of people have given me *that* excuse. You're the first one who was actually telling the truth."

"Can I put my hands down?"

"Of course," he said. He walked up to me and gave me my wallet back.

I pocketed it.

"I came here a couple weeks ago and some gang-bangers were stripping the wires out of the walls. A week before that, I chased a truck that had all your appliances in it. Dispatch made me break off pursuit and resume patrolling. We're spread so thin…"

I nodded. "Sure."

"Well, I apologize, Sir. You know, this is the only house in this neighborhood that hasn't seen a lick of flame. Were you insured?"

"No," I admitted.

"That's a shame. But I hope you can fix her up again. It would be a nice testament: the house that survived the nightmare."

"That's a nice thought," I said.

He held out his hand and I shook it. "Have a good day, Mr. Jacobs. As good as it can be."

"Thank you, Officer," I said.

He got in his car and left.

I finished my walk up the driveway.

27—The Old House

My grandfather's name was Jacob Jacobs. That must have been some kind of joke by my great-grandparents, who were dead by the time I had come into the world, and who my grandfather rarely mentioned. I called my grandfather *Pop*.

Pop was a film editor and a good one—not that I know anything about the subject—but if I gave you a list of his movies, you'd recognize most of them. He never had any time off between films. In Hollywood, that means you're good.

As Pop worked, Grandma, who I just called *Ma*, would take care of little Zeno. When I was seven, Ma succumbed to a long bout of pneumonia. About a month after her funeral, Pop retired and took over full time Zeno-raising duty.

Pop was hard, disciplined, and opinionated, but he liked to have a good time. We'd stay up late sometimes playing games—not video games, mind you—*real* ones: Chess, Stratego, Risk, Othello, Rummikub... Sometimes he'd instruct me about politics while we played, and current events were always favorite topics of his. Many times, the news made him angry, and sometimes enough so that he would talk of moving to Canada. But he was never really serious about that.

The NBC Nightly News was a staple of our family on the weeknights, and on Sundays, it was 60 Minutes. If I said a word while either of those shows were on, he would hold his finger up: *Quiet!* Only during the commercials could I ask questions or comment. He, however, commented continuously: *Morley Safer was better than this schmendrik! ... Oy, gevalt! They're back on this story again! ... Look at this schmuck—he's starstruck by the President; he'll never ask him a Mike Wallace question, you wait and see!*

School, news, and games were my daily routine until graduation, when it became work, news, and games. Though all my friends had clanned with others, I was happy with Pop. After Ma died, he'd have never asked me to leave because that would've left him alone. Pop had always needed someone to grumble to, and with the economy all gone to shit, that need of his was, for me, like having an iron-clad contract for free room and board.

But then he had his heart attack.

I was complacent and stupid, going out to have fun— as young people like to do. I left for a day-long excursion to Malibu with some friends. When we got there, it felt as though summer had come early. It was a warm, breezy day in mid-April. The waves were just right. Far from shore, the water peaks flittered in pinpoints of sunlight, and closer in, the breakers crashed in a baritone static. Everyone was surfing but me—I didn't have a board, and had never gotten enough practice to be any good at it. But I played in the surf, took note when the girls got in the lineup, and stared longingly when they dropped in and got into that wonderfully wide stance with their knees slightly bent. As it got toward evening, I began turning blue, so I made a fire and one by one, my friends abandoned the waves and gathered around. There was a girl there I'd known since second grade named Janie. I almost worked up the courage to ask her out, but decided to save it for the next time. That day was the last time I ever saw her, though.

One of Malibu's finest had ridden up on a quad, threatening to ticket us for the fire. So, we snuffed it with sand and rode back into town. After fifteen minutes or so, I felt Vic make a hard turn followed by an abrupt stop. He popped the trunk and helped me out.

"Sorry, Man," Vic said, motioning up the block. "I'll never get turned around if I don't let you out here."

I did a quick stretch and looked up Vista Street toward home. We'd stopped maybe ten houses short of mine. A fire truck, an ambulance, and a couple of police cars were clogging the street.

"Okay," I said.

I waved at my friends as Vic backed out onto Melrose, and then they were gone.

Beach sand abraded my toes as I walked up the sidewalk toward the scene. I wondered which neighbor had set a grease fire in their kitchen, or which of them had swallowed too many pills, or which of them had a clan war going. There was no sense in me that said it could have been *my* house, *my* family, *my* life that was about to be thrown into disarray.

We never think it'll happen to us.

That is, until they roll your loved one past you in a zipped-up body bag.

I was twenty-one years old and alone.

The two weeks I took off from work opened my eyes. Before, I had everything I needed: food, shelter, a ride when I needed one. My paychecks were small, but since everything was provided for, it had all been spending money. Pop's will made it very clear that everything was being passed on to me, but inheritance taxes swallowed most of his estate. I had to sell his car and most of his tools in the garage's woodshop. When I'd sold what I could, I had the house and the furniture but nothing more, and I needed to earn enough income for the property taxes, the electricity, the cable, the internet, the gas bill...

The day I returned to work, I sat at the desk busy, but daydreaming of other things. The most common theme of those dreams was being rich. Most young people do that, don't they? It would've been more productive to think about *how to get* rich, but like I said—I was stupid.

The executives had toured the facility while I was on leave, and Mr. Chandler had hired a catering company to provide lunch for them. I was signing paperwork as he opened the invoice. He gasped at the amount—it was a few thousand dollars—and it was being billed to him personally. He shrugged, saying, "Why are they billing me?" and then he shoved the invoice into the AP envelope.

The same envelope that would soon become my salvation.

Until the Hundred Days Riots.

And now, as I stepped into Pop's house for one last time, I wondered what he would've thought of the riots, the looting, and the curfew. Of the National Guard protecting the supermarkets. Of the U.S. Army being called in to quell the lawlessness.

I think he'd have gone apeshit.

The front window—glass, frame, and all—was gone. So was the front door, as well as the frame I had nailed it shut to. The house was not just emptied—it was stripped. The rugs were gone, and the wood flooring had been pulled up as well, leaving just a plywood subfloor. Not only were the appliances missing in the kitchen, but they had taken the plumbing, the sinks, the cabinets, even the valve in the wall that was for the refrigerator's ice maker. The dining room chandelier was gone—from its mount, a jagged tear went through the plaster along the ceiling. Similar tears were on the walls all over the house. I looked at an outlet—they took the cover, the receptacle, and ripped the copper wires clean out of the wall. The heating ducts that came up through the floor were missing, and through the holes you could see straight down to dirt.

The door leading from the house to the garage was missing. And the roll-up door as well. Even though I'd been the one to sell all Pop's tools, everything he'd built in there was gone—all of Pop's counters, drawers, and shelves. The water heater, along with the pipes bolted to the wall of the garage—gone.

Back inside the house, the toilet in the bathroom—gone. Pipe that the toilet bolts to—gone. The fiberglass tub, its sliding glass doors, the sink, the sink's cabinet, the medicine cabinet, the ventilation fan with its built-in light—all gone.

There was nothing left in the old house, other than a faint, familiar smell, the house's frame, and its roof.

Even outside, the avocado tree had been uprooted and carted off, along with all the rose bushes. All that was left were some decorative shrubs, the black junipers that erupted when Shasta was fetching the hose, and a brown stubbly lawn.

Truth told, I expected worse.

As I walked back down the driveway, a young, unkempt man approached me.

"Anything good in there?" he asked.

"Nah," I said, "it's cleaned out."

The man started to walk past me, but he stopped and turned around. "We could clan here, if you want."

I jiggled my leg, to feel the security of the gun in my cargo pocket. "No," I said, pulling on my shirt to highlight the regimental pin on it. "I'm already clanning with the Army."

He scowled at me and continued inside.

I headed north.

28—The Selma Park Shyster

Those same jack-barricades were there, spread out on the streets all around Ralph's. The supermarket's vehicular traffic was sidelined into a single lane for inspection. The National Guard went over every vehicle. The drivers and passengers were removed while soldiers examined everything with mirrors on poles. German Shepherds were led inside the vehicles to sniff.

Over at the pedestrian entrance, the Guard was searching everyone who arrived on foot.

I needed to ditch the pistol.

I wandered behind a smashed-out luggage store and found a cover to a service valve. Inside, there were sprinkler valves and spider webs. I glanced around and no one was watching, so I dumped the M-9 inside and dropped the cover back in place. That being done, I crossed Fountain Avenue to get in line.

These weren't the gentle searches you'd get at the airport or the train station. The Guard soldiers were getting *all up in it*. A young lady in a sundress was standing with her arms out, and a soldier wearing latex gloves started at her ankles and moved his hands inside her dress to her crotch. He forced her legs further apart. From a crouching position in front of her, he held her dress up slightly, putting his hand through her legs and up above her buttocks, and then he ran the backside of his hand firmly in the crack of her butt, down and over her genitals, and feeling palm-down up to her pubic bone. Next, he took both hands and ran them around her waist from her belly button to the small of her back.

While he was doing this, a second soldier had a rifle pointed at her head.

The first soldier stood. He ran his hands down her arms and back up to her armpits. From there, he immediately placed both his hands on both her breasts and squeezed. He rotated his hands to a different angle and squeezed again. Then, using two fingers of each hand, he felt under the top of the bra cups, and beneath the underwire. He worked the fingers around the strap to her back and then up to her shoulders. When he was done, he nodded to the second soldier who lowered his rifle. The lady retrieved her purse from a third soldier and went inside.

There were seven people ahead of me including a ten-year-old girl. They didn't do it any differently for the child.

When I got to the front, the rifle went up, aimed at my head.

"Put your arms out, Sir," the soldier said.

I did.

"If you have any weapons, even a pocketknife or knuckles or anything—tell me now and I'll retrieve it. If you don't tell me, Private Holt may shoot you. If he doesn't, we'll kick you out."

"I have a knife in a sheath on my belt," I said.

"If you move while I'm retrieving it, Private Holt will fire. Do you understand?"

"Yes."

He took it off my belt and handed it off.

The soldier stood back. "You may bring your arms down. Empty your pockets—*slowly*. Don't make any sudden movements."

All I had was my wallet. I put it in a Tupperware bowl that a third soldier held out for me.

"Is that everything?"

"Yes."

"Hold your arms up again. I'm going to do a full body search. Do not move at all, Sir."

The soldier did the same to me as he had done with the woman and the girl. The firmness of his knuckles made my balls ache, and when he got to my armpits, it tickled horribly. But the rifle aimed at my head turned the ticklishness into a panicky feeling.

Another soldier who had been swabbing my knife said, "No blood."

"Okay, Sir. You can relax." The rifle was lowered. Here's your wallet. Your knife has been tagged with your license number. When you're done shopping, go out the pedestrian exit, walk all the way around the outside of the fence, and they will have your weapon at the spot marked *Property Retrieval.* Have a nice day."

When I got inside Ralph's, there was something I had only seen at Disneyland before, back from Pop's time: *turnstiles.* There was a turnstile at the front door. In addition, each aisle had been segmented off with floor-to-ceiling chain-link fencing and the entrance to each aisle had a turnstile and a register. Mounted above each turnstile was a sign: ENTER HERE. And above each register: PAY HERE.

I found the ATM standing by the turnstile leading to produce. It had a sign as well—DEPOSITS ONLY/OUT OF CASH. There was no line in front of it. I put my card in and entered my pin. I selected BALANCE. It asked, *Would you like a receipt?* I selected *Yes.*

It said, *Please wait while your transaction is processed...*

What the receipt said was:

Your Account Balance is:
$2.30697206E09

I was numb. Mute. Some organ in my chest contracted, giving me a feeling of dread and nausea. I thought of Mr. Chandler's victory dance, and how he did his celebratory lap through the cubicles. I thought of Grace Van Horne holding that huge check, and her rapid gibbering and vapid posturing. Personally, I reacted like neither one of them. I just felt a little sick. I put the receipt in my wallet and left.

After a couple grueling hours of hiking, panting by the side of the road, and hiking some more, I had passed maybe two-hundred burned-out estates. Then there was a saddle between two scorched ridgelines. The homes hadn't been damaged there—where I found Shasta's old house. *This* house. The gate out front was padlocked, which was good news. If anybody currently lived here— back *then*, I mean—I didn't think it would've been chained and locked. The realtors had stopped putting up yard signs because they were an invitation to arson, so they listed all of the homes on websites where you had to enter your personal information to find out the address. The agents installed blinds on the windows and put the lights on timers—that way it would look like somebody was home. I followed the stone wall out there until I found a log to hop up from, and I jumped over the wall.

The landscaping was wild. I followed a weedy path around the back. The swimming pool was only half-full, and the water in it was dark green. Tadpoles swam around in it, and there were those funny little bugs skipping all over the place. I went from the pool to the French doors out back. Inside the house, everything was clean. A faded stick of lip gloss was sitting just inside the locked doors. I wondered if it had been Shasta's.

I turned back to the yard. The water slide had seen better days. It had become sun bleached and cracked. Some of the cracks ran deep enough in its surface that, if you would have used it, it would have dumped you in the water with a nice laceration.

That can be replaced, I thought. *And the landscaping can be trimmed. Yes, Shasta and I will fill this house again. Fill it with furniture. Fill it with pots and pans and dishes. Fill it with children—family. Fill it with love.*

I toured around, spending some time under the huge willow in the side yard. The swing on it was rotted and broke under my weight, so I went around front and tried to jimmy the garage open. I didn't have any luck.

I knew that every second I spent away from Shasta, she was worried, and I didn't want to be late for chow. I wheeled the garbage can over and scaled the wall again. I dropped down the other side and descended the hill into Hollywood.

On the way back, I retrieved my knife and pistol.

When I reentered the compound, the sergeant of the guard waved me through.

I made it to the front of the line at 5:45.

Shasta gave me that smile I loved so much. "Hey, handsome." Tears began to fall.

Dooley slid up beside her.

She wiped her face with an arm. "I'm sorry," she said.

"Naw, dem are tears of joy, now. You go eat, Shazza. I gots it."

"You sure?" she asked.

"Yep. You can take da night off."

She gave him a one-armed hug. "Thanks."

Dooley fixed two platters of steak and shrimp as Shasta came around front.

"Wow, is that for real?" I asked.

"Sho is. Once awhile they have us fix a treat like dis. Good fo morale. They is steak sauce and cocktail sauce on the tables."

"Thanks, Dooley."

"Any time, Mr. Jacobs, any time."

Shasta and I went to the tent.

I sat across from her so I could see her.

She cleared her throat. "I must've deveined like over 7,500 prawns today."

"Bet that was fun."

She raised an eyebrow. "Kinda monotonous, actually, and my hands keep cramping. After all that," she said, motioning to her plate, "he only gives me *six*."

I didn't think she was complaining—it was conversational griping. I played along. "Do you want some of mine?"

"Naw, I wouldn't steal yours. Don't you like shrimp?"

"Haven't had any since I was ten. Eleven, maybe."

Shasta filled a segment of her platter with cocktail sauce. She dipped the battered-and-fried prawn and popped it. She closed her eyes while she chewed. "Oh, so good!"

I tried one. It was delicious.

"Run into any trouble out there?" she asked.

"Almost," I said. "First a cop harassed me at the house, but I showed him my license with the house's address on it. He was cool after that. When the cop left, a guy came along asking if he could clan with me."

"Hope you told him to fuck off."

"You should see the place—it's..."

Shasta looked up from her platter. "It's what?"

"They took everything. *Everything*. The siding, the floor, the wires in the walls. All that's left are the frame and the roof."

Shasta stared at me.

I leaned toward her slightly. "Shasta—they took the avocado tree and the roses. They took *everything*."

She shook her head. "And you're losing your job..."

"They're shutting us down. I have to hold another meeting when we're done eating."

"How are we going to make it, Zeno? I mean, *that's it*, isn't it? Can we go with Sam? But—I don't want to quit my job. *God*, Zeno... It's the only job I ever liked! *God—*"

"*Shasta*—right now, let's just eat. We won't panic." I looked around and there was no one near, but still I lowered my voice. "Listen—we have come into a great deal of money."

She blinked at me. And leaned forward.

"The only problem is the law—"

Shasta whispered: "*What law!*"

I spoke up to a normal volume again. "Come on, Shasta—smile. This food is fit for royalty."

She cut a thin strip of beef from her steak, and sighed while chewing it. When she swallowed, she leaned forward, puckering as if to kiss. I followed her lead and moved in for it, and that's when she grabbed me behind the neck and pressed her forehead against mine—at an angle that held our lips apart. She raised her steak knife so it was in my field of vision. A wide grin appeared on her face and she spoke. "Tell you what, Zeno. If you get in trouble, I'm gonna do to your weenie what I did to these prawns." She nodded with our heads pressed together like that, making me nod too. "And I've practiced 7,500 times." She let go of my neck.

I didn't move.

She drowned her steak in sauce, and cut another strip—a thicker one. She chewed for a moment, and then spoke with her mouth full: "Zeno—this steak is *divine!*"

I sliced myself a chunk, and I chewed it without really tasting it. We'd just had our first fight. And Shasta won—no doubt about it.

She wolfed down her meal, but I was still working on my steak and salad. "Zeno," she said, "I have *good news.*" She said it as though it was a treat, like Dooley's hot-frosted cake.

I didn't know if we were still fighting. I nodded and chewed on a hunk of steak.

"I'm late."

I nodded at her. "Late for what, Babe?"

"No, Zeno. I'm *laaaaate.*"

I put on my best smile, but it was nervous. I leaned across the table as Shasta had just done. She met me partway and this time we did kiss.

"That is *good news*, Babe!"

"Do you *really* think so, Zeno? In *this* world?"

No was my first thought, but a man doesn't tell the woman he loves that. "Of course it is. Things won't be this way forever. Just you wait and see."

It took a while to get the folks up from downstairs, but they all straggled up eventually. I told them about Denver. I said that I would give them forty-eight hours to make up their minds, but they didn't need it. The vote was unanimous—they all wanted to go. They preferred Denver over the internment camp.

After the vote, Shasta talked me into helping out the guys with the dishes in the trailer. I let Shasta familiarize me with wash, rinse, sanitize; how you needed to use copper scrubbies on aluminum, stainless scrubbies on the stainless; she showed me the test strips used for measuring the sanitizer solution; she showed me how to tell the difference between clean and *clean*, the latter being so that food flavors couldn't transfer to the next dish. We had fun getting wet with the sprayer, and Shasta nailed Foster a few times. We laughed a lot.

We left the place spotless, and in doing so, we left ourselves dirty and wet. I wanted to change badly, so we walked together into the labyrinth. At one of the junctions, I turned toward the fox. She tugged me in a different direction.

"I want to go on the roof for a while, to see the city."

"Okay."

She led me through some passages to a place I recognized, where little ants were cutting leaves. The ladder was only a couple turns from there, and we climbed it and went up onto the roof. It was a cool night and we were soaked, so I held her close as we shivered. To the southeast, a bright red light rose into the sky and dimmed away. Another one went up moments later. And then another and another. When the sound arrived, its intensity was muffled by the miles it travelled getting to us: *dunn-dunn-dunn, dunn-dunn-dunn-dunn, dunn-dunn, dunn-dunn-dunn-dunn-dunn, POW, dunn, dunn-dunn-dunn, dunn-dunn-dunn-dunn-dunn, dunn-dunn.*

There was a flash and sparks in the air, all so far away that it was near the horizon. We couldn't tell if the battle was in a neighborhood, a commercial area, or a playground at a school—there was no way to know. The sound from the flash reached us a few seconds later as a boom followed by a sound like the crumpling of tin foil.

"Come on, Zeno," Shasta whispered. "Let's listen to the S-2."

We walked at first, but as the radios became audible, we tiptoed until we were directly above the camouflage nets. The outer wall extended above the flat roof by two feet. We sat and leaned back against it, becoming invisible observers.

"Grim-one-six, we have Blacksmith-niner-two heading your way. Pop smoke and see if we can lighten up some of that fire you're under, over."

"Roger, Remington-six."

There was a pause. We could see those tracers rising into the air again.

"Remington-six, Grim-one-six, over."

"Go ahead Grim-one-six."

The sound came: *dunn-dunn-dunn-dunn-dunn-dunn, dunn-dunn, dunn-dunn-dunn.*

"They lit us up with some Molotovs, but we neutralized them. Break. The coast is clear for Blacksmith. Over."

"Very good, Grim-one-six. Switch over to the Blacksmith net. Remington-six out."

We listened to some operational traffic for a while—much of it had to do with the guards around our compound. It was maybe ten minutes later when a garbled voice came across a staticky line.

"Can you clean that up any?" a voice below asked.

"I'll give it a shot, Sir," was the response.

It was still garbled, but we could understand it. "Remington-six, this is Blackjack-seven, over."

"Nice ta hear from ya, Blackjack. Go ahead, Sergeant Major."

"We've verified the identity of your Charlie, break. We caught him trying to cross into *Ciudad Juarez*, break. Motherfucker's on the Blackhawk Express to Guantan-amo, over."

A cry of celebration went through the S-2.

"All right, gentlemen. Let's get back to work."

Shasta whispered in my ear, *"El Consumidor?"*

"Maybe," I whispered back.

"Thanks for the good news, Blackjack-seven. Remington-six out."

Shasta yawned. I helped her up.

We looked out over what used to be Santa Monica, and past the 10 over toward Hollywood. All we could see was an array of orangey streetlamps. It occurred to me that the power had been back on for days, but we were still on the generator. I figured I could find one of the Blacksmith guys to help me get it switched back over, or maybe Mr. McClusky could do it before leaving... Then again, with HRW shutting down, it didn't really matter.

I thought of my fortune as we made our way to the ladder.

I had 2.3 billion of HRW's dollars in my account.

But was it really theirs?

No, it never had been. If it belonged to anyone, it was the property of Mr. McClusky's old boss, Mr. Kaufman, who had been squeezed out unfairly and unjustly. But he was long dead by then. So I didn't feel bad taking it.

We went down the ladder and to our cots. We changed and then I massaged Shasta's back until she slept. Then I worked on a mental list of all the wonderful things we could buy and do with all that money. My list must've had five hundred items on it before sleep finally took me unaware.

Throughout the riots, Thurman didn't just run occasional banner ads, he nearly monopolized the bottom of the television screen. He knew with all the destruction, people would be hungry to sue. More accurately put, people were desperate for the revenue produced by finding someone—*anyone*—to pin a little blame on. He was still running ads, so there was no doubt his offices were open. Still, there was no way I was going to call or visit his website from HRW because I was too paranoid someone would be listening in or monitoring my computer. So, I needed to walk out there and consult with him personally, and the next morning I told Shasta I needed to leave again. Since she had the day off, she said she would go with me. I was glad to have company for the walk, but I wasn't looking forward to Shasta being with me in the lawyer's office.

As I dressed, Shasta objected. "Oh, no, Mr. Stinky. You're going to take a shower and give yourself a shave. You look like a survivor from a shipwreck, for heaven's sake."

"Okay, okay..." I said. But she knew I wouldn't do any of that before my morning cup. "Coffee?"

"Sure, Zeno. Thanks."

I got a fiver and went. I didn't know my way from the fox to the sombreros, so I worked my way close to the labyrinth's exit and followed the sombreros from there. In the machine's place was a new one—the vending company must have replaced it while I was in Hollywood—and a paper sign had been taped to it that said:

**Please do not shoot
the coffee machine.**

I put the fiver in the slot and had it pour a cup, and then I walked back, gave it to Shasta, and told her why I needed another coin. After I'd gotten my coffee, I took a shower, shaved, and brushed my teeth. The image in the mirror was becoming unfamiliar, and I wondered when I'd be able to get a haircut. Since Shasta had never mentioned it, I suspected she wanted me to grow my hair out.

When I got back, she was admiring one of the fox paintings. It was black and white except for the fox, with a smooth, snowy slope and sparse spruces here and there. Shasta brushed the texture of the snow-paint lightly with her fingertips. It hadn't been glitter in the paint there, it was rougher—perhaps it was pulverized glass. She spoke to me, but continued caressing the canvas. "What's so important that we have to go into the city?"

"Money," I said.

"If you want to go to Denver, I'll go with you."

"I don't want to go to Denver. Do you?"

"No," she said, tracing a bank of snow. "If we have to leave, we should go with Sam."

"I'd rather not leave L.A."

"Okay," she said, and turned around. "Then where *do* we go?"

"This morning we are going to go see Thurgood Thurman the Third."

She turned to me, shocked. *"Esquire?"*

"Yeah," I admitted.

"The guy on TV?"

"Uh-huh."

She was nearly giddy now. *"The Selma Park* Shyster?"

His office wasn't at Selma Park, it was actually over on Wilcox. But Thurman was called that because some investigative reporters had filmed one of his lawyers having a conversation with a low-level gangster in Selma Park. "That's the one."

"About *money?*"

"Yeah."

"Oh, *God*," she said, "I can't wait to be in that room with you. Let's get some chow before we go."

29—Dystopia Now

HOLLYWOOD BOULEVARD
DO TELL, ZENO
WORDS LIKE BULLETS
CALL YOURSELF ZEE-JAY

Dressed in his retirement outfit of khaki trousers, a Hawaiian shirt, and a straw hat, Mr. McClusky stood just outside of the applicant entrance. He slid a pair of chrome-framed aviator sunglasses out of his shirt pocket, put them on, and smiled.

Shasta ran over and embraced him. Though Mr. McClusky's face was buried in her breasts, I could still see his grin—it stretched all the way to his ears.

"Will you have chow with us before you go?" Shasta asked.

Mr. McClusky pulled his face from my wife's bosom. "Better not—wanna make the trip non-stop, if you know what I mean. But you kids could walk me out to the motor coach."

Shasta let him take an arm, and we walked toward the far end of the south lot, moving at his speed—the crawl of the aged.

"Ain't gonna make another plea," he said to Shasta. "I'd be just tickled to have y'all along. I reserved three spaces in the park, right across from the lake. You could pitch a tent till Mr. Jacobs here finds work that pays well. Or, I could even help getcha a cheap trailer or somethin…"

"That's really kind of you, Mr. McClusky," I said. "But I've got some things to do, and we've both been here all our lives—"

"So you keep sayin," he said. "I left Nacogdoches when I was twelve. Ain't never pined for it since. Always been too many pretty women out here."

Shasta beamed at him.

He continued. "Los Angeles was different in those times, Mr. Jacobs—believe you me. Back then, everythang was cheap, the love was free, and the beach was just down the hill. It was like livin in heaven. But it all changed so quickly. There was the killin of Medgar Evers in '63, followed by President Kennedy's assassination. A little over a year later, Malcolm X gets done in. Then, as the elections were gettin goin, King was murdered and directly after, Andy Warhol took a bullet. Warhol survived, but while he's recoverin in the hospital, Sirhan Sirhan shoots Bobby Kennedy in the ear. All through this, we're goin *Peace, man*, but Tricky Dick steals the election, the government starts crackin down on everyone, and then they're declarin war on our drugs. Soon enough, we git Nixon Shock."

"Nixon *what?*" I asked.

"Nixon *Shock*—that's when President Nixon took us off the gold standard. The minimum wage had been $1.60 an hour, but that buck-sixty went a long ways cuz by law that buck portion was equal to one-thirty-fifth an ounce of gold. It was like makin sixty-five bucks an hour today. And today's wages are like makin fifteen cents an hour in '71. Ain't you never wondered why them CEOs are makin hundreds of millions a year?"

I shrugged. We made it to his RV.

Mr. McClusky faced me while still on Shasta's arm. "All them CEOs and executives ain't never left the gold standard, as we regular folk were forced to do. *Forced*, I say. See, givin the blacks their civil rights was somethin that needed to be forced upon us cuz there were so many ignorant racists out there. Forcin the civil rights laws was a good and just thang to do, but look at the resistance there was to it. There were hangins and cross burnins and people takin to the streets on both sides. I'll tell you what—the Vietnam War was another thang forced upon us, and *un*-justly so, and look at the resistance everyone had to *that*. There were people takin to the streets once more, people fleein to Canada and Mexico and Europe, people everywhere claimin to be conscientious objectors. But it wasn't the same with Nixon Shock. Overnight, everybody's dollars became junk, and there weren't no marches, there weren't no protests, there weren't no screams from a single damn soul t'all. Cuz no one really knew what was goin on.

"Now, I managed to keep myself afloat through the years by being mentally conscious and physically scarce—but I can't imagine what you kids'll do. Long ago, when I was your age, this was the loveliest place in the world—a real Garden of Eden. But it's a dystopia now. And you'll never make it here. Not cuzza the fires and the riots and the killins, but cuzza the system."

Shasta used her free hand to shine her necklace at me.

"Why would Lake Havasu be any different?" I asked.

"It's a small town. Most thangs are cheaper there—long as you stay away from the tourist traps—cuz tourists are suckers. I hope to sell my paintins to some of them suckers. I'm sure you can find a way to make a livin there too—a big-shot Director like you."

"Shasta and I will talk about it. We'll let you know."

Shasta gave Mr. McClusky another hug. "I'll miss you, Sammy."

When they were done, Mr. McClusky reached in through his RV's door, grabbed a pad of paper, and wrote on it. He ripped off a page and gave it to Shasta. "Here's my mobile."

"Thanks," she said.

Mr. McClusky got in, started up his RV, and pulled away toward the gate.

Shasta and I ate breakfast, and then walked out to Hollywood.

Shasta had to see the house. We didn't go inside; she accepted my description as truth.

Instead, we stood silently for a while, and then we walked north to Hollywood Boulevard, where we went east on the sidewalk. At La Brea, the boulevard was blocked by at least ten burned-out busses. A police car whooped at us as we approached the intersection. We stepped back to the front of a pizzeria, within some low shrubs. The cop drove up onto the sidewalk, scraping his driver's door on a bus stop bench, and gunned the accelerator. His vehicle bounced back into the street with a metallic crunch and then it sped away.

We passed the Four Ladies monument—it had been defaced with spray-painted penises, and the palm trees on the corner were just sticks rising into the air. The tops of them had all been burned off—how you set fire to the top of a fifty-foot tall palm tree, I don't know, but someone had done it.

Beyond there was a military recruiting center. It had been there as long as I'd been alive—longer, maybe. Like with the jewelry store on Melrose, some very angry people had been in there. It hadn't been set on fire, but it looked like someone had spent a week tearing things up with a chainsaw, and eventually, the roof gave out and collapsed in on the whole mess. After a couple more blocks, we came upon a twisted metal wreck on the street.

Shasta recognized it. "Oh my God, Zeno. That's the sign from the Roosevelt Hotel."

I nodded and looked up: the hotel didn't look damaged. The rioters just wanted to destroy the sign, I guess. We walked on.

The Kodak and El Capitan Theaters were both gutted. A Starbucks had been torched, but all the equipment from inside was sitting on the sidewalk in pristine condition. The Scientology building was pulverized—if it wasn't a wrecking crane that had done it, it had to have been explosives. I thought of the howitzers—*they could do damage like that*, I supposed. Spray-painted on the sidewalk all around the front of the building were more of those delta codes. I was certain by then those codes were where the police found bodies. From what I could tell, six people had died on the sidewalk out front. A short distance away, I saw an arrow pointing into the building:

$$\uparrow \Delta 1847\text{-}1881$$

I wondered if the bodies were still in there. Shasta tugged at me and we moved on. Further down the boulevard, the two steel antenna towers above the old Pacific Theater had drooped so they were leaning out over the front of the building.

We crossed Wilcox and headed south. The offices of Thurgood Thurman the Third, Esquire, were in the third building down.

A huge black man had me in both his hands: one at my right elbow, one at my right wrist.

"Now get it," he said. "Just get it with your thumb and index finger."

He allowed me to extend my hand into my cargo pocket. I squeezed the handle of my pistol as he instructed, and as I pulled it out, his hands still kept control.

"Now I'm going to let go of your wrist and take your gun. If you move, the next thing you'll hear is a snapping sound as your nose hits the pavement."

He took the pistol and pushed a button, shooting the clip out. He put the clip into his pocket and then cleared the weapon. He handed it back to me.

"You don't want it?" I asked.

"Only things that concern me are bullets and blades," he said and took hold of my arms again. "Put the gun back and unstrap your knife."

I did what he said.

He handed my knife to another fellow who looked just like him—they must have been brothers. The brother threw it into a cardboard box that was sitting against the building on the sidewalk.

"Anything else?" he asked me.

"No," I said.

"How about you?" he asked Shasta.

"Nope," she said.

He gave us a brief frisking and let us into the waiting room.

Shasta wandered over to a drinking fountain and sipped from it. At a desk by the door, a large, blonde woman held out a pen. The sticky-note pad she put in front of me said:

Your name and the reason for today's visit in fifteen words or less:

I took the pen and wrote:

Zeno Jacobs, I found 2.3 billion dollars and I want to keep it

The blonde lady ripped the sticky note off and went through a door. She was back in less than ten seconds.

"Take a seat anywhere, Sweetie," she said.

There was only one open seat. I offered it to Shasta and she sat. I took the floor in front of her and leaned back against her legs. All the people there wore the blank looks of those at the DMV or the plasma center. I thought we'd be there for a while, and it was like Shasta read my mind.

"We're going to be here for a while," she said. I could feel her hips shift forward as she slumped back in her seat.

Right then, some guy burst through the door that the receptionist had gone into a moment before. He was wearing a wrinkled business shirt that had its long sleeves rolled up above his elbows. The collar was unbuttoned, and his tie was loose and pulled away off center. He had two days' growth on his face and his hair was frazzled as if pulled on in frustration.

"Mr. Jacobs?" he called out.

I got to my feet and raised a hand. Shasta stood.

"Come right in, Mr. Jacobs."

"That was fast," Shasta told him.

We walked through the doorway.

"Well," the man replied as we walked, "we don't really have anyone take a number or do that *first-come, first-served* thing. What we've got here is legal triage, so to speak. And if the note Mr. Jacobs wrote is true, well, that bumps you right up to the top. *If* he's telling the truth, that is."

We reached the man's office door. As he held it open for us, Shasta shot me a *what the hell did you write on that paper?* look. We went inside. The man closed the door and sat at his desk, leaning forward and slapping both of his hands palms-down on the desk.

"My name's Stu Blubaum. I'm a full partner here at the firm. I'm the guy that always wins."

"Where's Thurgood Thurman the Third?" Shasta asked.

"Well, don't let the word get out, pretty lady, but in the spirit of our mutual need for honesty—I'll let you in on the secret."

Shasta and I stared at him. He was going for a dramatic pause. It worked.

Blubaum leaned back in his chair. "Thurgood Thurman the Third is a *dee-bee-aay*. The guy on TV is an actor who works out of New York—that way he's not seen around the streets of L.A. Anyway, the firm's real name is Goldman, Fuchs, and Blubaum. *Capiche?*"

We stared at him. I was hoping he'd say more.

He did. "You wouldn't believe how much business comes in because of a name. The name means *everything*. And Goldman, Fuchs, and Blubaum isn't a name with *verve*, it doesn't lend itself to memory, and it doesn't sell the product—which just happens to be the best fucking legal advice you'll ever find in this country." He smiled at us with bright white but slightly crooked teeth. "The name Thurgood Thurman the Third, *Esquire* does all those things and more. Yeah?"

Shasta and I nodded our heads at him.

"Now that I've been honest with you, I need you folks to reciprocate. *Quid pro quo*. Remember—I'm your legal counsel. Your story remains privileged. Slap me with the truth." He looked directly at me now. "You didn't find no 3.2 billion dollars. *So*—start from the beginning and tell me how you stole it."

Shasta turned her chair toward me. She folded her arms across her chest and crossed her legs. She tilted her head to the side slightly and raised her eyebrows. "Do tell, Zeno."

"Actually it's 2.3 billion, not 3.2 billion."

"Okay," Blubaum said, "a plastic fiver it *ain't.*"

"Billion?" Shasta asked. "Like with a *B?*"

I ignored her. "I filled out a request for a funds transfer at work. At HRW International. A transfer into my personal account."

"Wait," Blubaum said, "let's get this straight. These are company funds, right?"

"I don't know. Account 4114 was an artifact left over from the Pioneer Chicken days."

"Oh," Blubaum said, "I remember them."

I continued. "The account hadn't had any activity, except interest accrual, since the early 1980s."

"That might be so," Blubaum said. "But it's certainly not *your* money."

"Well," I continued, "it's all been sitting for decades, unnoticed in an orphaned account. See, the guy running the old company—Kaufman from Pioneer Chicken—couldn't figure out why the company was in the shit. Every time he looked up his cash reserves, the spreadsheet directed him to the wrong account. Account 5114 was the account used to pay for cook labor, and it got switched with 4114, the account where all his money was. It was a small error that would've been found by even a first-year accounting student. But before Kaufman could catch it, there was a hostile takeover and all the corporate Pioneer Chicken restaurants became Church's. All the old accounts were passed on as legacy accounts, and when the buyouts happened time and again—from Buyout A to Buyout Z—4114 has been there, with all that money in it earning interest. Nothing in the corporate ledger points to it, and no one's been aware of its existence. The only reason I found it was because we had an old employee, one that had been around that long."

Shasta kicked my chair. "*Sammy?*" she asked.

I continued for Blubaum. "So, I forged a letter from my boss asking Accounts Payable to transfer the money into my personal account. And they did."

"Just like that—no questions, no phone calls, no *nothing?*"

I brought out the ATM receipt and put it on the desk.

He examined the receipt, bouncing his finger along as he moved decimal places. He considered with a nod and looked at Shasta. "Did you know about this?"

"Not till just now," she said, glaring at me.

"Perhaps you should leave, pretty lady. I mean, once you hear all this, you're just as—"

"*No-no-no-no-no,*" she said, firing the words like bullets. "It's quite alright because *I can't believe a WORD he's SAYING!*"

Blubaum turned to me, smiling as though turned on.

I mouthed the word *sorry* to Shasta.

She responded by raising her eyebrows again, even higher this time.

"Lookit," Blubaum said. "Right now my team and I need to do some discovery. We need to see just how deep the shit that you've stepped into is, and we've got to do some immediate damage control. Lucky for you, the fact that The City of Angels is in the pits of Hades means that law enforcement—from the FBI to the fucking Litter Police— is so tied up that they don't have time for any of this white-collar shit. And that gives us time. Precious time. You wouldn't believe how many scams fail just because of a lack of time.

"Do you know if you're ever discovered, this will go down as the largest heist in history?"

I grimaced. Shasta began tapping her nails on the armrest of her chair.

"That would make the *next* largest only a billion. You know who that perp was?"

I shook my head.

Blubaum paused for effect again. "Saddam Hussein. Yeah, a billion bucks—U.S. currency, in hundreds." He grinned widely, turning his face back and forth between Shasta and me.

I was silent. I didn't dare look at Shasta's hateful stare.

Blubaum cleared his throat. "For now, I'm going to fill out this simple Limited Power of Attorney. This is going to give a trusted friend of mine control of your money. In return, he keeps the interest accrued during the time he has control of it—that's his fee. But he's going to set it up in a way that's much less obvious. And once the money's all invested, his fee goes down. What he's going to do for me is tell me your tax liability and set aside your withholdings and all that. And he's also going to let me know the proper, *um,* angle, to take when it comes to representing you—just in case a defense is needed. So, put your account number here and sign there."

I took a pen from his caddy, and he continued.

"Also, to make you feel more comfortable, here is a copy of my friend's CPA credentials and so forth. I put this packet together because the guy could legally take your money and run off to Mexico with it, but he's never done anything like that. He's a good man, and he's honest—in a slimy kind of way, granted—but he's honest.

"Once my team and I have settled on a course of action, I'll call and let you know how we'll proceed. What's your cell?"

"I don't have a phone," I said.

"Oh-*kayy*. Get one. Right away." He handed me his card. "As soon as you have it, text me your number. Just call yourself *Zee-Jay*, okay?"

"Okay. Where am I going to find a phone?"

"Go to Pavilions down on Vine. They've allowed some vendors to set up in their parking lot. All the utility companies are there, and most of the insurance companies—we've even got a little canopy there with a pretty girl."

I nodded.

Blubaum stood. "Oh. Then there's my fee."

I got to my feet.

Shasta was still watching me from the chair with her arms folded across her chest.

"How much?" I asked.

"It's fifty percent. After your tax withholdings, mind you, which I think is fair. I mean, if you'd've found the money, you'd've had to pay seventy-five. And if you *do* get stuck at *that* tax rate, I think 12.5 percent on gross is awfully modest for my fee. So, the more work my team and I put into it, the more we both make."

I looked over to Shasta. She shrugged sourly.

"Very well, Mr. Blubaum. I agree to fifty."

We shook hands.

30—Shadows Within The Labyrinth

We left the offices of Thurgood Thurman the Third, and the big guy outside gave me my bullets and knife back. Pavilions was directly south from there, so we headed that way. As we walked, Shasta hung her head and took dragging steps. I walked silently alongside her for a block, and then I noticed she'd stopped. I turned back to face her, but I couldn't find any words other than *What's wrong?*, so I just took her hand, a hand that felt as though it had no weight.

"Zeno," she said in a powerless voice, "I can't do this without you. I mean, all you have to do is look around. I need a *man*. I can't raise a child in this place without a *man*. You can't take unnecessary risks like this—"

I started to interrupt, but she stopped me with a squeeze of my hand.

"No, it was totally *unnecessary*. A couple million would have done it—not that I'd even approve of *that*—but, you know, enough for us to go to school, to be able to take the time to find a *real* job. But a *billion? Really?*"

"Two point—"

"*Shut up,*" she said. "Listen, Zeno: I love you to death. But I need you to be a *man*. A *man* will never do stupid things that could get him taken away from his family. I hope Thurman can sort this out, and if he does, that's good for us and good for our family. But I swear to God that if you ever put yourself at risk like this again, I will leave and try to find my folks in Montana. I need to have you *here*, not in jail. Understand?"

I nodded. "Absolutely."

She hugged me. "I love you, Zeno."

I squeezed back. "I love you."

Once Shasta's frustration with my illegalities was out, she seemed to be back to normal, and now she hypothesized about the pristine equipment in front of the Starbucks, saying maybe the machines had been looted, and the police may have found the stolen machines when they nabbed the looters, but when they went to return the items, the building was on fire. That made some sense. As I pondered it, she changed the subject to Mr. McClusky's paintings. She wanted them, but since we didn't have a house yet, she didn't know where we'd store them—still, she insisted we needed to save them. I nodded in agreement. After that, she got hungry. All she could talk about now was chow, how she couldn't wait to see what Dooley made, and probably because of her focus on it, my stomach began rumbling.

You know the Pavilions on Melrose and Vine—it's still there—but at that time, there was a hotel behind it that the National Guard had commandeered as a barracks. A razor-wire fence circled both buildings. We walked along the rear of the perimeter fence, and under the hotel was a parking lot where two soldiers eyeballed us as they guarded dozens of Hummers. We followed the fence on Vine, where there were signs of a fierce battle: a blackened hedge showed no signs of regrowth along the hotel's first floor, the paint above the hedge was black and flaking off, bullets had torn hundreds of pits into the building's stucco, the windows of the hotel were all gone, and where the windows used to be were now steel plates with small slits cut in them for viewing. Huge craters had been blown into the five lanes of Vine Street's blacktop in front of the hotel, and empty vehicle husks were strewn everywhere and in all configurations: right-side up, upside down, on the side, even one nose-down. There were body markers spray-painted everywhere, some of them with deltas and others with Xs—I figured the Xs were for the ones they'd killed in bandanas. Here the deltas were in the high two-thousands, but the Xs were in the low eighties.

Shasta and I were holding hands as we took this all in, and I guided her away from the concertina to the other side of the street, to where a small strip mall had been smashed and emptied. From one of the smashed stores, a skinny guy around our age started to angle in on us. He kept his distance at first, but suddenly he was right in front of us—turned around and walking backwards.

"Oh my God!" he said to Shasta. "You're *sooo* beautiful!"

I stepped forward between the guy and Shasta.

"Listen—I'll give you *anything*. Let's go party!"

"Go away," I said.

His eyes didn't even flick toward me. They stayed fixed upon Shasta.

"I've got *Oxies!* Oxycontin!" He motioned down the block. "From the CVS." He was slowing, trying to force me to stop.

I shoved him.

A long step backward brought him upright again. "My clan has the Roosevelt! It's the coolest place *ever*! And I've got a sound system made for a *movie theater*. Over a thousand CDs. Come on—when's the last time you've listened to any *music*? We can party—"

I shoved him again.

"—party hard. All night—"

This time, I pushed him as hard as I could.

"—*long*," he said as he threw the punch, a swing aimed at my head, one that I barely dodged.

I drew my knife and slashed a long line down his forearm.

He stood motionless, holding his wound and grunting, "*Fuck. Fuck. Fuck.*"

I sheathed the knife and took Shasta by the wrist. We stepped around the kid to the front of what used to be Yum-Yum Doughnuts—toward the turn onto Melrose. I kept looking back and he still hadn't moved by the time we'd rounded the corner, which was good.

If he would have, I'd've gone back and killed him.

"I gotta hide the knife," I told Shasta. "They test them for blood. We could get detained."

"Or you could like, *not cut people with it.*"

I was speechless, and I looked at her like, *What?*

She shrugged sarcastically.

We crossed a trafficless Melrose and went behind a blown-up gas station. There were no observers around, so I pulled up another water valve cover and dumped the knife and pistol inside. I kept the bullets, though—if somebody was watching and stole the pistol, at least they wouldn't be able to use it on us. *Then again*, I thought, *they'd have a knife...* I replaced the water valve's lid.

Shasta stood in front of me with her arms folded.

"What is it?" I asked.

"You don't have to be so protective, Zeno. I could've KO'd that loser with a flick of my finger."

I looked up at her, imagining going against her in a boxing ring, and I have to admit, she was right. The issue was the guy from the Roosevelt had scared *me*. But Shasta outclassed the dick by fifteen inches and at least seventy pounds, and since he had no weapon…

"I guess I overreacted," I said.

"*Yuuuh.*" She ruffled my hair. "You did. I can take care of myself, Zeno."

We crossed Melrose again and approached the entrance to Pavilions.

We went through the same thing I had gone through at Ralph's, where a guy points a gun at your head while the other one searches you. He asked me why I had bullets but no gun. I said since I knew I was going shopping, I left the gun at home—but I didn't want to risk getting back home to an armed intruder. He told me that I was a wise, wise man.

I winced as the soldier groped Shasta, but he was professional about it, so I took Dooley's advice: *You gotsta bear it—smile now, cry later.* I neither smiled nor cried, but I *did* bear it. I would feel the same way later when Shasta was a couple weeks shy of her due date and the doctor stuck his hand in to feel her cervix—a man just doesn't like another man's hands *on* or *in* his woman, that's all. The groping of Shasta didn't last forever and when it was over, they let us through the fence.

The parking lot was thick with rows and rows of canopies. We saw a gyros vendor and the hot meat smelled delicious. When I saw the credit card machine, I figured we should order some, but as the lady came over to help us, Shasta said *no* and tugged me away.

"Sorry, Babe," Shasta said. "Those vegetables look like they were prepped two weeks ago. The last thing we need is the runs."

There was a fry-bread vendor a little way up, and she guided me to it.

"We'll take an order," she told the fry cook. She told me, "We'll split it, and that way we don't spoil our chow."

As the dough sizzled, the cook rung me up—it was only twenty dollars. I slid my card and entered my PIN. When the bread was ready, Shasta tore it in half and gave me the larger of the two pieces. It was sweet, and a little cinnamonny. We'd gone down two aisles of tents before Shasta finished her half. I offered her the rest of mine and she gobbled it up in a couple of mouthfuls.

The AT&T tent was huge and they had big glass-display cases. I picked one out and the salesman upsold us a second phone. We waited forever as he activated and programmed them. When forever passed, he printed the contract and I signed it in all of the spots.

"I want to go inside," Shasta said.

"What do you need?"

"I want a new toothbrush. And shampoo—I've been, like, washing my hair with soap. That's not so good. And our clothes—I've been trying my best to wash them in the bathroom, but it would be nice to have a bucket of some kind. And if we could get you something other than those awful cargo shorts…"

"Okay." We both found a pocket to put our phones into, and we held hands as we walked into Pavilions.

A body covered in a blanket was next to the soldier at the door. There was blood soaking through that blanket. Shasta had been sure it was real—I think it was a prop meant to scare people. Either way, it was there.

Pavilions didn't install turnstiles or set up their registers along each of the aisles, but perhaps they should have. We got a cart and proceeded into the closest aisle, where the over-the-counter medicines and first-aid were. A courtesy clerk was trying to reorganize a section and the people around him were swiping products left and right, allowing bottles of cough syrup and tubes of ointment to fall all over the floor. We went into the next aisle, which had shampoo, conditioner, lotion, and all that, and when people found what they were looking for, it seemed that they would purposely knock a thing or two over when they went to grab it. It was purposeless mayhem that I couldn't comprehend. That experience in Pavilions sums up the civil riots for me fairly well: it was chaos for the sake of chaos, and there was no reason for it—they did it just because they *could*.

Shasta and I collected everything we needed. The line took an hour during which we both played with our new phones. After a while, I texted Blubaum: *ZJ*.

He replied:

Culpepper wants to meet. 1440
Idaho Ave, Santa Monica. 10 am
tomorrow.

I thumbed: *Ok.*

My shoulders ached since I'd carried everything back.
We had a bucket, laundry soap, moisturizing bar soap,
toothbrushes, toothpaste, floss, shampoo, conditioner,
lotion that smelled like coconuts, toilet paper, Kleenex,
nail polish in a color to match Shasta's necklace, eye liner,
lip gloss, razors, shaving cream, peanut butter, and some
pears—Shasta said she was *really* craving pears.

But what she wanted most at this moment was chow.

She tried to guess what it was by the smell.

"Oh, definitely more collard greens. And *carrots!*
The protein kinda smells like fried chicken."

"Well, let's drop off our stuff and we can go."

Shasta kissed me, and it landed near my eye. "Drop it
off and meet me inside, okay?" She bounded into the
DFAC trailer.

I let out a sigh. My hands were too full to get the
applicant door open. I set down the bucket, opened the
door, propped it with my foot, and picked up the bucket
again. When I went into the labyrinth, I was looking at
the far wall of the corridor, where the dolphin takes the
sombrero in its teeth. I saw the slightest of shadows
elongate over the painting, and it was the kind of shade

392

that you can barely see—but you can sense its movement, you know: something behind your eyes gets tickled by it.

Someone was in the labyrinth. I didn't think anything of it then—I figured someone was taking their fiver to the coffee machine. I followed the sombrero, and as I turned the corner, the shadow was now on that corridor's far wall. This time it started out sharp and dark, but it quickly diminished and blended into the light.

I turned where the fox's pink tail was poking out from behind a low shrub, and the shadow was along the far wall again. Whoever it was, they weren't getting coffee. I turned the next corner and for an instant, I saw the heel of a brown dress shoe at the next junction, and a complete, sharp shadow on the wall below a painting of the fox climbing a pile of stones among a field of angry, shivering sunflowers.

A feeling of dread visited me.

I continued to follow the fox to the dead end. There was no one there. I dropped off our groceries and sped off to chow.

It was chicken fried steak.

I wanted to watch some news, so we brought dinner to my cubicle, and as we ate, the office phone rang.

"HRW—this is Zeno."

"This is Bob. I have good news for you: I was able to reserve five Greyhounds. They're on their way from San Diego, so everyone needs to be ready to go to Denver in the morning. They'll pull up to the Army's gate on Pico at 6:30."

"Uh-huh."

"Don't worry about any of the equipment, but bring all the paperwork."

"What about the computers?"

"It's all leased, Zeno, and the information's on the network, not the PCs."

"Okay."

Bob's voice became exuberant. "Well—*aren't you excited?*"

I was caught off guard. "Excited about what?"

"To be coming to Denver!"

Oh, Jesus, I thought, *I never told her.* "Bob—my life's here. I can't leave L.A. It's my home."

There was a staticky silence, and then she said, "Oh. I'm sorry. I was looking forward to meeting you, Zeno. In person, that is."

I spun in my chair toward the camera. "Goodbye to you, Roberta." I waved and tried to smile. I knew that I'd miss her—in a way—and even now, I suppose I do. Even though I never knew what she looked like. I hung up on Bob and blew a soft kiss at the camera.

I turned to Shasta. "The employees are leaving for Denver at 6:30 in the morning. Think Dooley can make 'em a bagged lunch?"

"Yuh, sure. We'll get it ready tonight. I may not make it to bed till ten or eleven, though."

"That's okay. I'll be busy with all the employees packing up."

Shasta nodded and drizzled some dressing on her salad. "Oh—Dooley said the guy's name was Sancho Chucho Matapangpang." She giggled.

"Who?"

"The guy they caught crossing the border." She slapped me on the shoulder. "*Sancho Chucho Matapangpang*—isn't that a laugh riot?"

I shrugged and then picked up the phone, pressing INTERCOM: "*Attention, attention. The busses to Denver will arrive at 6:30 AM tomorrow morning. Please have all corporate and personal items upstairs by the applicant entrance by 6:15. Thank you.*"

Around one in the morning, the howitzers started firing volleys from the north lot. Each concussion rattled the suspended ceiling, turned the walls of the labyrinth into bass speakers, and struck my body like a flat-handed slap to the back.

After one particularly strong blast, Shasta propped herself up on her elbows, took hold of my hand, and gazed at me. "Am I awake, Zeno?" she asked. Her focus seemed to be light-years beyond me.

"I don't know."

"What a crazy, crazy life," she said, and she lay back down, asleep.

The volleys of fire continued throughout the night.

I couldn't go back to sleep then. I could've slept through the howitzer fire, but the evil behind those fleeting shadows earlier in the evening was hard for me to get off my mind. I stared at the ceiling, and Shasta was on her side with an arm around me. Even though the fluorescents were out in our dead end, the ones around the corner bathed the far wall in a harsh whiteness. I kept raising my head to look for motion in that light; it had been hours and there had been none.

Shasta's breathing changed. She took in deep lungfuls, releasing the breath again quickly. I turned my head to look at her, and her eyes were moving beneath her eyelids. Her arm twitched. "Are you still here?" she asked.

"Yes," I said. Then I added, "Where are you?"

"The waterfall by the gray-blue hillside. Are you coming?"

I looked at the wall again. "I don't know."

Shasta squeezed my waist.

"Oh, Jeeesus," Culpepper said. "I wish you people would consult me *before* you take the money. *Jeeesus.*" He was a middle-aged man with thick glasses and a toupee—it wasn't an unmatched color that gave it away, but rather the crooked way it was worn on his head. He had a stack of papers beside his keyboard. He typed, thumbed through the papers looking for something, and typed some more. "There will be a stack of forms as thick as a

Bible. We don't have the time for you to read any of it, so you're going to have to trust me. *Ha!* I wonder how many fortunes were lost with just that phrase: *You're going to have to trust me.*" Culpepper continued his back-and-forth between the papers and the keyboard. "If I were you, I'd trust me though. You see, even if you lose all of your money, at least you won't end up in jail."

Shasta jabbed me in my ribs.

I yawned audibly. Sleep had finally come a couple hours before sunrise and it seemed mere moments before I woke to help the employees carry everything to the Greyhounds. I needed a nap, and Culpepper's desk looked like a tempting place to rest my head. "I'm not a thief," I explained. "HRW, along with its last three incarnations, had no knowledge of the money from Pioneer. Listen: if a $500 bill is blowing down the sidewalk, how many people will go, 'That's not my money, so I'll leave it to blow away'?"

"Mr. Jacobs," Culpepper said as he continued to flip through papers, "I don't have to answer that—and you know it. You're a damned *fool.* If anyone has more wealth—in cash and equity—than the cumulative median income over the years they've worked, they *are* a thief. I'm willing to admit it myself—I make my money by stealing it from *fools* like you. Even so, the point is this: thievery is perfectly legal. Our economy is based on it. A thief that steals legally is called a *smart businessman.* A thief that steals *ill*–legally is called a *felon*. That's why you should have sought my advice first."

I dropped my head.

"You had a great-uncle in Macedonia. His name was Senad Ibro Šaranović—memorize that name. He was the owner of a foundry in Bitola that died without any relatives. Well, he had one relative now—*you*. I've filed all of the appropriate paperwork electronically. What I need to keep stored here are all the forms that require your signature." He pushed a button and the printer started shooting out papers. "I want you to back-date *everything*. Make it a date at least a week before you found that account."

"What about the deposit?" I asked. "If HRW doesn't have a record of the money transfer, surely the banks do."

"Yes. It took me all night to untie all those little strings bundling you all together, but now it just looks like a deposit from a foreign bank."

"And what about HRW's records?" Shasta asked.

"I wouldn't worry about them," Culpepper said. "This morning a representative from Delaware introduced HR-881. It's expected to pass unanimously."

"What's HR-881?" I asked.

"It's a bill that will make it illegal to file for new-hire and termination incentives on the same employee within five years of each other. I imagine that HRW International, at that point, will be liquidated."

Culpepper took the stack of papers from the printer and slapped them on the table in front of me. The stack was thick—not quite as thick as a bible, but thick. Shasta poked around on her phone while I flipped up the first page. I wished I had brought my signature stamp, but I hadn't, so I signed and endured the cramps that came. There was silence until I was done, when I handed the stack back.

"And now," Culpepper said, "I'm sure you want to know the results."

Shasta put her phone back in her pocket. I yawned, nodding *yes.*

"I was able to reduce your tax liability to only thirty-four percent. That means thirty-three for you and thirty-three for Thurman. I have taken your share, some $760 million, and assembled a portfolio. The money I make is based on the profits of your portfolio. Like Mr. Blubaum, I take fifty percent of the profits on your money and I pay zero percent of the losses. But in thirty-five years, I've never had any losses, so keep that in mind. I've left a hundred million in cash in your account because I presume you have a great many things to buy. A house. A car. Everything else that comes with being a *little bit rich.*" He said that last part with some flair.

He spoke again. "My advice to you is this: after that hundred million, find a way to live on the monthly payout of the portfolio, and never get into any debt of any kind." He motioned away from the building: *Out there.* "That's what started that whole mess in the first place."

I was awake now—*fully* awake. $760 million. I was like, *Wow.* "Thank you, Mr. Culpepper," I said.

He shook my hand. "Mr. Jacobs, if anybody— *anybody at all*—ever contacts you about the money, you instantly lawyer-up and zip it. Stay quiet and let us take care of it. Do you understand?"

"Yes." I turned away and helped Shasta up.

Culpepper went back to his computer.

"Have a nice day, Mr. Culpepper," I said, and then opened the door.

Culpepper let out a grunt.

We left. Up the street, Shasta spoke first. "Zeno—where should we go? I mean, we could go anywhere."

"Isn't L.A. your home?"

"Well, *yuh*, but there's nothing left of it."

I put an arm around her. "Your old home—the one on the hill—is empty, the fires never reached it, and I think we should buy it."

A smile started on her lips. It widened slowly. Then I had to kiss it.

From where we were standing, the salty air carried the ocean's odor upon it. I would've suggested going to the beach, and it would have been nice had I known we could be alone. It would have been romantic, I think. But I didn't.

We turned back toward the compound.

Feeling great.

Smiling.

And touching.

Then, even from blocks away, we could tell:

No noise. No smell of diesel exhaust. No concertina wire.

The Army was gone.

31—We Burn And Burn

Shasta's face twisted into a frown. She simply said, *"No."*

I hugged her. After a half-dozen thankless jobs, McDonald's and HRW among them, she'd landed a job that she actually enjoyed, one where she was in a team with cool people, one where she served hard-working, life-risking soldiers that she cared about. I think this really was the best way for her to lose that job in the chow trailer, though. But I wasn't going to tell her that. I held her for a while as she stood stiffly.

We walked past the Sparkletts truck. There were no more jack-barricades, no more fences, no more camo tents, no more radar dishes, no more Hummers. And no more chow hall. It had all been as it was before the Army had come, but it seemed much emptier now. We stepped softly toward the applicant door, as though we were at a funeral. Shasta's posture was one of defeat as we went inside.

There was a note on my cubicle wall. It said *SHASTA*. I took hold of it and handed it to her.

Shasta read the note. She smiled and cried. Then she said, "Here," and handed it to me. It read:

HEY SHASTA,

ONLY GOTS A SECOND BECOSE THEY ONLY GIVING US TWO HOURS TOO MOVE OUT. BUT I'M GONNA MISS WORKING WITH YOU. I WROTE MY EMAIL AND STUFF ON THE BACK. USE THAT ADRESS AND IT WILL FIND ME ANYWHERES OR WE CAN ALSO TALK WITH TEXTES BUT SOMETIMES I WONT GET BACK RIGHT AWAY. I WAS WORKING ON THAT BEANS AND FRANKS FOR SUPPER WHEN THEY PUT OUT WORD AND I HAD TO THROW AWAY FOUR POTS! BUT IT WAS GOING TOO BE GOOD. HERES THE RECEPY AND I HOPE YOU SEND ME A RECEPY BACK AND WE CAN KEAP IN TUCH THAT WAY. THANKS AGAN FOR ALL YOUR HELP WITH PREPING AND PEALING AND ALL THE HARD STUFF. AND MOST OF ALL THANK YOU FOR YOUR SMILES.

MUCH LOVE,

DOOLEY

When I looked back over, she had sat down and put her face in her hands.

"God, Zeno, everybody I care about always bails…"

I put my hand on her shoulder. "I'll be here."

She dropped her hands, exasperated. "Yuh, if you don't go to jail."

I kissed her wet cheek. There was nothing to say.

Inside the door, several dozen picnic lunches were left with cold sandwiches, potato salad, macaroni salad, Dooley's famous coleslaw, bags of Lay's and Fritos, and a bunch of cans of Hawaiian Punch. It was a surprise to me that Shasta was in a mood to eat—she loaded a plate with two tuna-salad sandwiches and grabbed several bags of chips.

I sat down with a roast beef sandwich. On the computer, camera crews were embedded with some of the arsonists as they threw flaming bottles at homes without Xs on the front door. A few minutes were spent high-lighting that, and then a different reporter began interviewing a soldier billeted at the Disneyland Hotel. The patch on his sleeve was different than our Brave Rifle guys. It had a shield with an eagle's head on it.

Shasta set down her sandwich. "This place is creepy, all empty like this."

I turned off the streaming video and faced her.

"I don't want to stay here tonight."

"Okay," I said.

"You're the billionaire, Zeno. Can all that money buy us a place to sleep?"

I bit my lower lip, not knowing what to say.

She punched me in the arm. "Where do we go?"

"Up the hill," I said, looking around as though someone might be listening. "To your old home. We'll have to break a window, but we're going to buy it anyway."

She glanced away from me, in thought.

"I'll get our stuff," I said, and got up.

The labyrinth was the same as it always was. All the familiar paintings that led to the dead end with the fox drifted past. When passing the painting where a pink tail becomes visible behind a shrub, a faint chemical odor became apparent. My first thought was of sooty exhaust, the kind that the Hercules tank breathed out by the cloudful. But after the next corner, the odor was stronger and unmistakable.

—that gasoline smell—

My face suddenly felt as though it had a rash on it, and my fingers began tingling. Ahead of me was one last corner, the dark corner—from when I'd rotated the fluorescent bulbs to put them out. I pro-ceeded slowly around it.

There was a person standing by our cots, and he must've been there a while because his eyes had adjusted to the dark—he was running a finger down the canvas on the wall, a look of awe upon his face. He wore a starched, button-down shirt with a sharp crease down the sleeve. Below it, a glossy belt held dress slacks around his waist; his shoes were shiny as well, reflecting the indirect light from beyond where I stood.

A five-gallon gas can was on its side atop our make-shift bed.

The guy's face turned toward me. Tiny craters darkened his cheeks in the reflected light.

He lowered his hand from the painting.

"It's *The Man*," Octavio said.

I reached into my cargo pocket and brought out the M-9. It was light. "Look, Octavio—"

Octavio began walking toward me. Slowly creeping. "No, *you* look! You *betray* me!"

The clip: it wasn't in the pistol's grip.

Octavio's walking became a stalk. *"You tell the Army about us!"*

I plunged my hand back into my cargo pocket and found the clip. *"No—"*

Now Octavio sprinted explosively. Instantly, he was right *there*.

And I was out of time.

I dropped the clip and went for Pop's knife. I had it out and halfway up.

Octavio's dress-shoed foot was in the air. As my brain registered that it was approaching, my throat was impacted. I collapsed backwards, unable to breathe.

The knife: *Gone.*

The gun: *Gone.*

Octavio landed a kick to my ribs.

I gasped and wheezed.

"You pucking betray us all, Man!"

Octavio sat on me with his knees on my biceps. He grabbed my cheeks with his left hand—pressing in hard with his thumb. I struggled as he crossed himself with his free hand. *"Santa María, madre de Dios, ruega Señora por nosotros pecadores, ahora y en la hora de nuestra muerte. Amén.*" He crossed himself again and released my face.

The gasoline fumes were thick and nauseating, but the sensation told me my breath was returning.

Octavio produced a matchbook. He lit a match and applied the flame to the edge of the book. The rows sputtered to life in a chain reaction.

"*Con llama, nos consumen y limpiar.* We *burn—we burn and burn!*"

I twisted my hips. I shook my torso. I whipped my legs. But I couldn't get free.

Octavio wound back for a roundhouse punch.

The world turned white.

Hundred Days Forever

32—The Edge Of The World

SEARCHING FOR SHASTA
CALL FOR HELP
I AM NEAR

I could feel only burning: the flame lashing my leg felt like hundreds of sharp little teeth tearing into my flesh.

A volumeless coughing shook me.

A dreadful vertigo spun me.

Though consciously distant, my body acted in panic.

It kicked off my flaming shoe. Tore off the smoking sock. Some skin went with it—*see?* The scars will always be with me.

As my mind returned to me, I stood, but the weight on this scorched foot brought searing pain and I swooned. I fell sideways into one of Mr. McClusky's canvases. My head punched a hole into its center. I flopped deadweighted to the floor, and the canvas fell atop me.

The thick, hot fumes threatened to take me out again.

I flung the painting at the building flames. The canvas combusted while still airborne.

Using my elbows and my good leg, I scooted backwards, but it was slow work with the pain and the coughing and the heat. I spoke to myself, within my head, loudly: *Get the fuck up!*

The ceiling tiles in the dead end collapsed. Hot sparks shot all around, but now I was being spared the brunt of the heat—the fire was immediately channeled upward through the suspended ceiling toward the higher roof of the HRW building. The flames ascended in swirls and vortices, and a cool breeze started, flowing from elsewhere in the labyrinth, past me, and into the fire. The lights went off and popped right back on again. I had to hurry—I knew how dark it would get if the lights went out for good.

I leaned against the wall, bracing myself and using my good leg to get to my feet. I walked away from the fire, every step on the left like treading on a griddle. My steps were uneven because of my lost shoe, so I kicked the other one off. I walked on, keeping my eyes on Mr. McClusky's paintings. The pink fox dashed backwards over snowy hills, and bounded head last into a leafy thicket. We were entering the woods together, him and I. Even past the familiar turns leading to the office—the same serpentine turns that silenced the sound of gunfire from when I shot up the coffee machine—there came echoey explosions of sappy pine. That meant the fire was hot, and spreading rapidly. When I exited the forest and was onto the beach, there were only two more turns before I'd be at the corridor that would lead me to my cubicle, and to Shasta. I took those turns, and beyond the end of the final corridor, where I should have seen cubicles, there was grayness, like a curtain had been drawn over the exit leading to the office.

There *was* the sound of the fire alarm: *Ehhhht. Ehhhht. Ehhhht...* I called above it: *"Shasta! Shasta, where are you?"* No answer came. My intention now was escape—to go for the applicant entrance, but in just five steps my vision blurred with tears. My first breath brought convulsive coughing. Then I slammed into a cubicle wall; banging my nose on it brought zigzagging stars to my vision. I turned around and the labyrinth's entrance had disappeared in the haze. I wiped my eyes. Above me, the ceiling was fluid and alive, like the surface of a pool right after everyone's gotten out—only it was orange instead of blue. Below the luminescent ceiling, the sprinkler pipes hung just above the now unmanned security cameras, and at the same level as the lights that were somehow still on. The sprinkler heads, like the cameras, showed no sign of life. I wiped my eyes once more, and walked back toward the labyrinth with my arms ahead of me. When my hands thumped the wall, I groped along its surface back to the entrance. Within the labyrinth's cleaner air, I hacked up a good measure of phlegm before moving on.

I followed the dolphin, which led to the north side of the labyrinth, and away from the inferno growing in the south end. I made turn after practiced turn, but my mind wasn't with me. The paintings became suddenly unfamiliar: seahorses swimming among playful fields of seaweed, clown fishes hiding in the center of a discarded tire, manta rays spinning around a whirlpool, a reef with flowery anemones. I turned a corner and hellfire flowed along the ceiling like an upside-down flood. I went back and followed a different passage.

I found a river in the paintings there and followed it.

To the center of the labyrinth.

In front of me was the *Waterfall by the Gray-Blue Hillside.*

A loud crack sounded—loud as a shotgun. The floor beneath me dropped an inch. Then the west wall within the center of the labyrinth fell away, collapsing to the first basement level, and a wave of heat blasted me in the face. The truth of the situation came to me immediately: if I couldn't find my way out, I'd be dead within minutes.

I left the way I'd come in—I followed the river that meandered away from the waterfall, not knowing where it would take me.

Under the ceiling tiles of the labyrinth, a foot-thick cloud of smoke now rolled, and in places it puffed downward to shoulder height. My hitching breath told me oxygen was becoming a rare commodity. I made turn after turn, following the river with its reedy banks, going the opposite way of a school of tiny minnows, but in the same direction of a large tortoise. Worry began to overwhelm my panic—the paintings seemed to repeat themselves, the minnows would swim to the left and reappear again on the right, while the tortoise continued swimming forward, mid-frame. I was going around a large square in the maze, over and over again!

I followed the square to a cross-junction. There were two walls per direction, eight walls in total. I ignored the two with turtles and minnows, and followed the only other path with water on the canvasses. In just three or four frames, a swampy area led to the open ocean. And in three more frames, I saw the fish.

It was the fish from the painting by the employee entrance.

He would lead me to *the life preserver!*—and out of this horrible inferno.

I chased the fish.

It took on a look of determination as it swam. Its fins rippled as it moved faster and faster through the water. Its tail kicked powerfully, and the peaks of the ocean's surface became a blur. As it raced onward, the blue sky darkened and soon, stars floated in the blackness.

A tremor jolted the floor. The lights went out. A sound came, a deep throaty noise, like the toppling of a six-story smokestack.

In my averted vision, I could see an oval, bluish glow and little white speckles. When I looked at it, it turned dark, and when I looked away again, it reappeared. I knew my eyes would adjust to the darkness in time, but the smoke building along the tile roof was thickening, and it was now at chest level. I plunged onward, lower to the ground. My leg objected and I ignored it. I kept on, following the glowing oval shapes into a turn. There was another junction. An orange luminescence on my left overpowered the glow-in-the-dark paint Mr. McClusky used on the fish. I turned right.

I found the fish again by keeping my eyes straight ahead. It kept up its furious pace. Then, where there should have been the next frame, there was only darkness. I continued forward and walked into a wall. I tumbled to the floor. The pin-pricky feeling returned to my throat. I fought unconsciousness as I worked my way to my knees. I crawled forward. Then I heard a ghostly voice, like the whisper of recent memory.

"The feather just blew over there..."

The smoke was so thick now, it made little difference being close to the floor. I had to constantly wipe tears from my eyes, and although my coughing was now constant, somehow I found the glowing fish again—it had dashed to the diagonal wall, where I caught it glinting in the dark, like the sparkletts had on Shasta's necklace. I turned toward the fish, on my hands and knees, going as fast as I could muster—not nearly as fast as the fish. The speed he was travelling at now made him look like a torpedo.

In the corridor ahead, there was a bright shape—a rectangle made from light.

I thought, *fire behind a doorway.*

I almost gave up. But above the rectangle, barely visible through the smoke, hung a word in dim, red light: EXIT.

As I got to my feet, my burned leg failed me again. I staggered against the wall opposite the fish, flipping a canvas onto the floor. Then I pushed out the door.

Coughing and wheezing, I turned and collapsed on the grass. The cool air tasted fresh and sweet. Smoke rushed through the open doorway and rose into the sky. I was facing in, the emergency exit's door held open by my back.

I looked up.

On the final canvas, the edge of the world was revealed—where all the planet's oceans pour off a craggily-edged seafloor into the abyss. Out beyond it was a star-speckled nothingness, seamless with the dark sky above. The fish—the same one that had been in the life preserver—had pierced the surface of the water falling off the edge. His face looked as determined as when he started his sprint, but now he also looked afraid. His fins were spread like wings as he flew out into the heavens. Without realizing it, I stood in front of the painting, feeling the slickness of the ocean, and how the texture of the water became cottony as it plunged over the edge. I touched the fish, and I was jolted with a flash of his emotions. It was a hallucination, I'm sure, but I experienced it, nonetheless.

Somewhere in my mind, I had always thought that the *Fish in the Life Preserver* was the last frame in that particular series—not the first. But I had never taken any time to stop and take a tour of the paintings...

Shasta came to mind when I took my hand off the painting. I left, and pushed the door shut behind me.

I had exited from the north side of the building.

I failed to look out into the parking lot—out toward where the Hercules had dragged the Eucalyptuses. My focus was near the building, where I felt Shasta might be waiting for me if she'd escaped. Toward the utilities enclosure, there was mud now where once there had been a lawn, and the impressions from the constant pacing of soldiers in the S-2 were still there. In the other direction, there was nothing but some holes where tall antennas were once anchored to the ground. I limped that way on the grass, avoiding the holes.

I rounded the corner on the west side of the building. When I got to the employee entrance, I felt the door handle. It wasn't hot, but when I opened the door, smoke came rushing out at me. I stepped inside, keeping low, and when the door shut behind me, I was left immediately in the dark. I took down the *Fish in the Life*

Preserver and used it to prop open the door. I took a couple breaths and hobbled quickly to the end of the first corridor.

"Shasta! Shasta!"

I got low to the ground and took a breath, waiting for a reply. This time, the smoke gagged me and I threw up. When the floor shifted again, I rushed back out the employee entrance and yanked the canvas free from the door.

I made off now for the applicant entrance, leaning the *Fish in the Life Preserver* against the southwest corner of the HRW building as I rounded it. I limped along in the grass, dragging my foot over the quarter-mile distance. When I got there, I tested the door handle the way I had before. Again—it wasn't hot.

When I thumbed the latch, the door exploded open.

I don't remember being airborne. But when I came to, I was some twenty feet away from the entrance. I felt my face and arms for burns. All I had were some scratches. And that was damn lucky, I think.

There was an unfamiliar bump in my pocket. It was my phone. As I grabbed it, I considered calling Shasta.

But stupidly, we hadn't exchanged numbers.

A crunching rumble sounded from under the plastic grating beside the building, and a dense cloud began rising through its slats. A tremor vibrated the ground I was sitting on. I feared that the basement levels might extend beyond the outside walls of the building, but all my trips downstairs told me that they didn't and that I was safe.

I thought of 911 as I held the phone. Just then, I had a strong, intuitive feeling—Shasta wasn't in there. No, Octavio had taken her. And if I ever wanted to see her again, there was only one person I could call and, luckily, it was one of the few numbers I knew by heart…

I called *(213) JIMENEZ*.

"¿Bueno?"

"Carlos—this is Zeno. *Necesito su ayuda.*"

"Okay. *¿Para qué?*"

"I need you to help me find Octavio—"

"I will call him."

"No—I need you to pick me up. I'll explain."

"Where you at?"

"At work. HRW."

"I am near. *Cinco minutos.*"

33—As If To Kiss It

The steel roof had finally collapsed, and a dense column of blackness raced into the sky above the HRW building. It was the time of day when the sun blinds you if you look westward—a time of full daylight, though also a time when the colors seem bleached from things. Carlos entered through the west lot and saw me. As I got into his pickup, I told him that Octavio had taken my wife.

"When you get married?" he asked.

"Remember Carson, I hadn't seen Carlos since the Hundred Days Riots began. It occurred to me throughout the years that I should've asked about Manuel—if he had been one of *los compañeros* killed at Tuna Canyon Road. I never asked if Manuel's wife and family had survived, or even if Carlos' wife, María, had. I *had been*

419

hungry to know how they were, but in the moment all I could think of was Shasta. I just *had* to find my wife—no matter the cost.

"Even now, I still don't know what happened to them all."

My heartbeat is quickening. Why *did* Octavio take Shasta? Had he gone totally mad? He left me for dead and took her. I never understood why. And I suppose now I'll never know.

"I visually examined Carlos as I belted myself in, and he didn't look battle worn like the soldiers in the DFAC line. He had an EP badge hanging down from the pocket of a nicely pressed, white shirt. Actually, he was dressed as if to go out dancing on a Friday night. 'There's been no Hundred Days here—in town—for at least a week,' I said. 'Why are you here?'

"Carlos nodded at me. 'Yes, we been in Indio for a few weeks now, *El Judío.* But we come back cuz we need some things, and we got them. Now we go back.'

"'Octavio came here with you?' I asked.

"'No,' he said, 'we come separately.'"

I asked respectfully, but demandingly: "Where is he, Carlos?"

Carlos looked me up and down. "Like I say, we come back to collect some things. We have friends in Indio—and from there, we will make our next move."

"Where would he go?"

"Other than Indio, I dunno."

I squeezed my hand into a fist and pounded the armrest. "What about the commune?"

"*No!* The Guard *destroy* East L.A. *Nuestra casa es un gran cráter.*"

I remembered Octavio telling me about the shelling. While I felt a measure of sadness at that, my desperation overwhelmed it. "We need to find Octavio—*now.*"

Carlos nodded. "If you don't want to call him, it's Indio. We were meeting there in three hours."

I nodded my agreement, and Carlos put the pickup in gear and accelerated. We were headed out the east parking lot's exit when I looked back into the late afternoon sun. Out in the north lot, on the far end, I saw the silhouette of an old, blocky car.

"Stop," I demanded.

Carlos jammed on the brakes.

"That's Octavio's car."

Carlos asked *"Where?"* as he executed a frantic, three-point turn.

I pointed toward the stacks of downed Eucalyptuses and Carlos floored the gas.

I bolted from the pickup while it was still in motion, and then cried out in pain. My screams quickly transitioned from senseless noise to my wife's name. I scanned the area through a fog of tears, limping on my burned foot.

She was sitting on one of the tree trunks. Her hair was out of its usual ponytail and was now all frazzled, with dark, slick locks here and there. She had the ivory complexion of the dead, and dappled upon it were splatters that were bright red, even in the early evening light.

Dazed and looking beyond me, she spoke lowly: "Hey, Zeno."

I balanced myself as well as I could on the one foot. *"Shasta—you okay?"*

"I dazzled him with a smile," she said.

"He lowered the gun," she said.

"I went to his neck as if to kiss it," she said.

"And I bit—like the first bite you take from an apple."

Shasta began to sob.

I rushed to sit beside her.

Carlos was by the Impala. *"Madre de Dios."*

Shasta wiped her tears, smudging the red spots under her eyes. There was a chunk of meat on her leg, raw and fleshy and darkish—like the thick part of a chicken leg. I brushed it off and it was sticky, like those toys you throw on a window—the ones that crawl slowly down the pane.

I wanted to hold her, but I was afraid to—I couldn't read her temperament.

"Told you I could take care of myself, didn't I?" she asked with despondent pride upon her face.

"I know," I said, pulling a messy strand of hair away from her face. *"Shhhhh..."*

Carlos shouted now, still by the driver's side of the Impala. *"¿Por que? Why?"*

The words exploded from Shasta like a bomb. *"He was going to kill me!"*

Carlos walked over. I was afraid—terribly afraid. It occurred to me that Shasta's DNA was on Octavio's neck. We needed the police so we could make a report, so we could explain what happened, so we could point to the fire and the smoke and the gun Octavio had held on Shasta. If we didn't, and the police had to come to us afterwards, the investigation would dig deep. And the most obvious thing in the world would be all my money.

I spoke to Carlos: *"Usted debe abandonar. Voy a teléfono a la policía."*

Shasta pushed away from me. "You speak *Spanish?*"

"Octavio no es un criminal," Carlos said.

"Octavio asesinados a dos *soldados."* I showed him my leg. *"¡Y me encendió en el fuego!"*

Shasta bumped her palm into my forehead. *"You:* speak English!" Then she looked at Carlos, as though he was pure evil. "And *you:* who the hell *are* you?"

I pivoted on the log so the three of us faced each other like the points of a triangle. "Carlos, this is my wife Shasta. Shasta, this is Carlos Jimenez—the leader of Hundred Days."

Shasta impaled me with a shocked look. More tears welled up as she got to her feet. She walked toward the HRW building, a place that was now a continuous, thick column of smoke.

Carlos eyeballed me, asking, "You still with us?"

I leaned toward him. *"Si."*

Shasta had stopped, and I turned to where she was now leaning against a light pole, facing away from us. I was going to reassert my intention to call the police, but Carlos had already gotten back into his pickup. He started it and drove away.

911 didn't take long—there were now few people left in L.A. When I hung up, I hobbled over beside Shasta and sat. But I couldn't think of anything to say.

We just watched the fire. Inside, the paintings Shasta had wanted to save were turning to ash. Today, their combined value would have been in the billions. Or maybe not—I think the value of a McClusky is somewhat determined by rarity. But I don't know. I'm no expert.

The detective arrived just after dark. When I pointed to the Impala, he knelt down by the open door, and he stayed there a couple minutes. Then he rose, shining his flashlight in our faces. "Mr. Jacobs—over here, please."

I squeezed Shasta's shoulder and used it to get to my feet. I limped over to the detective.

He was holding Octavio's blood-stained EP badge. "You can confirm for me that this is Octavio Mendez?" He shined the flashlight directly on the body's face.

It looked more like a child's face than an adult's, even with the pits and bumps ringing his face. He looked frozen in time, his expression like choking on something big, maybe a hunk of unchewed broccoli, or perhaps a Ping-Pong ball. He had covered his wound with his left hand, but the hand was now limp on his lap, and stained red between the fingers. Below where he had tried to hold in the spurting from his carotid—on the leather bench seat—there had drained a soda can's measure of blood. His right hand was down alongside his leg, with his index finger through the trigger guard of Dooley's gun. But the gun itself was up and over his fingers, being worn like some big-ass ring.

I looked at his shocked, pleading face. "Yeah, I was his boss. That's Octavio Mendez, all right. *El Consumidor*, if you prefer."

Shasta came over and stood beside me. She spat out a big, snotty gob that landed on Octavio's shoulder.

"*Enuffa that,*" the detective growled. "Get back."

Shasta and I walked arm-in-arm and did as we were told. In the sodium light, she looked like a character in the climax of a George Romero film. I tried to think of a way to wash her up. The thought failed. We sat against the lamppost she had found before, while the gore on her faded to brown.

An ambulance came. One of the paramedics treated and bandaged my burn. When he was done, he worked with his partner to bag up Octavio. As they transferred him onto a stretcher, the detective covered the back seat of his unmarked car with a blanket. He motioned for us to sit. We got in. As the detective got into the driver's seat, I saw a goofy-looking man with thick glasses approach the driver's side of the Impala. With a spray can mounted at the end of a long, metal stick, he painted a mark on the asphalt. The back of his jumpsuit said,

Google

HIS

which, like the spray-painted marks themselves, was a total mystery to me at the time. But a few years later, I would run into the acronym again, so I looked it up. It stood for *Historical Information Services* and, these days, it's just known as Google History. I went to their site and looked up Mr. Clean, or Δ892. His name was Notorious Roemer, and he had done time for a string of sexual assaults along the 5, from the Grapevine down to Newport Beach. That just left me with more questions, like, *Who the hell names their child Notorious?*

We spent twelve hours at the police station, where they kept Shasta and me separated. The story was the same each time it came out of my mouth, but they still wanted to hear it over and over and over. It was dawn before I saw Shasta again, now cleaned up and wearing blue overalls. We asked for a ride home, and they declined, ushering us into the station's lobby.

We left and walked from downtown all the way up here.

I had to do it on my burned leg, with police-issued flip-flops.

It was a long, painful, silent walk.

We sat together against that living room wall, where the loveseat is now, exhausted and staring. Shasta elbowed me in the ribs, right where Octavio had kicked me. I was too tired to react to the pain, though.

"Wish we had our Army cots," she said.

"You mad at me?"

"Yuh. But I'm too tired."

"Yeah."

"Yuh. Well, I'm going to sleep." She laid her head on my lap and was out immediately.

I sat and thought for a while, about when she would confront me regarding my involvement with Hundred Days, and about what I'd say. I mean, I didn't really *do* anything. Well, discounting the Vons truck robbery. And I didn't know Octavio was psycho. I mean...

I don't know what I mean.

I finally fell asleep. When I woke up, it was nearing sunset. I tried the sink for water, but there was no flow. I wandered the property looking for the water main and found Shasta sitting on top of the wall out there—past the kitchen window. I used an old milk crate as a step and climbed up.

"Whatcha doing?" I asked as I scooted close.

From the top of that wall you can see down into the valley. She pointed short of downtown and somewhat seaward. "Guess they're bussing people in for demolition. See the dust rising?"

"Yeah."

"Should be lots of jobs now, dontcha think, Zeno?"

"Yeah."

"Maybe that's how you end a depression: just blow it all up and start over."

It was an interesting hypothesis. "Yeah."

We were silent for a little while. I thought about the riots as we looked out across the city. In his speech, the governor said *violence is not the default condition of man.* In this moment, with the millions taken away to Camp Liberty, with the unknown thousands dead in the riots, with the unknown thousands missing and never to be heard from again, it was clear to me that violence really *was* the default. But, really now: when the violence comes—and it always does eventually—should it come in the form of anarchistic rioting? Or, should it come in the form of an oppositional force like Hundred Days, who had rules and regulations, limits and goals, and at least some rudimentary chain-of-command?

I'm not sure if answers exist for those questions.

Shasta and I sat there above the destruction, we two killers who struggled just to stay alive—but who also never left the place we'd known all our lives. We never had much to say to each other about the bad things that happened during the riots. We were ready to move on to our new life, a life where we were free from wage slavery, a life lacking unpaid mortgages and unpaid bills and unrealized dreams, a life where it would be the two of us—together forever.

She kissed me on the cheek and smiled. With what to her may have seemed a gentle push, she playfully launched me off the wall. There was a sharp stone below, and it cut a huge gash just around the backside of my hip. She hopped down to check on me. When she checked my burned leg, she saw the new injury, and she tore the legs of her coveralls off to make a pressure bandage from the cloth. She laughed the whole time she was wrapping me up. Especially when I wailed in pain.

I even faked a moan or two just to hear her laugh some more.

God, I miss the sound of it.

34—Our House

I got the water turned on myself. When I texted Blubaum the address, he set up an appointment with an agent. The agent came, and we pretended we hadn't broken in. We got the tour. I offered a measly million dollars—and the offer was accepted. But even at that price, I'm sure a killing was made in profit.

Furniture was easily ordered on my phone. The UPS driver that delivered it had an armed guard. I bribed them into giving me a ride, and once we got up north, we stopped at an ATM where I withdrew their fee—600 bucks. Then, I walked to a Toyota dealership and bought a car.

We got the place half furnished. We had a TV now, though we couldn't get cable or satellite hooked up. Every time we called, they would say, "Sorry, that service is currently not available in the Los Angeles area." So, it was antenna TV, and that actually worked out okay. I drained, scrubbed, and refilled the pool. I tore down the cracked-up water slide and paid another UPS guy to take it to the dump for me. Most importantly, Shasta and I spent an afternoon out in Simi Valley. The riots had never made it there. Everything we owned had been in the labyrinth, so we spent a lot of money on clothes. Shasta was able to find some maternity outfits. And we got plates, silverware, pots and pans—those kinds of things. And lots and lots of groceries. The car was stuffed by the time we headed back.

A month after the employees left town, HRW International went out of business. The company that started strong as Pioneer Chicken, floundered due to poor management, got bought up and treated like a lap dancer at a strip club, and eventually found its way into the termination business could no longer continue operations because Congress (members of whom had, no doubt, been listening to *El Consumidor*'s rantings) passed that bill Culpepper had talked about. Its passing destroyed HRW's business model, so its assets were liquidated.

Most of the days were routine until Shasta was fairly well along. We had ultrasound appointments. OB/GYN appointments. We would work on fixing one thing or another, we'd go out shopping until four or five, and we'd take all of the stuff we'd bought and get our house all set up.

That's what this place was.

Our house.

And we loved it.

We loved every second of our lives together.

Late one night, she woke me kissing and licking and biting my neck. She was naked, and her hand was upon me. She pulled me out of my remaining doze by putting her tongue in my mouth. I wiggled out of my pajama bottoms. She sat on top of me, leaning back, her hands squeezing the comforter under me. Her hair brushed back and forth over my toes. Her breasts had grown, and her nipples were darker. I looked at her stomach—she was showing now.

That was when it finally sunk in. Not when she had told me she was late, but then—when I could *see* it.

My wife and I would be raising a child.

And the thought was wonderful.

Shasta was just entering her second trimester. She awoke at her habitually early hour to shower. I made some coffee and turned on the TV. The riots had burned through Indio and Barstow, and now the fronts had moved onto Fresno, Las Vegas, Flagstaff, Phoenix, and San Diego.

Vegas had their own rioters, so out there, the two groups of *alborotadores*—the locals and the newcomers on the front—were initially engaged in a minor civil war. The Nevadans didn't appreciate Californians moving in on their turf—or, you could say, on their fuel. But even in Vegas, *Cien Días* had enough weight to insist on peace between the factions. So, they struck a deal, somewhat in the spirit of *Separate but Equal*. The Las Vegas group became the feared *Los Pirómanos*. Even today, they are considered the most effective penetrators, the most skilled infiltrators, the most ingenious fire starters.

The front didn't progress outward in an arc from L.A.—instead, it would proceed down roads and highways in convoys like families escaping the Dust Bowl. When they found new fuel, the front spread outward in a circle from wherever they stopped. The way they did this reminded me of bacterial colonies in a Petri dish, where one colony only spreads so far, but another starts a distance away. Before long, all of the colonies coalesce in cooperative competition for the rest of the nutrients.

As Phoenix began burning, an anchor on TV said, "The Hundred Days' Front has moved onto Phoenix, a desert city that's sure to be easy fuel for the rioters."

And it was.

One morning around then, Shasta made us some omelets and hash browns—just like Dooley's. They were absolutely delicious, and I told her so. When I noticed things like that, it always made her so happy.

After breakfast, we drove down the hill. Sections of Hollywood at this point were being fenced off as the utility companies took advantage of the lack of homes to improve the infrastructure. Those blocky transformer boxes appeared everywhere—they had installed new electrical lines underground. I went down Vista to the old house, but it was just flat, graded dirt now. Someone had approved the house's demolition, and they did it without my permission. That kinda burned me, you know. At the end of the block, there was a sign. It was a zoning change announcement. I figured the demolition had something to do with that—I had Shasta write down all of the info. Years later, I would sue the city for endorsing a quitclaim on my behalf, transferring my property without my consent (or any payment) to some developers. In an attempt to settle, they offered me fifteen years of free property taxes, up here on the hill. It seemed a rotten deal to me, but Culpepper disagreed, and over the years, as the periodic appraisals have increased my home's value exponentially, I could see how right he was.

Shasta and I moved on and she wanted to stop by the old HRW building. The lot was spotless other than those dead trees lying at the far end of the north lot. We drove around the building twice. Shasta pointed out, with a kind of dreamy disappointment, that the Sparkletts truck had been dragged away. Finally, I pulled up to where the DFAC trailer used to be, beside the applicant door.

We got out and walked up the sidewalk. A sign had been posted on the door:

EXTREME DANGER
DO NOT ENTER
CONDEMNED

I unlocked the door and peered inside. The stench of smoke was still strong. Inside, the floor was gone, the ceiling was gone, and I could see shadowy, twisted girders spanning a dark hole. That's all that was left of the HRW International building—the outer walls were fine, but everything else had collapsed all the way to the third basement.

I steadied myself at the doorframe and leaned in. Unexpected laughter came to me: way across a diagonal, on the opposite wall of the building, the elevator floated unharmed, certainly two inches below the ground floor that was no longer there.

I leaned back out and turned around.

"What's so funny?" Shasta asked.

"That damned elevator."

She didn't ask me to elaborate.

I closed the door and went over to that hard plastic grating that covered the riser from the basement. Its slats were smoke-streaked, but not melted. Beyond them, three stories down, Mr. Chandler's chair was still sitting there. I grabbed my keychain and fought the large Medico one off the ring. I dropped it through the grate and waited for the sound to come back to me.

It made several, satisfying *ting*s that echoed for a while.

We walked along the side of the building, toward the employee entrance. As we approached the southwest corner, I could see it was still there. In the months since the fire, it had remained untouched and un-blown-over. Leaning against the wall was the *Fish in the Life Preserver*.

When I held it up, Shasta squealed in delight.

I carried it back to the car, put it in the back seat, and we drove away, heading out for more shopping.

Before long, Shasta stopped going along with me on my shopping binges. One day, I came home with an electric shoe buffer. It was easily assembled, and I plugged it in by the front door. I was thumbing the button, allowing the pad to gently buff the skin of my now healed foot.

Shasta had snuck up behind me. "What's that?"

"A shoe buffer," I said, as though it was the most obvious thing in the world.

"Did you buy some fancy shoes?"

I shook my head. "Not yet."

She slapped my hand away from the buffer's switch. "Stop, Zeno."

I faced her. "Stop buffing my foot?"

"No! Stop buying shit you don't need!" She turned away, walking toward the kitchen. "You're worse than that looter with all the basketballs!"

I put my hands on my hips, pouting at the empty air in front of me.

35—Day 297 Of The Hundred Days Riots

In her spare time, Shasta kept busy with three hobbies: she scoured the internet for signs of her sister Cassie, she swapped picture mails with Mr. McClusky, and she experimented with new recipes for Dooley. Shasta was around seven months along when she invented a curry mix. It wasn't enough for her to send Dooley the recipe—she had a spice company manufacture the mixture. The place was somewhere near Sacramento, and we drove all the way out there to pick up a case of the mix. She sent it to Dooley asking him to use it for the soldiers—since it was manufactured in a food safe facility, the Army regulations would allow it.

Dooley did. And some four-star general was visiting the 3rd Cav that day. The spice company received an order for a hundred cases two weeks later. The company called Shasta and asked her to sign a licensing agreement.

Even now, I still get monthly checks from that agreement. It comes out to a half-million a year, which isn't so bad. I've seen recipes everywhere that call for "Shasta's Curry" in them, it's listed as an ingredient on some Lean Cuisine frozen dinners, and it's been written up favorably in otherwise bad restaurant reviews, as in "This place thinks that adding some Shasta's Curry to their rotten, overcooked chicken will keep me from noticing how poorly it tasted…"

After the licensing agreement, I had to know what the big deal was, so I asked her to make me some of Shasta's Famous Curried Chicken. When I did that, her mouth formed a big O.

"You *really* want to try it?" she asked. "It's kinda spicy."

"Spicy's okay," I said.

"I've just noticed that whenever you have a choice between spicy and not spicy, you choose *not spicy*."

"I want to try it, Shasta."

"Okay-okay-okay." She shook her hands as if she were drying them. Then she got up and put the remote in my hand. "Watch some TV. If you need a beer or something, call out and I'll bring you one. You want some chips and dips? An appetizer? *Hmmmm?*"

"*Sure*. Some chips, Babe."

She kissed me and ran off to the kitchen.

I turned on the TV.

KTLA was covering those people who had been hiding out, avoiding moving to the FEMA camp. You know, the homeless, the hungry, the poor, *poor* children in the aftermath. By this point, I'd paid an installer under the table so we could have satellite. I changed the channel to CNN, and an interview was on, mid-conversation. The caption said their location was just outside of Phoenix, in a place called Apache Junction.

"...no," a bandana-faced Hispanic man said, whom I recognized instantly as Carlos, "the value of a property is *exactly* this: the cost of the materials of the building, the cost of the labor to construct the building, and the arability of the soil the building is *on*. Which makes most properties in Phoenix worth about $40,000."

"So, in your view, why is there such a large discrepancy?" the reporter asked.

"The difference is from profiteering, which should not be counted in computing the real value of property. The profit for the builder, for the land seller, for the real estate agent, for the lumber house, for the wholesaler, for the shipper, for the architect—all of those are costs assumed by the buyer, but they don't add to the value of the property. Look—this is a $40,000 house that's on the market for $850,000. Part of the reason for this disparity is that profit seeking is out of control. And another reason is because property taxes are based on the appraised value of the home—it benefits the state for property values to skyrocket. But the real problem is this: when some desperate person finally succumbs to purchasing this home, because he cannot find anything cheaper that's close to family and close to his livelihood, he will purchase it with a thirty-year loan. By the time he's done paying that loan and its interest, he will have paid $1.7 million for a $40,000 home."

The police had been slow to publicize Octavio's death—they must've been confirming his identity or something—but at this point, it still wasn't public knowledge.

"Are you *El Consumidor*?" the reporter asked.

Carlos' eyes took on confusion. "Aren't we all?"

"It is now Day 297 of the Hundred Days Riots. Why are you and others still rioting past Day 100?"

"No, no: you do not understand the meaning. It was a hundred days in L.A., a hundred days in Long Beach, a hundred days in Riverside, and then a hundred days in Palm Springs. Right now, it's a hundred days in Phoenix. In this way, a hundred days becomes a hundred months, and a hundred months becomes a hundred years. It will be a hundred days *forever*. Or until the rules of the economy are changed. Until taxes and profits are fair again." Someone off screen handed Carlos a bottle. He lit the rag hanging off of the neck. "Until we all own homes for our families. Until we don't have to live in communes. Until there is no more clanning." Carlos threw the bottle through the house's window. As a fireball bloomed inside, he walked away.

The camera peered in through the broken window. The house was empty.

"Well," the reporter said, "it's clear they're not following their own rules anymore. This home clearly has an X on the door and that man burned it anyway..."

Actually, it was the real estate agents and the banks that caused that problem. Those corporations' first priority, when *Jimenez Loco* had mentioned the really big X, was to paint them on all of their properties. Eventually, every home was marked, so the symbol lost its meaning. Hundred Days changed its symbol to an upside-down A. I never found out what that meant, but I put one on my gate.

As Shasta came in with the chips, the scene changed to a helicopter view of a convoy. The caption read:

11th Armored Cavalry Regiment
Proceeds East on I-10 with Orders to
Deploy to Scottsdale and Paradise
Valley

This convoy had tanks. Lots and lots of tanks.

Shasta set down the chips and dip, and sat next to me. "Are those my Army friends?"

"Different ones."

"Yuh."

Shasta took my hand and placed it on her stomach. The baby stretched, pushing our hands up. We both smiled. After a moment of the three of us together, Shasta finished making dinner.

It's still my favorite dish.

But I haven't had it in years.

36—Cedars-Sinai

Of course, the time came.

When we arrived at Cedars-Sinai, they provided a wheelchair. Our prior visits to the OB/GYN had sped the check-in process some, but it didn't help that we arrived in the middle of the night. I didn't know precisely what time it was, I was just going with the flow—half awake, half asleep, and half hoping that the contractions would back off so, when we got to a room, there might be time for a nap. We did the *sign this, sign that, initial here* shit that was necessary to protect the jobs of sub-minimum-wage assemblers of pressure-sensitive signature pads in Pakistan and, of course, to keep the American lawyers at bay.

I wheeled Shasta along as a nurse guided us from the emergency department to the maternity ward. When we stopped at an elevator, Shasta was between contractions. I was rubbing her shoulders when her whole body jerked. She moaned, "*God, Zeno. It hurts.*"

I squeezed her shoulder and looked at the nurse.

The nurse drew back the corners of her mouth and shrugged, like, *Yeah, yeah, they all say that.*

Then: "*AH!*"

"Shasta! You okay?"

"*I don't know, Zeno, I don't know. It hurts it hurts it hurts!*" She started to breathe rapidly like she learned in the classes. We got in the elevator. It rose smoothly and quickly to the fourth floor and when the door glided open, the nurse led the way to the room. I wheeled Shasta along after her. The nurse held the door for us.

I remember—it was Room 4114.

"Okay," the nurse said, "let's get into bed." She operated something that lowered one side of the bed to make things easier.

I helped my wife out of the wheelchair. She did okay at first, but when she went to stand fully erect, she went "*OH!*" and bent into a ninety-degree angle at her waist. Her belly kept her from bending further.

"*Shasta—what is it?*"

"I don't know," she said, still breathing heavily. "It hurts really bad in my back—kinda on the right—*oh, I don't know…*"

I looked at the nurse again. She made the same face as before: *Yeah, yeah, they all say that.*

I helped Shasta change into her hospital gown and once I got it tied, I backed her butt to the bed. I supported her at the hips and lifted her legs. She made a little *ooof!* sound as I centered her. Once she was situated, she smiled at me with a questioning look on her face, as though she were saying, *Why me? Why now? Why can't this wait for just one more day?*

Or, at least till morning, I thought. I looked her in the eyes, hoping I had answered her telepathically. Her beauty was radiant just then, even though she'd gained like fifty pounds. *Eighty* pounds, maybe? I don't know— I'm not such a good judge of things, but she was as sexy to me then as she was when she came to work each day nearly naked. Maybe sexier.

The nurse raised the bed and began connecting equipment to her: some clamp for the tip of her finger, a cuff around her arm, and a strange elastic belt that went over her belly button and made a quiet sound like a police siren stuffed with cotton—only faster and at a much lower pitch. The nurse wiped the inside of Shasta's elbow and inserted a needle there as big around as a coffee stirrer. A tube went from the needle to this little clamping thing and over to this clear cylinder where you could see dripping, and then up to a bag of water on a stand. Next, the nurse set up another couple of sensors around Shasta's stomach and connected everything to a monitor. Another device now whirred lowly and dinged softly. The nurse left the room.

"Does it still hurt?" I asked.

"When we got in the elevator, it was like somebody had stabbed me, but I think it's okay now."

A monitor displayed squiggly little lines in different colors. They were all moving upwards, and when they got about two-thirds to the top of the screen, Shasta started doing her breathing thing, and she squeezed my hand so tightly I could feel my bones popping. As the lines dropped, she relaxed.

"Zeno," she said.

I leaned toward her. "Yeah."

"I'm thirsty."

The lines started moving up again. "I'll ask the nurse when she gets back." It wasn't a long wait. The nurse returned with a doctor before Shasta's next contraction.

Shasta was doing her breathing, and she suddenly went "*SHIT!*" and the nurse said, "No, no, just keep up your breathing." Shasta did as she was told, and the squiggly lines moved down again.

"She's thirsty," I told the nurse.

"I'll get some ice," she said and left.

The doctor was making adjustments to the bed. Shasta's legs moved up and the center part of the bed dropped away below her pelvis. The doctor put on some gloves and said, "Okay, just a little bit of pressure here—no big deal."

Shasta's mouth went to one side of her face and her eyes searched for nothing in particular on the ceiling.

"This is your *first* child?" the doctor asked.

"Yes," I said.

"Well, too late for an epidural," she said. All I could see of the doctor were crazy waves of blonde hair. "Eight centimeters… How long ago did her water break?"

"No more than an hour," I said.

"Huh," she said. Then she stood and left the room.

The squiggly lines moved up again. I helped Shasta through another contraction. Afterwards, the box monitoring her vitals suddenly screamed, *BEEP-BEEP-BEEP-BEEP,* giving me a surge of adrenaline, but then it stopped right away.

The nurse entered with a cup of ice.

"Still thirsty?" I asked.

Shasta bit her lower lip and nodded in anticipation. I gave her a chip of ice. She smiled and said, *"Fanks."*

The nurse produced a vial and a syringe. She filled the needle and, as she injected it near the spot where the water was dripping, she said, "This will make you feel sleepy. But you'll wake up for the important parts, okay?"

Shasta shifted the ice to a corner of her mouth. "Okay." She crunched and swallowed. She gave me a little closed-lip smile and then she was out.

It wasn't thirty seconds before she was awake again, letting out those huffs and puffs. As the squiggly lines on the monitor descended, she said *"Oh, God, Zeno—"* and she was out again. The doctor came back in and took her spot below Shasta's pelvis. About a minute later, Shasta awoke, saying, *"—I don't want to die..."* and resumed huffing and puffing. The box went *BEEP* once more and she lost consciousness.

I felt as though I was in a dream. I looked toward the doctor, asking, "Did you hear that?"

The mass of wavy blonde hair said, "Wow, ten centimeters."

The nurse was monitoring vitals. A printer sat below the monitor with the squiggly lines, and a long sheet of paper was coming out of it, like the receipt from a grocery store. The nurse lifted up a portion and considered, and she allowed it to hang down again.

The doctor said, "Looks like we're moving right along." Her hair disappeared below Shasta. "Okay, the head's crowned."

Shasta woke up calling my name.

I squeezed her hand. "I'm here."

She was going *puff-puff-puff-puff* and the nurse and the doctor watched the monitor. When the squiggly lines got where they wanted them, they said, "Okay, *PUSH!*" and Shasta did, grunting through her teeth. Her face flushed red from exertion. When the nurse said "Good, good, rest," Shasta flopped down, unconscious again.

They went through that only three more times before the baby came.

Oh, God, Zeno—I don't want to die.

That was all that was on my mind.

Shasta hadn't passed out after the last push. The squiggly lines kept moving. The doctor was using one of those rubber bulb things and it made a *squish-squish* sound. Our baby cried—it was a shaky, weak sound, like the distant bray of a sheep. The squiggly lines moved up and Shasta had another contraction.

"It's a girl," the doctor said unceremoniously—*another tumor born into the world.*

Shasta smiled tiredly, and then her body jerked—like it sometimes happens when you're trying to stay awake but failing.

"Zeno, it hurts," she said distantly. After that, her voice became suddenly stressed, as though she was searching for me. "Zeno...?"

I squeezed her hand: *I'm here.*

"Zeno..."

Every time she said my name, it struck terror into me. I needed to do something. But what could I do?

"Zeno..."

Convulsions came. The box went on full alarm with its BEEPs.

The doctor placed the baby into a clear plastic box on wheels. She barked an order to the nurse who filled a needle with something and shot it into the IV. The convulsions abated.

Shasta sprang awake again, but the box kept beeping.

"Zeno?"

"I'm here."

She found me with her eyes. "The baby?"

"She's fine," I said, but I didn't really know. I turned, saying, "Doctor—*what's wrong?*"

The doctor stood, her face a mask of disdain.

Shasta's face changed as well. She looked surprised and amazed. The box kept beeping, and Shasta looked past me as she propped herself up on an elbow. "Zeno! *Oh my God*—look!" Her eyes and head moved, following whatever she saw until she was staring nearly straight up. That damned box kept beeping. *And beeping.*

Shasta gasped and said, *"The giraffe!"*

I was so convinced of what she was seeing, I looked.

There was nothing there.

The box. Its incessant beeping. Kept on.

When I looked down again, Shasta had gone limp.

They kicked me out of the room while a team tried to resuscitate her. The baby was shuttled away some-where—to that cold, sterile place where they do all of those tests and eye drops and inoculations. And when the doctor and the nurses finally tore out of the room with their EKG records and clipboards, each one parroted an *I'm so sorry.* These people were not just leaving—they were *escaping.* I gave chase to the doctor, pursuing her wavy blonde hair down the corridor. I grabbed her by an elbow.

She shrieked.

"Excuse me, doctor—you need to *save* her!"

Her body went rigid. *"Get your hands off me!"*

I dropped my hand. "Please—"

"If you touch me again, it'll be *assault!* Hear me? Assault!"

"You can't just let Shasta die! Do your job! *What's wrong with you?"*

The doctor bared her teeth like an angry Rottweiler. She brought out her phone and aimed it at me. "Don't you follow me, or I swear to God I'll have you removed and charged with *assault*." She shook her phone at me, turned her back, and walked away.

I stood there. Frozen awhile. Maybe ten seconds or so.

Then I went in and laid my head down on my dead wife's lap. She still felt warm, and she still felt pregnant. Later—I'm not sure how long it was—an orderly showed up to take her away. When I rose, her skin looked like soap, and her lips looked stiff and colorless, like the lips of a fish. Her toenails had turned the color of pewter. I kissed Shasta one last time, on her forehead, and she was cold, so cold... The orderly rolled her away as I sat off to the side, crying into my hands.

. . .

You know—

Anytime I hear beeping now, I have a panic attack.
I have pills for it—for my...
Nothing in this house beeps.

"More coffee?" I ask.

"I'm good," Carson says.

"Death's always something that happens to Gramma, or to drug-addicted guitarists, or to skinny little babies half a world away. That's what young people like you think, dontcha Carson? But everybody was somebody to someone, y'know. *Was...* And people *go.* There's people going every second of every day, just dropping like flies, Carson. Some people go in their sleep. Some are gunned down in a robbery. Or in a drive-by. Or in a war. Some go after drinking the Kool-Aid listening to the PA blasting '*Mother! Mother! Mother!*' Some are killed by the Feds while holding their ten-month-old baby in their arms, or by the dozens within a fire started in their compound. Others go falling off ladders, slipping in bathtubs, tripping on stairs. They fall off cliffs, they crash in airplanes, they blow up in dance clubs all over the world. They mix the wrong tranquilizers. They choke on their own vomit at the kegger. They get pulled into machinery. They get buried alive in trenches. They get struck by lightning. Every year, somebody gets hit by a *meteor.*

"But if you think there's a lot of people dying, look at how many people are living.

"Some people keep on living, like me."

I slam my fist on the table. Our cups jitter. "For heaven's sake, why not Shasta?"

Carson's wise enough to realize it was a rhetorical question. It was a rhetorical fist pounding as well, and he neither jumped nor looked uncomfortable. He keeps the moment as it is. And I admire that.

I sigh. "Anyway..."

37—Hollywood Forever

The nursing staff prepared a checklist for me—each item for the legal protection of the hospital, of course. Ordinarily, they would come to the new mother's room and go through it all with her, but Shasta's room had a new woman in it—all the way from the FEMA camp, where I guess they didn't have medical services set up yet. Instead of screaming and puffing like most women do, this one was swearing and spitting like the possessed. *"Get this fucking thing outta me! It fucking burns! Betcha take it in the ass, dontcha bitch?!"* As I sat in a small plastic chair at the nurse's station, a chuckle stole its way into me. It has always pained me some that I found a reason to laugh so soon. I hadn't looked in, but over the years, I've always imagined it was that contemptible, curly-blonde haired doctor who was at the receiving end of that vile tongue lashing.

Anyway, I went around from place to place with this stupid checklist doing all these stupid things. In one, I sat across the desk from a man with a feminine lisp who blathered on for ten minutes, instructing me about how important it is to ease back into intercourse, to wait at least a month and then take it slow and gentle from there. You know, to give the episiotomy time to repair. And all the time I'm thinking, *Oh, God—please, just shut the fuck up and sign my form!*

Eventually, I made it down to the records office. A funny little redheaded girl was there in front of a computer. I sat and set my papers on her desk.

"Now, where's the mother?" she asked, being as peppy as she could be.

Tears spilled down my cheeks, surely an involuntary response to her *faux* cuteness. "Dead," I said.

She went wide-eyed. "I'm so sorry."

I shuffled my papers toward her.

She thumbed through them and found the one she needed. "May I have the mother's maiden name?"

"MacCalistaire."

"Have you chosen a name for your child?"

Shasta and I had discussed names. Hundreds of them. And we narrowed it down to five or six. Shasta had said, "We'll have to meet her to know which one is right."

Now, I couldn't think of any of them.

"Shasta Emily."

"*After your wife.* I think that's a very good way to honor her memory, Mr. Jacobs. So 'Shasta Emily Jacobs'—will you check the spelling?"

"No."

She grimaced at me. "I'm sorry?"

"Sheila. I want to name her Sheila..."

The woman appeared irritated, but she corrected the look in a flash. She changed the name and asked me to check it, and I nodded. A few moments later, I had more papers in my growing stack. As I got up, I noticed my phone buzzing.

It was Mr. McClusky.

I found a chair in the lobby and sat. "She didn't make it."

"Right."

I was at the edge of breaking down and gibbering like a fool, of blaming God and cursing Satan, of losing composure irreversably—the way one loses their virginity. How was I going to make it through? It was an impossible proposition for me to even get to the end of the stupid fucking checklist in my hand, not to mention getting to the end of the day...

"She came to me in a dream last night. Said goodbye."

Of course she did.

"I'm sorry, Mr. Jacobs. Really."

I fought away some tears. "Thanks."

"The baby?"

"Sheila," I said. "Sheila's just fine."

"My doormat's always out for you and yours."

I said my thanks and hung up.

After that, I put my phone on silent. The hospital was going to keep baby Sheila for a week because it was routine procedure when there was a fatality with the mother. I made it up north to shop for extras of all the necessities, you know: formula, bottles, diapers, diaper rash cream… But I spent most of my time at the hospital, and I slept in the waiting room.

On the morning of the day we were supposed to check out, an orderly woke me.

"Mr. Jacobs?"

I blinked dryly at the man. "What."

He held out a pen and a clipboard. "Sign here, please."

I scribbled and he handed me an envelope that said *Personal Effects.*

When I opened the envelope, I rotated it above my hand so I could catch her phone. The phone stayed put, but everything else spilled out onto the floor. They had broken Shasta's necklace and the beads were bouncing in a hundred different directions away from me. One of the sparkletts drifted onto my shoe. The wedding ring that she wore on the wrong finger rolled along the floor and a man in a doctor's coat stepped on it and staggered.

When he caught himself, he turned to me with a frown. "You need to pick this mess up," he said. "Somebody's going to *slip* and *break their neck!*"

I spent a half-hour on my hands and knees, collecting more dust bunnies than the tiny beads, and slipping

Shasta's effects one at a time into my pocket. When I found all that I could, it dawned on me that I still hadn't talked to the funeral home. There was a plot to purchase and a service to hold and all that. I told the nurse where I'd be.

It was about four miles and I needed the walk. When I entered the Hollywood Forever funeral home, an older gentleman approached to assist me. An EP badge hung like an award off the pocket of his perfectly tailored, black suit coat. He had a nice smile that was blended in equal measure with sorrow—it must have taken a lot of mirror-practice to get *that* look down. He asked me how he could be of service.

"I'm Zeno Jacobs. My wife is Shasta Jacobs."

"Oh yes, Sir. We have taken fine care of her." He went behind a counter and bent down, producing this *thing*. I call it that because I don't really know what else to call it. It could have been a plastic rendition of a German beer stein, or it could have been a cheap trophy with a removable lid. In either case, I didn't feel like drinking or celebrating a victory.

"*What's that?*" I demanded.

"An urn—your wife, Sir." The smile was gone and all that was left in his eyes was sorrow. He rotated the urn and there was a black-and-white label—the kind that gets spit out of those stupid little label machines. It said:

SHASTAH EMILY JACOBS

"You *cremated* her?"

"Sir," he said, backing off a step and bending ever-so-slightly at the waist. "I'm so sorry you hadn't contacted us. We called repeatedly and, after a certain time has passed, the state guidelines take over."

I took out my phone to look up the missed calls, but its battery was now dead. "My wife died in childbirth. I've been with our—" I felt numb.

The man spoke, presenting further excuses or justifications or whatever, and I showed him my palm. He presented the bill. I paid it.

Outside the funeral home was a bus stop.

I collapsed onto the bench.

My thoughts were vacuous—I was there for hours with my wife in that trophy-urn, her misspelled name adorning it crookedly. And while my thoughts were blank, my emotions were not. Wave after wave of feelings washed over me: sorrow, longing, panic, desperation, pain, anger... Yes, I was angry. Angry at myself. Angry at the doctors and nurses and the paper pushers and the mortician. And, most of all, angry at life. See:

I wanted to go with her. With Shasta. I couldn't bear doing it alone.

But I had Sheila to take care of now.

At some point, my ass began to ache—especially around my tailbone. In a way, the pain seemed appro-priate, and I think it was easier to suppress the emotional pain because of the physical pain. *Yeah.* So, I sat there feeling it. Maybe a couple hours later, a man in a really nice suit came along and stole the lid from Shasta's urn. "Here you go, Man," he said in a voice saturated with altruism. He dumped two ten-dollar coins inside. There was a little puff. He replaced the lid. "Do something good with it," he said, and he walked up the street and got into a Jaguar.

I chuckled for the second time since Shasta left.

Shasta's phone, which still had some juice, rang.

"Hey, Mr. Jacobs. Sorry to bug ya, but I been tryin to reach Shazza cuz she sent me dese textes when she went into labuh. Till now, all it do is rang and rang…"

"Hi, Dooley," I said.

I told him the bad news as I made my way back to the hospital.

Even though he was a soldier, he cried and cried.

38—Funny Blue Necklace

I'm in the home that Shasta and Sheila grew up in.
There's a magical feel here, as though it's an oasis in the Sahara, but it's only a house in the Hollywood hills with a well-manicured garden. Outside is a pool with a diving board and a slide. Two mongrels named *Mitzy* and *Tipsy* roam the place as though they own it, and Sheila loves them. I'm not sure I'd call this a fairy-tale life—that would be a bunch of nonsense—but it's as close as money can buy.

"I had just gotten Sheila home," I tell Carson. "I was warming water as she cried softly. It hadn't even been five minutes before the doorbell rang. I opened the door and a facsimile of my wife was there. She was shorter, and her eyes were brown instead of Shasta's blue. As the

459

baby cried, I stood staring at this woman who had my wife's smile.

"'Oh, hello there,' she said to baby Sheila. Then to me: 'My name's Cassie. I'm sorry, but I've been trying to find my sister, Shasta. Shasta MacCalistaire.'

"The moment was bizarre and sad. I told her I was Shasta's husband, and that I had terrible news. Cassie teared up right away—she said she had felt that something bad had happened. I asked her in and we talked as I fed little Sheila. I told Cassie everything, and she must have gone through two boxes of tissues. I invited her to stay through the new year. And she did..."

Cassie's a very different woman—darker than Shasta, with a wry, sarcastic sense of humor. She burns everything she cooks and claims to like it that way. I've tried to imagine Shasta and Cassie together, chatting about life and old boyfriends and whatnot. The contrast just shorts me out: I don't understand why the two were so close. But being an only child doesn't qualify me as an expert on family dynamics, I guess.

It was one night, early spring, and Cassie had just put Sheila to sleep. She was standing above the crib, singing a soft lullaby. I came up behind her, putting my hands on her hips. I planted a soft kiss on her neck. It was an instantaneous thing that lasted no longer than the blink of an eye. Afterward, I went to bed.

When I woke, she had her bags by the front door.

"Look," I said, "I didn't mean anything by that."

"Sure you did."

I was slain with regret. "No—please don't go."

"Zeno—it was wrong for me to play house here and *not* expect that to happen. But I can't." She closed her eyes and shook her head. "I just *can't*. I hope you understand."

A taxi sounded its horn from outside the front gate.

Cassie picked up her bags and she left, back to Montana.

"...and I was so thankful for it. Had it not been for Cassie, I'd've never learned to change a diaper or treat a rash or sterilize a bottle. She made it easier for me to get along without my wife. Not by much, but some. Some...

"After she left, she returned every year for Christmas. She'd always have the rest of the family in tow—Shasta's father and mother, Uncles Simon and Nick and their wives and children. Christmas time is always a fun time, with this house full of laughing, running, crying kids..."

And each Christmas, I'd lie awake well past the midnight hour, wishing Shasta was here with her family. It wasn't supposed to be this way. She was supposed to enjoy those times with us—with her father and mother, with Cassie and Sheila. With me.

One Christmas, when Sheila was seven, I was just drifting off with these regrets on my mind. My door opened and I was expecting my child, who would occasionally stumble in late at night, seeking comfort after a scary dream. I mumbled, "What's wrong, Honey?"

But the silhouette slinking toward me was adult.

Cassie slipped under my sheets and we made love for hours.

It was nothing like being with Shasta.

But it was a delightful flavor of rapture, nevertheless.

Like vanilla.

"... Ten years ago, Cassie had a husband in tow. And over those ten years, she's had a couple of children herself. But every year, she gives me the best gift I could ever receive. See, whenever Cassie catches my eye, she smiles, and those smiles are gifts I treasure—each and every one of them. She knows how much I love that smile..."

I look across the table and Carson is leaning toward me.

He's a good listener.

Score one for Carson.

The gong in my office sounds. I ask Carson to excuse me and I walk away. At my desk, I thumb my password into my tablet and check my messages.

The bills are endless. This month, my property taxes are due: $14.70 per thousand dollars appraised value. Last year, the state reappraised my home at $8.2 million, so the bill is for $120 thousand—over ten percent of what I paid for the home twenty years ago. The electric bill is $2457 this month. There's internet, satellite, wireless, gas, water, trash, landscaping, HOA, maid service, pool cleaning, and all the bundled insurance policies. And Sheila's registered for next quarter—there's a bill for her tuition: $26,219. Then there will be her dorm room, a meal card, textbooks, a parking pass, and fees and fees and more fees... I can't imagine *anybody* making it without stumbling across a couple billion dollars—or stealing it, as Mr. Culpepper likes to say.

A message blinks onscreen:

> *[s] @JimenezLoco:* ¿Estamos
> preparados para la fase2?

I reply:

> *[s] @ElJudío:* Ha sido un largo
> tiempo. Soy muy listo.

Another message comes shortly:

> *[s] @JimenezLoco:* No tenemos
> suficientes máscaras de
> gas.

I tap the side of the pad lightly while I think. The truth of the situation dawns on me:

> *[s] @ElJudío:* Tampoco a la
> policía.

I swipe away the conversation.

My time with Carson has left me thinking. Wondering.

I open up a search box and type `Doreen Crenshaw`. In a moment, there are a few portraits. I touch the face I recognize: she's beaming while being kissed on the cheek by a young man with vaguely Semitic features. Her profile page says, *Doreen Crenshaw only shares some information publicly.* A nearby link offers: *Send her a friend request.* My finger hovers over the link for an eternal moment while I visit the world in her picture.

Wherever Doreen has ended up, there's snow, and she's bundled up in layers with a knit cap on her head, but there's no sign of despair or pain or regret in her eyes. By the looks of the cabin in the background, as well as a Land Rover and a couple of shiny snowmobiles, she's somehow ended up well-off. The kid with her has been tagged. I brush his face with my finger and the words *Bertrand Crenshaw* appear. The two look happy in a way I've never been, and while I look every single one of my years old, Doreen looks maybe twenty-five.

I wonder. Wonder what she's done over the years. What she'll do in the years to come. Who she'll do it all with.

I put the pad in its dock, and go back out.

Carson's standing on the hearth, staring at the *Fish in the Life Preserver.* He's touching the canvas softly, feeling minute textures. The painting shows the surface of an ocean as an eight-year old would draw it, with curves drawn concave-up, and the ends of the curves joining together in tall chops. The water below is blue, as is the sky, but a peculiar tint is in the air, a tint I recognize now—it's smoke, smoke from the burning of cities, smoke from fires so hot it rises to the stratosphere. At the center of the painting floats a white life preserver, the kind with loops of rope attached along its slick circumference—so one can claw at it. Sticking through the center of the life preserver is a funny looking fish with one fin resting on the preserver and the other one waving. His smile is pure madness, and it consumes me.

"My wife loved that painting."

Carson jerks his hand away. "It's strange, Dad. Sometimes..." He blinks rapidly, steps off the hearth, and faces me. "I don't know—it's a little bit like standing between two facing mirrors. Do you know what I mean?"

I do. "That's what Shasta meant when she called the paintings timeful."

Carson goes, "Hmm."

All at once, the inevitability of Sheila being this guy's bride hits me. I take Carson by the shoulders and clear my throat. "Listen: I will never get my wife back. Nor will I raise another child. Now, you and Sheila seem to be getting serious, and that's fine. But don't you hurt her—*ever*—or you will pay quite dearly for it."

Carson appraises my resolve as the click-clacking of heels sounds from outside. The lock on the front door moves. Keys jingle and the door opens.

"Hey!" Sheila says. She's holding a huge, wrapped package, which she lays on its end, resting it against the settee in the foyer. She scans our faces as she walks near. "*Ooohhh*, you gentlemen must be involved in some serious *maaaan*-talk. What is it? The Dodgers?"

Carson and I look at each other. Then back to her.

Sheila walks behind me and massages my neck briefly.

"Well," she says, "as long as it's not '*I'll string you up by your balls if you ever hurt my daughter,*' then I guess I don't need to know."

She gives me a hard squeeze and goes back to the door to retrieve her keys.

Carson's looking at me like Sheila's a mind reader.

I shrug.

Sheila closes the door and hangs up her keys. She rushes to me, bends at her waist and knees, and embraces me. "Happy Birthday, Daddy," she whispers as she hooks an arm around mine. She walks me to the package she brought in.

It's a dull, stupid question: "What's this?"

"You'll have to open it and find out. It's from both of us, Daddy."

I turn and look at Carson.

"We saw it on Spring Break," he says.

"Lake Havasu?" I ask.

"*Yuh*—you know it!" Sheila says.

She jabs Carson in the ribs. "He was the one who dragged me through all the art galleries, Daddy. Kicking and screaming." She's prompting Carson to go on, but he seems at a loss for words. "Well, anyway, we had to get it for you. Go on and open it!"

I tear the Kraft paper wrapping. The back side of a framed canvas is revealed. Text on yellowed paper says:

Shasta Jacobs
by Sam McClusky

"Oh" is all I can manage to say.

But I know now... Now I know why Shasta and Mr. McClusky had disappeared into that labyrinth for so damn long.

I feel the sting of tears starting below my lower eyelids. I remember the first time Shasta and I kissed—how it made my heart quicken; a desperate, weak sensation coursing through me, but also an excitement, a thrill, a certainty of the fulfillment of all my dreams, the realization and excitement of all the things I'd never known I'd wanted in a woman. I feel that way again. Along with it: emptiness. I want my wife back. I want her touch. I want her smell, her taste, the sound of the laughter I so seldom heard from her—the laughter that this artist-slash-janitor so easily coaxed out of her.

I swallow.

And turn the canvas.

Shasta is standing in the center of the labyrinth in front of the waterfall by the gray-blue hillside. Mr. McClusky had captured the two-dimensional quality of the painting she stood in front of, but the water—the water*fall*—flows out of that painting, spilling over Shasta's head and her shoulders. Her right arm is above her chest, a finger touching one of the sparkletts on her necklace. Her other arm is out, steadying her balance in the sudden outpouring of the falling river. The look on her face is complex and perfectly captured: shock, surprise, an involuntary shriek of joy.

Through the fog that comes with sudden tears, I look at my full-grown daughter. The girl I used to hold in my arms. The girl who I bought a step stool for so we could cook together. The girl who I taught to swim, taught to ride a bike, taught to balance a checkbook.

It's been twenty years.

Mr. McClusky was right: *A flash in the pan.*

I look back to my wife's image again, lifting the frame so she's at eye level with me. It's startlingly lifelike. Like a photograph. Mr. McClusky certainly had a gift—one that I hadn't recognized because of the cartoony style of the paintings in the labyrinth.

My daughter goes to the mantel and takes down the *Fish in the Life Preserver.* She says, "Put it up here, Daddy."

I try to hang it, but the frame is too tall for the nail. So, I set the base of the painting on the mantel and lean it back.

The three of us stand back, staring silently.

After a minute, I extend my hand to Carson and he takes it. "Thank you, Son," I say.

Carson smiles in that charming way of his, a way I'm slightly less disgusted with now. "Sure thing, Dad. Happy birthday."

Sheila bends down and embraces me again. "Happy birthday, Daddy."

Her hair smells of jasmine.

I do my laps under a fossil moon, and I exit the pool exhausted. I dry myself and blot my trunks. I throw the towel over the arm of a patio chair; it slides off and slaps the deck. I go inside. I take a pill. And then decide on a dozen more.

Carson and Sheila have bailed—they are out having fun, as young people like to do. I sit on my leather couch in my damp trunks, enveloped in plushness. Above the mantel is my wife. A memory visits me in words: *How can one be warm alone?* My eyes close as I drift.

Often, Shasta comes to me in my sleep.

She has made love to me here, in this dreamland. It hasn't been often over the years, but it's wonderful when she does.

Many times, she'll have me lie on my stomach. She sits on my calves, asking me about things. *How is Sheila? Does she still want to be a teacher? Tell me about New Hollywood.* As we talk, she takes her fingernails and, ever so slowly, runs them up the back of my thighs and over

469

my buttocks. An electric sensation tightens my skin as her nails travel along my spine. Her fingernails reach the base of my neck and my body arches. She leans down. The warmth of her breasts is upon me. The whisper comes to my ear lightly, almost imperceptibly, as the wing beats of a nearby butterfly might, asking, "Are you asleep?"

"Yes," I say.

"Good," is her reply, "don't fall awake."

Her nails glide down my flanks; I'm enraptured in agonizing ecstasy. All around, her moist, strawberry breath lingers.

Sometimes, she...

She—

There is pounding, pounding on wood, coming to me from far, so *very* far away—distant enough that it could be in another world. The dogs yap above the sound of cracking, splintering snaps. There are voices shouting imperatives.

Where was I?

Sometimes...

This time, Shasta is riding a giraffe. It is muscular, organic, *alive.* She steadies it with a tug on its long, drooping reigns. Somehow, it balances well on three legs while gripping a dagger in its fourth.

Shasta spots me and cries, *"Zeno!"*

She smiles, and just like every other time, I'm smitten. A whip of the reigns starts the beast galloping. She speeds toward me upon it, thirty feet high in the air, her breasts giggling with each hoof strike, her hair streaming in wind-whipped locks, her silver ring bright on her pinky finger. I reach out to her, but she rides away, that funny blue necklace trailing behind her, the sparkletts glimmering in the falling sun's beams.

I wonder how many more times I'll wake without her.

I wonder, in this other world, if love is still the same.

I wonder when Shasta will finally bring me along.